BRAND OF DEATH

E. Craig McKay

published by

Greenleaf-Underhill

for Merlin

Other works of fiction by E. Craig McKay

Novels

Hit by the Dealer
Cross Country Hit
Hit with the Ladies
Ariel; Shieldmaiden of Middleworld

Short Stories

The Pledge
Life in a Box
Debbie Skips Dallas; Does Eagle Pass
Starpoint Rendezvous
Away With Words

Cover photography by James Wellington Marsh

Cover and interior design and layout by Greenleaf-Underhill

Brand of Death is Copyright © 2013 by E. Craig McKay

All rights reserved.

ISBN-13: 978-1482055566
ISBN-10: 1482055562

DEDICATION

To all those who work to preserve

life and the quality of life.

ACKNOWLEDGEMENTS

Valued input and critiques of drafts of this novel were provided by a number of friends. Their help is much appreciated.

The following are mentioned for special thanks:

Bill Morrissey, a professional capable of making the long shot count.
Bob Button, a lover of dogs and horses, an island cowboy.
Sally Cooknell, her extensive assistance with editing and proofreading has been invaluable.
JoAnne Gambarotto-McKay, my wife, my love, my best friend.

Chief Blue Horse

(Oglala Lakota: Sunka Wakan To in Standard Lakota Orthography)
(1822-July 16, 1908)
Chief of the Wagluhe Band of Oglala Lakota, warrior, statesman and educator. Blue Horse is notable in American history as one of the first Oglala Lakota U.S. Army Indian Scouts and signatory of The Treaty of Fort Laramie in 1868. Chief Blue Horse was known for his saving white men in distress and the iconic one-eyed Chief was popular subject for portraitists. Chief Blue Horse's life chronicles the history of the Oglala Lakota through the 19th and early 20th centuries. Chief Blue Horse and his brother Chief Red Cloud fought for over 50 years to deflect the worst effects of white rule; feed, clothe and educate their people and preserve sacred Oglala Lakota land and heritage.
- *source Wikopedia*

AUTHOR'S NOTES

For better or worse, the world has changed. People have continued to exhibit the same mixture of nobility and vulgarity which has so often characterised our history. It seems there have always been those who strive to create beauty and truth and those who are consumed with greed and envy. Oscar Wilde summed it up, 'We are all of us standing in the gutter, but some of us have our eyes fixed on the stars.'

My detective hero, Dr. Robert B. Pendergast, is representative of those who have dedicated their lives to the service of others. From frontier doctors, to doctors without frontiers, members of all branches of the medical professions are amongst those who exhibit that which is best in humans.

Murder mysteries are mirrors which reflect life through a glass, darkly. In this way they are a celebration of the process of illumination.

A personal note from the author:

One of the things often overlooked, in what might be loosely termed 'Cowboy' stories, is the number of Afro-American people who were amongst those who settled and explored the west of the United States. This book does not attempt to redress that lapse. However, I can tell you that two of the major characters in this novel are people of colour. I leave it to the reader to decide which.

BRAND OF DEATH

Part One: The Homecoming

"Don't imagine for a moment you are going on a picnic. Expect annoyance, discomfort, and some hardships. If you are disappointed, thank heaven."
- Omaha Herald describing travel by stagecoach in 1877

Cast of Caracters

The Artist – Not one to seek the spotlight; skilled at hiding in plain sight.

Brad Pendergast – Young medical student admires Sherlock Holmes.

Jacob E. Witherspoon – AKA Harry Plumber, Jacob is an enigmatic figure.

Frank Green – Personal passions haunt him; doesn't make friends easily.

Dr. Robert B. Pendergast – Likes chess, riddles, and puzzles of deduction.

Eddie Thompson – The young ostler sees a lot without being seen.

Miss Lily – She takes what she wants, but she gives good value in return.

Danny Lambert – His good time often proves a problem for his victims.

Clayton Edgett – Serves cold beer, free pours whiskey, but doesn't drink.

Jefferson Brooks – Mortician unsure of his sanity; others share his concern.

Clive Harrison – Works with iron; has potentially fatal artistic aspirations.

Luke Proctor – A man of potential, he has a shadowy past and a dark future.

Marshal Leroy Hopkins – A lawman investigates; who investigates him?

Carl Munds – The ambitious young deputy sees criminals everywhere.

Mrs. Hardy – Housekeeper to the doctor, she diagnoses and prescribes.

Willie Hardy – Young enough to be the doctor's child, some think he is.

Thomas Carter – A serious blacksmith and honest tradesman is his image.

Doris Proctor – She plays a lone hand; some of her cards are concealed.

Sam 'Shoe' Schuerman – Bossing a cattle drive is child's play, but murder?

Paul 'Badger' Matthews – Good at driving horses or playing poker.

Larry James – Herding cattle is lonely. He works hard and plays hard too.

Jim Thompson – His store provides more than needles, cloth and flour.

Violet Thompson – She means business; the Japanese say 'business is war'.

Lars Sorensen – It has been said that a man with a beard is hiding something.

Willard Wright – He claims to have no relatives. What are his connections?

Helga Sorensen – Is she actually more than a supportive wife and mother?

Jesus Fernandez Soza – Vengeance is a family tradition that he respects.

Charlie Lee – Local businessman talks loudly and has a big gun.

Andy Thompson – One of the Thompson boys, Andy is a chip off the block.

Paul Thurston – Second coach driver named Paul. A cameo appearance.

David Jones – Journalist extraordinaire. If he can't find news, he'll make it.

Preface

A Cruel Land and Isolated

The Artist was at work. The isolated canyon assured privacy. Actions would not be seen nor words overheard. The glow of the camp fire illuminated a face hardened by deprivation. A callused hand lifted a red hot iron from the flames. Deliberate steps moved toward the captive who lay struggling in bonds which would not yield to desperately straining limbs.

The victim cried out in terror. The ropes held and the dry ground offered no comfort. The brand was pressed cruelly against an upper thigh. Seared flesh sizzled and the odour of burned hair and skin filled the air.

"Now you belong to me," the Artist said with a twisted smile.

CHAPTER 1 ABOARD THE STAGECOACH

Brad was jolted awake as they hit a rut deeper than the thousands of others which lined the trail from Flagstaff to Sedona. The new road had cut the travel time to two days from four. It did not make it more comfortable. Brad Pendergast was taking a four-month break from his medical studies to visit his father at the homestead in Red Rocks, renamed Sedona in 1901. Carl Schnebly, after whose wife the town had been named, had been instrumental in having the road to Flagstaff shortened by cutting through the mountains. Although the opening of the Schnebly Road in 1901 had led to an improved stagecoach schedule, Brad was wishing he had taken his father's advice and rented a horse at the railway stop in Flagstaff.

Across from him, the only other passenger seemed to be asleep. Brad had spent almost fifty hours in the man's company and knew little about him. It was intriguing. Most people were more than willing to talk about themselves, their plans, their hopes. This man was a puzzle.

A little over fifteen years ago a British author, Arthur C. Doyle, had published a series of stories which Brad had recently read. The Tales of Sherlock Holmes displayed the use of deductive powers to solve crimes. Brad had been acquiring similar skills at medical school to diagnose illness. Doyle was said to have based Sherlock Holmes on the observational skills of a Doctor Bell from the Edinburgh Royal Infirmary. Brad Pendergast had tried to apply the same deductive method with patients he met at the teaching hospital in Boston, with mixed results.

Brad decided to employ the methods of Sherlock Holmes to see what he could glean about the man across from him. The man looked to be in his late thirties and was wearing traveling clothes which seemed well used. His hands were not hardened by manual labour and his manner of speech indicated some formal education. He wore boots which seemed to have been well cared for. Brad noted a gouge which had scored the inside of the right boot. Of greatest interest was a leather satchel which contained documents which Brad had seen the traveler examine during the passage.

Clearly, Brad thought, this man is a traveling salesman for some manufacturing company back east. The scar along the inner edge of the boot suggested to Brad the marks he had noticed on the boots of printers working the treadle of printing presses or paper cutters. Yet another possibility was that this man had scuffed his boot while operating the crank of one of the new automobiles or motorized bicycles which had begun appearing in the streets of Boston.

The traveler had a four foot long case of what might be trade samples propped in one corner of the coach. Clearly he valued the contents too highly to strap them on the exterior roof racks like other baggage. What could he be hoping to sell in Sedona?

The town had long been a stopping off point for prospectors rushing off toward the new gold mines of the west. But by the turn of the century that had died out. By 1906 there were only a score of permanent residents. His father had managed to make a living providing medical care for both locals and transients, but Brad knew that it was the old doctor's independent nature which had brought him here and kept him here.

When his fellow traveler reached up to lift the brim of his hat, Brad decided to test the validity of his deductions with a few probing questions.

"We'll be getting into Sedona in a half hour or so now," Brad offered. "You can see the first of the red peaks over the rise."

The other lifted his boots off the seat beside Brad and leaned forward to look in the indicated direction. "Supposed to be a hotel in town, The Horn Saloon," he said by way of reply.

"The Horn is downtown, cheap, and popular." Brad told him. "It's either stay there or at the Schnebly house. The rooms at The Horn are clean enough, but nothing fancy. You do a lot of traveling, I guess."

"I do some."

"We don't see a lot of salesmen in Sedona," Brad prodded.

"I don't suppose you do," the man said straight-faced. "Cowboys more like, I imagine."

"Tucson's more of a cattle town than Sedona," Brad answered. "You work with supplies for cattlemen, do you?" Brad wondered what kind of goods cattlemen would buy.

"I wouldn't say that," the older man replied, making no effort to clear up Brad's confusion. "Will your father be meeting you at the stage?" he continued.

With a start Brad realized that although he had managed to learn next to nothing about his fellow passenger in the past two days, he had for his part told this man all about himself and his childhood growing up in the outskirts of what until 1901 had been called Red Rocks. He had mentioned his wife Alice back in Boston, his attendance at medical school, his father's practice here in Arizona, and even his hopes to convince Doctor Pendergast to come and live with him and Alice. He wondered if he wasn't behaving more like Dr. Watson than Holmes. Certainly his fellow passenger was better at asking questions than answering them.

CHAPTER 2 MAIN STREET, SEDONA

He's no salesman, that's for sure. Unless he's peddlin' dynamite.
–Bad Day at Black Rock

Frank Green was walking down to the courthouse from the marshal's office when the stage rolled in. He saw Dr. Pendergast seated on a buggy watching the stagecoach pull to a stop. Frank had heard that the doctor's son was coming for a visit. Apparently, Brad was here.

Frank watched the coach door swing open with anticipation. He had only met young Pendergast once, but had found him a pleasant young man.

The man who stepped down first from the confines of the coach holding a hat in his left hand was not Brad Pendergast, but there was something familiar about him. Frank set the thought aside as he saw the doctor's son pass down a case to the stranger and then emerge with a smile for his father. Then something in the way the tall stranger placed his hat just so on his head triggered a memory for Frank. It had been a couple of years, but he knew him. Frank wasn't altogether happy to see this man. With a sense of foreboding he passed out of the sunlit street and into his shadowy office.

* * *

Brad waved to his father as he stepped down from the stagecoach. The old doctor was sitting quietly on the seat of the two-wheeled cart, but he climbed down as nimbly as a younger man might and came forward to embrace his son.

"Welcome home, Brad. You're putting on a little weight there, son, but it suits you. Alice must be feeding you well."

"She's a good cook, Dad, and we're very happy together. She wanted to come out to visit with you too, but one of the reasons she didn't is why I've come out now to talk with you," Brad told him with a twinkle in his eye.

"Well, we've got time to talk, but I can guess at what your meaning might be," Dr. Pendergast told his son.

The two Pendergast men had long engaged in a competition of riddles and puzzles which they discovered or created to test each other. Brad remembered one of his father's favourites. Question: How is a mouse like a lot of hay? Answer: Cattle eat it / Cat'ill eat it.

"Well, I think this is one puzzle that you won't guess," Brad told his father.

The stagecoach driver called out and Brad went over to receive his baggage as it was passed down. As he carried it over to load it onto the rear of the small cart, his dad smiled serenely and climbed up to take the reins.

Brad was no sooner seated beside him on the buckboard seat when his father surprised him by saying, "I imagine I've got a grandchild on the way. I'm very glad to hear it."

CHAPTER 3 THE HORN

A man walks into a bar...

"So, you new in town?" Lil asked, though she knew full well he was. She had watched him step down from the stagecoach just before noon. The stranger was tall, an inch or so short of six foot, and lanky, in a way that made him seem to take up way more space than he had any need to. He wasn't bad looking; he wasn't what you'd call good looking either. His hair was dark and had a sort of natural ruffled look to it and his chocolate brown eyes made him look softer than she suspected he was. She wouldn't kick him out of bed, but she wouldn't be offering him a cut rate either.

"New as water falling from the heavens," he said, setting down his glass. Jake was new to Sedona; he'd been new to many towns. In his line there was no point in staying put.

"Hear you plan to settle here; hear you're looking to buy some property," she added.

"Might be," Jake told her. He knew it didn't pay to be too communicative.

"Looking to raise some cattle, are you?" she probed.

"Could raise cattle; could plant crops," Jake answered. "Haven't decided yet. Depends upon the land and the market."

"Market's good right now for ready money," she said suggestively.

"Might raise something," Jake agreed. "Depends on the price of the land."

"Land's not cheap around here," she told him. "But, it's pretty fine land."

Jake turned toward her and considered his situation; he rolled a cigarette with one hand without looking down, and asked, "You might happen to know where some property is available, might you?"

The woman was standing close beside him at the bar. She was standing too close for someone who didn't know the man close by whom she was standing. But she was used to that. She had learned that there were two types of men: those that wanted company and those that didn't. Those that did sometimes found it in the bottle if they didn't find it elsewhere. Didn't pay to let them go to drink.

She had sized up the stranger when he got off the Monday morning stagecoach. Lil had seen a lot of men; she knew this one was looking for action. Might be that he wanted her kind of action; might be that he wanted something else. She meant to find out which. He was easy to talk with; didn't push back like some did and was pleasant enough, in a crusty sort of way. On reconsideration, if it weren't for her professional guidelines, she might have considered a pro bono offer in his case.

Frank Green, the town clerk, had come in at lunch hour. Now he was back for an evening visit. Frank needed a little something to get him through the afternoon. Then after work he came to get a snoot full to get him through the night. Frank was as queer as the bar was straight. In a town like this there wasn't much Frank could do about his needs, without getting shot that is, so he buried his desires in whiskey and beer. Early on Lil had tried to spark some reaction from him but that had gone nowhere.

There was no use talking to Frank after seven o'clock each evening. By that point he was past the point of making sense. Most nights he ended up talking to himself at the end of the bar.

Frank was at his best at about noon. He was talkative, lively, almost cheerful. Today he had told her about the stranger's inquiries about landholding near town and whether some might be for sale. Now it seemed that Frank was in his cups and she planned to see for herself what this stranger was all about.

Jake bought her a second cocktail, which looked as if it might be mostly fizzy water designed to keep her sober. He asked her what it was and she offered him a taste. He was surprised by the potency of the harmless looking beverage. "Hey," he said in surprise, "That drink packs quite a wallop. You're not just another pretty face, are you?"

"I can handle my liquor, a horse, and a gun. I've got a fair inkling of the major life skills."

"Maybe you could show me some place I might like to settle down," he said with a smile. It was a pleasant smile, not full of itself. As strangers went, he was not as strange as some.

"Happens that I do know the lay of the land," she told him.

"So, are you the official greeter and sales agent 'round here?" he asked quietly.

"I'm more into short term rental," Lil said as she pressed the side of her leg against his. He didn't move away. "I'm Lily," she told him. "My full name's Elizabeth; my mom named me after the virgin queen." She smiled coyly and added, "But my friends call me Lil. I'd like you to call me Lil."

"My name's Harry," Jake said with a warm, ingratiating smile. "Everyone knows me as Hank," he told her without the least indication that he was lying through his teeth. Truth was Jake had used so many names he was starting to recycle them. There actually used to be some people who knew him as Jake. They were mostly all dead now he supposed.

Jake turned a bit more toward Lil and glanced past her down the bar to where Frank was apparently lost in contemplation of a beer and whiskey chaser.

Although Jake had recognized Frank in the land office, the clerk had not shown any indication that he had seen Jake before. Now, in the bar, Jake had noticed the clerk checking them out. Jake always kept an eye out to see what was happening around him. It didn't pay not to.

"Fella at the end of the bar seemed to be checking me out," he told Lil. "I saw him over at the court house. What's his story?"

Without looking, Lil replied, "You mean the man with dark curly hair and a wispy moustache that looks like it's been painted on with a single horsehair?" she asked. When Jake nodded, she said, "That's Frank. He's only been in town a year or so."

Jake took another look at Frank in the mirror behind the bar. "He's not looking now, but earlier he was giving us, or you, or me, a lot of attention."

Lil laughed softly. It was a deep-throated laugh with a bit of a purr to it. "He's not actually my type; he might hope you are his."

Jake wondered if that was it or if Frank had recognised him after all.

CHAPTER 4 THE HORN

Clay Allison was one of the most notorious and downright deranged outlaws of the Old West. His gravestone reads: ~Gentleman. Gun Fighter. He never killed a man that did not need killing."
- Anonymous attribution

Watching them from the far side of the room, sitting in the corner so as to have his back to two walls at once, was Danny Lambert. Danny loved Lil as much as he loved anyone, which wasn't saying much. Truth was what Danny felt for Lil was lust tempered by the general loathing he felt toward most living things. Right now Danny was considering how he was going to kill the stranger. He imagined that he would just get him alone and smack him with a hulk of pipe or something similar. No use wasting bullets.

* * *

While Frank and Danny watched Jake and Lil, another pair of eyes watched Danny. Jefferson Brooks was the town mortician. Over the past few years business had picked up. He thought Danny had a hand in that. Jefferson appreciated his efforts.

The stranger looked as if he could take care of himself, but he was sailing pretty close to the wind chatting up Lil in front of Danny. Jefferson wondered if he might look forward to a commission real soon. He'd noticed that some of Lil's former clients had turned up dead.

* * *

Behind the bar, absently drying a glass while keeping an eye on the customers, stood The Horn's purveyor of beer and spirits. Being bartender at The Horn was as tranquil as Clayton Edgett had expected. When he came to town six years ago he had found a sleepy, back-country community that was off the main trail heading west. People had settled in what was then called 'Red Rocks' seemingly because they didn't have the energy to go further with a desert lying before them. Many of them were failed silver miners who had thought better of it and turned to farming. Some settlers who were near springs or pockets of water had planted crops which had done well enough. In other parts of the region crops dried up and died in the poor arid dust that passed for topsoil. Most of the outlying land was too flat for goats and too dry for anything save cactus and tumbleweed. Future projects would bring irrigation to those areas but for the moment the main occupations involved horses and cattle. The people who did that would come to town to drink and play poker, but they weren't town folk.

Three cowboys had given up an attempt to start a poker game for lack of other players. They sat at a table drinking beer and swapping stories. Clayton knew Sam and Larry, but the third was unfamiliar. Cattle drives often passed close to Sedona because of the available water in creeks and small ponds. Probably he was from one of those.

Clayton had taken the job as bartender at the only hotel in town thinking that the one thing people could do here was drink. Since there wasn't much else to do, he figured he'd have steady work.

It was mostly a group of regulars who frequented The Horn. They ordered simple drinks, beer or whiskey, and they didn't start fights much. But Clayton had worked in more lively bars in Tombstone and Flagstaff. From experience he knew how to watch for trouble. He always kept an eye out in case some trouble developed. If it did, he wanted to stay out of the line of fire.

Tonight there was a hint of tension in the air. He'd taken note of the attention the stranger was attracting. Clayton poured drinks for him when requested, but the rest of the time he stayed as far down the bar as he could.

* * *

Jake had noticed Danny when he first came in. He had identified him as either harmlessly peculiar or a mad-dog killer. Jake had chosen a place at the bar from which he could watch Danny in the mirror between the necks of a row of bottles without Danny noticing until he could decide which kind of odd the man was.

Danny's reaction to the attention Lil was paying to Jake suggested that Danny had some interest in her.

"Who's the hombre in the corner, Lil? Your husband?" he asked without looking around.

Lil raised her glass and let her eyes sweep the room without looking at anything in particular. She gave Jake a playful shove on the shoulder and laughed gaily. "Why, that's Danny," she said quietly while smiling. "He'll probably try to kill you when you leave, Hank."

"That so? And here I was just starting to like being alive," Jake replied.

Lil took a sip of her drink and said, "Course if you decide to stay the night you will be able to spot him coming at you in the morning light."

CHAPTER 5 THE HORN

Down at the end of the bar, Frank wasn't as drunk as usual for this time of the evening. He had been surreptitiously topping up his drink with water and nursing it. He wanted to keep an eye on the stranger who had identified himself as Harry Plumber at the town hall just before noon. Frank didn't let on, but knew this man wasn't Harry Plumber. Fact was, Frank remembered him from Texas. That was when the real Harry Plumber was killed in Eagle Pass about two years ago.

Why he was here, passing himself off as someone he wasn't and pretending to be looking to buy some land, Frank meant to find out. He suspected that it involved someone's death.
* * *
Danny saw Lil put her hand on the stranger's shoulder and wondered if maybe he should kill her too. Then he started to consider other things he could do to her instead and his eyes glazed over. He remembered the fun he and his brother, Tom, had with that family of settlers that had lost a wagon wheel down south of the Comstock arroyo last year. Those were good times. Sometimes he regretted killing Tom.

There wasn't much that Danny considered regretting. That was lucky 'cause a man who had killed his brother, his father, his mother, and two cousins might find a lot of regretting to do once he got started. That didn't even include the casual killing of strangers that Danny had got up to in his short life. Danny was twenty-four. Some would call it a life of random violence. He had already killed about twenty people, a stray dog, and a balky mule. Danny's life would fit the description: short, brutish, and ugly. To general relief someone would finally put a bullet through him.

When that happened, the jury that would convict his killer would do so without leaving the box. The deputy marshal at the time would suggest that if the shooter had killed only Danny he would have deserved a medal.

* * *

Jake did stay part of the night with Lil. He slipped out of bed at two a.m. Tuesday morning and dressed quietly. He left five dollars on the dresser and slipped down the back stairs and out the back door without disturbing the old guard dog that was asleep in the hall. Jake had learned to move silently. It was important for a hunter.

* * *

Frank had watched the stranger who he knew wasn't Harry Plumber and Lil for a couple of hours. When they headed upstairs just after midnight, he decided that he would have to wait until morning to find out more. He turned his attention to Danny Lambert. Frank knew that Danny was both dangerous and unpredictable. He didn't trust Danny in or out of his sight, but he was more nervous when he knew he was nearby.

There were three rules Frank had to avoid a problem with Danny. He never spoke to Danny, he never let himself be alone with him, and he never made eye contact with him. So far it was working.

CHAPTER 6 THE PENDERGAST RANCH

The last time Brad had visited his father he had been dismayed to find signs of casual neglect creeping over the property. The sudden death of his mother, Katherine Pendergast, had been sorrowful for Brad, but it had come as a crushing blow to Robert Pendergast. Brad's parents had met back east when the now elderly doctor was a young man. They'd been married almost forty years and Brad suspected that his father was not adjusting well to being alone. Worries about his father, plus Alice's announcement, had prompted Brad's present visit.

On the ride out from town, Brad was pleased to find his father more vivacious than he had been. When they reached the homestead he noted a number of small changes which denoted greater care being taken. There were new flowers planted beside the house and he saw clothing hung out to dry which included a child's trousers. A hobby horse stood leaning against the gate post. His surprise must have been obvious because his father replied to his unvoiced question.

"Looks as if wee Willie's been out here to greet us. He must have been distracted by a butterfly, or something else more interesting than an old doctor and his son."

"Wee Willie!" Brad exclaimed. "Who is wee Willie?"

"You're not the only one with new life springing up around you, son. I've got a young lad here again too," Dr. Pendergast said with a grin. He watched the confusion on Brad's face for a second and then took pity on him. "No, I haven't been sowing my ancient seed on fertile ground. I acquired a housekeeper, Mrs. Hardy, and she came complete with a young lad."

As the doctor brought the cart to a stop in front of the house, the door opened and a young woman dressed in a gingham frock came out with a boy of about five by her side. Dr. Pendergast tied up the horse to a rail and took Brad across to meet Mrs. Hardy and her son William.

After unloading Brad's bag the two men led the horse over to the drive shed where they unharnessed her.

Brad went immediately to see the other horse in the second stall. The horse shied, not recognising him at first, and then came forward to take in Brad's odour while he in turn caressed her neck. "It's good to see you, Cornflower," he said with affection. "Are you getting enough attention?"

"She is indeed. Mrs. Hardy takes her out for a ride on a regular basis. And young William is always out here to offer her and Grey a carrot," his father responded.

The doctor checked the feed and water for both horses and Brad removed his jacket to brush the cart horse, Grey, down. The mare had been named after Henry Grey, the author of Grey's Anatomy. The textbook was first published in America in 1859, the year Robert Pendergast turned thirteen. Robert's father had bought a copy and reading it had set the then young Pendergast's mind on becoming a medical practitioner. Naming a chestnut horse Grey was typical of the doctor's sense of humour.

While father and son completed the joyful tasks of caring for their horses, Dr. Pendergast explained the presence of Mrs. Hardy.

"Martha Hardy and her husband, John, came out here from Buffalo a little over six years ago. When John Hardy was fording a storm-swollen stream his horse went down and rolled on him. I took her on as a housekeeper and it's helped us both. Eventually she will need to move to a larger center, but for now she is happy to be here, and having a young boy around this place has taken me out of myself and helped me move on. I'm happy to have her and William here, and overjoyed to learn that I will soon be a grandfather."

"How did you ever guess that Alice is pregnant?" Brad asked. "I thought I would surprise you."

"I'll explain that later," the doctor told him. "Now let's go inside. Mrs. Hardy will have prepared lunch for us."

CHAPTER 7 THE SMITHY

Down at the village smithy, the apprentice blacksmith, Clive Harrison, was about to finish his day's work. After an uneasy evening going over his options, Clive was locking up his trunk when Eddie Thompson came sauntering through the stable doors. Eddie was whistling and seemed in high spirits. The young son of a local merchant was a willing worker and reliable. Clive gave the youngster a run-down on the horses stabled for the night. There were the regulars, but with the Wingfield crew bringing new horses for Wells Fargo and the ranch hands who often appeared unannounced and ended up staying in town overnight, the horses to be cared for changed unpredictably sometimes.

Tonight Clive had something on his mind other than the stables. He had some entanglements which threatened to drag him into serious trouble. Tonight he intended to cut one of the ties that bind.

CHAPTER 8 THE PENDERGAST RANCH

After a day of surprises and a splendid supper which left them both vowing to eat less in future, father and son settled across the chessboard from each other. Since they seldom played except against each other, they were fairly evenly matched.

Brad Pendergast pushed his king's bishop's pawn forward and held up his hand in signal for his father to pause before making his answering move. Brad sat back in his chair and looked up at his father. They had fallen easily into the habits of his youth and were still in the opening stages of the third and deciding game of chess when he thought of a possible answer to the question he'd been pondering since their meeting in town.

"I've got it," he declared. "Dr. Hawkins must have told you about Alice's pregnancy. You two were in school together and I know you stay in touch."

"James Hawkins would never divulge private information about a patient, Brad. You should know that," his father replied with a mock serious tone.

"Well, then I give up," Brad declared in frustration. "I can't imagine how you knew that Alice and I were expecting a child. We only found out ourselves two weeks ago."

"I didn't know," his father told him with a self-satisfied grin. "I deduced it."

"Explain how," Brad challenged him.

Dr. Pendergast settled back in his chair and said, "Actually, it was fairly easy. There were only a few reasons you would have suddenly taken a break from your studies and come out here to see me. You could have given up your dream of becoming a physician or for some infraction you might have been expelled from the college; both of these possibilities I knew to be unlikely just by examining your smug demeanour. Next I ruled out the possibility of a breakup in your marriage. You yourself had just assured me that married life suited you both fine. The possibility that either you or Alice had fallen ill was clearly not the case; you would hardly have left the sickbed of your wife and lover at the very moment that she needed you. Your own good health was immediately obvious to me by your robust appearance and obvious good spirits."

Clearly much pleased with himself and enjoying the chance to display his acumen, Dr. Pendergast paused and examined the chess board before concluding, "Having ruled out those possible causes of your precipitous action of rushing out here with some news which you were sure would please me, it was child's play to anticipate the most natural fruit of a happy, healthy marriage: a child."

Brad was about to respond when his father added, "By the way, I think you will find that you have left a serious opening in your pawn wall." With an air of finality, Pendergast senior slid his queen across the board and declared, "Check and mate!"

CHAPTER 9 PROCTOR'S ROOM & BOARD

Luke was uneasy. He'd agreed to meet here, but it was the last place he wanted to be seen. The open area near the house was lit up by a gibbous moon and there was a light showing in one of the side windows, so he had retreated into the shadow of some bushes. The night breeze carried a chill and he realized that he needed to take a piss.

He checked once more to see if anyone was approaching from the street and turned toward an old barrel to relieve himself. Just as he was starting to button up, he thought he heard something behind him. He made a quarter turn to his right and caught a glimpse of something moving down out of the darkness. As the hammer made contact with his skull, Luke's muscles relaxed. His lifeless body fell forward onto the newly dampened soil.

* * *

The Artist straddled the body and swung downward with a backhanded blow which made a satisfying crunch. The old bastard had gone down without a sound. He smiled in satisfaction as he raised the weapon and gave the unresisting body one more smack alongside the ear for good luck. He dropped the hammer beside the body and began to check the pockets.

While he was still bent over the body pulling Luke's jacket back he heard a noise from the front of the house. Against the ambient light from the street he could make out the outline of someone approaching.

CHAPTER 10 THE HORN

Frank had stayed pretty sober. He turned his mind to what he knew of the killing of Harry Plumber. The night Harry died he had been playing poker at the back of the old Casino Real Hotel, Eagle Pass, Texas.

The Harry Plumber Frank had known was a bit of a nighthawk. Frank had been working part-time as a night clerk at the hotel, so he saw a lot of Harry. The day clerk told him that he had never seen Harry cross the front doorstep during the day. Well, it made sense. Harry was a gambler. Fact was, he was the best poker player Frank had ever seen. Harry would join the game late, maybe around ten at night and play almost 'til daybreak. It made sense that he had to sleep sometime.

Harry had a ranch out near the base of the small rolling hills that sat back about a mile from the bank of the Rio Grande. He turned up one day at the land registry office with a bill of sale and a deed transfer certificate signed by Jesus Fernandez and witnessed by a local lawyer. Jesus Fernandez had apparently departed for parts unknown. Jesus had relatives who disputed the sale, but in the absence of proof to the contrary, the transfer stood. Plumber moved into the large adobe farmhouse.

Townsfolk didn't ask too many questions once it became common knowledge how ready he was to spend money among the local merchants. Harry Plumber kept to himself other than coming into town three or four times a week to play poker. Rest of the time he was at his ranch. He had a double fence of barbed wire strung around the whole 160 acres and guard dogs roamed the inner perimeter of the property. Seems he liked privacy. He didn't bother anyone, and no one bothered Harry until the stranger came to town.

The stranger had walked in one night Plumber was playing poker. Frank thought he called himself Willkie Collins then. Even at the time the name had sounded a bit phony, like he'd made it up, or heard it some place.

Plumber had won a big pot with a full house. The stranger, a person then unknown to Frank, but now passing himself off as Harry Plumber in Sedona, was standing watching the game. This person said something to one of the losers in that hand and that cowpoke asked to have the deck passed over to him. When he got it he counted the cards out slowly so as everyone could see how many there were. It turned out that the deck had only 49 cards in it. Three cards were found lying under the table. Everyone naturally assumed that Plumber had somehow managed to take some replacement cards to fill his hand.

One of the men at the table was down a lot of money and Plumber had a huge pile of chips in front of him. He called Plumber a cheat and went for his gun. Plumber got his out first and shot him in the shoulder. The game broke up and everyone headed for home. The next morning Plumber was found dead near the entrance to his ranch.

There was nothing to tie the stranger to his death, but Frank remembered that something the stranger had said started the fight, and the stranger had checked out and left town the next morning.

CHAPTER 11 THE HORN

Jake had a good memory for faces. He had noticed Frank at the court house and had recognised him as someone he'd seen in Eagle Pass, where they'd both been the night Harry Plumber had died. There were plenty of reasons for someone to kill Harry Plumber. Harry had probably killed Jesus Fernandez and taken over his land. Without a body it was hard to prove that Fernandez was dead or that he hadn't willingly signed the deed over to Plumber. Jake had tried to find out. Before long Harry turned up dead.

Now Jake was calling himself Harry and he was in Sedona. Was it just coincidence that Frank was here too?

CHAPTER 12 GOING TO PROCTOR'S

Frank made sure Danny was not watching him as he left the bar. He was more sober than he had been for weeks at this time of night and he wanted to get home and to bed. He'd waited for the stranger to come back down to the bar, but finally he'd given up and left.

It was almost three and the main street was quite deserted. A moon which was almost full cast a cool light down the roadway. He stepped down from the long wooden porch and crossed toward his boarding house. The side door itself was in shadow, he'd need to fumble about to find the opening for his key. One night last week he had lost his key somewhere and had spent the night huddled up on the wicker sofa beside the door. Even though it was mid-June he had woken up shaking from the cold.

As he neared the lighted area near the door, he heard a noise off to his right. He turned and saw someone in the shadows over by the large trash barrel. The silhouette looked odd until he realised that it was one person bending over someone else who seemed to be lying on the ground.

"Are you okay there?" he called out and the figure turned towards him.

CHAPTER 13 THE HORN

Lil was a light sleeper. When she woke and found the man she knew as Hank gone, she was surprised. It was not unusual for a man to decide he had better get on home, or out of the hotel at least, once his sexual appetite had been satisfied. But it was not often that a sleeping partner could get out of bed without waking her. She checked the clock on the town hall across the street and found it was almost three a.m. The place where the stranger had lain was cold. He'd been gone for more than a few minutes.

She tried the door. It was locked. Her toe touched something and she groped on the floor and found the room key. The stranger had locked the door after going out and had pushed the key back under the door. That was mighty thoughtful.

She went over to the side window and looked out on the alley beside the hotel. It was brightly illuminated by the almost full moon and completely deserted. Lil lit the small lamp on the dresser and found the five one-dollar bills. She wasn't insulted.

CHAPTER 14 PROCTOR'S

As the figure took a step toward Frank, the moonlight revealed the face of Clive Harrison, one of the other lodgers at Mrs. Proctor's boarding house. Frank had had fantasies about Clive. His apprenticeship with the smith, Carter, had given tone and shape to the muscles of his arms and shoulders, but there remained a delicacy to his features. The contrast of masculine prowess and beauty was remarkable. Clive's sensitive eyes, pools of clear water in the ruddy complexion, were excitingly alluring. Frank had been on the point of coming on to Clive several times, but the memory of being driven out of other towns held him back. When the other boarder, Willard Wright, made a comment about Frank watching Clive, it was a warning. The job Frank had as town clerk was a good one; any revelation of his sexual proclivities would threaten that.

Now, as the expression on Clive's face became clear in the light,

Frank realised that something was wrong. There was something dark with a reddish hue on Clive's hands; it looked like blood. "What is it, Clive?" he asked.

Clive's answer was simple, "It's a body."

CHAPTER 15 THE HORN

Jake was moving back down the alley beside The Horn when he saw Lil's window light up and her silhouette pass in front of the lantern. He wondered if she had heard him leave after all. He hadn't thought she woke when he slipped out of bed.

He considered going back to spend the rest of the night. He had some unfinished business for the morning, but that was hours away and would have to wait. Then he decided to leave things as they were and moved on down the alley.

CHAPTER 16 DRIVING TOWARD SEDONA

"Red rocks, nothing but big red rocks," Doc Pendergast mumbled to his son Brad as he brought the buggy around the turn and within sight of Sedona's main street. "Used to be called Red Rocks around here. Now they've gone and changed the name to Sedona. Well, it once was Camp Lincoln, that was back in 1865, and then they changed that to Fort Verde. Guess it might as well be named after Carl Schnebly's wife, Sedona. Horrible thing to lose their daughter like that. The girl loved horses; and a horse accident killed her." Brad's father realized that he'd been sort of talking to himself and stopped. "That's what happens when you live alone, Brad. You become your own best company. You take care of your Alice, hear."

It hurt Brad to see how hard the loss of his mother had hit his father. He was glad he'd been able to take a semester off from his studies to come home for a visit. Alice was waiting for him back in Boston. "I'll do that, Dad; and we both want you to be with us."

Brad considered how often the bolt-out-of-the-blue can destroy our dreams. It was like that with the Schneblys. A few years ago the government had authorised a post office here and Carl had proposed the name Schnebly Station. The government response that the name was too long caused Carl to choose his wife's name, Sedona, which was approved. Everything seemed fine until the riding accident which had killed their daughter. Their hopes and plans were shattered by that. Most people said they thought that the Schneblys would even leave Sedona.

Martha Hardy had been blindsided in the same way. Seize the day, Brad reminded himself. You never know when the uncertainty of life will catch up with you. The world is a big place and even with the miracles of modern transportation, travel meant separation. He was sunk in contemplation about how the family could be together when his father laid a hand on his arm.

As if reading Brad's thoughts, the old doctor suggested, "When you finish your studies find yourself a town where they've got a nice blue lake."

Brad was following in his father's footsteps as far as becoming a doctor, and he also agreed with him about where to settle down. He didn't want to be in a big town, but it would be nice to be near a body of open water. The importance of water was emphasized living here, so close to a desert. Most people heading west decided to load up with enough water at Maripoca Wells to last across the desert from Maripoca to Gila Bend. Here in Sedona they didn't see the big wagon trains. It was mostly folk heading up Munds Trail toward Flagstaff. Now it would be the new road he reminded himself. But, everyone knew how vital water was.

You could pick out the areas with water from any high point of ground. Where there was water green things grew. There were farms near those areas growing produce. But when you raised your eyes and looked toward the uplands the desert plants took over. Cactus, creosote bushes and purple sage covered the hills. In the early morning light he could pick out some yellow-flowering blackbrush. In spring there would be wildflowers on the lower hills. At higher elevations they would give way to clusters of juniper, and ponderosa pines.

Brad had already decided to look for a place near a large town where he and Alice would be comfortable to raise a family and where his father could retire to enjoy the rest of his life. He pictured his dad sitting at the end of a wooden pier with a fishing pole in one hand and a book in the other. There could even be more than one grandchild to fish with him.

In the right setting he wouldn't even mind the early morning calls. He was riding into town with his father now in response to a message brought out to their homestead by Deputy Carl Munds. The deputy had not even got down from his horse, just relayed the message from the marshal to come to Mrs. Proctor's boarding house to look at a dead man.

CHAPTER 17 PROCTOR'S

Clive sat on a bench in Mrs. Proctor's back garden. He was holding his hands apart, like Marshal Hopkins had told him to. Hopkins had said something about protecting the evidence. Clive had no idea what he was talking about, but he sat quietly waiting for the marshal to tell him he could wash up.

He had told them that he got the blood on his hands when he bent down to see if he could help whoever was lying on the ground there under the bushes. That seemed likely, but the marshal had insisted that he wait and show his hands to the doctor before washing up.

It seemed pretty foolish to Clive. But the marshal had been real serious, so Clive just sat there.

* * *

Marshal Leroy Hopkins was standing where he could watch Clive and the body at the same time. He was asking Frank Green to tell him again about finding Clive and the body.

"Like I told you the first time, Marshal, I was just coming home and happened to see Clive over by the body. It wasn't like I saw anything or heard anything. I just saw him there and asked what was wrong."

"What made you think something was wrong?" the marshal asked.

"Well, maybe I didn't use those exact words," Frank said. "Maybe what I said was 'Who's there?' or something like that."

"What caused you to ask 'Who's there'?" Hopkins asked then.

Frank paused and thought a bit. They'd been over this ground a lot and he wasn't sure now exactly what he had said. He looked at the marshal in the light spilling out of the side windows of Mrs. Proctor's and replied. "To tell you the truth I think I heard something, and then when I saw Clive's face and the blood on his hands it made me think maybe something bad had happened."

The marshal just nodded and told Frank that he could go off to bed now if he wanted.

Frank nodded back and headed into the house. He looked over at Clive on his way in and wondered what really had happened. Clive had told him that he had just found the body, but if he had he was standing there a long time looking at it. Frank hadn't seen him go over to it or anything.

Just before Frank reached for the door, the marshal called out to him and had him wait on the step. Dr. Pendergast was arriving

CHAPTER 18 PROCTOR'S

Doctor Pendergast and his son pulled up in front and Brad waved to the marshal and Frank who he picked out standing by the boarding house side door. The father climbed down from the buckboard and moved briskly toward Leroy. He had just turned sixty, but still had a spring in his step.

The marshal waved to him and he headed back toward where a few early risers had gathered out of natural curiosity. He introduced Brad to Frank Green and had Green repeat his story to the doctor. Then Frank was released to go to bed.

The glow of the rising sun was painting the clouds along the eastern horizon as Brad and his father approached the blanket-shrouded body which still lay face down as it had been found. Although Clive had by his own account bloodied his hands checking the corpse, even he had not turned it over. Marshal Hopkins had kept everyone away and covered it to preserve the evidence. There was a small ball-peen hammer lying on the dry grass next to the body. The rounded peen was covered in blood.

Dr. Pendergast eased the gray woollen blanket back from the body and examined the wound in the growing daylight. The back of the male victim's head was caved in and would certainly account in itself for his morbidity. There were no other obvious signs of trauma and the doctor asked his son to aid him in rolling the cold and now stiffening body over onto its back. He examined the stiffness of various joints beginning with the fingers and progressing to major joints. He proceeded to a cursory examination of the side of the face which had been next to the ground and the sides of the arms. He had the marshal move the onlookers back to one side and took a rectal temperature reading while Brad discretely screened the body from the view of the crowd.

Once finished his preliminary examination, Pendergast covered the corpse again and called Marshal Hopkins over to him.

"Cause of death is probably the blow, or I should say blows, to the head. The progress of rigor mortis is slower of a night as warm as we have just experienced," he told the marshal. "But by a rough calculation, based upon body temperature, I would say that he's been dead at least four and as many as seven hours." The doctor pulled out his pocket watch and noted that it was almost 7:15 before adding, "That would make it after midnight but earlier than 3:30 at the latest. Has Mrs. Proctor been told?"

"Mrs. Proctor?" the marshal replied in surprise. "What should she be told?"

The doctor frowned and replied, "I thought you would have known. That's Luke Proctor, her husband, lying there dead. I haven't seen him in more than twenty years, since he ran off with that young girl, but that's him sure enough."

CHAPTER 19 THE JAIL

Bright morning sunshine did its best to penetrate the grimy windows of the jailhouse. The result was more murky than sparkling and the mood was no brighter. It had been decided to keep secret the news that the dead man's identity was known until interviews could be conducted with people who were connected and/or might be considered suspects.

Marshal Hopkins, Deputy Munds, Dr. Pendergast and his son Brad, were gathered around the marshal's desk. The desk had two side drawers and a central shallow one in the middle. The side drawers had pretty good locks on them.

The marshal kept his extra ammunition in the bottom side drawer, his handcuffs and leg irons in the top side drawer, along with a bowie knife he'd taken off a drunk cowboy some years back, and a notepad and a couple of pencils were in the centre drawer. The notepad was his filing system, his calendar and his pay book. He'd had the same pad for four years, ever since he'd taken over as marshal. He had it open on the desk in front of him and was scratching under his chin with the stub of a seriously chewed pencil.

"There are several people we want to talk with about this killing," Hopkins concluded. "I've already spoken with Frank Green, but I got a feeling he's holding something back; we'll speak with him again."

"Who you wanna see first, Marshal?" Carl Munds asked. Carl was keen. He had been deputy for almost a year and had complained more than once that most of his time was spent locking up drunks or running errands for the marshal. It was clear to everyone present that he was looking forward to a murder investigation.

"Well, I suppose we should talk to Clive again. I'd like to hear about how he found the body," Hopkins said while tapping his nose with the pencil. "Then we can see Doris Proctor, Frank Green, Clayton Edgett and the stranger. who came in on the stage What's his name, Carl?"

Carl looked pleased to be asked and pulled out a piece of paper he'd collected at the hotel that morning. "Harry Plumber. He checked in yesterday afternoon at The Horn. Didn't have much in the way of luggage. Pretty strange him coming all the way out here from Chicago with only a suitcase, a little hand bag and a case. I reckon he killed Luke Proctor, sure enough."

"Well, Carl, we have to give the man a trial before we hang him. So let's just go slow here. Might be good to get some proof to give the judge first," Hopkins said with a smile.

Brad cleared his throat and when the marshal looked over he said, "I think you'll find out that he's a salesman, Marshal. I came over on the stage with him from Flagstaff yesterday."

"Is that what he claimed to be?" Dr. Pendergast asked. His furrowed brows seemed to indicate his doubt on the matter.

Brad reddened a little and replied, "Well..., he didn't so much as admit that. But I gathered that was his line of work."

Hopkins turned back to his deputy. "Did you tell him not to leave town until we talked to him, like I asked?"

"Sure did, Marshal. Went right up and knocked on his door. He pretended like he was just waking up."

"Might be he was, Carl. It was about 7:30 when you went over to the hotel. I heard from Frank that the stranger might have spent some time with Lil late last night. Thing like that can cause a man to sleep in," the marshal replied.

"Well, if he was with Lil all night there's a chance we can rule him out, Marshal," Brad Pendergast suggested. "We might want to check with Lil to see if she can vouch for his whereabouts."

"That's a good idea, Brad," Hopkins acknowledged. He added Lil's name and the name Harry Plumber to the list of persons to be interviewed. Then he turned to Carl Munds. "Deputy," he said, thinking that he might as well acknowledge Carl's official capacity and give the young fella a thrill. Hopkins had noticed that Carl liked to use the title 'Marshal' when activities were the least bit official. The marshal appreciated the fact that young Carl was eager, but he was still only 23 and Hopkins wanted to bring him along gradually. At 47, Leroy Hopkins still had a desire to help keep the peace, but he knew that in a few more years he might want to step back and let a younger man take up the reins. "I'd like you to tell these people we want to talk with them. Have Frank, Lil, Clayton, and this stranger, Harry Plumber, stand by to be called when we need them. Frank will be coming into the town hall any time now. He can stay there until we call him. I don't want the other three to leave the hotel or talk to each other until we meet with them. Then collect Clive and bring him in here."

"Right, Marshal," Munds shot back. "I'll take care of that."

Brad Pendergast found himself amused by the seriousness of the deputy. He thought for a moment that the young man was going to salute Leroy. Instead he hurried out of the office looking like a man on a mission.

Hopkins turned to Dr. Pendergast and tapped his front teeth with the pencil stub. "Did you know Luke Proctor well, doctor?"

"Well enough," Pendergast senior replied. "I set up practice here back in 1870. Luke Proctor came here with Doris Proctor in the early 80s. He took off on her a few years after that, but I'd already seen enough of him to know he was a waste of space."

"Mrs. Proctor must have been pretty young when she started running that boarding house," Hopkins ventured.

"She was no more than the age of your deputy, Leroy. But, although she was a slip of a girl, she was a strong woman, even then, and running a boarding house in a town like this has made her stronger yet."

"Strong enough to kill Luke Proctor?" Hopkins asked and began to worry the blunt end of the pencil with his right canine tooth.

CHAPTER 20 THE JAIL

Clive Harrison worked at the livery stable. He was good with animals. Even though he had a slight, almost fragile build, and weighed not much over a hundred pounds, Brad had seen him calm and control a stallion who had bolted and seemed ready to kick down the smithy doors. Clive didn't have the build to become a smith himself, but he knew a lot about handling livestock. He had lived at Mrs. Proctor's since he had come to town from Tucson three years earlier.

When Carl brought him into the marshal's office, Clive had the same wild look in his eye as a wild beast at bay. 'What has this man so spooked?' Brad wondered. Certainly it would be upsetting for most people to stumble upon a dead body, but Clive's state of agitation seemed well beyond what Brad would have expected.

The marshal had set up another chair at the end of the desk such that the person being interviewed could be seen by the four investigators without sitting apart from them. Leroy indicated that Clive should take that chair and Carl Munds returned to the chair he had previously occupied.

While Carl was off arranging the availability of the people to be questioned, Hopkins had asked Dr. Pendergast if he and Brad would join him in questioning people. "I'd like to have your opinion of the truthfulness of these folk. Some of them you know better than I do."

Now Leroy took the lead and explained the situation to Clive. "This is all just for our information, Clive. Nobody's accusing you of anything," he said. "We just want to find out if you saw anything that might help us find whoever killed the man."

Brad watched Clive and thought that the young man became more nervous rather than less when Leroy said that. Clive's hands were on his knees and his body swayed forward and back as if he were about to spring to his feet.

"Could you just tell us where you were last night and how you came to find the body?" Hopkins asked and sat back in his chair to let Clive answer. Leroy held the stub of pencil between fingers of his right hand and began to roll it back and forth with his thumb as if rolling a cigarette.

"I had to see to the horses from the evening stagecoach and settle the regulars for the night," Clive told them. "Wells Fargo will collect them in the morning, but they have an arrangement to do the evening exchange here," he explained. "I walked home and was about to go inside when I heard a groan from over in the shadows. When I went over to look I found someone lying there. I tried to help him and got blood on my hands. Then Frank came along and I told him about the body."

"You heard a groan?" Hopkins asked and stole a look at the old doctor.

From where he was seated Brad could see Dr. Pendergast run a finger up the side of his nose and pull down the skin below the eye away from Clive. It was a sign which Brad read as meaning somewhere between 'My eye!' and 'I doubt it.'

"Well," Clive paused and then said, "I heard something and it made me look over that way and I saw someone lying there. I didn't know he was dead or anything. I just thought maybe he was sleeping there. Sometimes boarders forget their key and have to wait until someone comes by. That exact thing happened to Frank Green just a few weeks ago. You ask him if it didn't."

It occurred to Brad that Clive was working pretty hard trying to justify his actions. It didn't seem like the behaviour of an innocent man.

The marshal reached into his desk and drew out the hammer which Dr. Pendergast had confirmed was the murder weapon. He held it up and asked Clive, "Have you ever seen this before?"

Clive registered surprise and reached out for the tool. He examined the head and handle before responding, "I don't think so. It's pretty light for the kind of work we do, so I don't think it's one of Thomas's," he replied in reference to the blacksmith, Thomas Carter, with whom he worked. "Was this what was used to kill that fella?"

"Looks like it," the marshal replied and put the hammer back into the top drawer of his desk.

The marshal stopped with the drawer still open when Clive said, "I can tell you something about that hammer though."

"I thought you said you didn't know it," Carl said aggressively.

"I haven't seen it before, I don't think," Clive explained. "But there's a mark on the bottom of the handle that might mean something."

Hopkins took the hammer back out of the drawer and looked at the bottom. He passed it to Carl Munds who had taken the chair at his right hand. Carl looked at it and passed it on to Brad. There was a circle with what looked like an 'X' or a cross inside a circle cut roughly into the base of the handle. Brad passed the hammer on to his father and waited to hear Clive's explanation.

"That mark, a circle divided into four parts, is a symbol that was used by the Yavapai, the tribe of people who were in this territory when the Spaniards arrived. It looks a bit like a cross, so the Spaniards thought that the people were already Christians," Clive explained. "It's a common enough symbol around these parts."

Leroy asked a few more questions about the time of night and how long he was near the body before Frank came along. Then he asked Clive if he had seen anyone else about in the street on the way home.

"Matter of fact, I did," said Clive with a sort of puzzled look on his face. "I saw Jefferson Brooks. He was coming out from behind Sorensen's Lumberyard. Don't know why he would be out there that time of night."

Leroy Hopkins asked if anyone else had any questions and Dr. Pendergast raised a hand.

"You go right ahead, Doc," the marshal told him. "We're all just trying to find out what happened, is all."

"Well, Clive, you said that you heard a sound over from where the body was lying. Could it have been someone moving off through the bushes?"

Clive paused as if pondering something. Brad wondered if Clive would pounce on this as another excuse for claiming to have heard a sound. He thought that his father had just offered Clive a way out.

After thinking for another second or two Clive shook his head. "No," he said, "It wasn't that sort of a sound. It was more of a whooshing sound, but low and mournful. It could have been a snore or a sort of a huff, but it sounded like a groan sort of."

The doctor sat back with a speculative air. The marshal looked around the room and his deputy indicated that he had a question. Leroy nodded approval and Carl asked, "You came to town from Tucson a few years back, didn't you?"

Clive looked puzzled but responded without hesitation. "Yep, I worked for A.C. Soza."

"A.C.?"

"Antonio Campa Soza," Clive explained. "There are so many members of the Soza family in the cattle business near Tucson that everyone specifies which one when talking about them. A.C. has a spread right near the cathedral. Right handy for the stock auctions."

"What caused you to leave your job there and move here?" Carl asked in a tone which suggested that leaving a job was suspicious behavior.

"I thought I might be able to pick up some blacksmithing practice here," Clive explained. "Most of the time at A.C.'s I looked after the horses, but I got interested in the wide variety of brands the Soza family used. Here I help Thomas when he's got shoes to put on and he lets me practice working iron. I'm hoping to maybe start a business. There's good money in fine iron work like making tools and decorative pieces like window grills and gates."

Carl looked sceptical, but seemed to have run out of questions.

Leroy thanked Clive for his help and told him he was free to go.

Brad saw a look of relief and sadness pass over Clive's visage. He couldn't help thinking that something was wrong here. Clive seemed like a man with something to hide.

When it became clear that the marshal was finished with Clive for the moment, Dr. Pendergast addressed the young man. "Clive, it seems that Brad and I will be staying in town for the day. Would you please take our buggy and Grey over to the livery stables with you and take care of her needs?"

Clive was familiar with the doctor's horse, but Brad smiled when he thought of the surprise many people exhibited when they first heard Dr. Pendergast refer to the brown mare as 'Grey".

Clive readily agreed to stable Grey and quietly left the office.

CHAPTER 21 THE JAIL

The door had barely closed behind Clive when Carl Munds exploded with, "He's the one, Marshal. What kind of story is that? He's trying to claim that a dead man groaned. He's a sly type. I'll bet he was fired in Tucson for stealing something or other."

"Hold on there, Carl," Leroy cautioned. "There might be another explanation. What do you think about his claim, Doctor?"

Brad saw his father reach up his left hand and massage his neck. Then the old practitioner nodded his head slowly and said, "Well, your deputy might be right about Clive lying about the groan, but there is another possibility which might explain it."

All eyes were on the doctor, but he in turn directed his gaze at his son. He posed a question to Brad in the manner of a teacher grilling a student.

"Brad, can you suggest a bodily function which continues after death and might give rise to a noise such as Clive described?" he asked.

Brad thought for a second and then smiled in understanding. "There are several things the body keeps doing after death, some for a few seconds, some for a longer period, but the one which might cause the body to expel gas and perhaps emit a sound is digestion."

His father just nodded his head in satisfaction.

"Do you mean that the dead body farted?" asked the deputy.

"It could be that," Brad replied. "Or air released up the throat might cause the vocal cords to vibrate and create a sound very like a groan. That phenomenon is sometimes called a 'death rattle'."

"So, Clive might have heard what he thought was a groan," the marshal concluded.

"Yes," said the doctor. "But something else he said is more interesting."

"What's that?" the deputy asked.

"He said that he saw Jefferson Brooks coming out from behind the lumberyard. There is a reason why someone might do that without being interested in lumber."

"Yes, I thought of that too," agreed Leroy. "If a person were leaving Mrs. Proctor's back garden and didn't want to be seen, they might pass behind the lumberyard next door."

He looked around for his pencil and found it in his hand. As he reached for his notebook he said, "Carl, I think we should add Jefferson Brooks' name to our list."

CHAPTER 22 THE JAIL

Before Carl arrived with Mrs. Proctor, Hopkins asked the doctor about his secondary examination of the body.

Dr. Pendergast assured the marshal that the cause of death had been the blows to the head. "The first blow would have been enough to cause unconsciousness, perhaps even death by itself. Certainly Luke

Proctor was dead after the second blow was struck. The third blow was unnecessary."

"Sounds like someone was trying to make sure he was dead," Leroy speculated "Would it take a strong man to administer the blows?"

"Not at all," Dr. Pendergast assured him. "The skull is easy enough to crush with a hammer of the type found. If he were taken by surprise a woman could have done it as easily as a man."

Before the marshal could ask more, Carl Munds returned with Mrs. Proctor.

Doris Proctor was not a big woman in any sense. She stood a little over five feet tall and was what in a young woman would be called slim. As she neared middle age, folk were more likely to regard her as being wiry. She was a fine featured woman with delicate hands and large clear eyes. She reminded Brad of someone, but he couldn't think who exactly. Perhaps she made him think of one of the young nursing students who he had met during his classes at the teaching hospital.

His wife, Alice, had seemed a bit concerned when she saw how pretty some of the young girls he trained beside were, but he had reminded her that he had seen enough naked bodies in his dissection classes to cure him of any purely physical attraction.

The marshal rose and ushered Doris Proctor to the chair recently vacated by Clive. Brad looked for signs of nervousness and concluded that she seemed completely at ease. She looked around the room, ran her finger under the edge of the desk, and took note of the smeared glass in the window.

"Looks to me as if this place could stand to be cleaned up a bit, Marshal."

Leroy Hopkins looked at the window and allowed his eyes to sweep around the room. He rubbed the left side of his chin with the pencil. Feeling the stubble from his overnight growth of beard, he looked at the pencil as if it were somehow to blame and set it down on top of his notebook. "I reckon you're right about that, Mrs. Proctor. Just as soon as I get time, I aim to take care of that." He opened the top drawer of his desk and started to reach inside. Then he seemed to think better of it and closed it again. He picked up the pencil and began taping it against his palm. "What do you know about the man found dead on your property?" he asked finally.

"I know that Clive didn't kill him, Marshal," she told him. "It was a major topic of discussion over breakfast this morning. Clive was quite upset, naturally, and Frank Green said he thought you suspected him. Frank was so upset he barely touched his breakfast this morning, just rushed off to work. My only other boarder at present, Willard Wright, claimed to have slept through the whole commotion."

"What about you, Missus? Did you sleep through it as well?" Leroy asked.

"Certainly not! I'm a light sleeper, always have been. When I heard you arrive I looked out and saw you talking with Frank. Then I got dressed when I heard Dr. Pendergast and his son arrive," she continued. "How are you, Brad? I heard you were back visiting. How's everything back east? You'll be finishing up your studies pretty soon, won't you?"

"Yes, Ma'am," Brad managed before the marshal intervened. "Hold on there," Leroy said raising both hands palm outward. Brad noticed that he was holding the pencil between his right index finger and middle finger like a cigarette. "We're conducting an investigation here, Doris. You can socialize with Brad later."

Brad had to fight to avoid laughing. He knew that Mrs. Proctor was always aware of every bit of gossip and all the comings and goings of the townsfolk. He had seen her standing just inside her back door keeping an eye on things when he and his father had arrived at her house a few hours earlier.

"Mrs. Proctor," Marshal Hopkins continued, "We believe that there is a possibility that you may know the man who was killed last night." He paused to let that sink in and then added "Would you be willing to look at the body and see if you can identify him?"

"That's not necessary, Marshal. I know who he is." She replied with determination. "He's Luke Proctor, my husband. I killed him."

CHAPTER 23 THE SMITHY

Thomas Carter was adding fuel to the forge and preparing some iron rods when Clive arrived. He looked up and nodded a greeting.

"Sorry, Thomas. I had to talk with Marshal Hopkins about what happened last night."

"I heard about it. You feeling okay to work?"

"I'm fine, Thomas. The horses need tending to. I'll get right to that. If you need me, I'll be out in the stalls."

Clive passed on through the smithy and entered the stables which stood as a separate building behind it. He checked each of the stalls and picked up a fork to start mucking out. As he passed the chest he used to store his personal tools and some of the practice pieces he'd been working on, he wondered if he should clear it out and get rid of some of his work. It wouldn't do to have the marshal find out about his personal iron work.

CHAPTER 24 THE JAIL

Carl started to say something in response to Doris Proctor's calm announcement. Leroy Hopkins held up his right hand for silence and then pointed the tip of the pencil at Doris Proctor and asked, "Are you admitting that you killed your husband, Luke Proctor?"

"Course I am. Didn't I just say so?" she replied in a voice devoid of emotion.

"Why did you kill him, Doris?" Hopkins asked gently.

"I'm not going to talk about it. I did it and that's all you need to know."

"Did you shoot him?"

"Don't be draft, Leroy," Doris replied. "Everyone in town knows his head was bashed in."

The confession, coming as it did was less than convincing. Brad sensed that Mrs. Proctor was determined, but innocent. He could understand why she might be glad to see Luke Proctor dead, but he couldn't imagine her killing him out of passion after all these years.

The marshal made several other attempts to draw her out, but she finally just refused to respond. Faced with her silence, there was nothing he could do but move on. He wasn't about to lock her up here. The facilities weren't exactly suitable for a woman prisoner. He asked her to promise not to leave town and sent her home to look after her business.

Two minutes later Carl was standing at the window watching her walk back toward her boarding house, which was a few hundred feet down the street on the opposite side, next to Sorensen's lumberyard and building supplies. It was almost directly across from The Horn. "You think she'll make a run for it, Marshal? You think we should set up a stakeout?" he asked while keeping one eye on the retreating figure.

"If she was going to run she would have left before now," Hopkins countered. "Besides, I don't suppose she really did kill him," he added with a smile at Dr. Pendergast who nodded agreement.

Brad felt he was missing something. "Why in heaven's name would she confess to killing him if she didn't?" he asked.

"Could be she's trying to protect someone else," Marshal Hopkins answered.

"Well, who the hell would that be?" Carl Munds demanded.

Brad suddenly realized what it was about Mrs. Proctor that had reminded him of someone he'd seen recently. "Clive," he replied. "Clive is a relation of hers. Could be a nephew, or . . ."

"Or a son," his father finished the thought for him. "Doris Proctor was born Doris Harrison. About eight months after Luke Proctor left town I delivered a boy child of Doris Proctor. She had gone to Tucson to stay with her mother and when she came back to Red Rocks she left the boy in her mother's care."

"You knew this all along," Brad said. "So, Clive did kill Luke Proctor."

"Should I go pick him up, Marshal?" Carl asked. Brad thought he saw Carl look toward the drawer where the handcuffs were kept.

Dr. Pendergast and Leroy exchanged glances of exasperation with the young men they had to curb. "Brad," his father said, "Just because Doris Proctor is worried that her son might have done something and is trying to protect him, doesn't mean that he is guilty."

Brad sat back sheepishly, but Carl spoke up and attention shifted to him. "Well, it must have been someone Luke Proctor knew pretty well to allow them to get behind him with a hammer."

Dr. Pendergast gave a little cough and said, "Not if he was taken by surprise, which seems likely."

Leroy Hopkins looked sharply at the doctor. "What makes you think that he was taken by surprise?"

"Well, there were no defensive wounds, and I noticed a small detail while I was making my second examination," the doctor answered. "It doesn't prove anything, but it could explain how someone could have come up behind him."

The marshal and deputy both looked perplexed. Brad had assisted his father in the examination, but he couldn't think of any aspect of the corpse which could suggest a surprise attack.

"Like I said, it isn't proof," Dr. Pendergast said. "But, I noticed that his fly was open."

Carl laughed. "He was taking a piss when someone smacked him?"

"It's possible," the doctor confirmed.

The marshal leaned back and peered out the window to catch sight of the town hall clock. "It's gettin' on towards noon, I was hoping to talk again with Frank Green before he got over to the Horn at lunch, but I also don't want Lil, Clayton, and the stranger, Harry Plumber, to start comparing stories," he said thoughtfully. "Here's what we'll do. Carl, you go over to the clerk's office and tell Frank that the town will be buying him lunch today. Then you get him to order something and get the hotel to bring it over. Have lunch with him yourself, if you like, but don't be discussing the murder with him. I want to have him fresh when we all meet with him after lunch."

After Carl had gone off to isolate Frank, Hopkins turned to the two Pendergast men and said, "We can interview Lil, Clayton, and the stranger over at the hotel." Hopkins tore out the page he'd written the names of people to be talked to. He shoved his notebook back into the center drawer of the desk and rose to his feet.. Brad noticed that by habit the marshal tucked the stub of a pencil into his right front pocket.

CHAPTER 25 THE HORN

Clayton was behind the bar getting glasses and stock organized for the lunch regulars, which on a Tuesday in June were not many, when Hopkins and his two companions walked into the saloon. According to town bylaw liquor was not to be served before noon, and state law set a curfew of 2:00 a.m., but in Sedona no one watched the clocks very closely. There were two of the Wingfield ranch hands having a beer with a Wells Fargo driver who was on a layover from the night before. In addition to raising cattle, the Wingfields supplied some of the horses for the stagecoach line, so the beer could be considered a business lunch, Leroy supposed.

He recognized the two cowboys at the bar. One, Sam Schuerman, was a cattle drive boss. His nickname was 'Shoe', or sometimes "Sure Shoe" based on his nature of hurrying the cattle and the drivers. Everyone lost a few on the way to market. 'Sure Shoe' lost fewer than most. Both Sam and the lanky cowboy beside him, Larry James, were locals. Their families had been homesteaders. Neither had ever caused Leroy any trouble and he was willing to cut them some slack. An early beer was certainly nothing worth making a fuss about. The driver would be leaving town when the stagecoach from Tucson pulled in.

Hopkins made a point of not noticing that the two men had mugs of beer and went over to stand across the bar from Clayton Edgett. "Clay," he said without preamble, "I need to talk with you, Lil and this stranger Harry Plumber. I know you have work to do, so I can talk with you later. Can you tell me where Lil and the stranger are?"

"Lil's in her room, Leroy. Been there all morning ever since Carl Munds came over here telling everyone to avoid talking to each other and, in the case of the stranger, not to leave town."

"Where's the stranger at then?" Hopkins asked.

"He's out in the lobby, Marshal. He doesn't look too happy, but I followed Carl's instructions and avoided him," the bartender replied.

"Well, Lil will keep, I reckon. We'll go talk to this Harry Plumber and then go up to see Lil," he said. "We'd still like to meet with you later."

"No problem, Marshal," Clayton replied. "I'll be here 'til six. I've got tonight off."

The three men headed out to the small hotel lobby which was to the left of the saloon. There they found the stranger seated in an overstuffed chair reading what looked like a handwritten document of several pages. As he saw them approaching, he closed the cover on his reading material and slipped it back into a leather briefcase which was leaning against one of the chair legs. His eyes met Brad's and he acknowledged their familiarity with a quick nod..

"Morning, Mr. Plumber," the marshal said by way of greeting. "This is Dr. Pendergast and his son, Brad. They're sort of assisting me in the investigation into the dead fella we found. I wonder if we might ask you some questions."

"I'll be quite willing to help you all I can, Marshall," the stranger responded. He had his long legs stretched out on a horsehair hassock and as he said this he let his feet fall off one on each side of the footstool and leaned forward. He reached down and lifted the leather briefcase onto his lap. "But before we start talking, there's something you ought to see." He reached into the leather satchel and brought out a white envelope. Then he stood up and set the briefcase on the chair. He took a folded sheet of paper from the envelope and handed it to the marshal. With the other hand he held up a badge.

CHAPTER 26 THE HORN

Leroy Hopkins read the paper carefully and then said, "Well, I can't say I like having this dropped on me like this. You should have come to see me as soon as you arrived in town." He passed the letter to the doctor who read it quickly and gave a little, told-you-so smile to his son as he passed it on.

"It wasn't that simple, Marshal. I had to be sure the person I'm investigating didn't find out who I was," the stranger replied. "If he had tumbled to the fact that he was being investigated, he might have taken off on me."

Brad Pendergast, having finally had a chance to see the letter, said, "'Jacob', your real name's 'Jacob E. Witherspoon' and you're a Pinkerton Agent?"

"I prefer 'Jake' to 'Jacob', and in fact I'd be obliged if you kept that to yourselves and call me Harry Plumber, or Hank while I'm still investigating," Jake said and held out his hand for the letter.

Hopkins reached over and took the piece of paper out of Brad's hand. He looked it over again. "It says here that you're a Pinkerton man alright, but there's no mention of you working on something at the moment. What's this investigation all about?" he said with a serious tone of voice. Then he added, "How do I know that you didn't kill the real Jacob Witherspoon and take this paper from him?"

"You can contact the Pinkerton Agency in Chicago," Jake told him. "They'll confirm my identity, but the subject of my investigation has to remain private. I'm dealing with some dangerous people, Marshal. I've got to be careful."

"I can't say I'm too happy being kept in the dark; but I'll contact your office and if they confirm your identity, we can come to some accommodation," Hopkins replied. The marshal took his pencil and folded sheet of paper out of his pocket. He went over to the hotel counter and copied some information onto his sheet before pocketing the sheet. He set the pencil down on the counter and then thought better of it and put it in his pocket as well. He handed the letter back to the stranger, looked him in the eyes and said, "In the meantime I'd like you to tell us where you were last night."

"I spent much of last night with a lady, Marshal. Then, I was alone in my room from about 3:00 a.m. until your deputy woke me up this morning," Jake informed them.

"Half the town knows you went upstairs with Lil last night," Hopkins agreed. "Can she vouch for your whereabouts until 3:00?"

"She seemed to be asleep when I left, but I imagine she can tell you where I was 'til she fell asleep."

"And what time was it that you left?" Hopkins asked.

"A little before 3:00. My room was just down the hall," Jake replied.

"Did you go straight to your room?" the marshal persisted.

Brad noticed the stranger's eyes slide away toward the window before he responded. "Fact is, I went for a bit of a walk before heading to my room. I wanted to check on something, Marshal."

"What were you checking on at 3:00 in the morning that couldn't wait for morning?" the marshal asked. "And where were you checking it out?"

"Curiosity, Marshal, I wanted to see who was still at the bar. I took a quick look and I headed off to bed. I was asleep by a few minutes after 3:00."

Brad reached out a hand to touch the marshal's arm. Then he whispered to him "Why'd he leave the bar in the first place if he was waiting for someone there?"

Hopkins smiled a little and said, "Why don't you ask our friend here that yourself, Brad. I'm sure we all were wondering."

Finding everyone looking at him, Brad reddened a little. Then he coughed lightly and said, "Seems a bit odd to me that you're supposed to be investigating this suspect, and you go off to Lil's room instead of keeping an eye on him."

Jake smiled and nodded as if he agreed. Then he sat back down in the chair he'd been in when they arrived and answered, "Even I don't work 24 hours a day. I choose when I follow someone and who I talk to. Sometimes I even take a bit of time off for my own pleasure. You can understand that, can't you, young man?"

Brad realized that the stranger was right. He didn't have to account for his work habits to them. Young Pendergast looked over at the marshal who took over for him.

"I'll check out your story 'Hank'. But don't be leaving town until I tell you I'm satisfied." There was a bit of emphasis on the way Hopkins said 'Hank'.

The stranger nodded. He drew the same document he'd been looking at before, or another like it, from his briefcase. He settled back in his chair and turned his attention to the document. The three men looked at each other and the marshal signalled with his head for them to head back into the bar.

CHAPTER 27 THE HORN

"Man seems pretty sure of himself, I'd say," Dr. Pendergast ventured once they were out of earshot. They were standing together just outside the saloon door. The room had cleared out. Clayton was washing up some glasses at the far end of the bar.

"Either he has nothing to hide, or he's hiding it well," Hopkins responded. "I'll telegraph Pinkertons and see if they back up his story. I've known the Pinks to resort to some underhanded dealing when breaking up unions, but they don't usually creep around back alleys smashing in heads with hammers. We'll let the man alone until we know more about him."

"I'm sorry about asking that stupid question," Brad said. "He made me look like an idiot."

"We were all wondering the same thing," his father replied. "Asking questions is never wrong; it's sometimes more important than physical evidence."

"Speaking of that," the marshal said, "I noticed that Frank had no noticeable splashes of blood on his clothes, hands, or face. Do you think he could have struck the blows with that hammer and have avoided getting bloody?"

"That's a good point, Leroy," the doctor said. "I had wondered about that too. I've seen hunters get bloody just picking up a few ducks or a brace of rabbits. Frank didn't seem to have any spots of blood on his face, where drops might well have landed. If they had been there it might have told us something, but their absence doesn't prove that he didn't bash in Luke Proctor's head. I noticed that the only blood on Clive was on his hands, but the same caveat applies."

"So, either of them could have killed him without getting big splashes of blood?" Hopkins said by way of confirmation.

"Or both," Brad added helpfully. "Even having blood on you doesn't prove much. Take your deputy, Carl. I noticed that he had a smear of blood on his sleeve just from moving the body."

"I saw that too," the doctor confirmed. "I wondered about it at the time. I don't know how he managed to get his upper sleeve bloody that way just moving the body."

"Carl's about as clumsy as they come," Hopkins said with a smile. "He trips over the doorway at the jail almost every time he comes in. I don't know that he could handle a hammer well enough to hit a head first try. I often worry when he's got a gun in his hand."

"Speaking about hammers," the doctor continued. "Clive said he'd never seen that hammer; said it was too light for blacksmithing. But he talked about doing some fancy iron work, branding irons and stuff with a lot of detail. Seems to me that he might well need a smaller hammer for that sort of work."

"Or it might be about the right size for a woman who was handy and did her own repairs to keep," Brad suggested.

"Well, since Mrs. Proctor's already confessed, I don't see much point showing it to her. She'd just claim it was hers to support her story," Hopkins exclaimed. Brad noticed that the marshal had taken his pencil out and was rolling it around in his right hand. Poker players talk about someone having a 'tell', a facial expression or body gesture which betrays their emotions. He wondered what the marshal's manipulation of that pencil could tell him.

He got his answer about Leroy's present thought process when Hopkins said, "Guess we should add another person to our list. We can show that hammer to our smith, Thomas Carter. Might be he will recognise it."

"You might find out something interesting about Doris Proctor by asking her about it," Dr. Pendergast suggested with a glint in his eye.

"But she'll just claim it as hers, like I said," Hopkins said with a frown.

"Oh, I don't mean show it to her," the doctor continued. "Just ask her to describe it. In fact, why not show her some other hammer and ask her to show how she held it, or something like that. It might at least convince us that she didn't do it. If it is hers she would certainly know about that divided circle symbol on the handle."

"Speaking of symbols, Marshal," Brad said, putting one hand on Leroy's arm. "When our friend in there was taking out that collection of papers I happened to notice that one of them had drawings of diagrams on it. There might be some connection to that hammer. Might be some kind of code."

Leroy Hopkins and his father both looked at Brad as if he was talking nonsense. "Can't see why he'd need a code for something he keeps in a case," the marshal responded. "But even if it were that would be his business, I reckon."

Embarrassed again, Brad looked away from Marshal Hopkins and through the saloon doors. More to change the subject than for any other reason he said, "Clayton looks as if he's not busy now, Marshal, do you want to talk to him right away?"

"Might as well," Hopkins agreed. "I want to find out for certain when Frank left the bar and if Clayton noticed anyone leaving about 2:00 or so."

CHAPTER 28 THE HORN

Clayton looked up as they approached the bar. "I hear someone was killed last night."

"Do you know something about that?"

"Only what everyone in town is saying, Marshal. This morning one of the maids told me that Clive killed someone called Luke Proctor, Mrs. Proctor's husband that left town years ago. That was before my time here in Sedona. Clive wasn't in here last night, if that's what you want to know."

Brad had almost forgotten how quickly word spread in a sleepy town. Nothing went unnoticed.

Clayton leaned across the bar and said, "Hope this won't take long, Leroy. Business tends to pick up about this time of day."

"Just a few questions, Clayton," Hopkins assured him. "You were at the bar last night until closing, were you?"

"If I wasn't the stock would all be drunk and the till empty" Clayton replied. "I could use an assistant; but it's hard to find one who won't drink the merchandise."

"Frank Green was in here all night, was he?" Hopkins continued.

"Pretty much," Clayton agreed. "He was at his spot at the end of the bar. Wasn't drinking as much as usual, and he left about the same time as the stranger."

If Hopkins was surprised by this information, he didn't show it. He asked the bartender, "Did you notice what time that was?"

"Well, I'd say it was near onto midnight, maybe a bit after, because Jefferson Brooks came in just about then," Clayton told them. "He's an odd duck. Often enough he comes in at that time as if it were noon. Guess in his business night's a good time to work."

"How long did he stay?" the marshal continued. Brad could see Hopkins' right hand working its way into the top of his pocket.

"'Bout an hour, I'd say. That's usually how long it takes him to drink two beers," the bartender told them.

"Did you notice anyone else come in or go out around that time?" Hopkins continued. He had unfolded his note sheet and was tapping the surface with the point of the pencil.

"Well, Marshal, I was busy enough and people come and go all night. A lot of the ranch hands prefer to relieve themselves out in the alley, not being too used to indoor plumbing. Matter of fact though," he said, rubbing his chin as if recalling the night before, "I did notice Danny going out the door at about 1:30. He was back in his corner the next time I looked that way though. So, he couldn't have been gone long."

Hopkins wrote something on the paper and asked, "Was Danny here late?"

"He left at about 3:00, right after Frank. I wondered about if he was following Frank; Danny's an odd one too if it comes to that."

This time Hopkins did react. He set down his pencil, rubbed the back of his neck with his right hand and said, "Hold on there, Clayton. You told us that Frank left at about midnight. He couldn't leave at midnight and also leave at 1:30 and 3:00."

The bartender had been holding a cloth in one hand and fussing with glasses while answering the marshal's queries. Now he set the glass down and seemed to be surprised himself. "That's right. He did leave. He must have come back sometime later. Can't say I noticed. One minute he was gone, then he was back again. People come and go, Marshal; I just serve drinks."

CHAPTER 29 THE HORN

As Clayton was saying this, Carl Munds came in through the front door and joined them at the bar. Brad noticed that Carl had a few spots of gravy on his shirt front and what was either blood or ketchup smeared across one cheek.

"Well, when did he leave again, or is he still here?" Hopkins asked the bartender with a bit of exasperation showing through.

"Guess it was more like just before 3:00, like I told you, Marshal," Clayton said as if Hopkins should know. "'Cause that was why I wondered if Danny was following him that time 'cause he also went out the second, or third time, whatever it was." He paused for a second and added, "Say, you don't suppose Danny had something to do with that guy gettin' killed, do ya?"

Marshal Hopkins looked over towards the bottles standing up on the shelf behind the bar and took a deep breath before he consulted his notes and summed up, "So, the stranger, Hank, went upstairs with Lil around midnight; Frank left by the front door at the same time; Jefferson Brooks came in at midnight and left at 1:00; and both Frank and Danny left at about 1:30 and again just before 3:00. Is that all correct?" he asked looking at Clayton.

"Yeah," Clayton said nodding vigorously. "Except Frank went out first and Danny left a few minutes later, like."

"Did anyone else leave between 1:00 and 3:00?" Hopkins asked.

"Not that I noticed," the bartender said holding up his two hands, palms outward, as if confirming that he didn't know anything else.

"And you were here all night at the bar, were you?" Hopkins asked.

"Absolutely," Hopkins agreed. "Except when I had to go down and connect another keg of beer," he added.

"Down to the cellar?" Hopkins asked laying his pencil down on the bar and then grabbing at it as it started to roll away.

"Well, yeah. That's where the kegs are. It's too warm up here to store beer, Marshal," Clayton said with a look of hurt innocence.

Leroy Hopkins clasped his hands together and asked, "When was that, Clayton? When was it that you left the bar to change the keg?"

"That was at about 1:30. Say, that was probably why I didn't see Frank come back in."

Hopkins made a note and circled it. He looked around to see if anyone else had any questions. Brad and Dr. Pendergast shook their heads to decline and Carl looked as if he was trying to catch up. Hopkins nodded and said, "Thanks, Clayton. Let me know if you remember anything else, will you?"

"Sure will, Marshal. Always willing to help out," Clayton said. He picked up his towel and started polishing a glass. Brad thought the glass already looked as clean as most of the others.

CHAPTER 30 THE HORN

They walked to the back of the saloon and went through a double set of doors which led to a set of stairs to the first floor up. As soon as the doors were closed behind them Hopkins gathered the four men into a circle. "Well?" he said and waited for comment.

"Not the most reliable of witnesses," Dr. Pendergast ventured. "I wouldn't want to see a man hanged on his testimony." He paused and then added, "Or a woman either."

"I wonder why Frank didn't mention his absence from the bar earlier," Brad mused. "And this Danny fellow. I don't know him at all."

"He's a bad one," Hopkins explained. "He wasn't in town when you were growing up. Kept to the spread his family had down south a way. He's killed more than one man, I'm sure. But there's been no proof. If I were Frank, I'd keep an eye out for him."

Carl had been looking avidly from one speaker to another. Now he ventured a comment. "I reckon that Danny's behind this killing," he declared. "Frank Green is terrified of him for some reason."

"Well, Frank has his own reasons for being nervous, I imagine," Hopkins responded. "I'm all in favor of looking at Danny for this murder; but, we're going to tie him to something eventually anyway. Maybe we should just try to find the guilty party for this one. Danny will wait."

"What's all this about Frank leaving twice, Marshal? Frank told us that he left just before 3:00. If he's lying about that, chances are he's lying about other things too," Carl said with a determined tone in his voice.

'Carl won't be happy 'til someone gets strung up for this one,' Brad thought.

Hopkins turned to the deputy and directed him, "I'd like to see what Frank's answer is to that question, Carl. I'm going to talk with him now, but I'd like to send off a telegram to this address. Our stranger claims to be a Pinkerton man. I'd like to check out his claim. See if you can get one of theThompson boys to take the wording to Schnebly's. Join us at the courthouse as soon as the telegram is on its way."

CHAPTER 31 THE COURTHOUSE

On the way over to the courthouse Hopkins stopped off at his office. The two Pendergasts waited outside while he went in. He came out carrying a small burlap bag which Brad guessed contained the hammer. The clerk's office in Sedona was not fancy. Frank had a desk and a chair and a three-drawer filing cabinet. There was a counter which separated the area where Frank worked from the door, and provided a surface upon which those who could read and write could look at local documents and/or fill out requests for claim registration or land transfer.

Frank was sitting at his desk when the three men entered. There was one extra chair in the office, so the four of them gathered at the counter and Hopkins posed his questions.

The marshal folded back the top of the bag such that the symbol on the bottom of the handle was visible. While the Pendergasts looked on with interest, Hopkins called Frank's attention to the symbol on the hammer and asked if he'd seen it before.

Frank took his time looking at the circle with two crossed lines and replied, "Not that I know of, Marshal. If that's what was used for the killing I wouldn't have been able to see it in the darkness."

"Frank," he said. "We've got a bit of a problem with what you told us earlier."

"How's that, Marshal?" Frank asked. "I just told you what happened." Brad thought that Frank seemed more surprised than nervous. At that point Carl came in the front door and joined the group. He nodded to Hopkins and then drew up to the counter and leaned against the edge of it.

"Well, you told us that you left the bar just before 3:00, Frank," Hopkins said. He said it gently, Brad thought, as if he didn't really want to spring what he now knew on Frank.

"That's right, Marshal," Frank confirmed. "That's when I did leave. If anyone says otherwise they're wrong."

"Let me put it another way, Frank. Was that the only time you left the bar?" There was something about the way Leroy Hopkins asked the question which caused Brad to wonder if he wasn't trying to protect Frank Green.

Frank paused to consider the question. Deputy Carl Munds was leaning forward, his eyes were fixed upon the town clerk as if anticipating evasion by Frank. Brad allowed his attention to drift over to watch his father and noticed that the doctor was watching Hopkins, rather than Frank. Brad sensed that there was a lot riding on Frank's response.

As if a light had just gone off for him, Frank spread his hands open before him in a gesture which Brad interpreted as indicating openness. His answer seemed almost anti-climactic. "Well, I did step outside briefly at about midnight," he said. "Fact is that Jefferson Brooks asked me to take a look outside. He said that he'd been followed by someone from his shop and he asked me to see if there was someone hanging around outside."

"And was there?" Hopkins asked.

"Not that I saw," Frank told him.

"So, you just took a look outside and came right back in, did you?" the marshal persisted.

Green looked around as if wondering what all the questions were about. Brad wondered himself what Hopkins was doing. It almost sounded as if he was coaching Frank.

"Well, not directly," Frank answered. "I watched the door for a minute or so and then stepped into the alley beside the hotel."

Carl couldn't control himself. "And why would you do that?" he demanded.

CHAPTER 32 THE HORN

Lil was fed up. Well, more accurately, she was starting to feel a little hungry. Carl Munds had told her to wait for the marshal in her room, but that was almost four hours ago. She had gone back to bed, but hadn't been able to rest easy knowing that Marshal Leroy Hopkins was going to be visiting. Hopkins was a strange man. Lil couldn't quite make out what it was about him that she found so unusual, but she sensed that he was hiding something.

She had spent most of the morning sorting through her clothing and deciding which of the garments had outlived their usefulness. She had even taken time to write a long and rambling letter to her sister. Evelyn was a born missionary. For years she had tried to convince Lil that a life of prayer and devotion was more rewarding than all the gold in the world. Lil avoided most of the details of her daily, and nightly, activities and concentrated on describing the scenery and the weather.

Concluding her message with a wish that Evelyn was well and happy, she sealed the letter, shoved clothes deemed useless into a burlap bag, and headed down to the bar.

Clayton was rearranging some of the glasses on a shelf in front of the plate-glass mirror. Lil caught his eyes in the glass and waved. "Any chance of getting breakfast at this hour, Clay?"

Still holding a glass in his right hand, the bartender turned and said, "Well, sure, Lil. Did you talk with the marshal?"

"I sat up in my room for the last four hours since Carl woke me up and I haven't seen a soul," she replied. "Have you seen him?"

Clayton noticed the glass in his hand and set it down on the bar. "He was just here. I thought they were on their way up to your room when they left."

"Well, if you see them again tell them I'm in the restaurant," she told him and headed out the door which led toward the hotel lobby and dining area.

CHAPTER 33 THE HORN

Jake looked up from his document and was pleased to see Lil come though the archway into the lobby. "Good morning, or rather good afternoon," he called out cheerfully.

"Good morning to you, Hank. Have you seen the marshal lately?" Lil asked. She noticed that Hank had a small ruler in one hand. He seemed to be measuring something on a chart he had spread out on the front desk. As she walked toward him he folded the piece of paper and slipped it and the ruler into his briefcase.

Jake smiled. "As a matter of fact, he was here a few minutes ago. Apparently someone was killed last night and he's interviewing everyone in sight. Did he talk to you?"

"No! I've been cooling my heels in my room waiting for him. I just decided to have a late breakfast. Who was killed; was it Danny?"

"Do you mean was Danny killed, or was Danny the killer?"

"Either would be likely. Maybe the town would get lucky and he'd be both."

Jake had to smile at that. "Would you mind if I joined you for a late breakfast? I started the day with black coffee and burnt toast."

"Someone should have warned you. Our cook can fry eggs without breaking a yoke, but he tends to forget the toast until it starts smoking," Lil told him. "I'd enjoy your company over breakfast, or perhaps we should call it lunch."

CHAPTER 34 THE COURTHOUSE

In the courthouse office Frank was looking at Carl as if he were an idiot. "I went into the alley because I had to pee, and the alley is marginally cleaner than the john at the bar. Have you seen that place?"

"He's got you there, Carl," the marshal declared. "Even the mice won't piss in there."

"No, no, I meant why were you watching the door?" Carl clarified.

Frank sighed and replied, "I never like to turn my back on Danny. I wanted to make sure I wasn't being followed."

"And were you?" Hopkins asked.

"No," Frank responded "And by the way, Carl, I went out one other time to pee also about an hour later." He paused and turned back to the marshal. "I wasn't followed that time either, I checked, always do."

"Did you go back in right away?" Carl asked. Brad could see that Carl was trying to make up for being made to look foolish.

"Not right away, no. I walked to the back of the hotel and looked up at Lil's window to see if that stranger was there or not. He's who you should be checking out, not me."

"Why is that, Frank? What do you know about the stranger?" the marshal asked with renewed interest.

"For one thing I know his name's not Harry Plumber, like he's been claiming. I knew Harry Plumber. The stranger might have killed him." Frank said with determination.

CHAPTER 35 THE HORN

Jake was working his way through a second breakfast, a plate of fried eggs and ham with some flapjacks instead of toast. Lil had opted for the cook's speciality, Eggs Ranchero and home fries. She was starting to feel more human.

"What did Marshal Hopkins want to know, Hank?" she inquired while sipping tentatively at the coffee. Like the toast, their cook had a habit of neglecting the coffee. Sometimes it tasted burnt too.

"I think he wanted to know if I killed the fella," Jake told her. He had a bit of a twinkle in his eye as he said it.

"Did you?" she asked.

"Not that I recall," he grinned. "I was otherwise occupied."

Lil added a bit of sugar and gave her coffee a stir. It wasn't the best coffee she'd had here, nor the worst. "I suppose it depends when he was killed. I woke up to a cold bed. I thought you might stay 'til morning."

"Never like to outstay my welcome. Thought I'd give you a little space," he answered.

"Well it was nice of you to lock the door on the way out." She met his eyes and asked frankly, "You still thinking of settling down around here?"

Before Jake could respond, Lil looked up and exclaimed, "Well, look what the cat dragged in. I thought you'd gone fishing, Marshal."

The four men stood at the doorway and Marshal Hopkins stood with his hat in his hand and an abashed expression on his weather-lined face. "Well, Miss Lily . . ." he began.

"If you want to talk with me, Marshal, I suggest you pull up a chair," Lil told him with a bright smile. "I've ordered breakfast, but I don't mind chatting while I eat."

"Fact is I haven't had lunch myself, Lil," Leroy Hopkins responded. "If you and Mr. Plumber don't mind the company I'd enjoy that."

Jake rose and pulled back a chair to indicate his agreement and the marshal turned to Carl Munds. "Carl, you had lunch with Frank, so I'd be obliged if you'd ride back out to Schnebly's to see if we have a reply to our telegram."

"You got it, Marshal," Carl replied. Brad thought he looked relieved to have something physical to do.

"You're welcome to join us too, Dr. Pendergast. I haven't had a chance to talk with Brad since he got back," Lil offered.

Brad hadn't been a frequent customer of The Horn nor ever one of Lil's, but in a small town everyone knows everyone else and there are very few secrets. The marshal, Brad and his father seated themselves while Carl went out to the front of the hotel. When the three men were seated at the table with Lil and Hank, they all ordered the daily special of hash browns, pork chops, and beans.

"So, tell me everything," Lil commanded Brad.

CHAPTER 36   THE SMITHY

Clive was starting to wonder what he'd gotten himself into. He should never have agreed to meet with his father. He should never have talked to Larry James. Most of all, he should never have let Frank Green find him near the body. Now his mother was claiming she'd killed her estranged husband, and Clive could only think of one way to keep her from being convicted and hung.

CHAPTER 37 THE SMITHY

Carl paused in the doorway of the smithy and let his eyes adjust to the dim interior. The smith, Thomas Carter, was turning a bar of iron with a gloved hand and repeatedly pulling down on the handle which drove the bellows. His face was alternately cast into shadow and lit by a ruddy glow. Carter was the strongest man in town. When a wagon had collapsed at the feed store and trapped a farmer against the side of a shed, Carl had seen Carter lift the axle unaided. Later, Carl and three others had tried unsuccessfully to duplicate the feat. What was the smith thinking of taking on a weakling like Clive as an apprentice?

As the deputy entered the smithy, Carter paused in his action with the bellows and thrust the iron bar deep within the glowing coals. He turned toward Carl while slipping off his gauntlets and helping himself to a mug of well water.

"Mornin', Carl," Carter greeted him, "Lookin' to ride out again? Clive is out in the stables right now. He noticed that your horse could stand to be reshod."

"Morning, Thomas, I'll see to that later. I've got official business out at the Schnebly place right now."

Thomas Carter had another sip of water and took care to wipe the smile off his face. The position as assistant to the marshal had gone to the young man's head. Well, he was young; probably he'd grow into the position.

"There's something else, Thomas," Carl said. He glanced around as he said this as if to ensure that there was no one within sight or earshot. "Marshal wants to have a private word with you. Probably be over later today."

"Well, he knows where to find me, Carl," Carter said with mock seriousness. The deputy nodded briskly, as if he'd just delivered important information, and made his way through the smithy toward the stables.

Clive was in one of the stalls near the back working away with a hoof pick on the front shoe of a gray gelding. As Carl approached he held up a piece of stone he'd just pried out and tossed it into a bin. He bent over the foot and pulled a brush from a pocket of his leather apron and began brushing briskly at the hoof. Without raising his head he called out, "Star's pretty close to losing a shoe from the right front, Carl. If you're heading out, take it easy with her."

"Not going far, Clive, but I'll get Thomas to reshoe her now. Do you have another horse I can use while Star's being fitted?" As he said this, Carl loosened the cinches and began lifting his saddle off the back of his horse. Clive finished up with the gelding and came over to give him a hand.

"There's a bay one of the outriders for the stage uses from time to time, Carl. He's not going to be back this way for week or so. She could use the exercise."

"Fine, I'll be back directly to get her," Carl told him. As he started toward the smithy to arrange reshoeing of Star, Carl turned back toward Clive. "That fella you found dead last night, Clive, did you ever see him before?"

After a slight pause, during which his eyes slid over toward the open doorway, Clive said, "I haven't really seen him yet. It was pretty dark where he was lying and he was face down."

A minute later, Carl came back, mounted the bay and rode off. Clive wiped his hands on his apron and then walked with determination toward the smithy.

CHAPTER 38 THE HORN

Brad reddened a bit and said "Things are going well, Miss Lily. I've got another year of studies and then I'll start looking for a spot to open an office."

"Not planning to take over your father's practice?" she prodded.

"Not much of a practice left, Lil," the older Pendergast interjected. "I have hardly enough patients to keep occupied. A young doctor needs more of a challenge."

"Sedona was busier when you started here. After the gold rush quieted down, people moved on," Brad explained. "I'd just like to find a larger community."

"I suppose your wife would also like a larger town?"

"Alice and I share my father's love of open space, but, yes a bit larger would be good."

Jake sensed that he was in the way and said, "Well, if you folk will excuse me, I'm going to stretch my legs a bit." He pushed his chair back, nodded to Lil and the others and sauntered off.

Lil watched him leave and then said, "Looks like you frightened Hank off, Marshal."

"I think he realized that I have a few questions to ask you, Miss Lily."

"Ask away, Marshal."

"We're just trying to eliminate suspects, Miss Lily," Hopkins explained. He looked ill at ease and seemed reluctant to ask his questions. "Could you just tell me if you went out of the hotel at all last night?"

Lil seemed to be enjoying the marshal's discomfort. She reached up and toyed with her earring before responding. "Hell, Leroy, the whole town knows I was in the saloon last night until midnight and then headed up to my room with Hank. I had company who could vouch for my whereabouts when that fella was killed."

Leroy seemed relieved to get the ball rolling a bit. "Well, I wonder if you could just tell me what time your company left, Miss Lily."

The question seemed to take Lil back a pace. She looked more serious as she said, "I know for sure he was gone at 3:00; I'm not exactly sure how much earlier he left."

CHAPTER 39 THE SMITHY

Clive listened to Carl ride off and went back to examine another of the gelding's hooves. He was bent forward with the right front hoof between his legs when something blocked out the light. He raised his head in expectation of seeing Thomas Carter coming to ask for assistance at the forge. Before he could make out who it was, a heavy blow came down across his neck and the lower part of his skull. His limp body pitched forward into the trampled straw.

CHAPTER 40 BROOKS' MORTUARY

Jefferson Brooks had no sense of humour. He knew that well and had tried to remedy the failing. He didn't want to live down to the common expectation of most people. Folk thought that his profession was ghoulish enough without thinking him obsessed with death.

He had tried to develop a pleasant manner of speech. He even went as far as to memorize jokes and to try to fit them into conversation. However the effect on others was never what he hoped for. An awkward silence succeeded his attempts at levity.

His physique was against him for one thing. Jefferson was tall, thin, with a natural stoop which gave him somewhat the appearance of a vulture. His long arms, and his habit of carrying them clasped in front of his chest had led to his nickname, 'Mantis', as in praying mantis.

He had obtained a pamphlet outlining the theories of an Austrian physician, Sigmund Freud, who had put forward the idea that what drives us is buried in our unconscious. Although we are not aware of them, these drives continue to impact us dramatically, according to Dr. Freud. Jefferson had also read the Stevenson novel, Strange Case of Dr. Jekyll and Mr. Hyde.

Jefferson was much worried by one fact which seemed to bring the theories of Dr. Freud and the imaginings of Stevenson together. He was a sleepwalker. He had on occasion awakened to find himself in a room other than his bedroom, and once standing in the open door of his house. Was it possible that he was living two lives?

CHAPTER 41 THE HORN

The marshal and Dr. Pendergast exchanged meaningful glances. Brad knew what they were thinking. Either Harry, who claimed he was Jake, or Lily, could conceivably have killed Luke Proctor.

To Lil the marshal said only, "I've one more question for you, Miss Lily. Did you know Luke Proctor well?"

"As far as I know I still don't know him, Marshal. Am I supposed to?"

"Not that I know of, Miss Lily. I just wondered," replied Hopkins.

"Hold on there, Leroy," Lil demanded. "You asked 'did I know?' Is that the name of this fella that was killed?"

Leroy Hopkins just nodded politely and the three men excused themselves.

CHAPTER 42 SCHNEBLY'S LODGE

Carl had the response telegram in his back pocket. It was addressed to Leroy Hopkins, U.S. Marshal. If it had been a letter Carl wouldn't have opened it. But a telegram was sort of different. The telegram operators at both ends had read it, It wasn't in a sealed envelope. Well, it was in an envelope, but not tightly sealed, and there was no stamp.

Carl read it. The telegram from Pinkerton's agency confirmed that they had an agent assigned to Sedona (which they referred to as Red Rocks) and they had provided a description which fitted the stranger pretty well. They had also included some test questions to which the real Jacob E. Witherspoon would know the answers.

Carl was eager to get back to town to deliver the message. He was mindful of what Clive had said about Star having a loose shoe. He should have noticed himself. Star was a good horse; Carl hoped to still be riding Star when he made marshal; he thought the name suited.

As he passed the smithy door, Carl waved to Thomas Carter who was pounding away at a bar of iron and rode around to the stables. He dismounted and looked around for Clive. If he wasn't helping Carter, the young apprentice was usually in the stables. Carl led his borrowed horse into the cool shadows of the enclosure and started down toward the compartment he used. As he approached the stall he saw something odd lying between the feet of the gray gelding in the adjoining box stall. Clive's body was stretched out on the ground.

* * *

The Artist watched Carl rush out of the stables and hurry toward the hotel. It seemed likely that the deputy had found Clive. Two deaths within 24 hours would create quite a stir in Sedona.

CHAPTER 43 THE HORN

Jake was sitting on a bench outside the Horn waiting for the stagecoach when the marshal and the two Pendergasts came out onto the porch. He nodded and watched the three men step down into the street and start across toward the marshal's office.

Then three things happened at once. The stagecoach made the turn into town and started down the main street, Lil came out the front door of the hotel, and Carl came out of the smithy and started running down the street waving his arms and calling out, "Marshal, Marshal!"

* * *

Frank was watching from the front window of the courthouse. Carl was sure excited. Frank was surprised to see Clay Edgett standing in the door to the saloon. It was unusual to see Clay anywhere but behind his bar.

His attention was diverted from watching Carl running and Clay watching by the sound of the front door to the office opening. He turned and watched Jefferson Brooks walk in. Frank was perhaps the closest thing Jefferson had to a friend and even Frank always felt ill at ease around the mortician. Jefferson dressed habitually in black and spoke in a ponderous way that made conversation difficult. On one occasion Frank had been present when the undertaker had tried to tell a joke. The sombre manner of his delivery had made it seem as if he were recounting a tragedy. The period of silence which followed it had yawned like an abyss.

Frank wondered what business could bring him to the land and registry office.

CHAPTER 44 THOMPSON'S DRY GOODS

Doris Proctor was coming out of Thompson's dry goods store. She had a basket over one arm and a bolt of broadcloth tucked under the other.

The basket contained a set of bone buttons and a few other supplies she had specially ordered to make a new top coat for Clive. She had noticed that he had begun wearing his present coat to work and it was starting to look a bit shabby. The bags of flour, salt, and sugar that she bought would be delivered along with the other heavy items, but she was taking personal charge of these special items.

Doris was midway through instructions to Jim Thompson's eldest girl, Violet, when she caught sight of Carl Munds running out of the nearby smithy. Carl turned wild eyes towards her and seemed surprised to see her there. Then he looked toward The Horn and started calling out, "Marshal, Marshal!"

Now she stood frozen in place as Carl approached Marshal Hopkins and the Pendergasts in front of the hotel.

Carl was speaking quickly and loudly. Doris heard Clive's name spoken and looked back toward the smithy where the brawny smith could be seen emerging, carrying Clive's limp body in his arms.

Doris was no weakling, but her head spun and she felt faint with fear. Dropping her basket and letting the bolt of cloth tumble into the dust, she ran, her heart in her mouth, toward Thomas Carter and his precious cargo.

CHAPTER 45 THE JAIL

Brad listened as Carl told Hopkins of his discovery.

"Clive's dead, Marshal. Just like the other. His head's been bashed in," Carl exclaimed. "I found him when I got back. Someone's killed him too."

Turning his attention toward the smithy, Brad saw Tom Carter emerge from the shadows carrying Clive's body. Something about the care with which the smith cradled the slim young man made Brad think there was hope. He urged his father to join him and then hurried ahead to meet Carter.

CHAPTER 46 THE COURTHOUSE

Frank joined Jefferson in the doorway and they watched side by side as the Pendergasts moved toward Thomas Carter. Quickly though young Brad moved, Doris was there before him. Carter stood holding Clive as if he weighed nothing while Doris crowded close. As Brad Pendergast drew near, Carter could be heard to say "Alive, he's still alive!"

The stagecoach was drawing to a stop in front of The Horn but all attention was on the small but growing group around Carter. Brad Pendergast had taken off his coat and the smith was following Dr. Pendergast's instructions and setting Clive's limp body on the edge of the boardwalk with Brad's coat cushioning his head.

By common accord Frank and Jefferson crossed the street and joined the others. Marshal Hopkins was kneeling beside the doctor and Dr. Pendergast directed his first words to him.

"The boy's been knocked out, but he is still alive. He must be moved very gently to a proper bed."

Hopkins looked around and picked out Lars Sorensen who had joined what amounted to a fair percentage of the townsfolk in the main street. "Lars," he said, "We need to fashion a stretcher to move Clive. Do you have the makings in your yard?"

"I've got some eight-foot rails that will serve. We can fasten some rope or a blanket across them," Lars replied.

Doris Porter rose from her spot next to Clive on the boardwalk and pointed back toward the dry goods store. "There's a bolt of broadcloth that will work, Lars. Use that."

Violet, who had come out of Thompson's and gathered up the items which had spilled from Doris's basket, now set them aside and lifted the bolt of cloth. Brad rushed over to take possession of the cloth and then followed Lars who was hurrying off toward his lumberyard.

Lily and Jake had come up to stand beside the marshal. Now she spoke up. "You can bring Clive to the hotel, Leroy. We've got a cot behind the front desk where he can be laid down."

Before the marshal could respond, Doris spoke again. "If you bring him to my place we can place him on the daybed in the parlor. There I can care for him."

Hopkins looked to Dr. Pendergast who nodded agreement. "He may not come around for some time. I'd like to see him somewhere quiet."

CHAPTER 47 THE HORN

Clayton Edgett watched from the doorway of The Horn saloon. The excitement in the street was quieting down. Lars Sorensen and Thomas Carter were bearing the makeshift stretcher toward Mrs. Proctor's boarding house under the watchful eyes of Dr. Pendergast and Doris Proctor. Clayton imagined that a number of the men of the town would gather in The Horn to share stories and opinions. He could look forward to a busy afternoon.

His attention shifted to the Wells Fargo loading area. There, amongst the parcels of freight sat a polished cowhide suitcase. Beside the suitcase, removing a pair of buckskin gloves, stood a well-dressed man in the prime of life. His clothes were well tailored and his black hair and moustache shone with the lustre of a rich pomade.

CHAPTER 48 PROCTOR'S

Dr. Pendergast directed Mrs. Proctor to let Clive rest as undisturbed as possible and to contact him if Clive showed any signs of worsening or of coming around. "Rest is the best thing for him at present," he told her. "The effects of the injury he has suffered are uncertain. We must wait."

Hopkins, Brad and Carl stood together by the parlor archway. Now, as Dr. Pendergast moved toward them they prepared to take their leave of Mrs. Proctor.

As they walked down the drive toward the main street, Brad spoke. "I'd almost forgotten how well a small town pulls together at a time of crisis. It's like being part of one big family."

"Except for one thing," his father corrected.

"What's that?" Brad asked.

"One of these people attacked him."

CHAPTER 49 THE COURTHOUSE

As they walked back to the courthouse Jefferson Brooks seemed excited; Frank might even say that the old fellow was animated. His sallow, sunken cheeks seemed to have acquired a touch of color. He was breathing rapidly and his eyes had an almost lively character to them. Frank had seldom seen him like this. Could it be the prospect of another cadaver which so invigorated the usually impassive mortician? Surely not; that would be disgusting. Someone had to look after the dead, but to relish the prospect was revolting.

Frank ushered Jefferson into his office area expecting to learn the reason for his unusual visit. He was astonished by the first words spoken.

"Just like his father. There must be a connection."

CHAPTER 50 THE HORN

Jake stepped up beside Jesus Soza and said, "Welcome to Sedona. You have come at an interesting moment."

At 57, Jesus Fernandez Soza was an impressive individual. He had grown up as the eldest son of a minor branch of the Soza family which had arrived in Tres Alamos in the latter half of the 19th century. Jesus had built up a sizable cattle operation north of Tucson which had recently been experiencing serious losses of cattle under mysterious circumstances. He had contacted Pinkertons seeking assistance in solving the problem. Jake was that assistance.

"So it seems," responded Jesus. "You must be Mr. Witherspoon."

Jake was aware of Clayton's presence, possibly within earshot. He responded carefully. "Please call me Hank. But let's get you checked in and settled. We can talk more privately in my room."

CHAPTER 51 THE COURTHOUSE

"Just like whose father, Jefferson? What are you talking about?" Frank demanded. He wondered if the mortician had finally gone insane. Sniffing all that embalming fluid had to kill brain cells. Brooks may have slipped over the edge into madness. Lord knows he'd never seemed to have too firm a grip on reality.

"Clive's, of course. Who else has just been hit over the head like his father before him?" Jefferson countered.

Now Frank was really puzzled. Granted he was a newcomer to Sedona, but he'd never heard anyone speak of Clive's father, let alone say that he'd been bludgeoned to death. In response to Jefferson's comment he merely replied, "I don't know anything about his father. Was he hit over the head too?"

"Of course, I was forgetting. You're not from here. You wouldn't know."

"Know what?" Frank inquired, confusion turning to annoyance.

"Clive's mother is Doris Proctor; his father was Luke Proctor."

CHAPTER 52 THE JAIL

"Thomas Carter is one strong man," Carl remarked. "He would have no trouble smashing in someone's skull. We should find out where he was last night, Marshal. He might'a done Luke, too."

Carl suspects everyone, Brad thought. He was on the verge of pointing out that Carter seemed to have saved Clive's life when his father put a hand on his arm to restrain him. They waited to hear Marshal Hopkins' response.

Hopkins just looked at Carl and said calmly. "Let's go do that, deputy. Where was Clive when you found him, and where was Carter?"

"Why, Clive was lying on the floor of the stall right under that gray gelding he was tending to when I left. Carter was in at the forge. I didn't see him when I got back 'cause I rode straight to the stables. He was working at the forge when I ran through there after I found Clive."

"Speaking of your errand, Carl, was there an answer to my telegram?"

Carl put his hand to his forehead and said, "I plumb forgot with finding Clive and all. Yes, I've got the reply right here." He reached into a back pocket and produced a Western Union envelope which he handed to Hopkins.

CHAPTER 53 PROCTOR'S

Doris Proctor was sitting on a dining room chair she'd drawn up beside Clive. He hadn't moved since they'd settled him on the daybed. He looked deadly pale, but his breathing seemed normal enough. Dr. Pendergast had made up a special sort of bandage which fitted on the back of Clive's head and kept pressure off the point where he had been hit. The doctor had instructed her to avoid moving Clive and to send for him if the boy showed any change. She was gently feeling Clive's forehead to check for signs of a fever when Willard Wright came in the side door.

Willard came into the parlor with his cap in hand and said, "Lars suggested that I quit work early today. He thought as you might need me to help with Clive or to do something else for you while you're busy tending to him."

"That was right thoughtful of you and Lars, Willard. I appreciate that."

Willard looked ill at ease. Clearly he had something on his mind. Finally he gave voice to his concern. "Mrs. Proctor, I just thought you should know. People are saying as how Clive's your son. They asked me and I didn't know what to say."

Doris was tempted to tell him that it was no one's business, but she knew that wouldn't wash. In a small frontier town everyone wanted to know everything. Besides, Willard was not a busybody. He was usually quiet and kept to himself. Willard had come north to Red Rocks in 1888 as a teenage orphan. Most people knew little of his history, but he'd confided to Doris that he'd lost his family to an Apache attack at their homestead near Redington along the San Pedro River. Since then he'd worked at the lumberyard and helped out on odd jobs on ranches.

Doris had risen when Willard entered the room. Now she settled back onto the chair and motioned for Willard to sit as well. He looked around and then drew up another chair from the table. He perched on the edge of it and turned his cap nervously in his hands.

"My husband, Luke Proctor, was gone before you came here, Willard. Clive is my son, but he was raised by my mother as her own. For a long time he thought he was my brother, but we told him the truth when he was fifteen. When he came here we saw no reason to tell those folk who didn't know. Those who did know have been supportive and kept it our secret. I guess the time has come to make it public."

Willard had reddened during her recital. Now he stood and said in a tone of pain and sincerity, "I think he's pretty lucky to have a mother like you, Mrs. Proctor. I'll just go up and change out of my work clothes. Then I'll be here to do whatever you need."

As he left the room Doris found herself wondering what had brought Luke Proctor back to Sedona now and if that was connected to the attack on Clive.

CHAPTER 54 THE JAIL

"Do you suspect Carter of attacking Proctor and Clive?" Brad asked.

"Not really. For one thing, if Thomas Carter had hit Clive, he'd be dead, not just knocked out," Hopkins told him.

"Don't forget that Carter was the one who discovered Clive was still alive and carried him out to us," Dr. Pendergast added. "If he wanted him dead he could have finished him off then."

"He might just be trying to look innocent," Carl insisted. "The smithy is right next to the stable. How come he didn't hear Clive being attacked?"

"Let's go ask him that too," Hopkins suggested. "But first let me read this telegram."

"It says Pinkertons have an agent here, Marshal," Carl volunteered. He flushed as he realized that he was admitting to having read the message and then added, "They sent some questions you can use to confirm his identity."

Hopkins opened and read the telegram. "So it does, Carl. I guess we'll ask the questions, but that sort of eliminates him as a suspect."

Brad thought he detected a trace of disappointment in Carl. He punched the deputy lightly on the arm and said, "Cheer up, Carl; we eliminate until we have one left."

"Yeah, and then what?"

"We keep him."

* * *

The Artist was angry, and a bit nervous. Clive was supposed to be dead. Dead men tell no tales, right? If Clive started telling what he knew, the marshal might start connecting the dots. Something had to be done to make sure he didn't start talking.

CHAPTER 55 THE HORN

Clayton poured beer for the men. The stagecoach driver and the outrider, Tom, had come in with Sam Schuerman and Larry James. The driver was asking about the crowd in the street when the stage arrived.

"First thing we saw was your deputy running down the street flapping his arms like he was trying to take flight," the driver said with a laugh. The driver was a regular on layover. Clayton thought his name was Paul, but everyone seemed to call him 'Badger.'

"Carl's okay," Sam said with a smile, "But he gets a bit het up sometimes."

"Then your blacksmith comes out carrying his apprentice like a rag doll," the driver continued. "It made me think of that Frankenstein character from the book."

"Monster," Clayton corrected. "The doctor was Frankenstein, the monster is the one you mean."

"Well, anyway, you catch my drift. It looked as if he was carrying a sacrifice or something," the driver explained. "Sure was odd."

The outrider took a sip of his beer and said, "I heard that someone was killed last night."

CHAPTER 56 THE SMITHY

Thomas Carter was not in the smithy when the four investigators arrived. There was a bar of iron heating in the forge and a mug of water sat on the window ledge.

"He's run off," Carl declared. "That proves it. He must have killed both of them. We should form a posse and run him down, Marshal."

Dr. Pendergast took a sip from the mug of water. He smiled as he set it down and examined the bar of iron. "The water is still cool and the bar is not yet overly heated. I suggest that our worthy smith has not been gone long and will return."

Brad took up the prognosis. "Water drawn cool from the well will come to room temperature quickly enough, and Carter would not bother heating iron he did not mean to beat."

"Are you looking for me, Marshal?" Thomas Carter asked from the back door of the smithy. "Since I'm on my own here, I was out seeing to the horses."

CHAPTER 57 THE COURTHOUSE

Jefferson filled Frank Green in on the details of Luke Proctor's abrupt departure and Doris Proctor's decision to establish her boarding house to avoid losing the property. "She had her hands more than full, running a boarding house, without having to raise a young boy on her own at the same time," Jefferson told him. "She could have just gone home to her mother, I suppose, but Doris Proctor has a lot of gumption. I have a lot of respect for her."

Frank thought that there was something odd about a mother giving up contact with her son like that, but he had to admit that his own emotions would be considered odd by many.

CHAPTER 58 THE SMITHY

"I was meaning to talk with you earlier, Thomas, but things just seem to keep happening," Hopkins told the smith. "You know Brad Pendergast, don't you?"

"Sure, Marshal. I did some work on the doctor's wagon and Bradley took an interest and assisted me with the job. Have you decided to give up medicine for buggy making, Brad?"

"I'm going to be sticking with medicine, Thomas," Brad replied. "But if you want to get in on something, you should see what they're doing with the new safety bicycles back east. People have even attached motors to them. Some are claiming they will replace carriages."

The big smith rubbed his chin and replied, "I reckon they won't be able to carry much with just two wheels and for crossing the desert I'd want something more reliable."

"I'd like to see one keep up to a horse over rough ground," Carl scoffed. "They might be alright on paved streets, but we won't be paving that road Schnebly built any time soon. Even the stagecoach has to go slow on that."

With the air of someone pulling back the reins of a runaway wagon, Hopkins turned the discussion back to the problem at hand. "I was wondering about last night, Thomas. Where were you, say about midnight?"

"Where I usually am at that time, Leroy, I was in bed asleep."

"So you couldn't say how late Clive Harrison was here at the stables?"

"Nope, I wasn't here."

"He claimed to have stayed on doing work at the forge," Carl put in.

Carter dismissed the implied doubt in Carl's question by simply responding, "If he said he was, he probably was." He looked at each of the four men in turn and added, "Clive's a good worker. He starts early and works late. Even so, he's always ready to help out with some shoeing or forging."

"What about today?" Hopkins continued. "Did you hear anything today when Clive was attacked?"

"I was pounding out a piece of iron. You don't hear much over the sound of that. I only went back after Carl came running through here as if the building was on fire," Thomas explained.

Brad stole a look at Carl, who was fidgeting as if the deputy would rather not be reminded that it was Thomas Carter, not himself, who had realised that Clive was still alive.

Carter paused and then added, "Matter of fact, I'd like to show you something in the stables."

The men followed Carter back to the stables. He led them to a handmade wooden trunk. The lid stood open and they could see a number of tools and forged iron articles.

"This is Clive's personal storage," Carter told them. "He keeps pieces he's working on in here. From time to time he shows me something he's fashioning. Sometimes he asks advice; other times it's just to show me something he's proud of. Clive has a great touch for detailed or elaborate iron work."

"You found it open like this?" Hopkins asked.

"Yes, when I came back to tend to the horses I noticed it standing open. It may have been open earlier, but I don't think it was."

"Did Clive keep it locked?"

"Yes, and the lock was forced," Carter told him. "It wasn't a strong lock. Anyone could have opened it with this." He reached down and picked up a small pry bar which lay on the ground.

"Was anything taken?" Carl asked.

"I don't know for sure, but it seems to me there was more in here," Carter said with a shrug. "It's Clive's personal work, Marshal. I don't like to seem to be prying, so I only get involved if he asks me to. I'll take a look at it and let you know if anything seems odd."

"Please do that," Hopkins told him. "You don't have to do it right now, but have a look and let me know."

"Which stall was it you found Clive in, Carl?" Brad asked.

"The one second to the back, next to my Star," Carl said leading the way down toward that enclosure. "I see you moved the gray gelding up near the front, Thomas," Carl called out over his shoulder.

"Thought you might want to examine the stall," Carter responded. "Other than picking Clive up and moving the gray I haven't touched anything."

Brad wondered what Sherlock Holmes would have made of the trodden dung and straw covered floor of the stall. He imagined him crawling about the enclosure on his knees with a magnifying glass and tweezers. With a shake of his head he dismissed the image.

Dr. Pendergast gripped Hopkins by the elbow and pointed to a dark chunk of material lying along one side of the stall. Hopkins used a pitch fork to move aside a clump of straw which was partially covering it. The doctor stooped down and examined what looked like a foot-long piece of dark wood. He picked it up and examined the underside.

"I think this is what Clive was struck down with," he suggested. "There's a bit of what looks like blood on the edge." He hefted the object with two hands and added, "This isn't wood though. It's more like rock."

"It's petrified rock," Carter told him. "Clive had a piece. That looks like it." Carter moved closer to Dr. Pendergast and looked at the fragment. "I think that's the piece. He kept it on the window ledge near his tools."

"We'll want to keep this as evidence," Hopkins said. Carter made no comment and Dr. Pendergast handed the petrified wood to Carl.

"Thanks, Thomas," Hopkins told him. "If there's nothing else you can tell us, we'll look over the stall and let you know if we have any other questions."

"Well, there is one thing you should know, Marshal. That stranger who arrived yesterday came asking questions. He said he was thinking of buying a spread here and wanted to meet the smith."

"Did that seem strange to you, Thomas?" Hopkins asked.

"Not in itself it didn't, but he seemed more interested in looking around the smithy and asking questions about Clive than talking about his own plans."

CHAPTER 60 MAIN STREET SEDONA

Jake and Jesus were crossing the street on their way to the marshal's office when they heard a call from their right and turned to see Marshal Hopkins, Deputy Munds and the two Pendergasts coming down the street toward them. Jake and Jesus stopped where they were and waited as the group approached.

When they were close enough to talk without shouting, Leroy Hopkins held up the telegram he had received and said, "I've received confirmation of what you told me, Hank. I just need a moment alone with you."

Jake raised a hand in recognition and replied, "Probably won't be necessary. I'd like to introduce you to Mr. J. F. Soza, Marshal. I was sent out here to do some work for him. Because of the death last night and the attack today, we've decided to turn the matter over to you. Could we discuss this in your office?"

CHAPTER 61 THE COURTHOUSE

"So, what did you come to see me about?" Frank asked Jefferson. "With all the excitement, I didn't get to ask."

"It's about some land, Frank. When he left town so suddenly years ago, Luke Proctor owed some money to some cattlemen. He also owed me some. His wife, Doris, didn't have any, so I just sort of wrote it off as bad luck," Jefferson explained.

Frank waited to hear Jefferson out. He couldn't quite see where this was going, so he just waited until Jefferson picked up his tale again.

"Luke had title to the land around his house and him turning up dead like that, got me thinking," the mortician continued. "I believe that Sorensen's lumberyard is sitting on part of that land."

"And if it is, Jefferson, what then?"

The face of Jefferson contorted itself into what looked like a grimace.

Frank thought the man was undergoing a stroke, or a fit of some sort. Then he realized that Jefferson was doing something unusual. He was smiling.

CHAPTER 62 THE JAIL

Once inside the marshal's office, Hopkins went to his desk and encouraged the others to take a seat. They were one chair short, so Brad sat on the edge of a chest near the window. He wondered what business this Mr. Soza could have which required a Pinkerton agent being despatched. The man's appearance suggested a certain level of wealth. He was wearing expensive fitted clothing and a silver bracelet with turquoise stones encircled his left wrist. His hair was neatly cut and brushed straight back. The black hair had a luxuriant shine to it which suggested use of a hair oil. His shoes were expensive and the shirt looked like it was tailor-made. Brad took note of the well-manicured finger nails and the fact that his hands bore no calluses, common amongst those who engaged in manual labour. Upon consideration, Brad decided that Mr. Soza was a foreign banker, perhaps from Spain or Italy. Undoubtedly some financial scandal was about to be revealed and Pinkertons had been called in to try to recover stolen funds.

Hopkins took the piece of petrified wood from Carl and set it on the floor beside his desk. Brad was watching Mr. Soza closely and noticed how his eyes focused upon the artefact. He wondered if the banker knew what it was.

His father seemed not to be paying much attention to Mr. Soza. Brad wondered if he had stolen a match on his father this time. He resolved to wait until the proper moment to reveal his insights into Mr. Soza's profession and to question him.

As soon as they were all settled, Marshal Hopkins pulled out the telegram and said, "Mr. Witherspoon, you have identified yourself to me as a Pinkerton employee on assignment. I have received a telegram from the head office of Pinkertons which acknowledges that one Jacob E. Witherspoon has been sent to Sedona. The telegram contains two questions which you should have no difficulty answering. I suggest we get that out of the way first." Brad noticed that the stub of a pencil had suddenly reappeared in the marshal's hand.

"Agreed, Marshal. What are the questions?"

"What does the initial 'E' stand for in your name?"

With a sense of accepting the inevitable, Jake responded, "Ezekiel."

"What is the town of your birth?"

"Albany," Jake replied. "Do I pass?"

"You do. You told us that you and Mr. Soza were on your way here to lay your cards on the table. Why don't you go ahead and do that. Then we'll all know where we stand."

"Mr. Soza and I had arranged to meet here in Sedona. Now that there has been one murder and an apparent attempt at a second, we are agreed that you should know all that we do." Jake opened the briefcase which he had on his lap and removed a number of papers from it. Brad could see that there were drawings or diagrams on several of the sheets and a map on another. Jake spread the six pieces of paper on the marshal's desk. "As you probably know, the Soza family has been in the Tucson region cattle trade for more than forty-five years. In fact they established a large ranch near Tres Alamos in 1860. The Soza family has a Tucson location just behind the San Agustin Cathedral."

Brad sat quietly on the chest. He was grateful he hadn't spoken out loud concerning his deduction that Mr. Soza was a banker. He looked out the window and his attention was attracted to Danny Lambert standing outside The Horn in conversation with Sam and Larry. He wondered what the Wingfield ranch cowboys could have in common with a loose cannon like Danny.

Jake was continuing with his presentation. "Recently they have experienced a major increase in rustling activities. Many of the cattle have gone missing near Sedona, specifically the Oak Creek Canyon route which is used to reach the Flagstaff rail head." Jake directed the marshal's attention to a map which showed the cattle drive trails, the Oak Creek Canyon route.

"Rustling has always been a problem for cattlemen," Hopkins agreed. "What makes this special?"

Jesus Soza spoke for the first time. "Normally we have been able to prevent resale of rustled cattle by monitoring for altered brands at stock markets. However, we believe that some sophisticated rebranding on cattle has been going on. Show them the overlays, Mr. Witherspoon."

Brad and the others gathered around the documents on the desk as Jake prepared the demonstration. He pointed to a sheet with a number of brands illustrated. "This is a family illustration of all Soza brands."

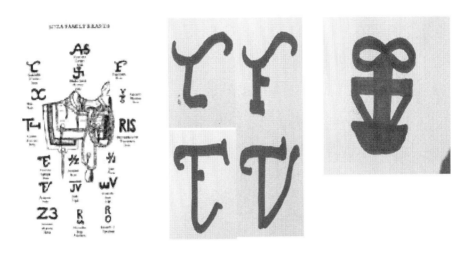

Jake unfolded a second sheet with four of the brands handdrawn in an enlarged size. "These are the brands which are being used, or have been used in recent years by the Soza family," Jake explained. He took a piece of onion skin paper from his briefcase. There was a new brand on the sheet. Jake showed the sheet to everyone and then placed it over the sheet of four Soza brands. He aligned the new brand over each of the Soza brands in turn. It could be clearly seen that the new brand could be positioned to cover all parts of each of the Soza brands.

Carl could not contain himself. "Rustlers have always used running irons and altered brands to hide their activities," he exclaimed. "There's nothing new here."

Brad knew that Carl had actually been involved in a cattle drive once. He probably did know something about the actions of rustlers, but Brad suspected that Carl was upset that an outsider seemed to be telling the Sedona law enforcement their business.

Jake wasn't fazed by Carl's outburst. He turned to Jesus Soza and invited him to comment.

"It is true, Deputy. Crooks have often tried to alter brands to escape discovery. But these are perfect brands. Brands have been forged to overlay our brands and produce brands for newly formed cattle companies. It has been impossible for us to prove that our cattle have been stolen."

There was a brief silence into which Dr. Pendergast inserted a comment which was both simple and concise. "In other words, a skilled blacksmith is involved."

* * *

When he came downstairs at Proctor's boarding house, Willard found Mrs. Proctor standing bent over Clive who was breathing quickly and producing high-pitched groans. As Willard moved up beside her, his landlady reached out to him and said, "Find Dr. Pendergast, Willard. I think Clive's coming to."

* * *

Jesus Soza followed up on the doctor's comment by saying, "I understand that there was an attack on the blacksmith's assistant, Marshal. Could there be a connection there?"

Hopkins rolled the little pencil between the palms of his hands. He looked out the window and then at each of the people in the room. Finally he took the stub of wood between his thumb and right index finger and waved it forward and back several times. He looked a bit like a priest sprinkling holy water. Brad wondered what significance the Austrian, Dr. Freud, would attribute to that guesture.

It was seeming as if Hopkins was not going to respond at all when he said, "There are six of us in this room. If we are going to solve this puzzle we need to share our information. We also need to keep the information from becoming common knowledge. I would like your assurance, Mr. Soza, and yours too Jake, that you will not repeat this information to anyone else until we have resolved the problem at hand."

Mr. Soza spoke first. "You have my assurance, Marshal, that I will treat what I'm told as confidential."

"I will have to inform my employers of the outcome, but I have a free hand in this matter and will not release information without your permission, Marshal Hopkins.," Jake replied.

"Good," Hopkins said. "There is at least one connection which is not widely known. The smith's assistant, Clive, is the son of the man killed earlier this morning."

"Both were struck over the head, I believe," Jake interjected. "Was the same weapon used?"

"No," Hopkins replied. "A hammer was used to kill Luke Proctor. Clive was struck down with this piece of petrified wood." Hopkins picked up the weapon and pointed out the traces of blood with the tip of his pencil.

"The Paiute Indians think that those chunks are weapons of Shinarav, the wolf god," Jesus Soza offered. "Do you have any indication of native involvement?"

CHAPTER 63 THE HORN

Lil thought of the saloon as her office and The Horn as her place of business. She was pleased to see that her office was starting to fill up early today. She had seen Jake meet up with the law and the medical profession and head off across to the jail. There was a well-dressed individual with them who looked as if he might be a potential client. The hotel registry identified him as one J. F. Soza. Soza was a name she'd heard associated with money. Money was good. Maybe Mr. Soza would be coming by the office later.

Danny Lambert was not in his usual spot by the wall. He was sitting at a table with two of the Wingfield ranch hands, Sam and Larry. Charlie Lee, The Horn's owner, was sitting with his back to Lil, but there was no mistaking his plaid waistcoat. There was another man sitting at the table with them. Lil thought that man was a Wells Fargo driver she'd heard called 'Badger'. Charlie was shuffling a deck of cards. It looked as if a poker game was about to break out.

CHAPTER 64 MAIN STREET SEDONA

Willard was excited. Maybe Clive was going to be okay. He ran first toward the smithy. He'd last seen the doctor and his son going in there with the marshal and deputy Munds. He found the smithy empty and called out for Carter. A muffled response came from the stables and Carter emerged carrying a twisted piece of metal in his hand.

Thomas had an odd expression on his face. Willard thought the smith looked concerned, perhaps even guilty, as if he'd been caught with his fingers in the cookie jar.

"Where's the doctor, Thomas? Clive's coming around," Willard demanded.

"They all left here a while ago," Carter responded. "Probably back at the marshal's."

Willard turned on his heal and hurried off. Was Carter hiding something, he wondered? Did he know something? Then he saw Jefferson and Frank coming out of the registry and called out to them.

CHAPTER 65 THE HORN

Charlie Lee was a businessman first and foremost. He seldom did anything which was not directed toward making money. He could have chosen to live in Chicago or New York and done business there, but he preferred the wide open spaces and the relaxed life of the frontier. His investments were varied. He held some equity investments in Western Union and Wells Fargo. The services they provided, communication and money transfer, were essential in a country as big as America. He had done very nicely on those investments. He had missed the boat, so to speak, on the railroad. By the time he had enough capital to invest there, the early profits had been made. Land was a long-term investment, but it was sure and safe. He had seen the humourist, Mark Twain, on a speaking tour and loved his line, 'Buy land. They're not making it anymore.'

Charlie encouraged people to call him, 'Charlie'. It sounded more harmless somehow, more like a regular guy. He owned a lot of land near Sedona and had a financial stake in some of the ranches and local businesses as well as holding a majority interest in The Horn. He was a good businessman. He knew the value of knowing the names of his customers and was willing to buy a round once in a while to encourage the regulars. Charlie was well aware that poker games encouraged drinking. The winners celebrated and the losers drowned their sorrows.

CHAPTER 66 THE JAIL

"That's it," Carl exclaimed. "There's got to be some Indian massacre behind this! Show him the hammer that was used."

"Whoa there, Carl," Leroy suggested. "Let's not go off half-cocked now." He unlocked his desk and lifted out the hammer. "We never did get around to showing it to Doris Proctor, but I reckon we can rule her out. She's not likely to have attacked her son. I can see her killing her husband, there's probably plenty of candidates for that job, but Clive is a likable enough lad."

"So why did she confess?" Carl continued.

Brad had been thinking about Doris Proctor's confession. He was about to suggest some possible motivations when the marshal said, "To protect her son, Carl. That's reason enough."

Jake raised his hand and said, "Just a second, Marshal. Are you saying that someone confessed to killing this fellow and she's the mother of Clive Harrison?"

"That's right," Hopkins acknowledged. "But, I'm pretty sure she was just protecting her son."

"So, the fellow who was killed was named Harrison and he had a son with Mrs. Proctor?" Jake continued. "What happened to Mr. Proctor?"

"The man killed was Luke Proctor," Brad told him, hoping to clear things up. "He was married to Doris Proctor. Doris Proctor is Clive's mother; Luke Proctor was Clive's father. There was no Mr. Harrison." Brad thought for a second and then corrected himself, "Well, Doris Proctor's mother was married to a Harrison, I suppose."

Jesus Fernandez Soza jumped in. "Mr. Clive Harrison was named after his grandmother's husband. That makes sense. My second name is Fernandez because that was my mother's maiden name."

The marshal cut short the speculation by saying, "Something like that, Mr. Soza. Anyway, here's the hammer that was used to kill Luke Proctor." Hopkins held up the hammer and then turned it to display the symbol of an X or cross on the bottom of the handle.

"Ah, yes. That is a sign used by the Yavapai," Mr. Soza agreed. "When the first Spanish missionaries first met them they thought that they had already adopted Christianity. The Spaniards called them Cruzados because they wore crosses in their hair. But the symbol of the cross is not related to the Paiute peoples. The X shape depicts the division representing the four tribes that make up the nation."

"So the attacks were made by two different natives?" Carl asked.

"I think we can safely assume that no Indian tribes were involved in either death, Carl," Dr. Pendergast declared. "Also, it seems likely that the same person attacked Luke and Clive."

"One thing about that strikes me as odd," Hopkins said. "Luke was killed outright. You said yourself that the first blow would have been enough. Why is it that the same person hits Clive with this big chunk of rock, or something as hard as rock anyway, and Clive is only knocked out?"

Dr. Pendergast picked up the hammer and pointed to the rounded peen at the rear of the hammer. "Because this peen is round, the force is transmitted as if from a single point. It crushed the skull easily. The piece of petrified wood on the other hand is more or less flat at the spot that it contacted Clive's head. Although it felled Clive and rendered him unconscious, it did not crack the skull."

"So the person who hit Clive was probably trying to kill him?" Hopkins confirmed. "He just underestimated the force needed with this different weapon?"

"I think it most likely," the doctor confirmed. "Luke was killed in the dark of night. The killer was concealed by darkness and struck several times. The attack on Clive was in daylight and a place where someone might arrive at any moment. There was a certain urgency to get away unseen, I imagine."

Jake was nodding quietly. Now he sat up and said, "Seems as if the two attacks were connected and that the connection includes our rustling. Clive was attacked to keep him from talking; perhaps his father knew something which got him killed."

CHAPTER 67 THE COURTHOUSE

Frank found a smiling Jefferson Brooks more disturbing than his normal taciturn self. It was as if a bird of prey gave vent to a charming song.

"It just occurred to me that Mrs. Proctor would probably inherit that land. But she'd have to know about the deed."

"You're thinking about the money Luke owed you, aren't you?" Frank asked.

Jefferson shook his head ruefully. "Actually I'd given up on that debt years ago, and I have no proof that he owed me anything. I just thought Doris Proctor might as well get what she deserves. Lord knows she's had a tough time of it."

Wondering to himself if maybe he had become too cynical, Frank dug out the land title records and confirmed Jefferson's affirmation. The land next to Mrs. Proctor's boarding house was registered in the name of Luke Proctor. Frank wondered how it was that Lars Sorensen was using the land without title. A further search of documents provided no answer.

"So, the record shows the land belongs, or belonged, to Luke Proctor. Is it possible that Lars bought it and didn't register it?" Brooks asked Frank.

"This may sound a little too simple, Jefferson. But why don't we ask Lars?" Frank suggested. "It's possible he has a bill of sale but didn't change the registration document."

Frank stuck a 'closed' sign in the window and the two men set off to ask Lars. As they emerged from the office, Willard Wright ran by. He called out to them "Where's the doctor at? Clive's coming to."

Both men stared at Willard. Then Frank said, "Try the marshal's office." Willard ran on and they watched as he burst in the marshal's door.

CHAPTER 68 THE JAIL

"If that's the case, Marshal, shouldn't you be keeping a watch on Clive? The person who attacked him may just try to finish the job before he can say anything."

As Jake was saying this, the door was flung open and Willard Wright called out, "Come quick, Doctor; Clive's waking up."

CHAPTER 69 THE HORN

Lil sauntered over to the poker table and gave the Wingfield boys a smile. She wondered why Danny was playing. He wasn't normally involved in poker. Most players who knew him would prefer not to be involved in a game with him. If you beat him at the table, you might not be seen again.

Charlie Lee wouldn't have to worry. Lil had never seen Charlie walk away from the table a winner. If he got ahead he played until he was back even before he quit. Charlie was making too much selling drinks and renting rooms to risk it by scoring a win at cards.

In fact, Lil had received a pleasant surprise the first time she talked with Charlie three years ago when she set up her own business at The Horn. He had joined her over lunch one day and laid out some ground rules for her. Charlie didn't want a kickback and he didn't want a taste of the goods. He gave her a good monthly rate for room and board and told her that he would tell Clayton and the part-time bartender, Jim Thompson, to watch her back.

"There's somethings I want in return," he had informed her. "I want you to be pleasant with all the customers of the hotel, even if they aren't customers of yours and I don't want any trouble. If someone gives you a problem come to me. You'll find that I'm fair."

At first Lil had thought that there would be a catch, but as time went on she realized that Charlie was just taking care of business. The one time a drunken ranch hand had got out of line Clayton had sent for the marshal who had solved the problem very simply. Hopkins had listened to Lil, Clayton, and the cowboy and provided a choice for the drunk. He could either go home right then or spend the night in jail and face a fine in the morning.

It had all worked out for the best. The ranch hand had even turned up a few days later to deliver a shamefaced apology.

CHAPTER 70 THE COURTHOUSE

In a small town people take an interest. So, rather than walk down to Sorensen's lumberyard right away, Frank and Jefferson waited to see what would happen.

Willard never actually got inside the marshal's office. He opened the door and they could hear him speaking to someone. Then Dr. Pendergast and his son came out and started off toward Proctor's boarding house with Carl trailing behind them.

CHAPTER 71 THE JAIL

Marshal Hopkins took his deputy by the arm and said, "Stay with Clive until I come to join you. If you need to send for me, send Brad Pendergast. I don't want Clive left alone until I get to talk with him."

Carl nodded and hurried after the others.

Hopkins closed the door behind Carl and invited Jake and Jesus to join him at his desk. He examined the drawing of brands, still spread on his desk, and said, "There's something that's not clear to me here."

CHAPTER 72 THE LUMBERYARD

Lars was in the tool shed seated behind a trestle table. He was recording the figures from the inventory he and Willard had conducted before he sent Willard home for the rest of the day. He looked up when the door opened. Frank Green and a serious looking Jefferson Brooks came in.

"Do you have a moment, Lars?" Frank asked.

"Of course," Lars responded setting down his pencil and pointing toward two chairs beside the table. "How can I help you?"

CHAPTER 73 THE HORN

"The game's seven-card stud, fellas; two down, four up, one down; nothing wild; cards talk," Sam declared. "High card deals." He let Charlie Lee, who was sitting to his right cut the deck and then started dealing cards one at a time, face up. Paul Matthews got a seven, Larry a ten, Danny a king and Charlie a jack. Sam turned a ten of clubs up for himself and passed the deck to Danny Lambert.

Danny gathered the cards together and began shuffling. "What's the maximum bet, Sam?" he asked. "Any limit?"

"Let's keep it friendly, shall we fellas?" Charlie suggested. "How about a nickel ante, three raise limit and maximum bet ten cents?"

There was general agreement and Danny started to deal the first hand.

* * *

The Artist considered his options. It was going to be harder to get to Clive now, but he had to be silenced.

CHAPTER 74 PROCTOR'S

The image of his father bending over Clive stirred memories for Brad. His first memories as a child were watching him treat patients. Brad admired his father. More than anything else he had wanted to be like him.

Doris Proctor held onto Clive's hand as Dr. Pendergast examined his eyes and spoke to him gently. At length the seasoned practitioner stood back and said, "Lie quiet now, Clive. Try not to move your head too much." He put a hand on Doris's shoulder and told her, "He'll be alright, now. Just keep him warm and still."

The men drew back to the hallway and gathered close to the rear entrance. "He can't speak coherently yet. He may not be able to tell us anything about receiving the blow. The mind sometimes forgets periods of pain, especially if they lead to unconsciousness," the doctor told Carl. "We need to let him rest."

"The marshal told me to stay with him," Carl informed the others. "It's starting to get dark; are you planning to stay in town, Dr. Pendergast?"

"No, there's nothing more to do for Clive at the moment. I've got some sleeping powders I'll leave with Doris. Brad and I will head back to the house and check on things there." He went back into the parlor and spoke quietly with Doris Proctor.

CHAPTER 73 THE LUMBERYARD

Frank waited to see if Jefferson wanted to speak. When he didn't, Frank cleared his throat and directed a question to Lars. "Fact is, Lars, I was going over the land registry records and it turns out there's no record of your ownership of this land your lumberyard is on."

The tall Dane's face clouded over and became dark red. Frank had never seen Lars angry; was this it? Lars stood up. For a second Frank thought he was going to reach across the narrow table and throttle him. Then he realised that Lars was embarrassed, not angry.

"I was here before you came to town, Mr. Green. So you do not know. I arrived with very little money and with my family to support. I began working in lumber because I know wood and construction. But I had no money to buy land," Lars Sorensen explained. "I rented, and continue to rent this land."

"But, you have a house built on the land," Jefferson protested. "How can that be?"

"I built our house at the back of the property with my own hands," Lars explained. "It is built as a temporary home using wedges in place of nails. When we can afford to buy some land we will move it there. I was told by my landlord that I could do so."

"So, you have been renting the land from Luke Proctor all these years?" Frank asked.

"Who is Luke Proctor?" Lars demanded. "I rent this land from Mr. Charlie Lee."

CHAPTER 76 THE JAIL

Hopkins arranged the piece of semi-transparent paper over one of the Soza brands on the master sheet. He arranged it such that it completely overlapped the Soza brand. Then he moved the top sheet to another Soza main brand. The same new brand covered and obliterated that brand as well. Jesus Soza came over and showed him how the same brand, turned upside down could be used to cover yet another Soza brand.

"These Soza brands have been in use for many years. We could develop new brands, but that would not solve the real problem." Jesus said. His voice carried a note of sadness and determination. "There is money and organization behind this. It's not just a few rogue cowboys grabbing a few strays and hustling them off. These 'cover brands' are being registered and the rustled cattle added to legitimate stock of large cattle operations. Unless we can prove their involvement they will just develop new cover brands."

"What about posting guards and picking off the rustlers when they try to grab some cattle?" Hopkins suggested.

"We are doing what we can," Jesus Soza explained. "The problem is that it is harder to guard cattle than to find some unprotected."

"We need to make connections which allow us to bring legal actions against the companies. Locating the smith making the brands is only useful if it leads further," Jake added.

Hopkins considered the map of cattle trail and the proximity of the Wingfield ranch to the Oak Creek Canyon route. "Do you have any reason to suspect someone near Sedona?" he asked.

Jesus started to answer, but Jake spoke first. "I'd rather not single anyone out without a bit more proof, Marshal. I'm hoping that Clive Harrison can tell us something."

"That being the case, we'll have to hope that this attack makes him willing to speak," Hopkins suggested. "I intend to mount a guard over the Proctor boarding house tonight. Are you carrying a gun, Jake?"

"I never travel unarmed," Jake replied patting the left breast of his jacket. He removed a gun unlike anything Hopkins had ever handled. "This gun was released last year. It's the Colt model 1905. Pinkertons received one of the first shipments." Jake made the gun safe by dropping out a slim magazine and sliding back the upper part of the gun. He handed it over to Hopkins.

The marshal hefted the sleek handgun. "It's pretty short barrelled. How accurate is it?"

"If we get some time, I'll demonstrate it for you, Marshal. It's very accurate and has knockdown power. The first self-loading pistol developed for the army was .38 ACP caliber. This one is in .45 ACP." Jake took out one of the stubby bullets and passed it over to the marshal.

Jesus had come over to stand beside Leroy Hopkins as he examined the pistol. "The bullet's a lot shorter than my .45 ammunition. How does the power compare?"

"Everything has been improved for this gun," Jake explained. "This cartridge is not like the Smith & Wesson .45 Schofield. The smokeless powder used in the .45 ACP produces higher muzzle velocity. It has greater accuracy and more impact energy than the long colt .45. This gun has gone through serious testing. You'll probably see all army officers carrying this gun."

Jesus was examining Jake's weapon and Hopkins was comparing a .45 long colt bullet from his own sidearm, a Remington 1875. Jake laid his pistol down beside the marshal's revolver and remarked, "The biggest advantage is I can carry the gun concealed. You'd have trouble tucking that sidearm of yours out of sight, Marshal."

Leroy looked up with a wry smile and said, "Actually, Jake, I don't shoot people that often. I find that if people know I have a gun they're less likely to raise a fuss."

"Still, I'm surprised that you're still using a single-action revolver," Jake continued "Even before the self-loader, a lot of people had switched to a double-action."

Leroy was considering a response when the door burst open again.

E. Craig McKay

BRAND OF DEATH

Part Two: On the Run

CHAPTER 77 THE HORN

Paul gathered in the pot and Danny gathered in the loose cards. Larry quickly passed him the rest of the deck. They'd been once round the table and Paul was the big winner so far. He'd taken Danny's money twice on the showdown. Sam knew that Danny wasn't an experienced player. Paul had sucked him in when Danny couldn't possibly have had the better hand.

Now as Danny shuffled, Paul pushed his luck. With a bit of a smirk he prodded Danny, "Why'd you stay in that hand? Did you think I was bluffing?"

Danny did not respond, but his face darkened

Sam suspected that Danny had not even considered the possibility that Paul had filled a flush. With three diamonds showing, the possibility had seemed likely enough to cause the other players to drop out, but not Danny. Danny not only called, he had raised the maximum. Sam noted that Paul was living up to his nickname, 'Badger'. He wondered if Paul realized how dangerous Danny could be.

Larry cut the deck and Danny dealt two cards down and one up to each of the players. By the time there were four cards up, only Danny, Paul, and Charlie were still in. Charlie was dominating with a pair of kings showing, but Paul had a possible gut-shot straight and Danny had an ace and two tens showing.

When Charlie checked, Paul raised and Danny raised again after him. Charlie looked at his cards, regarded with interest the two players still in, and folded. Paul raised again and Danny called.

The tension was palpable. Lil had withdrawn to the bar and she and Clayton were watching the card game from across the room.

Sam could see that Danny was excited and 'Badger' was determined. Danny dealt the seventh and final card. With two tens showing, Danny was under the gun. After checking out his own final card, Danny bet the maximum.

Paul raised back and Danny paused. He took a long read on Paul and said, "You haven't looked at your last card."

"Maybe I don't need to," Paul replied with a mocking tone.

"Meaning what?" Danny demanded.

"Meaning maybe I've already got a straight," Paul replied.

"Do you?"

"Call me and see. I'm pretty sure you have the losing hand," Paul crowed.

Danny called and flipped up three tens. Paul laughed and turned up his straight. As Paul reached out for the pot, Danny said, "How'd you get that?"

Paul froze and turned serious. "What do you mean? You dealt." He started to rake in his winnings and then realized that Danny was standing up. His gun was in his hand.

"What the . . ." Paul said just before Danny put a shot into his chest. Paul went over backwards and Larry and Sam leaned away from the space he had left. Charlie, sitting on the far side of Danny just tried to become invisible. Danny walked around the table to his right and put two more bullets into Paul's belly.

Clayton had ducked down behind the bar and Lil was frozen at the far end of it.

Danny reached down with one hand and scooped up the small stack of bills from the spot where Paul had been sitting. He tucked them into a pocket. He picked up Paul's beer and drank it before turning and walking calmly out of the saloon.

CHAPTER 78 PROCTOR'S

Dr. Pendergast and Brad paused outside Proctor's boarding house. Brad surveyed the area where Luke Proctor's body had been found about fourteen hours earlier.

"This attack on Clive proves one thing anyway," he told his father. "Clive wasn't responsible for the attack on Luke Proctor."

"I wouldn't jump to that conclusion," the doctor responded.

"Well, you have to admit that the two events are connected," Brad insisted. "It must have been someone who had it in for the Proctors."

Instead of answering directly, Dr. Pendergast replied, "Oh, I think that the connection was not necessarily a familial one."

Before Brad could sort out what he meant by that, he was distracted by a loud noise which seemed to come from The Horn. The two Pendergasts turned toward the hotel and heard two more reports. "Those are gunshots," Brad declared.

The saloon door swung open and Danny Lambert came out. He turned left and ran toward the Pendergasts before veering in toward the smithy and livery stable. He had just entered the gaping door of the smithy when Clayton peeked out of The Horn and, seeing the street deserted, hurried across to the jail house.

A few seconds later Danny rode out into main street atop Carl's horse, Star. He was riding bare-back with a simple lead rope and halter. Star reared as Danny dug in his heels and horse and rider rose as one in silhouette against the glow of the western sky. Then Star plunged forward and galloped away toward the western end of town. Danny had the lead rope wrapped around his right hand and the fingers of his left hand tangled in Star's flowing mane.

"You have to admit," Dr. Pendergast declared, "That Danny Lambert is a fine horseman."

"That's Carl's horse, dad. He's a horse thief."

The doctor's mouth creased with a wry smile. "Yes, he's that too."

CHAPTER 79 THE JAIL

Leroy turned to see who was coming through the door in such a hurry. This time it was Clayton. His face was flushed. "Come quick, Marshal. Danny's killed someone."

Hopkins shoved the cartridge he'd been showing the others back into his revolver and stood up knocking his chair over in his haste. He peered past Clayton's form which half blocked the doorway in time to see Carl's Star with Danny aboard sweep down main street to the west. Clayton leapt out of the way as Leroy moved forward and brought up his gun.

Danny was fifty feet away and moving. Hopkins steadied his right forearm against the left-hand frame of the door and drew a bead on the dwindling outline. He made a small adjustment upward and fired once. Danny Lambert's upper body collapsed forward along the neck of the galloping horse. Star lowered his head as if the horse himself were ducking and continued his headlong flight out of town.

"You hit him, Marshal," Clayton exclaimed.

"I don't think so," Hopkins responded. "I was mostly shooting for effect. There was always the chance that Danny might have fallen off. Carl's got a good horse there. I was being careful to avoid hitting Star."

CHAPTER 80 MAIN STREET, SEDONA

Father and son stood and watched Danny Lambert moving as one with the horse. Suddenly the marshal erupted from his office, braced himself against the doorframe and took a low percentage shot. "Did he hit him?" Brad asked as Danny's body draped itself over the neck of the horse and seemed about to slide off the right flank.

Dr. Pendergast regarded the motion of horse and rider for a second and replied, "I don't think so. If he were hit high with one of the heavy slugs Hopkins uses he'd have been knocked down. Besides, look at his left heel."

As Brad directed his attention to the left foot he could see what his father meant. Danny looked as if he were just lying lifeless, but his left heel was dug in, urging the horse to turn left toward the south fork.

"Danny must have done something more than just borrow a horse," Dr. Pendergast ventured. "Hopkins is no hothead. He wouldn't have shot, even as a warning, without good reason."

CHAPTER 81 MAIN STREET, SEDONA

As if the sound of Leroy's shot was an all-clear notice, people spilled out of The Horn to stare off at the sight of Danny taking the south fork as he swept past the shed where Jefferson Brooks stored his funeral wagon. Charlie Lee was the first to comment.

"Isn't that Carl's horse?" he asked "Why didn't he take his own horse?"

* * *

Frank, Jefferson, and Lars were standing at the open gateway of Sorensen's lumberyard. They had not taken much note of the earlier shots which had been muffled thumps such as might result from a slamming door. But the crack of Marshal Hopkins' lone shot had drawn them outside to investigate.

Half the town was staring off to the west. It seemed as if they were waiting for the arrival of some important personage.

Frank noticed that the marshal was talking earnestly with the man who called himself by dead Harry Plumber's name. Clayton and a well-dressed stranger were behind them. Dr. Pendergast and his son stood in the street in front of Proctor's.

"What's happening?" Frank called out to them.

Brad swung around and yelled back, "He stole Carl's horse."

A figure broke past the row of bushes along Proctor's driveway and into the street. "What! Who stole my horse?" Carl bellowed.

"Danny Lambert," Brad told him. "The marshal took a shot at him, but I think he missed."

Carl looked around and saw everyone still looking off to the west. For a moment it seemed as if Carl was going to run off down the street after his horse. Then he seemed to gather himself and strode off toward the smithy.

* * *

Lambert was a useful tool, the Artist thought. But it might have been better if the marshal's shot had killed him. Danny knew enough to cause trouble if he talked. If a posse was formed, the Artist might have to join up to make sure he was taken dead rather than alive.

CHAPTER 82 THE HORN

"I thought Danny was going to start spraying bullets all over the room. Did you see the look in his eyes?" Larry asked Sam.

"Lambert's a loose cannon," Sam replied. "Paul was crazy to provoke him."

Charlie Lee was standing beside Sam. "Paul had a mouth bigger than his brain," was his terse response.

Lil had been watching the poker table from across the room when Danny had pulled his gun. Because she was so far away she could see the reactions of all the players. Paul had been completely taken by surprise, but the other three men almost seemed to be expecting it. Charlie had leaned back from the table while Danny was dealing the final cards of the hand. Larry and Sam were both watching Danny. Neither of them paid any attention to Paul. When Paul was lying dead, Larry and Sam had risen from their chairs as Danny walked out the door, but Charlie had remained seated with a strange expression on his face. Where had she seen that look before? It was familiar, but she couldn't quite place it for a moment. Then it clicked. It was satisfaction. She had seen that same expression on Charlie's face before when things worked out to his liking.

Now, as the three men stood watching the edge of town as if expecting Danny to ride back, she turned her attention to Hank. He was talking with the marshal. Hopkins had his left hand on Hank's arm and was looking off toward the north as if waiting for Danny to tumble from his mount. Lil had thought Danny was hit at first, but then saw that he was just taking shelter along the horse's straining neck.

Clayton was in conversation with the well-dressed newcomer. She had been somewhat surprised by Clayton rushing off across the street like that. He usually tried to avoid getting involved. Now he was over there in the thick of it.

CHAPTER 83 THE SMITHY

Down at the smithy, Carter and the young stable hand, Eddie, stood side by side just under the eaves of the weatherbeaten structure. Carter held a hammer in one hand and had the other on Eddie Thompson's shoulder. Even Violet had come out of the general store and further down the street, the Pendergasts were in conversation with deputy Carl Munds and Willard Wright. Beyond them Lars Sorensen was with Frank Green and Jefferson Brooks. What strange collections of humanity the crisis had revealed.

Lily wondered what Hank could be discussing so seriously with Marshal Hopkins.

CHAPTER 84 MAIN STREET, SEDONA

Willard watched Carl move off down the street. Carl sure liked that horse. What had possessed Danny to steal it? He turned to the doctor and his son. They had been outside when the final shot was fired. They could tell him what they'd seen.

Willard joined the Pendergasts at the end of the driveway. He was struck by the similarity between father and son. Brad was a competent and popular young man, and good looking. He'd make a good doctor, and with his father's contacts he'd be able to set up a profitable practice wherever he liked.

"What's all the ruckus about?" he asked. "Isn't Carl supposed to stay here to protect Clive?"

"Danny Lambert rode off on Carl's horse," Brad answered.

"I want to go talk to the marshal. Would you stay here until Carl or someone else comes, Brad?" Dr. Pendergast asked.

Willard could see that Brad was disappointed not to be included. He made a suggestion he knew Brad would welcome. "Heck," he said, "I can stay with Clive. I live here anyway."

CHAPTER 85 MAIN STREET, SEDONA

Frank watched the group in front of Proctor's split up. Carl was marching into the smithy and the two Pendergasts started off toward Marshal Hopkins while Willard turned back toward the boarding house.

"Willard's not working today?" he asked Lars.

"He asked for the rest of the day off to help Mrs. Proctor," Lars responded. "I only employ him a few days a week anyway. Now that the new road building is over, I probably won't even need him that much. Mrs. Proctor could use the help. She's got her hands full right now I guess."

"You said you didn't know Luke Proctor, Lars," Jefferson said. "He was the man they found dead in the bushes between your yard and Proctor's boarding house. He was Doris Proctor's husband and Clive's father."

Lars bristled. "Well, I've never heard of him before," Lars responded hotly. He was staring at Jefferson. After a short, but pregnant pause he added, "We saw you poking around the far side of the lot last night. What were you looking for?"

CHAPTER 86 THE SMITHY

Thomas was talking to the ostler, Eddie, when Carl stormed into the smithy.

"Where the hell were you when Danny made off with my horse, Carter?" Carl shouted.

Thomas Carter turned calmly toward the deputy without speaking and then said quietly over his shoulder to Eddie, "Take Danny's horse back to the stall and then bring me the piece of iron that's sitting on Clive's trunk please, Eddie."

Danny's quarter horse was standing in the back corner of the smithy. Eddie took it by the short rope attached to a working halter and led it out the back of the smithy toward the stables. Thomas picked up a mug and took a drink of water. After wiping his mouth on the back of his hand he replied, "Well, deputy, Eddie and I were working on Lambert's horse when he ran in here. When he realised that his horse wasn't fit to ride with half its shoes being refitted, he took yours, which I just finished reshoeing. I noticed he was in a hurry and that he had his gun out and ready to use, so I didn't argue with him."

Carl's anger cooled as he realised he was yelling at the wrong person. His face reddened and he fought to find a response. Before he could think of anything to say, Eddie came back holding a piece of wrought iron. He handed it to Thomas who held it up for Carl to see.

"I found this among Clive's practice pieces," he said simply. "It looks like a branding iron to me."

CHAPTER 87 SOUTH OF SEDONA

He was three miles out of town before he thought, 'What next?' Danny had shot the Wells Fargo driver, Paul, partially because Paul was being annoying and partially because Paul was winning. The main reason he'd shot him though was that he was making Danny look foolish. Danny didn't like looking foolish. Well, who was the fool now? The more Danny thought about that question, the less certain he was of the answer.

Sure Paul was dead, but Danny had limited choices open to him. Shooting someone during a poker game was a serious crime; stealing a horse was a very serious crime.

Danny had taken the fork south mostly because turning left kept his body shielded behind the horse's neck. He was pretty sure Marshal Hopkins wouldn't shoot a horse, especially his deputy's horse. Now as he thought about it, going north made more sense than heading south. He could reach Mexico if he had to, but what would he do there without money? He considered the possibility that having shot one Wells Fargo driver for pocket change he could shoot some more and pick up some serious money. Even Danny knew that would be a mistake. Wells Fargo coaches often had an outrider or someone aboard with a rifle and/or shotgun. Passengers were even known to get involved in a firefight. It was not a job for a gang of one.

He could turn north under cover of darkness and hope that the search for him looked south. He'd find somewhere to lie low until sundown. Sometime soon he was going to need a saddle and proper bridle with a bit. He could already feel the strain of riding bareback.

CHAPTER 88 PROCTOR'S

Willard Wright had followed Carl out of the house. Doris was alone with Clive for the first time. Her son was lying quietly, but his eyes were open. She had prepared the sleeping draught in some warm lemonade with honey, but before he took a sip she asked, "Do you know who did this, son?"

Clive wet his lips with his tongue and replied, "I thought you did Luke; I didn't see who hit me." His eyes searched his mother's face. "If you didn't kill Luke, then maybe he was telling the truth for once."

"What about?" Doris asked quietly. Willard was coming in the door. She leaned her ear down beside Clive's mouth.

"Charlie Lee and Danny Lambert," Clive whispered.

CHAPTER 89 THE JAIL

"So, Clayton, what happened?" Hopkins asked. "Who did Danny shoot? Was there a reason or was it just Danny being Danny?"

"He shot the Wells Fargo man, the driver Paul they call Badger," Clayton replied. "They were playing poker and Danny accused him of cheating and shot him."

"Who else saw the shooting?"

"There were three others playing. Sam and Larry from the Wingfield crew and Charlie Lee were at the table. Lil and I were the only others in the saloon," Clayton explained. "They'd only been playing for about a half hour when the fight broke out."

"Did the Wells Fargo driver go for his gun?" Hopkins asked.

Clayton paused to think and said, "I don't think so, Marshal. I think he had both hands on the table at the time."

"You were watching him?"

Clayton thought again and said, "Not exactly. I wasn't paying that much attention until their voices were raised. Then I looked up 'cause it sounded like trouble brewing."

"What happened next?"

"Danny jumped up, shot him once and then walked over and shot him twice more while he was lying there. I ducked down and the next thing I saw was Danny charging out the door."

"Nobody else pulled a gun?" the marshal asked.

"Not that I saw, Marshal. Lil probably had a better view than I did." As he said this Clayton looked across the street and added, "I better get back to the saloon, Leroy. Excitement makes people thirsty."

"Okay, Clay. Send Charlie Lee over here, would you?"

Clayton stepped down into the street and started across to The Horn. Hopkins noticed that he looked both ways before he crossed. Brad and Dr. Pendergast arrived and Hopkins could see Carl coming towards him too.

The marshal turned to Jake and Jesus. "I'm going to have to deal with this. I'd like you to meet in the office with Dr. Pendergast and his son to share what you've told me and find out how Clive is. Danny Lambert's a wild card, but I want to find out if there's a connection to the attacks on Luke and Clive."

Brad and the doctor arrived and Hopkins asked, "How's Clive?"

"He's resting with a sleeping potion. He'll probably be out all night now," Dr. Pendergast told the marshal. "Willard and Doris are with him."

"Well there doesn't seem to be much doubt that the Wells Fargo driver is dead, Doc. But I guess you should look at him to make it official. We'll have to contact Wells Fargo to find out what to do with the body. After that I'd like you two to share ideas with our visiting Pinkerton agent and Mr. Soza," Hopkins told Dr. Pendergast.

The doctor started across to The Horn after Clayton. Brad waited beside Hopkins with Jake and Jesus.

CHAPTER 90 THE JAIL

As the bartender headed back to the saloon, Carl approached the marshal and the three other men standing beside him. He was carrying the branding iron in one hand.

Hopkins saw Clayton pause on the way into The Horn to speak with Charlie Lee. Lee looked up, saw Hopkins, and started across the street behind Carl.

"If any other man had shot toward my horse I'd be angry, Marshal," Carl began.

"You know I was just trying to get Lambert off Star," Hopkins told him. "I shot so high that bullet is probably still coming down."

"Well, I appreciate that," Carl replied "But I want to go after him before he sells Star or rides him to Mexico."

"Write up a description of Star and Danny," Hopkins suggested. "We'll put out a bulletin on the wire right away." Hopkins was a bit surprised that Carl was as controlled as he seemed. Perhaps the deputy was growing into his position. "I notice that you've armed yourself with a bar of iron, Carl. Are you planning to use that on Lambert?"

Carl looked down at the iron bar as if he couldn't remember what it was. He handed it to Hopkins and explained that Thomas had found it among Clive's property.

"Take this inside the office, Carl. I'll deal with Charlie Lee and be in directly."

CHAPTER 91 THE HORN

Lil was waiting in the bar as Clayton came back into the saloon followed closely by Dr. Pendergast. The doctor went over to examine the dead man while Clayton joined Lil by the bar.

Sam and Larry had drifted back inside and were watching the doctor examine Paul. It was a short examination.

"He's dead," the doctor pronounced "Any one of the shots probably would have killed him. Cover him up with something if you like, Clay. I expect Jefferson Brooks will be by directly. Tell him I'll be by his place to examine the body more closely later."

Sam and Larry draped a blanket which had been lying neglected on the piano bench across Paul's inert form and sauntered over to the bar looking a bit thirsty. Clayton lifted a beer mug and both men nodded agreement. Except for the blanket-covered body lying on the floor, things returned to normal.

CHAPTER 92 MAIN STREET, SEDONA

Charlie Lee confirmed Clayton's account of the shooting, adding only that he thought Paul had provoked Danny.

"I'm not saying Danny had any right to shoot, Marshal. But, 'Badger' was being a bit of an idiot. It doesn't take much to provoke Danny."

"Okay. That's good enough for now, Charlie. I've got some stuff to do here now. Could you ask the two cowboys to hang around town until I get time to talk with them?" He indicated Sam and Larry with a head gesture.

Charlie Lee smiled and asked, "Is it okay if they entertain others who might want to drink with them to hear the story?"

"I can't see as how that would cause a problem. Just as long as no one else gets killed, they can drink and tell stories. My plate is pretty full right now. I might be a while."

Charlie was practically rubbing his hands in anticipation of a busy night at the saloon. As Dr. Pendergast walked back across the street he encountered Charlie about half way. The doctor thought the bar owner looked pretty cheerful for someone who had just witnessed a murder.

"Death is apparently good for the saloon business," he commented to Hopkins as he and the marshal crossed the street to the office to join the others.

CHAPTER 93 THE HORN

Charlie could see that Jefferson had given thought to business as well. The ever-ready mortician crept into The Horn saloon moments after Leroy and the doctor left it. Charlie was at the bar in conversation with Clayton and the saloon was starting to fill up. When he saw Jefferson, Charlie walked over to him, pointed at the blanket and told him that the doctor would be down to examine the corpse at Brooks' parlor later. Then he turned his attention back to Clayton, and his mind back to profit. "Do you have enough stock available? How about beer? I'm going to send for one of the Thompson boys to help out. It looks like a busy evening building up."
* * *

When the likelihood of a commission to be made occurred to Jefferson, the vulture instinct took over Jefferson's thoughts. He was drawn to The Horn like a scavenger to a carcass. As he made a beeline for the saloon, Frank left him and headed back toward the land transfer office to lock up for the night.

He couldn't help wondering why Lars would be paying rent to

Charlie Lee. Had Lee acquired the land from Luke Proctor and failed to register the deed change? Those were other unanswered questions the meeting with Lars had raised.

CHAPTER 94 THE JAIL

Jesus was bent over the marshal's desk comparing the branding iron Carl had brought with the designs on Jake's document.

Carl looked up from a notice he was preparing and said, "I've got a description of Danny and Star prepared for the bulletin, Marshal. Should I say 'Wanted Dead or Alive', or just 'Dead'?"

"I don't think it would matter," Hopkins responded. "Danny's not likely to surrender and I don't know too many men willing to try to take him alive. That would give him a chance to go for his gun. Most would rather just gun him down instead."

While Hopkins looked over the draft of a wire to be sent out, Brad went over to his father and said, "I was thinking about Mrs. Hardy and her son out at our place. I know Danny headed south, but he could swing north and head up toward Oak Creek Canyon. That would take him pretty close to our homestead. If we're going to stay in town tonight I can pick up the Hardys. I'll get Cornflower while I'm there. He'll be missing Grey and I don't want him left where Danny could help himself."

Dr. Pendergast agreed immediately. "I don't like the idea of Mrs. Hardy being out there alone either, Brad. Take the buggy and get her and Willie. I'll put them up at the Schnebly lodge until things settle down. They'll be safe there. Schnebly mounts a guard each night since he keeps some federal funds in a safe."

The deputy overheard their comments and jumped in with an offer. "Danny's going to be looking to pick up some money and a saddle," Carl said, "How about I ride out with Brad and take a look, Marshal? I could take the wire to the telegraph office on the way back."

CHAPTER 95 THE JAIL

Leroy Hopkins could see that Carl was keen to get out looking for Danny and Star. Well, mostly Star probably. It wouldn't hurt to have him go out with Brad to bring the housekeeper and her son in closer to town. "That's a good idea, Deputy. I've got a few suggestions about how this notice can be expanded. I'll have it taken out to Schnebly's."

"What's missing, Marshal?"

"You've got a very good description of Star, but the details about Danny Lambert are a bit sketchy," Hopkins suggested. "Seems like you're more interested in getting Star back than finding Lambert."

"That would be about right. Star is worth more," Carl replied. He didn't bother to smile.

Hopkins smiled for both of them. "Come back here as soon as you can. It's getting too dark to do anything about tracking Lambert now. We'll make some plans to start a search of the area in the morning."

"I'll get a horse from the livery and go into Schnebly's on the way out to alert them that Danny's on the run.," Carl added. "They can keep a special eye out."

Hopkins considered and then said, "Good enough, but also ask them to get a room ready for the night for Mrs. Hardy and rejoin Brad before you head back with her and the young lad. I don't want anyone else shot."

As Carl hurried out the door the deputy could be heard to mutter something which sounded like "Except Danny."

CHAPTER 96 NEAR SEDONA

After thinking over his options, Danny had decided to head north. He knew that going into Flagstaff was a bad idea. There would be a reward on his head sure enough. But, if he could skirt the town and head west he might be able to find easy pickings near Vivian, a new gold mining center on the route toward California that had just opened up in 1902. Some fella named Taddock had found gold there and a boom town was springing up.

Danny had some camping gear and ammunition stashed up Oak Creek Canyon. One way or another he would get some horse tack. The route west from Flagstaff was well enough traveled that he could pick up supplies and anything he needed. This was especially true since he wasn't too particular how he came by it.

He circled wide to the west of Sedona and worked his way slowly north. It was heading on toward evening. He figured he'd bed down in a concealed area he knew and head on out by morning light. He knew the canyon well enough, but it was treacherous to travel at night in the hills.

CHAPTER 97 THE HORN

Lil was wondering what Jake was up to. He seemed to be part of the inner circle of the guardians of the peace, judging by the time he and this Mr. Soza from Tucson were spending in the company of the marshal and the two Pendergasts. The doctor had often assisted Marshal Hopkins in solving little problems which involved medical matters. Not that there was much of that sort in Sedona, as Red Rocks was now called. Unlike some small towns which had become boisterous centers of action in the Wild West, Red Rocks had dwindled as the Indian wars ended and the gold fields petered out. The new name, Sedona, suited the small community which was largely agricultural now. Cattle drives and outfitting of speculators heading west provided some trade, but aside from the occasional drunk ranch hand, life was usually fairly sedate in Sedona.

The saloon was busy. Locals were quizzing the Wingfield crew members, Larry and Sam, about 'the shootout', as it was being called now. The drama had grown with time and the actions of the two ranch hands had grown in proportion. Charlie Lee did nothing to exaggerate his own part, but he encouraged Larry and Sam.

Lil was confused. She had been unable to get Jake out of her mind. This was not normal. She was a professional; she shouldn't get emotionally involved. So why was she thinking about him?

CHAPTER 98 COURTHOUSE

Back at his office, Frank took a quick look through the land registry records before closing up for the night. There was no indication that Charlie Lee had any rights to the land Lars Sorensen was apparently paying him rent to use.

He closed the files and arranged his desk for the morning. Everything was in order, but he sat without moving and remembered his time in Eagle Pass. Harry Plumber had made a lot of enemies because he was a hard-nosed businessman. But Frank had loved him. There was a soft side to Harry that the world in general never saw. Like Frank, he had come from a broken family; like Frank he had difficulty making friends. But Harry Plumber was driven to succeed financially. Perhaps he wanted to prove something; maybe he was just looking for security. It brought him into conflict and may have contributed to his death.

Harry's death had devastated Frank. He had moved to Arizona to try to start anew. Now that man who caused his death was here and calling himself Harry Plumber. The marshal clearly wasn't taking Frank's claim that the man was an impostor seriously. What could Frank do?

He must do something ... anything.

CHAPTER 99 LUMBERYARD

A few planks of pine to build some coffins wouldn't mean much for business, Lars reflected. He had made some sales of building supplies during the construction of the new road people were calling the Schnebly road, but sales had dropped off lately. It was alright for some. The saloon would be busy and Jefferson Brooks would make some profit out of burying the Wells Fargo driver and the other dead guy. Now the mortician was sniffing around and asking questions about who owned the property Lars used to store his stock and house his family.

Was Brooks thinking of buying the land out from under him? If this dead man, Luke Proctor, had been the husband of Doris Proctor, how did that affect the land?

When Lars had arrived with his wife and young daughter, Charlie Lee had offered to rent this land and made no objection to Lars constructing a small house as long as it was temporary. No one else had made any claims on the land.

Now Lars was concerned. Maybe he should go talk to Mr. Lee about it. On the other hand, if Charlie Lee was pulling a fast one, maybe Lars should ask Doris Proctor about the property first.

CHAPTER 100 THE JAIL

"There is no question that this branding iron is designed to modify some of our brands," Jesus Soza declared. "It seems that this young blacksmith was mixed up with the rustlers."

"Thomas told Carl that he found this in Clive's trunk and Clive was attacked. Maybe that attack was intended to shut Clive up," Dr. Pendergast speculated.

"You said that Clive was unable to give any description of the person who knocked him out," Hopkins added, "Seems to me that he knows more than he's saying."

"He might well be telling the truth about not seeing the person, or remembering the attack, but we need to find out what he does know," the doctor concluded. "Unfortunately, the sleeping powder I gave Doris to administer to him will put him out for the next eight hours or so."

Jake had been examining the branding iron and listening. Now he set down the iron with a clank and said, "In that case, that young man is in danger. We should mount a guard on the boarding house."

CHAPTER 101 THE ROAD TO THE RANCH

Carl had harnessed up Grey to the buggy and had arranged to use the gray gelding again to accompany Brad out to the Pendergast homestead. Mrs. Hardy could drive the buggy back to the Schnebly place. Brad would ride back on Cornflower.

The sun had set and the gathering twilight limited visibility, but Carl pulled up at the forks and peered off to the south. He rejoined Brad a few moments later and rode along beside the buggy in silence. After a few minutes he called out, "I'll turn off up ahead and go to Schnebly's. I'll tell them that we'll be coming back with Mrs. Hardy and her son. That way they can prepare a room for her."

Brad suspected that the deputy was looking for an excuse to look for Lambert, but it wasn't his place to tell Carl what to do. "Be careful," he warned, and watched as the deputy peeled off to the west and encouraged his mount to a little more speed.

Brad turned his attention back to the road and clucked quietly to Grey. The chestnut mare was an excellent cart horse. She seemed to enjoy trotting along pulling the light buggy and presented an impressive sight the way she stood upright between the shafts.

He had to admit he was enjoying his visit. Despite the series of unusual events, Sedona was a pleasant relief from the bustle of Boston. He was a country boy at heart. He missed Alice and part of him wanted to hurry back to her, but he looked forward to finishing his studies and beginning a rural practice of his own. Maybe Sedona would not be a bad choice after all.

He was deep in thought when he heard hoofbeats behind or off to his left. At first he thought it was Carl returning. He couldn't be sure what the sound was because of the sounds of Grey's movements and the gentle creaking of the harness. He looked back but could make out nothing in the gloom. Then the hoofbeats, or whatever else had made the sounds, died away and he drove on.

A few minutes later he pulled up in front of the old house where he was born and grew up. Memories flooded back. The front door opened and light flooded out into the yard. For a moment he flashed on an image of his mother welcoming him home. Then the diminutive form of the boy came into the doorway and he made out the features of Mrs. Hardy.

CHAPTER 102 OUTSIDE SEDONA

There was partial light from the waxing gibbous moon which had risen high in the eastern sky at sunset but it was partially obscured by clouds. Danny was trying to make time by using the roadway when he became aware that he was overtaking a wagon of some sort. He drew up and let the vehicle pull ahead. From the sound it was a light cart or buggy and it was moving fairly slowly. Danny let it pull ahead and then edged off the road to the east. He would have to go slower himself. It wasn't worth the risk of being spotted. He wanted folk to assume he'd continued south.

He wished he had taken the time to throw his own saddle on this horse. Now he was facing the necessity of riding on through the night or making a cold camp. He missed the flint and extra ammunition which was in his saddle bags.

The deputy's horse was compliant enough, but over the rough terrain of the canyon and the shale-covered slopes a proper set of reins and stirrups would be useful. He had fashioned a jury-rigged rein with the lead rope attached to the work halter the blacksmith had been using, but he wanted better than that for the treacherous slopes of the high passes. 'Damn Carter for picking that time to re-shoe the horse. I should have shot him and that loon-faced stable boy and taken my pick of their tack and gear,' he thought.

Danny knew it was useless to have regrets now. If wishes were horses, then beggars would ride, was the old saying. If he had not ridden out of town when he did, rifles would have come out and he'd have been pinned down. As it was the marshal had got off a shot at him and that one shot could have laid him low, or at least have taken the horse down, which would have amounted to the same thing. Unhorsed and with only a handgun he'd have been easy picking for someone with a rifle. He wouldn't put it past Charlie Lee to cut him down from the saloon doorway.

Well, wait till he got to the old mine and equipped himself again. They haven't seen the end of Danny Lambert yet. He'd put a few more in the ground before it came his turn.

CHAPTER 103 PROCTOR'S

Meanwhile, back in town, Marshal Hopkins had taken Jake's suggestion seriously that Clive could be in danger. He left the three others working in the office and went over to Proctor's himself. Doris seemed pleased to see him. She let him use the parlor table to work and settled down in a wing chair next to the daybed where Clive lay fast asleep.

Working quickly the marshal finished composing a wire which could be sent out to law enforcement offices. He thought the description of Danny Lambert accurate and detailed enough to help identify him. If they could get someone in town to produce a half decent drawing of Danny he could send it to towns and communities by stagecoach. A man on a horse can move faster than a stagecoach, for a short time, but a man traveling alone has to stop to rest and sleep. A stagecoach can move almost twenty-four hours per day by changing teams of horses and driver teams.

Danny would be hard pressed to stay ahead of 'wanted' posters calling for his arrest or execution.

He looked up to find that Doris was asleep sitting in the chair. Rather than disturb her he crept up the stairs and called out to Willard who was in his room. Hopkins handed the document to the young man and asked him to take it out to the telegraph office at Schnebly's.

"Thomas, or the ostler, will provide you with a horse. Tell them to put it on my account," he told Willard as the young man grabbed a jacket and headed toward the door. "Ask whoever's at the stable to have five or six of the Wells Fargo horses available for us in the morning. Some of the posse will need horses." As an afterthought Hopkins added, "Remind them that Carl will need a horse as well, and keep an eye open. Danny's still out there somewhere."

Hopkins reflected on Carl's affection for Star. It would be hard to dissuade the deputy from continuing the chase wherever it led. As likely as not Danny was well on his way to Mexico by now. They'd be lucky to pick up his trail. Their best hope was that he'd get himself shot along the way.

CHAPTER 104 THE RANCH

All things considered, Mrs. Hardy took less time gathering clothes and personal items for her and her son than Brad might have expected. They were ready to load their bags into the buggy before Carl arrived. Brad had Cornflower saddled and bridled and had grabbed a change of clothes for himself and his father and was wondering whether he should wait for the deputy or start back toward town when Carl came riding up. He sized up the situation and sat waiting in his saddle while Brad helped the Hardys into the buggy and loaded their baggage behind.

Brad found he had lost the practised ease of mounting up, but once in the saddle he felt comfortable enough.

"You're sure you're okay driving the buggy, Mrs. Hardy?" he asked.

"Land, yes!" she assured him. "I've been handling horses since I was William's age."

Truth was she looked more at ease than he had felt on the way out from town, Brad thought. He brought Cornflower over closer to Carl and said in a low voice, "I thought I heard you catching up with the buggy just after you went off toward Schnebly's. Did you forget something and start back?"

CHAPTER 105 PROCTOR'S

As Willard opened the door a bearded giant loomed up on the step. Willard froze for a second and then cried out, "You scared the hell out of me. Is there a problem at the yard?"

Hopkins had moved to the door with one hand on his gun. He relaxed as he recognized Lars Sorensen illuminated by the light spilling out of the open doorway. Leroy looked back to see if Doris Proctor had been awakened and saw that she had. The landlady was sitting upright and blinking. Clive was still dead to the world though breathing well enough.

"No problem. I was coming to speak with Mrs. Proctor," Lars explained.

"You go ahead, Willard," Hopkins said. "If you don't mind, when you get back to town have one of the men from my office come over here."

"Sure enough, Marshal," Willard called out as he disappeared into the darkness.

Willard was glad to have something active to do. He'd been brooding in his room. Doris had refused his offer to take over for her watching Clive. Willard could see that she was worn out. He'd like to see her take a break, but she was determined to stay by Clive's side. Well, that was natural enough. He had decided to get some rest himself now so that he could take over the vigil if she finally succumbed to fatigue.

Now the marshal was here to assist. There was no point in hanging around.

The deputy, Carl, was practically the same age as he was, Willard thought. Maybe if Willard did something useful to prove his worth the marshal would value him more. Willard imagined the marshal asking him to become a deputy. He felt certain that he could fulfil the duties. Hell, Carl wasn't anything special. It should be possible to outshine him. Willard intended to do just that. He'd start out as an errand boy, but he'd end up marshal. Just see if he didn't.

CHAPTER 106 THE HORN

Lil was bored. She'd heard the account of the shooting retold more times than she had thought possible. The only thing of interest was to watch the story grow and the role of the participants become more glorious. The last time she had overheard Larry telling the story he had practically become the major player in the piece. Since she had witnessed the whole event, Larry's current version, in which he tried to pull Paul to safety and told Danny to back down, made her want to break into laughter.

Sam was more reticent about his own role in the drama. She suspected that he was feeling pangs of guilt for putting Paul at the table with Danny. Danny was trouble waiting to happen and Paul could never control his mouth.

Charlie Lee was clearly relishing the business the episode had generated. Sam might dwell on Paul's death, but Charlie was never one to let profits take a back seat. Lil had overheard one of the Wells Fargo outriders, who was staying over in town for the night, ask Charlie about when Danny had ridden right by the front door of The Horn on his way out of town.

"Couldn't you get a shot off at him then?" he'd demanded. The drinks had been flowing for some time now. Lil noticed that everyone was becoming an expert on gunfights and the strategy involved in unhorsing a rider.

Charlie pointed out that he did not usually carry a gun during business hours. Then he changed the subject to a detailed description of his new rifle. Lil had heard it all before.

"The very same rifle, mind you, that our President, Theodore Roosevelt, carried with him during his safari into darkest Africa," Charlie proclaimed now and went on to praise the power and accuracy of the gun to anyone who would listen. Tonight he had an eager audience. Everyone wanted to talk guns and shooting.

CHAPTER 107 THE RANCH

Carl thought about what Brad had just said. "I went straight to Schnebly's after I left you. On the way here I went off to the west a bit to check out the ford at the creek, but I was never close to you and the buggy," he insisted. "I was checking to see signs of anyone crossing the creek lately, but it was getting too dark to see much."

"Well, I'm sure I heard a horse. You don't suppose it could have been Danny, do you?" Brad speculated. In a way, that made sense as an explanation of what had happened. Surely if it was some innocent traveler they would have ridden up and exchanged greetings. The unknown rider had seemed to pull back and maybe even get off the road.

Brad could see that Carl was starting to get excited by the possibility. He didn't want Carl to ride off alone to investigate, so he suggested, "Why don't we take a lantern and have a look at the spot the rider would have crossed."

"Get two lanterns," Carl countered. "We'll take a good look."

CHAPTER 108 THE HORN

Charlie Lee was in great spirits. They had sold more beer tonight than they usually sold in a week. Clayton had more than he could deal with himself. Young Andy Thompson was kept busy clearing and washing glasses and bringing up bottles of liquor. The Thompson boys certainly knew how to work. He might be able to find other jobs for Andy.

As he circulated through the room, Charlie found a number of men talking about hunting Danny Lambert down. Of course, that was liquor talking. By the sober light of morning these brave words would evaporate like morning dew in the desert sun.

He would personally be glad if Danny was never seen again. He'd done what he could to control the hothead over the past year. It was good to see the back of him now. If a posse was formed in the morning, Charlie intended to be part of it. Being involved in publicly spirited ventures, such as hunting down and blasting away a troublemaker, would increase his standing in the community. That could be good for business.

CHAPTER 109 THE ROAD TO SEDONA

When they reached the point in the road where he had heard the sound of hoofbeats, Brad had Mrs. Hardy stop the buggy. He and Carl went forward with the lanterns, one at each side of the road. Just where he had thought they'd be, the tracks were clearly outlined in the ground where they drew off on the eastern edge. Carl got down and examined the sharply-edged imprints cut into the dusty soil. They would be obliterated by even a light breeze, but in the still air of evening they were clear to read.

"I'm pretty sure these tracks were made by Star," he declared. "These are from new shoes. Thomas replaced Star's just yesterday."

Brad thought Carl was going to suggest going after Lambert right then, but the deputy showed uncharacteristic restraint.

"Let's get Mrs. Hardy settled for the night at Schnebly's and go tell the marshal. We need to get a posse organized."

CHAPTER 110 PROCTOR'S

Doris Proctor placed her hand lightly on her son's forehead. He was sleeping easily and there was no sign of fever. She rose from the wing chair and came into the small vestibule "Why Lars, what brings you here so late? Are you looking for Willard?"

Lars looked ill at ease. Now that he was here he wasn't sure how to broach the subject. The marshal was watching him closely and he could see Clive lying stretched out under a blanket in the farther room. "How is Clive doing?" he asked.

"He's resting quiet. Doc says he just needs to rest. Thanks for your concern." In the face of continued silence, Doris looked around and said, "Willard ought to be around here somewhere. I must have dozed off."

"Willard went on an errand for me, Doris," Hopkins explained. "He'll be back shortly, I imagine."

Lars gathered himself and said, "Actually, it was you I wanted to talk with, Mrs. Proctor."

"Whatever about, Lars?"

The big man let his eye slide over Leroy Hopkins. "You might as well hear this too, Marshal." Then he turned back to Doris, "The thing is, I had a visit from Frank Green and Jefferson Brooks today. They were asking about the land my lumberyard sits on. I've been paying rent to Mr. Charlie Lee ever since I arrived. Now, Frank tells me that you own the land."

CHAPTER 111 MAIN STREET, SEDONA

After providing Willard with a horse, Thomas Carter had given Eddie Thompson instructions about which Wells Fargo horses could be provided for the posse. He told the ostler to send for him if there was any trouble during the night. As he walked toward his house at the western end of town he passed in front of the saloon at The Horn. There was a lot of action for a midweek night. The shooting was creating quite a stir in town and the local watering hole was where men gathered to gossip. They wouldn't like to hear it described that way, but that's what it amounted to, he reasoned.

Carter enjoyed a cool beer as much as any man, but he preferred to take it in the shade of a tree or in the contemplative silence out behind the smithy. Standing around in a crowded bar while red-eyed drunks shouted nonsense at one another didn't appeal to him. The rush to the saloon seemed as senseless as a stampede of cattle. Besides, in his opinion, which he carefully kept to himself, Charlie Lee was a pompous, self-centered, pretentious waste of space.

CHAPTER 112   THE HORN

As Charlie wandered back toward the bar, Lil motioned for him to come over. She could see that he was flushed with entrepreneurial excitement. Men were easy to read. It was clear to Lil that Charlie had a hunger for money. He was good at spotting an opportunity to turn a profit and loathe to let any chance slip by. Tonight he was in his element.

"Big crowd tonight," she commented.

"Maybe we should arrange for a shooting every Tuesday afternoon," he joked. "Can't say I'm sorry to see the last of Danny," he declared. Then he grew serious and added, "Paul was a decent man. He should never have taunted Lambert."

"What's going to happen about Danny?" Lil inquired. "You were over talking with the marshal."

"He just wanted to know what I saw." Charlie paused and added, "If Danny has any sense at all he won't stop riding 'til he reaches Mexico."

"No one ever suggested that Danny Lambert had any sense at all," Lil countered. "What about the two new fellas, Hank and that

Mexican gentleman, Mr. Soza, who arrived on the stage. They seem to be pretty thick with Marshal Hopkins."

Charlie tugged at his earlobe and took in the boisterous socializing going on around the room. He met Lil's eyes and responded, "Good question, Lil. It almost seems like they've become official investigators. I wonder just who they are."

CHAPTER 113 SCHNEBLY'S

The driveway which led westward to the Schnebly house was as broad as the main road and less heavily traveled. Carl Schnebly was a real operator. He had a hand in everything local. He ran the post office and the telegraph and provided overnight rooms of a better quality than those offered by The Horn hotel. The setting was impressive. Little was visible now in darkness, but Brad knew that the creek which ran behind the main house was jammed with trout. He and his father had fished the lower reaches of the waterway. As a young boy he had wandered the natural forest pathways made by deer and bears. Plants were lush and bountiful. He had gathered berries along the banks of the creeks.

As they neared the front of the house, Brad was jolted out of his reverie by Carl. "Look who's coming out on the porch. Isn't that Willard Wright?"

"He was supposed to be with Clive and Mrs. Proctor," Brad responded. "Maybe there's a problem."

They urged their mounts forward and rode toward the Schnebly house while Mrs. Hardy brought up the rear.

Willard heard and then saw them approaching as they advanced out of the darkness. He raised a hand in greeting and descended the steps to await their arrival.

CHAPTER 114 PROCTOR'S

"I think you're mistaken, Lars," Doris exclaimed. "I've never owned that land."

"According to Frank Green that land is registered to one Luke Proctor and that makes it yours now."

"I never knew anything about that good-for-nothing Luke Proctor owning anything of value or doing anything worthwhile," Doris responded hotly. She stopped herself and gazed over at Clive lying easy in the daybed. Her eyes, which had been sparks of fire, softened momentarily and she added, "The one good thing he did for me was to give me that boy, and that was only a side effect of him taking his pleasure."

"Well, there must be something to it. Jefferson Brooks backed up the claim," Lars explained. "They came to ask how it was that I'm using the land and I told them that I rent it from Charlie Lee." He paused to let his explanation seep in.

"And why is that?" Leroy Hopkins asked. His eyes were fixed on Lars and Lars felt himself becoming confused.

"He offered to rent it to me when I asked about available land," Lars replied "I naturally thought it was his to offer." He looked from the marshal to Doris Proctor and back again. "Now I don't know what to think," he finished lamely.

Doris and Lars both turned to look at Hopkins. He was the unofficial local mediator. It was typical for town folk to turn to him for direction in small disputes.

The marshal had never known Lars to tell a lie or to treat any customer other than honestly. On the other hand, it seemed odd that Charlie would try to get away with renting land he didn't own. He would know that sooner or later the truth would come out and that would make him look bad. Hopkins knew that appearances were very important to Charlie Lee.

"Seems to me," Hopkins told them, "That we need to ask Mr. Lee to explain."

CHAPTER 115 BROOK'S MORTUARY

'People don't warm to me easily,' Jefferson thought as he regarded himself in the mirror over the sink in his work area. He had noticed that people sometimes seemed uncomfortable in his presence. Part of it was his occupation, but his appearance was against him too. He had an unnatural pallor to face and hands which, though congenital, was increased by his avoidance of the sun. The comparison of his pale skin to the ruddy tan sported by the outdoor types who made up the male population of Sedona was as striking as it was to be expected. While the majority of the country folk spent many hours outside herding animals, tending crops, or mending fences or outbuildings, Jefferson worked in the dim seclusion required by the nature of his trade.

While he was collecting the corpse of the Wells Fargo driver he'd been aware of the silence which had accompanied his arrival and departure. It was as if he were some sort of pariah. No one realized that his was an honorable profession like any other. The dead required care as did the dying and those temporarily alive.

No one thought anything of Charlie Lee making a good profit out of the shooting. If Lars was to be believed Charlie was also making money by renting out a widow's land.

'But just because I prepare the dead for proper burial, they act as if I'm a vulture of death. Sometimes people respect a predator more than they do a vulture, even though a vulture does no harm,' he thought. 'And I'm not a vulture,' he added peevishly.

* * *

The Artist had been secretly relieved to see Danny ride out of town and turn south. That would mislead the locals. He had done a bit of work with Lambert and knew a bit more than most about Danny. He knew Danny had a campsite up a dead-end canyon just off the Oak Creek cattle trail. Danny would probably go there sometime to pick up supplies, even if he intended to go south eventually. While the law was searching for Lambert down south of town, the Artist would slip north and see if he could dry gulch his sometime partner. There was bound to be some reward offered and it would be just as well to shut Danny up before he could get to trial. Danny knew where some of the bodies were buried, and they weren't proverbial ones.

CHAPTER 116 SCHNEBLY'S

Willard stopped at the bottom of the steps and waited for Carl and Brad to draw near. Carl seemed worked up about something.

"What's going on?" Carl demanded as he strove to quiet a horse strange to his use. "I thought you were at Proctor's."

"I was," Willard told him. "Then the marshal arrived and asked me to bring out something for the telegraph. I think it's about Lambert." He held up an envelope for Carl's inspection.

Carl took the offered document and examined it. "We'd better get back to town. Now we know where Lambert is heading we've got a chance to catch him."

"How do you know where Danny is going?" Willard asked.

"We found some tracks," Carl told him.

Carl was pretty full of himself over the discovery, Willard thought. Still he had to admit that it would narrow down the area to search. Well, if they caught up to Danny Lambert, Willard would make sure he was there. Carl would find that he wasn't the only one with sharp eyes and the wits to use them.

Willard considered who was likely to join the posse. A lot of people would talk big but avoid the inherent danger of a manhunt. He was tired of being looked over and considered only good enough to stack lumber and weigh out sacks of nails. His chance would come; he'd show them all what he was made of.

CHAPTER 117 THE HORN

Lil was taking a break. She had settled into a wicker chair outside the reception area of the hotel and was smoking a hand-rolled. The cool night air was a welcome relief from the crowded saloon. The moonlight cast sharp shadows across the unpainted decking where the stagecoach usually discharged its cargo.

She was about to flick the last of her cigarette into the roadway when her attention was drawn to the three riders moving down the main street at a good pace. She was surprised to find Brad Pendergast,

Willard Wright and Deputy Munds arriving together. They pulled up in front of the marshal's office and Carl leapt off his mount and rushed inside leaving Brad to hold his horse.

Curiosity overcame her. She wandered across the street and sidled up to Brad.

"Hi again," she said by way of opening. "What's up?"

"Oh, hello Miss Lily," Brad responded. "We just brought Mrs. Hardy in from the ranch."

"You sure did arrive in a hurry to announce that," Lil teased him. "I guess the marshal must be real eager to know she's here." She paused and added, "Where is she by the way? I don't see her."

Brad's blush would have been evident, had it not been dark. As it was, Lil could infer that from the confused nature of his response. "Well, . . . she's not actually 'here'. We took her to Schnebly's."

"Oh, I see. That's why Carl is in such a hurry to tell Marshal Hopkins!" Lil said. The taunt in her voice was evident to both Willard and Brad.

Willard snorted in amusement. Brad groaned. Why did Lil always enjoy teasing him so much, Brad wondered? He reflected on some of the theories of human behavior he had studied and was struck by a possibility. Maybe it was because she liked him. It was a bit like a young girl teasing a boy she fancies. Despite her occupation and apparent self-confidence, Lil was at heart a simple woman.

Gathering himself together he responded, "I suppose that I didn't explain that very well, Miss Lily. Carl is in a hurry to inform the marshal that we found some tracks which might lead us to Danny Lambert."

"Are you considering getting involved in a manhunt, Brad?" Lil asked, the concern clear in her face. "I thought doctors were more interested in saving lives."

"I'm not actually a doctor yet, and I wasn't planning to shoot anyone. It's not even certain that there will be an attempt to catch Danny."

"If there is a posse formed I'll join up," Willard declared.

Lil looked from one to the other in puzzlement. Why were men so ready to get involved in wars and violence? She was about to speak again when the door opened and Carl came back out.

"The marshal's over at Proctor's. I'll head over there."

Willard slapped himself and interjected, "Sorry, I could have told you that. He asked me to send someone over there when I got back."

Dr. Pendergast had come to the open door behind Carl. "I'll go with you, Carl. I'd like to look in on Clive anyway."

As the two men walked off toward the boarding house, the tall form of Jake Witherspoon emerged from the office to fill the doorway. He saw Lil standing beside Brad and stepped down to approach her.

"I think I need to explain something to you, Lil," he began.

"What's that, Hank?" Lil asked.

"First of all, I'm not Hank," he said with an abashed grimace.

CHAPTER 118 THE JAIL

Carl was striding purposefully toward the Proctor boarding house. He was clearly a man with a mission. He would be the one to tell the marshal about the tracks headed north.

Brad tied up the horses and he and Willard moved discretely inside to give Jake and Lil some privacy. Near the marshal's desk, Jesus Soza was examining the partially formed branding iron Thomas Carter had discovered amongst Clive's tools and practice pieces.

"What does that iron tell you?" Brad asked Jesus.

"Clearly it's connected with the rustling. Some of the people in this town must be involved as well." Jesus laid the iron on the desk and turned his full attention on Brad. Brad noted that the cattleman's forehead was creased with frown lines. "This rise in rustling comes at the worst possible time," Jesus continued. "The great cattle herds of the past century have been reduced to thirty or forty percent of their size twenty years ago."

"The drought," Brad prompted.

"Yes," Jesus agreed. "The droughts of 1885 and 1886 were dreadful, but 1892 and 1893 were worse. We've begun breeding herds and selling registered animals."

"Those herds must be easier to protect," Brad speculated.

"They are," Jesus agreed, "But we are still shipping most yearling steers north and those cattle drives have been targeted."

"And you suspected a connection with Sedona?"

"People talk," Soza explained. "It became clear that someone in Sedona was involved. Now with this branding iron we have a piece of the puzzle. I want to hear what your young blacksmith has to say."

CHAPTER 119 PROCTOR'S

Doris Proctor, wearing an apron and a smile, opened the door to the three men. She ushered them in and led them into the parlor where Marshal Hopkins sat with a cup of tea in one hand and a muffin in the other. Dr. Pendergast went directly to examine Clive while Carl cast a covetous eye on the muffin.

Willard wandered over toward the sofa and watched the doctor as he inspected the wound and checked Clive's pulse and respiration.

"Has he been sleeping straight through?" the doctor asked.

"Mostly he has, doctor," Doris replied. "But about ten minutes ago he woke and asked for a drink. That bent glass straw you left allowed him to drink without moving his head much. He seemed much better and his face is less flushed."

"He seems stable. There's no undue swelling near the wound. I believe he just needs rest," Dr. Pendergast told her. "Don't move him at all for now. In the morning we'll see about having him sit up. Do you have a bed pan in case he needs to relieve himself in the night?"

"Right beside the sofa," she assured him. "I've nursed sick men before now."

Carl was standing beside Hopkins holding the envelope Willard had given him outside Schnebly's. As he handed it to the marshal he said, "We found some tracks crossing the main road and heading north east, Marshal. I'm almost certain they were made by Star. Lambert must be heading toward Oak Creek Canyon."

"Good work, Carl," Hopkins told him and was gratified to see Carl's face light up. "There's a chance he might go to ground up that way. There are abandoned mines and hidden gullies all through those hills.

I'll send another wire to Flagstaff tomorrow and we can work our way north while they come south. I don't want a big posse tripping all over itself though."

Willard had come over to join the two law officers. "I'd like to volunteer to help out, Marshal," he told Hopkins.

CHAPTER 120 THE JAIL

Jake paused and waited for Lil to respond. Although he was used to traveling under false names and conducting investigations without revealing his true role, he felt strangely uncomfortable in this instance. There was something oddly innocent about this working girl that touched him. He wanted to be honest with her.

"So, your real name is Jake Witherspoon," she said. There was the edge of a laugh in her voice which encouraged him. "That sounds like a banker or a lawyer's name, not a detective."

"I think my father would have preferred me to have entered either of those professions," Jake agreed. "As a young man I wanted adventure. So, here I am."

"It seems that you have brought it to Sedona," she exclaimed. "Normally this is a quiet little town."

Jake turned serious. "Since you now know who I am and what I am, maybe you can help me with why I'm here," he told her.

"Why are you here? I guess it's not to buy land."

"No, far from that," Jake told her. "Come on inside and meet my client. You may have heard something that could help us."

CHAPTER 121 LUMBERYARD

The more Lars thought about it the less he liked it. Charlie Lee had never actually told him that he owned the land; he had just told Lars that he would rent it to him. Was it that simple? Had Charlie just tricked him into renting land that Charlie didn't own?

How gullible he had been. He had arrived in town and asked about land for sale or rent. There were signs up in the land registry office offering to sell property, but Lars couldn't afford any of the land offered for sale. Then he had asked Mr. Lee if he knew of any that was affordable. Charlie had said that he didn't know of any for sale, but that he could rent the acre lot next to Proctor's boarding house to him.

Lars hadn't asked to see proof that Mr. Lee owned the land. Who would ask? The rent asked was reasonable. Lars was happy to find land to rent at that price. He'd offered to sign a lease, but Charlie had said that wasn't necessary.

Now, in view of what he had learned from Mr. Green and Mr. Brooks, Lars was starting to wonder if he hadn't been taken for a ride.

He was ashamed to let his wife, Helga, know how foolish he had been. After supper he told her that he was going to The Horn to talk with Mr. Lee without telling her the topic. He tucked his young son and daughter into their bunk beds, slipped his canvas jacket over his shoulders, and headed toward The Horn with resolute steps.

CHAPTER 122 PROCTOR'S

"Thank you, Willard. We'll be happy to have you with us," Hopkins told the young man. "We will probably leave at sunrise tomorrow. Come to the office tomorrow. Bring your rifle, a lunch and a bed roll. We won't plan to be out overnight, but be prepared."

Hopkins approached Dr. Pendergast and Doris Proctor who were discussing medical matters. "Doris," he said, "Do you have room to put up the doctor and his son overnight? The town will pay for their room and board."

"Lord love a duck!" Doris exclaimed, "Of course I've got room, but you don't think I'd charge the doctor and his good son for being here and taking care of my boy, do you?"

Leroy Hopkins smiled at the expression and said, "Thank you, Doris. No, I guess I wouldn't, but the town will still pay something toward their keep."

Turning back to the other two men, Hopkins said, "Tomorrow may be a long day, and we've still got some planning to do, Carl. Let's head back to the office. I want to speak with Charlie Lee and the two

Wingfield boys. Willard, you get some rest. We may be long in the saddle tomorrow tracking Danny Lambert."

As Carl and Leroy moved toward the door, there was a stirring on the sofa. Clive was moving. Doris cried out and moved close to him.

"Danny, Danny and Charlie. . . . They killed him. . . . They wanted me," Clive cried out. His eyes were open, focussed on nothing.

The doctor had one hand on his wrist and was watching his eye movement in consternation. After the brief outburst Clive fell silent. His eyes closed. His forehead was beaded in a cold sweat.

Hopkins strode across the room and bent to whisper in Dr. Pendergast's ear. The doctor shook his head and replied, "He was delirious. He may just have been repeating words that you were using. He'll be unable to respond right now. Perhaps in the morning he'll be able to talk clearly. For now he needs to sleep and heal."

CHAPTER 123 THE HORN

Lars was not a habitual client of The Horn saloon. What little liquor he drank was consumed at home and in moderation. He had no money to waste buying bar liquor. He entered the saloon and was astonished by the noise and commotion. He spotted Charlie Lee standing at the bar in conversation with Clayton. As Lars made his way through the crowd many of the townsfolk reacted with surprise seeing him in the bar. Several men offered to buy him a beer, but he thanked them and continued to make his way toward the bar. He had a mind to confront Charlie Lee and demand some straight answers.

CHAPTER 124 THE JAIL

Jake introduced Lil to Jesus Soza. He explained how Pinkertons had dispatched him to help the Soza family track down the ring of rustlers.

"How is rustling connected with the two killings we've had in Sedona?" Lil asked.

"It may not be, but there was also the attack on the blacksmith's apprentice, Clive. Let me show you what we found amongst his affairs." Jake held up the branding iron for Lil to see.

"That looks like the kind of thing I would expect a blacksmith to make," Lil said. "I don't see how that connects with rustling. Don't blacksmiths make that sort of wrought iron all the time?"

Jesus reached out to take the iron from Jake's hands. "Here," he said, "Let me show you." He moved over to the marshal's desk and spread out the diagram of Soza family brands for Lil to examine. "This branding iron is capable of covering up many of our cattle brands and make it seem that the cattle belong to this newly formed cattle company. Records we've obtained from the combined cattle markets show that this new company, registered as Lazy-8 Livestock, has sold far more cattle then they have purchased or could possibly have bred. In fact, the very name, Lazy-8. seems to have been chosen to facilitate use of a brand which could cover ours."

Jake showed Lil how the semi-transparent image of the brand of Lazy-8 could be superimposed over several of the Soza brands to completely cover them.

"Then Clive was involved with the rustlers," Lil concluded.

"It certainly seems so. We're hoping he will tell us when he can speak again," Jake told her.

"You said that I might be able to help you. How can I do that?" Lil asked.

"I'm hoping that you may have overheard something, or might just have some local information which people aren't likely to share with two out-of-towners like Jesus and me," Jake explained.

"There's nothing like a few drinks to set people to saying things that they don't mean to let slip, or perhaps without even realizing what they've said," Jesus added.

CHAPTER 125 THE HORN

Frank had joined the gathering at The Horn. He'd lived in Sedona for almost two years, but they events of the past twenty hours represented more dramatic change than he had seen during that entire period. The saloon had an almost festive atmosphere with Sam and

Larry the twin centers of attention. Although Charlie and Clayton had been witnesses, they had both turned their attention to serving the paying customers and seemed happy to let Sam and Larry bathe in the limelight.

Lil had slipped out of the saloon without Frank noticing and now he saw the bearded lumberman, Lars, making his way toward the bar. Frank was at his usual place down at the end and it happened that Clayton and Charlie were standing nearby discussing the supplies of beer and whisky available. Charlie was making notes about replacement supplies to be ordered and Clayton was totalling up the consumption. Neither of them saw Lars approaching, his eyes fixed on Charlie.

Frank sidled over and leaned unobtrusively closer to Charlie. Something interesting was going on and Frank wanted to hear what was said.

CHAPTER 126   PROCTOR'S

The noise from The Horn saloon drifted down the street on the still night air. Hopkins took Carl by the arm and said. "Seems to be a fair crowd at the bar, Carl. We might as well go on over and sign up volunteers for a posse right now. I'd like to ride out early tomorrow morning."

"It will be one hung-over posse from the sound of it," Carl suggested.

"We'll take our pick of those sober enough to show up," Leroy said. "I don't want too many anyway."
* * *

The lawmen were not the only ones with their minds set on preparations for an organized search. The Artist also turned his thoughts to the morrow. Somehow he needed to ensure that Danny Lambert was not taken alive.

That might not be too difficult, given Danny's disposition to violence rather than reason. But, the Artist knew that if by any chance Danny were captured and taken into custody while still able to speak it would be necessary to silence him. If witnesses were present, more than one

person might have to die. The Artist was prepared to see that happen.
* * *

"Do you really mean to ride out with the posse tomorrow, Willard?" Doris Proctor asked. His declaration to do so had surprised Doris. She had never known him to carry a handgun. Like most men he had a shotgun and a rifle for hunting, but he was not one she could picture riding out in a posse. He was always polite and seemed so sensitive.

Willard seemed a bit surprised by the question. "I'm sorry, Mrs. Proctor," he offered. "I should have asked first if you needed me to help you out here, what with Clive laid up and all."

"No, no. It's not that, Willard. The doctor and I can manage fine. It just surprised me, that's all," she told him.

Willard looked a bit chagrined. "It just seemed that I should offer," he explained.

"Well, I'll make up some sandwiches for you and put them in the icebox. You'll have to get away early enough but there will be coffee in a pot on the corner of the woodstove and there are muffins in the bread box."

"Thank you kindly, Mrs. Proctor," Willard said politely. "If you don't mind I'll go up to bed now and be off in the morning."

CHAPTER 127 PROCTOR'S

Willard headed off up the stairs and Doris went back into the parlor where Dr. Pendergast was settled in the wing chair looking through a recent issue of The Arizona Silver Belt.

"Can I get you a cup of coffee, Doctor?" Doris asked.

"I'm just fine, Mrs. Proctor. If you'd like to lie down and have a rest yourself, I'll be here with Clive."

"I'll go up and prepare a room for you and Brad now," Doris replied, "But if there's anything you'd like just help yourself. I'll have a lie down later on."

Left on his own for the first time in hours, Dr. Pendergast read over the lead editorial by Joseph Hamill. He noted with surprise that it was being proposed that the newspaper become a daily. Pendergast was a progressive thinker and approved of the strong editorials which had been written by Hamill and indeed those of the former editor, Aaron Hackney, until his death in 1899.

He set the newspaper down on his knees and thought about what he had told the marshal. Was it just delirium which caused Clive to call out Danny's and Charlie's name, or was it rational? If there was meaning to the outburst, what could it be? "They killed him," Clive had said. Who were they? Who did they kill? Was he saying that Danny and Charlie had killed Luke Proctor? Or was he talking about the death of Paul? But, it couldn't be Paul's death he was speaking about. Clive was unconscious before that happen, wasn't he? How could he know anything about that?

CHAPTER 128 THE HORN

"Hello, Mr. Lee. Could I talk with you?" Lars asked. His normally deep voice seemed tight as if under stress.

Frank could tell that Charlie noticed the difference too. Charlie was a man of above average height, but Lars had come up so close to him that Charlie had to tilt his head back to meet the firm gaze Lars held him with.

"Why, Lars! What brings you into this den of iniquity?" Lee asked with forced jocosity.

Out of the corner of his eye, Frank saw Clayton move back from the bar. Clayton always took care to stay out of the line of fire. The instant he thought that, Frank looked to see if Lars was carrying a gun. With relief he assured himself that both of the Norse giant's hands were empty. 'Mind you,' he thought, 'Lars would hardly need a weapon to kill someone.'

Lars Sorensen was not a man to mince words. "I've been told that you don't own the land you've been charging me rent on," he challenged Charlie. Lars seemed to notice Frank for the first time and seemed about to appeal to the town clerk to back up his claim.

Frank realized that he might be caught up in the confrontation and wished he was not quite so close.

"I never said I did," Charlie said with seeming lack of concern. "Let me buy you a beer."

Lars brushed away the suggestion with the air of a bear swatting at a fly. His face darkened as he replied in slow measured words, "I don't want beer; I want to know why you tricked me." His hands hung motionless, but Lars seemed to grow even larger as he towered over the businessman.

"Hold on," Charlie said in sudden realization that Lars was in deadly earnest. "No one tricked you. Luke Proctor owned that land and he signed it over to me because of money he owed me. I had every right to rent it to you."

Now Lars seemed puzzled. "But Mr. Green told me that the land is not in your name." He now turned his attention to Frank and seemed about to demand confirmation.

Before Frank could say anything, Charlie Lee calmed things by saying, "That's correct, Lars. I hold the land as security for the debt and have the right to use it as I like, including renting it. You have to admit that the rent I charge you is reasonable."

Lars paused. "Yes, you charge me a fair rent," he admitted. "It has allowed us to live here."

"I have a document in my safe which I will show to you and Frank here," Charlie went on. "When Luke Proctor disappeared I didn't want to trouble his wife about the debt. She had no money to pay it off and I had no desire to buy the land, so I let the matter lie. When you wanted to rent some land I thought that I might as well get some of my money back," he added.

Frank could feel the tension dissolve. As Lars stood considering what Charlie Lee had said, Frank spoke to Charlie. "I just learned this afternoon that the dead man was Mrs. Proctor's absent husband. Now the ownership of the land will revert to her."

"I suppose it will," Charlie admitted. "Today has been pretty busy so far. I hadn't even thought about that." He considered the situation for a moment and then said, "I like Doris Proctor. I'd be willing to write that debt off now in return for the rent I've collected over the past few years. We can consider that Luke's debt died with him." He smiled and told Lars, "You can probably rent the property from Doris Proctor. I'm sure she can use the income."

Noticing that all seemed calm, Clayton had drifted back down the bar. Now he spoke. "We've got visitors," he commented. He drew attention to the swinging doors where Marshal Hopkins and Deputy Munds stood watching the milling crowd.

CHAPTER 129 THE JAIL

"You must hear a lot of gossip in the bar, Lil." Jake suggested. "People tend to say things they shouldn't when they've had a few drinks."

"I probably hear more confessions than a priest," Lil said with a smile.

"What about talk about cattle drives?" Jake suggested.

"Sure, the boys like to brag about how tough a drive was, or how far they've come. I don't remember anyone talking about rustling though." She thought a while and then said, "We did have a crew in last year who were grumbling about losing their bonus because they had so many strays."

"We've been losing almost twice as many steers on drives in the last three years," Jesus told her. "The crews may lose their bonus; we're losing even more, and the losses seem to be occurring largely between here and Flagstaff."

Lily considered Jesus' words and then ventured a comment. "The only thing that comes to mind is a discussion I happened to overhear in the bar one afternoon last week," she said. Her eyes had taken on a far-away look and she clasped her hands together and raised them to her chin.

While Lily was gathering her thought, Jake noticed that her eyes, which he had thought of as cornflower blue, had seemed to take on an aquamarine tint in the lamplight and that her lips pressed together in thought described a perfect arc beneath a pert, little nose. Jake was not an insensitive man, and he was used to analysing people and his reactions to them. His reaction to Lily was not the rational investigative reaction he had to most people. If he was examining someone else's emotional reaction he would have said they were those of a person infatuated. In fact, he decided, he might think they were those of a person in love.

CHAPTER 130 THE HORN

Hopkins had spoken with Frank, Lars, Charlie and Clayton. He had been told about the misunderstanding about the land and was pleased to hear that Doris Proctor would finally be reaping something worthwhile from her husband's existence. He invited the four men to join the posse on the next day and received conditional agreement from them all.

Next he drew Sam Schuerman and Larry James aside and got their account of what had happened during the poker game. He sensed that the tale had grown in the telling, but the major details were clear. Danny had pulled a gun and shot Paul. Paul had shot his mouth off, but had done nothing to warrant being shot. He asked them to join the posse. He was especially keen to have these two men because of their intimate knowledge of the canyon. They both vowed to turn up early the next morning.

Now he was standing on the bar addressing the crowd. "You all know about Danny Lambert's actions in here today. We're going to ride out tomorrow morning to see if he's still in the vicinity. If he's gone, he's gone. But if he's still hanging around I want to see him stand trial."

There were murmurs of approval and somebody at the rear of the mass of men called out, "Hang him."

"We'll see about hanging him after the trial," Marshal Hopkins suggested. "In the meantime we want to get him into custody." He waited to get their attention again and said, "We need a few men with horses and rifles to ride out tomorrow morning. I'd appreciate seeing as many of you who are willing to lend a hand out front of the hotel tomorrow morning at 6:30. We have an arrangement with Wells Fargo to supply horses to those who lack mounts, but we'd like you to bring your own guns, rifles if you have one. If you don't have a rifle, we can supply one. Bring a bed roll with you too, we might camp overnight."

There were a numbers of cries of general support and a number of men called out, "I'll be there" and "Sure enuf." Hopkins knew that most would roll over in bed in the morning and decide to stay there, but he imagined that a few of them would actually show up.

There was a certain amount of backslapping and words of encouragement as Leroy and Carl departed. As they crossed the street Carl said, "I sure hope he puts up a fight and we have to shoot him." He thought a bit and then added, "If he's injured my horse, I may just shoot him anyway."

CHAPTER 131 BROOK'S MORTUARY

Jefferson considered going to The Horn for a nightcap, but didn't relish the idea of dealing with the crowd. They would be pretty drunk by now. Jefferson had trouble relating to people in normal circumstances. When they were intoxicated he found them impossible. He paused and considered that thought for a minute. That wasn't quite true, was it? When they were intoxicated enough, say with formaldehyde, they were quiet and tractable. On the whole, Jefferson preferred to associate with people who were dead.

The corpse of Paul Matthews was quiet. The preservatives had replaced the corruptible blood. The body was neatly arranged in his storage vault. It was of his own design and Jefferson thought of it as a temporary resting place for the corpse. After life's fitful fever he sleeps well. What was that from? The Scottish play wasn't it? But the king in Macbeth had been killed as a result of a plot. This unfortunate Wells Fargo driver had been killed in hot blood, not by cold treason.

Thinking of death and dealing with it usually had a calming effect on Jefferson. Tonight he found himself wondering about the possible connections between the sudden epidemic of violence in Sedona. He decided that he would go for a drink after all. Maybe Frank would still be sober enough to talk to.

Jefferson hung up his lab coat and slipped a black worsted jacket over his shoulders. He enjoyed walking alone at night. The darkness could conceal many ugly things.

CHAPTER 132 THE JAIL

Brad listened to Jesus and wondered where Luke Proctor could fit into this cattle rustling scheme. From what his father had told him, Luke Proctor was basically a good-for-nothing. He had been too lazy to succeed at anything he turned his hand to. In addition to all his other failings he was a drunk. He might have been hanging around his wife's boarding house hoping to lay his hands on some money, but how would that tie in with rustling?

Clive had been producing, or at least practicing producing what amounted to a tool for rustling. But what did that have to do with his estranged father? Was there a connection with the Wells Fargo driver, Paul? Could Danny Lambert be connected?

Brad strove to apply the deductive reasoning Sherlock Holmes used in solving mysteries.

What was the common element? The attack on Clive took place in the livery stable. The branding iron was discovered there too. Danny had stolen a horse after shooting Paul. Paul was a stage coach driver. He worked with horses. Was there a connection between Luke Proctor and the livery stable which had been overlooked? What about Thomas Carter? Carter had been nearby when Clive was attacked. It was only Carter's word that the branding iron had been amongst Clive's tools. It seemed strangely coincidental that Carl's horse, Star, had been unavailable when Carl wanted to use him to ride out to Schnebly's but then ready to go with fresh shoes when Danny needed a steed. Brad was pulled out of his reverie by the arrival of the marshal and deputy.

Carl was all het up as he came through the door. "We're organising a posse. Are you fellas in?"

CHAPTER 133 THE HORN

Andy Thompson set another tray of clean glasses on the serving platform at the rear of the bar. It was just in time. Clayton had just pulled beer into the last pair of clean glasses remaining.

He had been kept busy, but with Andy handling the glasses and clearing used mugs and glasses from the tables, all was flowing smoothly.

It would be a lot more efficient if people would keep track of their glasses and reuse them, but trying to get cowboys to behave was more difficult than herding cattle. Not that Clayton knew the least thing about herding cattle, but they couldn't be any more cantankerous than these cowpokes were or they'd never get to market.

Charlie Lee was in a funny mood tonight. Right after Marshal Hopkins announced the intention to have a posse head out after Danny Lambert, Charlie had come by to talk with Clayton.

"I'm going to join up with the posse, Clay," Charlie had declared. "Are you with us?"

A number of thoughts ran through Clayton's head. First and foremost, he didn't like putting himself in danger. Then there was the fact that joining the posse would involve getting up very early. The way the bar was jumping tonight it was going to be a long night anyway. Clayton had a rifle, but it was an old 1862 Henry Rifle he'd picked up second hand years ago. He had thought he might do some hunting when he moved out west, but he hadn't. It was years since he had even touched the rifle.

"Well," he began, "It looks as if we'll be keeping the bar open pretty late tonight, Mr. Lee. There's a lot of beer yet to be sold." Clayton knew that the profit motive was the major driving factor in most of Charlie Lee's decisions. Surely he wouldn't want Clayton to go with the posse at the cost of ready money.

"Normally I'd agree with you there, Clay," Charlie said literally sweeping his hand across the surface of the bar as if thus brushing Clayton's objection aside. "The marshal has requested that we close the bar at midnight tonight to help out." Charlie paused and then added,

"Since we're supposed to close at midnight every night anyway, I didn't see as how I could disagree."

Clayton swallowed and raised his next protest. "What about tomorrow's business? Someone has to be here to open the bar at noon."

"I imagine it's going to be pretty quiet here tomorrow afternoon with a lot of the men with the posse," Charlie responded. "When they get back we'll be open to slake their collective thirsts. I'll get Andy Thompson to come around early with one of his sisters to clean up and prepare things." His eyes took on a contemplative look and he added, "Those Thompsons are all good workers. I may have been missing something there."

"It's been a long time since I shot my rifle. I'm not sure I would be much help," Clay elaborated

"I don't expect we'll be doing any shooting. Hell, Danny's crazy, but he's not stupid. He's probably halfway to Mexico right now. We'll be lucky to find any tracks."

"I'd like to join in," Clayton replied. He'd just thought of a foolproof objection. "Fact is I don't have any ammunition for my rifle. I've been meaning to get some ordered though Jim Thompson, but I haven't got around to it."

Charlie Lee was very well aware of Clayton's desire to avoid joining the posse. He phrased his next question carefully. "I'm sorry to hear that, Clay. Other than that you'd be willing to help out, would you?"

Clayton paused and then offered a tentative, "Well, sure."

"You've got a Henry rifle in .44 caliber. Is that right?"

"Yeah," Clayton admitted, "But it's an old 1862 model. Hard to get the rim fire ammunition it needs."

"You're in luck. I happen to have some .44 rim fire left over from when I got my new Winchester," Charlie said in a tone which brooked no further objection. "You're welcome to it."

Clayton knew he was snookered. Forcing a smile he replied, "Great."

He watched Charlie Lee go back to working the crowd and encouraging the festive atmosphere. Clayton wondered why his boss was so keen on the two of them joining the posse.

CHAPTER 134 PROCTOR'S

There was silence in the house. Willard lay on his back and stared at the clouds drifting across the sky. Occasionally stars were revealed. Once there was a brief flash of a shooting star. He was thinking about Clive's outburst. Clive must have spoken with his father. Willard wondered what else had passed between them.

Tomorrow a posse was going out to look for Danny. From what he'd overheard Carl tell the marshal it's likely they would be heading up Oak Creek Canyon. There were hundreds of small side canyons which could provide a hiding place. Would Danny have gone to earth in one of them? Willard didn't think he would. Those minor canyons had no other exit that a man on a horse could use. Lambert wouldn't box himself in like that. There were a few large enough to end in a gradual slope a horse could climb. If he was still in the canyon tomorrow that is where Danny would be.

Willard had a plan. He hoped to be the one who found Danny. If all went well it would help him become a deputy.

CHAPTER 135 THE HORN

The marshal was standing on the bar making a speech when Jefferson arrived. Deputy Carl Munds was standing at his side looking self-important as usual. Jefferson listened to the plea for men to turn out for the posse in the morning. He decided that he wanted to be part of the action. It would be his chance to fit in. Of course there was always the chance he would get to kill Danny. That would be a win-win situation, wouldn't it?

Frank had seen Jefferson arrive. As Charlie moved to speak with Clayton, Jefferson took the open space at the bar. Lars was getting ready to leave, but Frank asked him to stay and tell Jefferson about the land matter. They assured Lars that Doris Proctor would probably be happy to let Lars continue to rent the land but make payment to her.

"She could certainly use the income," Jefferson agreed. "It may be some time before Clive can get back to work and she can't very well evict her son."

"I hope you are right," Lars said. "It would be hard for me to start over."

"Are you going to join the posse, Lars?" Frank asked. "We could use a good man like you."

"When you say we, does that mean that you're planning to join up?" asked Jefferson in surprise.

"I certainly am," Frank declared. "People like Danny need to be stopped." Privately Frank was glad Danny had done something so stupid. This would eliminate Danny as a threat to him and also provide him a chance to act macho. There was nothing like helping to run down an outlaw to give one the seal of approval.

"Well, I'm with you," Jefferson declared. "You'll come too, won't you, Lars?"

Lars hesitated as if thinking it over. He had privately decided that he should be involved, but he didn't want to look too eager. "I will have to speak with Helga before making such a decision, but perhaps, yes, I should go also."

CHAPTER 136 THE JAIL

When Leroy and Carl got back to the office they found Brad, Jake and Jesus gathered around the desk with Lil making notes on a map. They had drawn circles on the map representing the farthest away Danny could travel on horseback in the coming days. Working on the assumption that Danny was probably headed north or north-east the Oak Creek Canyon formed the focus. Jesus was excited because it would give him and Jake a chance to examine the area where most of the cattle losses were taking place.

"If you don't mind us coming along, this will give me a chance to get a sense of the territory," Jake explained.

"Good idea, and we'd be pleased to have your assistance," Hopkins agreed. "We can supply you with horses. What do you have in the way of weapons?"

"In addition to my handgun I almost always travel with two rifles,"

Jake announced. "Jesus only has his revolver with him, but he can use the Winchester Model 1894 which is my back up. I'm now using the Model 1895 as my primary rifle. It's convenient because I've got both chambered in .30-.30"

"What's the difference between the 1894 and the 1895 then," Carl asked, "If they're both .30-.30 lever action?"

"The main difference is that the model 1895 has a box magazine," Jake explained. "President Roosevelt has one in .405 caliber. He used it game hunting in Africa and called it 'Big Medicine'."

"As a matter of fact, Charlie Lee has one of those guns," said Hopkins. "He bought one of the 1904 models in the large caliber. He made a point of showing it to me. Seemed pretty proud of it."

"Well, I can see you boys are going to be pretty busy comparing the size of your guns," Lil teased. "I'm going to head back to The Horn."

Jesus was a bit taken aback by her comment. Carl and Hopkins were familiar with Lil's direct way of speaking and took it in stride. Jake laughed and said, "Actually, we should all get some rest before tomorrow. We all meet here in the morning, is that it, Marshal?"

"That's right. See you at sunrise," Hopkins agreed. Jesus, Jake and Lil left for the hotel and Hopkins turned his attention to Brad. "You and your dad will be put up at Proctor's. I know that the doctor will be staying to keep an eye on Clive tomorrow. Will you stay in town too?"

"I'd like to ride out with you," Brad told him. "I don't intend to shoot at anyone, but I might be some help if there are any injuries."

"We'll be glad to have you. I'll see you in the morning. Carl and I have a bit of planning to do now, if you want to get to bed, go ahead."

Brad thanked the marshal and left him and the deputy to their preparations. As he walked toward Proctor's boarding house he took stock of his deductive success so far. He had been wrong about Jake being a salesman; the case he had thought held trade samples was actually carrying rifles; and Jesus Soza was a cattleman, not a banker. Sherlock Holmes had made it look easy. Well, tomorrow was another day. He would keep his eyes open and be on the lookout for clues along the trail.

CHAPTER 137 SEDONA

Frank and Jefferson left The Horn saloon together. Charlie watched the unlikely pair pass through the door and speculated upon their relationship. Both were haunted, both were outsiders and misfits. Charlie knew that Frank was terrified of being persecuted and Jefferson was just plain weird. He thought that Frank was probably harmless and hoped that Jefferson was.

* * *

Helga heard the front door open and recognized the familiar sounds of Lars shucking off his shoes and fumbling to hang up his jacket in the darkened entranceway. She listened as he negotiated his way carefully through their living area without lighting a lamp. Lars was a big man, but he was capable of moving quietly and she knew that he felt things much more deeply than he allowed others to see.

She imagined him traversing the darkened room and pictured him peering into the children's room to ensure himself that they were tucked in and sleeping peacefully. Her eyes were well adjusted to the darkness and she could pick out his head and shoulders against the pale light filtering through into the house from the front window.

She lay motionless as he dropped his clothing onto the floor and slid, almost gracefully into the bed beside her. Helga knew he was trying not to disturb her sleep, if asleep she was. As he settled back against the pillow and adjusted the covers she reached out to show him that she was awake.

"Did you speak with Mr. Lee?" she asked.

"Yes," he replied. "I believe all is well. There is no need to worry," he assured her.

"Good. I like it here. The children will be safe and Nora has begun to make friends."

"Tomorrow there is something which I need to do," Lars told her. "I must get up early."

"How early?"

"At dawn, I think. They are riding out to look for Danny Lambert. It is important that I show my support for our community," he explained.

"Be careful," she told him. "We need you."

"I will be," he comforted her.

Lars pounded the pillow with a big right hand and pulled the covers up to his chin. As he felt Helga's body relax and she drifted toward sleep he lay staring into the darkness. All might still be well, but he must move carefully tomorrow. Much depended on his actions.

* * *

Jesus bid them goodnight and headed up to his room. Jake spoke quietly to Lil and they moved to the bench by the Wells Fargo loading point.

"I don't want to drink anything tonight. Tomorrow is a working day," Jake explained. "But I want to apologize for not telling you who I am before."

"There's no need for that. I understand you needed to conceal your purpose here," Lil replied. "Be careful tomorrow."

"Thank you, Lil. We will be gone for most of the day I imagine. If I get back in time I'd like to see you."

"See me?" she asked. There was a laugh in her tone and feigned shock on her face.

"Yes," Jake said simply "If I'm back in time I'd like to have dinner with you."

Lil fell silent and then responded quietly, "That sounds nice."

* * *

Carl and Hopkins were ready to call it a night. They had decided to wait until morning to make final decisions on deployment. It would depend upon who showed up.

Carl headed off toward his room over Thompson's Dry Goods and Leroy Hopkins moved into the empty cell for the night. The morning would come soon enough.

As he drifted off, Hopkins thought about the seeming coincidence of the attack on Luke Proctor and the shooting in the saloon just when a Pinkerton agent came to town. Jake seemed straight enough, but . . .

CHAPTER 138 SEDONA

Thomas Carter woke early. He had almost taken Clive for granted during the past year. Now he was remembering what it had been like working the forge himself and trying to look after the horses with only occasional help from young boys or girls who would play a part for a year or two and then move on to their intended life occupation.

The young Thompson boy had been at the stable alone for almost seven hours. Thomas knew he must hurry to the smithy to assist his young charge prepare horses for the marshal.

* * *

Clayton was awake, but grumpy. He hadn't got to bed until two hours past midnight. It was all very well for his boss to agree to close at midnight, it was quite another to convince a room full of drunken cowboys and would-be cowboys. By the time he got the last two out of the saloon it was more like 1:30.

On top of that he had not slept well. He'd dreamed that he'd met up with Danny Lambert in a box canyon. He'd reasonably offered to let Danny pass and promised to keep his mouth shut. But Danny wasn't having any of it. Danny had gone for his gun and when Clayton had looked for his he found that the cartridges Charlie had given him were actually mini-cigars.

He had woken in a cold sweat and found the light of dawn spilling into his room.

Much as he would have liked to roll over and go back to sleep, he knew he had to get up or face the wrath of Charlie Lee.

* * *

Doris sat up with a start. She was seated in the wing chair and realized that she must have drifted off. Clive lay on his back on the sofa. His breathing was regular and his forehead felt cool. Dr. Pendergast was bending over his patient. Doris heard a noise from the kitchen and remembered that Willard had said he would join the group of men riding out to search for Danny Lambert. She hoped nothing would happen to Willard. He was always so thoughtful.

A hushed voice from the kitchen alerted her to the presence of a second person. She checked Clive again and went toward the kitchen where she found Brad Pendergast pouring coffee into two mugs. He was dressed warmly and Willard was standing close beside him.

"Brad," she said softly, "Are you really going out with the posse?"

* * *

Lil opened her eyes and lay motionless. There had been a sound. She listened carefully and heard the rustle of something being slipped under her door. Then she heard footsteps departing down the hall. She had gone to bed early, without bothering to join the crowd in the saloon.

She rolled over and went back to sleep.

CHAPTER 139 THE HORN

Charlie passed effortlessly from a state of unconsciousness to being fully awake. It was always thus. He never dozed or awakened slowly. His mind was immediately on the projects of the day. He splashed water on his face and shaved carefully.

He chose appropriate clothing and dressed with care. He strapped on a tooled brown leather belt and carefully adjusted the tie-down laces so they would not bind. His handgun had been chosen for appearance and prestige. The Remington model 1890 was an attractive gun which suited his hand well. The nickel finish alone made the gun stand out and Charlie had custom black walnut grips which had decorative inlaid mother-of-pearl.

He was even more proud of his new rifle, a Winchester 1904. He had a matching tooled leather saddle-mount holster for it. Charlie didn't shoot much, but when he rode out on his big chestnut mare he looked good. Appearances were important. Sometimes they were all that mattered.

The rifle was almost identical to the president's Winchester. The .405 caliber center fire cartridge was somewhat ridiculous for Charlie. A hunter would be unlikely to find a rhino anywhere in Arizona. But Lee liked the connection with Roosevelt. Charlie was a good looking man and he knew it. He admired Oliver Winchester, to whom he bore some facial resemblance, and had hats of a similar flat top style to those worn by the successful gun manufacturer shipped west at considerable expense. Carefully knotting a black ribbon tie and slipping into a buckskin riding jacket which complemented the shade of his horse completed his sartorial preparations. He considered his image in the full length mirror by his door. Yes, that would do nicely.

He was almost out the door when he remembered the ammunition for Clayton. He pulled open a bottom drawer and lifted out a tan cardboard box with green label marked 50 Winchester .44 flat, rimfire. He wouldn't let Clayton beg off for want of ammunition.

CHAPTER 140 THE HORN

Jesus was seated on the edge of the bed with a pair of supple deerskin gloves in one hand. In a serious contemplative mood he stared out through the window at the glow of dawn. He missed his wife and children. He pictured them rising to meet the new day in Tucson. For almost a year now, his youngest daughter, Maria Carla, had begun rising early to aid her mother in the kitchen to prepare a light breakfast for the family. Soon she would be old enough to be a real aid to the family. Then soon, too soon, she would be courted and married and start a family of her own. The river of life moves ever onward. It either carries us with it, if we are strong enough to remain afloat, or it leaves us as jetsam on the riverbank. Maria Carla was strong and beautiful; she would do well.

As he sat lost in thought, a light knock came to the door and he heard Jake speak his name. He opened the door and found the Pinkerton agent with a saddlebag hanging across his chest and a lever action carbine in either hand.

CHAPTER 141 SEDONA

Jake had slept well and woke at the first buzz of the alarm clock on the table by his bed. He had laid out his clothing and equipment the night before. Both Winchesters were loaded and the breeches closed on an empty chamber. His pistol had been loaded with new rounds and was tucked into a holster which would fit out of sight under his left arm.

He dressed and sat briefly at the small desk to write a note for Lil. He walked it to her room on the floor above and slipped it under her door. Then he returned to his room to gather his gear before knocking on Jesus Soza's door next to his own.

* * *

Frank had a hangover and a sense of foreboding. What was he doing? Chances were he would regret riding out with these locals. He had been born in postwar Charleston. It had been almost ten years after the end of hostilities, but Frank suspected that the antebellum Charleston which his mother remembered so fondly was gone forever.

His father had been wounded during the war and would never talk about those times. When Frank was nine they had moved to San Antonio and by the time he was twenty-four both his parents were dead. His father had died of complications from his war injuries and Frank's mother had dwindled away as if life held no further interest for her.

With the suspicion that nothing good would come of it, Frank put on a new pair of boots, a cowboy hat he seldom wore and walked self-consciously toward the jail through the chill air of a cloudless morning.

* * *

Lars slipped out of bed and went to look in on his son and daughter. Nora was sleeping quietly with the covers tucked neatly under her chin. His seven-year-old, Morten, had rolled in his bedclothes and lay in a tangled mess.

Helga came up behind Lars and pressed her head against his left bicep. Lars was tempted to go back to bed with her but remembered the task which lay before him. He began to dress as Helga wrapped some bread and cheese for his lunch.

He had no handgun, but his hunting rifle was reliable. He had traded two weeks work as a carpenter to a former horse soldier from Colorado for the rifle. It was a cavalry issue Model 1865 Spencer

Carbine manufactured by the Spencer and Burnside Rifle Company. The 56 gauge Spencer ammunition was still available since the rifle had been used widely in campaigns against hostile Native American tribes following the Civil War. Lars had no trouble keeping his family in meat and fish from the forests and streams near Sedona.

* * *

Willard rose quietly and dressed in silence. He packed a small canvas pack with a blanket and a few other things he might need if the posse ended up camping overnight. It didn't seem likely, but Willard wanted to be prepared. This was his chance to make an impression. If he could play a prominent part in taking Danny Lambert, the marshal was sure to notice him.

He went downstairs to check on Mrs. Proctor and the old doctor. When he reached the foot of the stairs he was surprised to find Brad Pendergast already in the kitchen. Brad looked up with the coffee pot in one hand and reached for a second mug.

Before he could say anything, Mrs. Proctor came in from the hall.

CHAPTER 142 THE HORN

There was a voice. It seemed far away. Larry wanted it to go away completely, but it kept on calling him. Larry opened his eyes a crack and realized that someone was bending over him. There was a bright piercing light. He could make no sense of what was happening. Was he injured? His head hurt like hell and his mouth was dry as death. What had happened to him?

He tried to turn away but a hand on his shoulder turned him back toward the light. The voice spoke his name and Larry realized it was Sam. What was Sam doing in his dream?

He tried to focus. Then he remembered: drinking, the saloon, people buying him drinks, more drinking and stumbling upstairs. Sam was shaking him and telling him to get dressed. He remembered the shooting, the marshal forming a posse, Sam and him being drafted into the group to go after Danny Lambert.

"Leave, leave me. I'm okay. Just let me lie here a moment." He called out weakly. His head was pounding; his eyes couldn't deal with the light.

Sam's commanding voice was worse than the light. "You can rest in the saddle, cowpoke. Marshal expects us to be with him. We will be."

Larry and Sam had been through a lot together. They'd been into Mexico together and they'd done some crazy things. Larry had never seen Sam laid low by liquor and he'd never seen him bested in a fight. Course that might be 'cause Sam didn't tend to overindulge the way Larry had to admit he did, and Sam picked his fights. There wasn't much Sam couldn't handle, but he knew how to walk away from a bad situation.

Once on a cattle drive near Tucson they'd run into a small party of Apache who were looking kind of longingly at the herd. Some folk would have put on a show of force and threatened the natives. Sam didn't. Sam went right up to the leader of the hunting party and diffused the situation. He sat tall in the saddle and waited for the Apache to speak. Not much conversation passed between them. Sam shared some tobacco with the native and the two men sized each other up. Apparently both were shrewd enough to realize that they would both lose by fighting, 'cause the hunting party went on by and the cattle drive continued toward Tucson. Sam gained a lot of respect among cattlemen from that encounter.

Larry knew that Sam was right this time too. He threw back the covers, pulled on his pants, and headed down the hall to the indoor facilities. It didn't seem right that a man could have a dry mouth and have to pee at the same time.

CHAPTER 143 BROOK'S MORTUARY

Alone in the small alcove off his work area the mortician leaned over the dry sink and poured water over his head. He bathed his face in the cool water and applied a little pomade to his coal black hair. He wore it drawn straight back in a pompadour. He made a concession to the somewhat festive nature of the day's outing by choosing his gray hat.

He had slept sufficiently and risen early. Sleep never came easily to Jefferson, but that didn't seem to matter. The big sleep would come soon enough. Death held no fear for him. He imagined it as being the same as before he was born. That time was uneventful enough, as far as he could remember, and what you couldn't remember didn't matter either.

There were those that talked about life after death and some said there was reincarnation. If there was, Jefferson would deal with that when it came. For now he concentrated on the present.

Chances were nothing would come from all this fuss of riding out in a posse. Danny was probably halfway to Mexico by now.

Still if the posse did come across Danny there might be some shooting, and shooting often led to business for Jefferson Brooks. He didn't intend to get out front, or to actually shoot too much. However, if some undertaking was required, he was more than willing to undertake it.

Jefferson almost smiled at his little joke, but he didn't. He'd found that people didn't react well when he smiled and over the years he learned to avoid it, even in private.

CHAPTER 144 PROCTOR'S

The confusion which often came with waking in a strange bed soon passed, and Brad thought about his father. He had offered to spell-off Doris and his dad in their vigil by Clive's side, but both had insisted that he get to bed since he would be on horseback and they could rest quietly during the day to come.

He reached for his pocket watch on the side table and saw that it was almost six. A doctor should be able to rise at any moment ready for action he reminded himself, but it always took him a minute or so to let life's aspects fall into place. Would he have chosen to be a doctor if his father had not been one? He didn't know for sure, but the profession seemed right to him. Already he had experienced the feelings of satisfaction and dismay which came with the job. He doubted that he would find a better calling.

Brad washed quickly and ran a razor over his smooth cheeks. He was pleased to have little body hair and only a sparse beard. It made maintaining personal hygiene easier. Brad was a great believer in the theories of personal cleanliness espoused by Dr. Joseph Lister, recently made Baron Lister. Lister himself had a thin beard which he wore as wispy side whiskers. Brad thought that his own features were not unlike those displayed in early images of Dr. Lister.

Brad dressed and descended to the parlor, where he found his father seated across the room from Clive and reading the newspaper. Doris Proctor was snoring lightly in the wing chair. Clive appeared to be resting easily.

Brad nodded to his father and signalled that he would go to the kitchen. He lifted his hand and mimicked drinking in silent query as to whether the doctor would like a coffee. When his father smiled and shook his head, Brad moved back into the hall and crossed to the kitchen.

He had just found mugs and sugar when Willard came down to join him. Brad started to pour for both of them and then realized that Doris Proctor had entered by the hall door.

"You boys had better be careful, hear." She instructed them. Turning to the young Pendergast she told him, "Brad, your father would like a word with you before you go."

Brad left the room and Doris spoke quietly to Willard. "I don't know why men are always so ready to take up arms," she said. "Mending takes longer than hurting. You take care, Willard. You're a good looking young man. Don't get yourself shot up."

Willard promised he'd be careful. He was touched by Mrs. Proctor's kind words, but he meant to achieve something for himself today.

When Brad joined up with him outside, Willard thought the young Pendergast seemed lost in thought. Was it something the old doctor had told him?

CHAPTER 145 THE JAIL

Carl was eager to get going. He arrived at the office to find Leroy

Hopkins seated at the desk examining a detailed map of Oak Creek Canyon.

He greeted his leader with a cheerful "Morning, Marshal. Do you expect a good turnout?"

"Hard to say," Leroy responded. "No one liked Danny much, but everyone knows he's dangerous."

Carl peered over the marshal's shoulder at the map. "Where do you suppose Lambert is headed, Marshal? Will we stand a chance of catching up to him?"

Hopkins reached out and circled an area partway up toward Flagstaff. "He couldn't have gone too far in that terrain at night," he assured Carl. "If we get away soon enough we might pick up his trail. He won't want to pass too close to Flagstaff, so he will pass on the east or west side if he's going to continue north. I think that our best bet is to head up Cibola Pass and head on north toward the junction near Oak Creek. There are lots of places he could turn off before West Fork, of course. We'll just have to see what turns up. I'm hoping Sam Schuerman will be able to give us some insights. He knows that area better than most."

Carl felt his hopes diminish. Marshal Hopkins was right. It was a big area and there were lots of passes leading up out of the canyon that Danny could take to frustrate pursuit.

There was noise in the street and marshal and deputy went to the door to greet the earliest volunteers to arrive.

CHAPTER 146 NORTH OF SEDONA

'Thunder' and 'damnation' were words which floated through his mind. Danny was in a mood to kill someone. Anyone would do. He had spent a miserable night under some low growing Hackberry trees surrounded by Snakeweed Broom. He had no ground sheet, no blanket, and nothing to eat. He woke shaking with cold and aching from riding without stirrups. How did native riders stand it? Just a few hours of riding with his legs hanging down without support had left him with difficulty standing.

He had turned north along Soldiers Pass, but had been forced to stop when the horse slipped on some loose shale in the darkness. He'd damn near been thrown. If he hadn't been in desperate need of a mount he would have shot the horse right then. As it was he had to scramble all over hell's half acre to find a place with enough ground cover to conceal him and the stupid horse.

The situation was not good. He had an incompetent horse, makeshift harness, no food, no rifle, and damn little money. He almost regretted killing that smart-assed Wells Fargo driver. He did wish he'd waited and killed him somewhere private. Paul deserved killing, but now Danny was in a jam with no easy fix. He wouldn't want to ride far without getting a saddle from somewhere. He had half a mind to ride back into Sedona and get his own horse. The other half of his mind knew that was really stupid.

He took stock of the situation. The one good thing he had going for him was that the whole town had seen him head south. No one would expect him to be heading up Oak Creek Canyon. Luckily, he had a stash laid away up in the foothills of Sterling Pass. He didn't plan on continuing up that way, but he needed to get his hands on a rifle. Most things worth killing, either for food or money, won't let you get near enough to pick them off with a hand gun. The rifle he had stashed wasn't great, but it had better range than his revolver.

Danny walked straight legged over to the scrub willow where he had hobbled Star. Because he had no length of rope to hobble and tether the horse properly, Danny had used his belt and a few woody vines. It wasn't fancy, but it had worked.

He remembered that later today he would have a rifle and a tinder box as well as other materials stashed at the mine. He could shoot something and have a hot meal. He brightened at the prospect and spoke with uncharacteristic gentleness to his mount, "No offence meant, horse," he said, "But I'd rather have my paint here."

CHAPTER 147 MAIN STREET, SEDONA

There were four men approaching the meeting point for the posse.

Jake and Jesus each carried rifles. Clayton had his Henry rifle tucked under his arm and a forlorn look on his face. Charlie Lee was proudly strutting across the street with his fancy new Winchester held over his shoulder, muzzle down, and the nickel finish of his six-shooter sparkling in the reflected glory of the rising sun.

Hopkins could see two more men coming from the west and Lars, Brad, and Willard were approaching from the east.

"Break out the rifles, Carl," he said without looking toward the deputy. "We've got us a posse."

* * *

Frank saw Jefferson approaching from the west end of town. Who was that walking beside him? It was Thomas Carter. Frank hadn't expected the smith to be part of the posse. As they neared the group Thomas peeled off and continued toward the smithy. Jefferson picked Frank out of the crowd and came up beside him.

* * *

The Artist was pleased to see the good turnout. There was nothing like a group of men with guns to lead to a lynching. He might not even have to kill Danny himself.

CHAPTER 148 MAIN STREET, SEDONA

Larry and Sam crossed from The Horn and joined the crowd in front of the jail. Hopkins gestured with his hand to quiet everyone down to make himself heard.

There were some people present he hadn't expected. The posse was going to take some organizing to make sure manageable units were formed. Rather than hurt anyone's feelings, Leroy decided to include all who had turned out. He wanted to get mounted up and under way as quickly as possible. He spoke privately with Sam Schuerman and Larry James and obtained their agreement to function as unit leaders.

"I need a show of hands of anyone who needs a horse supplied," he said simply.

Brad noted with amusement that Hopkins had delegated note taking to Carl. Carl even had Leroy's stubby pencil in his hand.

Only four men indicated need of a mount: Lars, Frank, Clayton, and Jesus. Jesus had arrived by stagecoach and the other three were men whose main work was done in town and didn't keep a horse.

Carl took down the names and Hopkins asked if there was anyone present without a rifle and ammunition.

Only Frank, Jefferson, and Willard raised their hand in response to this question. While Carl took down their names Leroy cast his eye on Brad. He motioned for Brad to come forward and spoke directly to him. "Do you have a rifle with you, Brad?"

Brad shook his head and replied, "I don't intend to do any shooting, Marshal. I'm just coming along to provide first aid if it's needed."

"I don't want anyone with us without a rifle. You don't have to shoot, but I want you armed if you're coming with us."

Brad held up a hand in sign of submission. "Okay, Marshal. I'll carry a gun, but I won't shoot unless I have to."

Hopkins nodded and turned his attention back to the list Carl had passed him. "Okay, Lars, Frank, Clayton, and Jesus go to the livery stable. Thomas Carter will see about getting you saddled up." He looked again at the list and added, "Frank, I'll have a rifle for you when you get your horse."

Leroy Hopkins looked over his list of those needing a rifle and called Jefferson, Willard, and Brad to come forward.

CHAPTER 149 MAIN STREET, SEDONA

The marshal's office had a supply of rifles to be used by temporary deputies should need arise to appoint some. Carl had laid six of them on the desk and set a box of ammunition beside each one. The rifles were Winchester Model 1873 chambered for the .44-40 cartridge. Newer models had been produced in various calibers, but this set had been purchased by the state and supplied at a special price to law officers. Both Leroy and Carl had used the rifles for occasional hunting as well as for regular shooting practice, but they were normally kept locked up. The marshal was an excellent shot. Had he been using a rifle instead of his side arm Hopkins would have brought Danny down sure enough.

He handed a rifle to each of the men and had each demonstrate that they knew how to make the gun safe and how to load and fire it. He instructed them to carry it with the chamber empty and to only lever a cartridge into firing position on command by himself or a designated squad leader. Neither Brad, Jefferson nor Willard had any questions about the use and handling of the gun.

When the marshal was convinced that all three knew how to safely transport and handle the rifles he moved back outside to check the guns and rifles of the assembled posse volunteers. He had completed the examination and was reminding Clayton of the danger of carrying the Henry rifle with a round under the hammer when Carl came back with the men who had needed a horse supplied.

"We're all set, Marshal," Carl announced in an almost military tone.

Hopkins avoided smiling with difficult. Carl was a good deputy, just a little over-eager right now. He stepped back up onto the landing and called for everyone's attention.

* * *

The Artist waited patiently. His opportunity was coming, but it could not be hurried.

CHAPTER 150 THE HORN

The commotion in front of the hotel kept intruding into Lily's attempts to doze. She finally gave up. She lay on her back thinking about the posse that was forming and the possibilities that raised. She thought about Jake being shot. He was a good man, from what she'd known of him. She hoped he would stay clear of trouble. She didn't expect them to find hide nor hair of Danny; she just hoped they wouldn't shoot each other.

Men were strange creatures. They were ready to throw themselves into a foolishly dangerous adventure at a moment's notice, but most took forever to make a serious commitment to the important things in life, and half of those who did couldn't live up to it. Seeing Doris Proctor nursing her son, Clive, had touched something deep in Lily.

Having a child was perhaps too much for her to hope for, but she was beginning to sense the loneliness of her life.

A gleam of light reflected off her dresser mirror and created a small rainbow on the wall. She put such brooding thoughts behind her and thought again of Jake. Early as it was, Lily decided to get dressed and go down to watch the posse ride out of town. Her eye caught the white folded paper on the floor by the door and she remembered hearing it being shoved under the during the night, or early morning.

She picked it up and unfolded it. As she did a hand drawn image of a lily growing out of a heart fell out. She looked closely at the drawing and realized that the name Jacob was engraved across the heart.

Lily was not easy to surprise when it came to men. What she read in the note surprised her. Jake had perhaps meant it to be a simple pleasantry. Nevertheless, the note expressed affection for her in a way that touched the young girl in her. She went to her bottom drawer and took out something small which she carried with her as she hurried downstairs.

CHAPTER 151 THE SMITHY

Thomas Carter and Eddie Thompson had saddles and bridles on all the horses designated for the posse. The forge was banked up and could wait.

"As soon as the posse leaves, you get on home, Eddie. I appreciate your filling in for Clive. Are you okay to do the same again tonight? If you want I can make up a bed here in the loft and share the watch."

"I'm fine to work again tonight, Mr. Carter," Eddie told him. "I can get my brother Andy to help out too if you need it."

Thomas knew that the Thompsons were all good workers. Their father had arrived in Sedona, called Red Rocks then, with nothing but a wagon of stock and a pregnant wife. He'd started off selling door to door and had helped build the store he now owned in return for reduced rent until he could buy it. The family knew how to work and how to save money. Others, with better prospects had fallen by the way side while the Thompsons had grown strong and multiplied. Charlie

Lee was a good businessman, but he was only one man. Charlie was involved in plenty, but the Thompsons had a hand in most everything else going on.

CHAPTER 152 MAIN STREET, SEDONA

"Listen up now, men," Marshal Hopkins called out. A hush settled and Hopkins explained that each of the posse members would be deputized. He explained that they had reason to believe that Danny Lambert was heading north and that the area of search would be the Oak Creek Canyon and smaller passes leading off east and west.

"As temporary deputies you will all answer to me and in my absence to Deputy Munds. But to allow us to cover as much territory as possible looking for signs of Lambert, I'm going to divide the posse into four individual units each under the direction of a leader who is familiar with the terrain. You will each be assigned to one of the units. We will stay together whenever possible but if it is necessary to spread out to conduct a search you will be expected to stay with your unit leader and follow his directions. Brad, you and Lars will be with me in unit one. Deputy Carl Munds will lead unit two with Jesus and Jake. Sam and Larry know the canyon as well as any of us. I'd like Sam to lead unit three with Willard, Jefferson, and Frank. Larry, you will lead unit four with Clayton and Charlie. I'll be directing the posse when we're traveling together and will give specific instructions to unit leaders if a unit is sent off on its own."

Hopkins paused to allow what he had said to sink in. He was pleased to see the men move to stand in their assigned unit. He was counting at least partially on Sam and Larry's experience keeping groups moving in concert during cattle drives to help keep this odd grouping of individuals from wandering all over the place and shooting each other.

The marshal raised his hand and spoke again. "Our objective is to find Danny Lambert if we can and to bring him back to town to stand trial. No one will fire their gun without being directed to do so. If you are fired upon you should take cover and return fire only if you are directed to do so and have a clear target. I don't want anyone getting hurt. Now I'd like all of you to get your horse and meet up out front of the smithy. I'm going to meet briefly now with the unit leaders; we'll all meet up in five minutes ready to ride out."

CHAPTER 153 NORTH OF SEDONA

As he picked his way over the ridge and started his descent into the main canyon, Danny considered his options. He could go to his stash in the old mine to pick up some gear and move on west, but the mine was up the Sterling Pass. That pass led up into the Secret Mountains. That route would be difficult anytime; without a saddle it would be dangerous.

He could probably stay undetected at the mine for some time. But, although there was some money and ammunition stashed, there was no food. He couldn't shoot something or start a fire there for fear of attracting attention. Besides, he wanted to get out of the Red Rock area before word about the shooting got out ahead of him.

He could count on a day or so if people thought he had gone south. The Lambert homestead was south of Sedona and it would be natural for them to expect him to pass by there. That was their mistake. His family were all dead and he had left nothing of value there. He had slept there sometimes, but that was over.

He could head straight north up Oak Creek and outdistance pursuit, if there was any. Problem was he was low on ammunition. He had used three shots on that useless Paul. He had ammunition in his saddle bags but they were back in Sedona. Even if he met someone whose horse and saddle he could acquire, he might have to use up one or more of his remaining three cartridges. He might need to buy more. The .41 caliber used in his 'Thunderer' version of the Colt 1877 was not common; he might have to kill more than once to get more cartridges that way. He decided he'd be better off to go to the mine even if it meant retracing his steps.

'Courthouse Rock' near Sedona

CHAPTER 154 MAIN STREET, SEDONA

There was sense of eagerness in the group of men which was contagious. Brad had seen mob mentality turn sensible people into fools. He hoped this expedition would not turn ugly. Leroy Hopkins was a good marshal who commanded respect. Brad trusted the marshal.

He was troubled by what his father had told him on parting. Clive had roused during the night and spoke to the physician who sat close at hand. The short message was conveyed to Dr. Pendergast with urgent sincerity: 'They killed him. Stop them.'

The message was enigmatic, but rational. The death of Luke Proctor, or perhaps Paul Matthews, had been planned by more than one person. The doctor had concluded that Clive's warning must refer to the death of Luke Proctor, since Clive had been struck down and lay unconscious when the shooting of the driver Paul had occurred. Brad was not so certain. It seemed possible to him that Clive may have overheard something while lying apparently senseless.

Either way, the possibility of a conspiracy suggested connection to a widespread danger. Clive's half-finished branding iron seemed to suggest a connection to the rustling. Could Luke Proctor have been killed to shut him up? Was it possible that Paul was privy to some information which threatened the rustlers? Paul traveled from town to town. He might have heard some rumour about Sedona. Luke had been absent from the town for years. What could have drawn him back now?

The two men had met a violent death, and Clive had been attacked within a few short hours following the arrival of Jake Witherspoon. Was the Pinkerton agent everything he claimed to be? The marshal seemed convinced, but could the telegram be a fake? What could have caused Jake to leave Miss Lily's bed in the early morning if not to attack Clive's father? Brad felt a flush of sexual desire at the thought of his own dear wife perhaps even now rising to begin her day. It would take something very important to draw him from her side in the early morning. What had drawn Jake?

Brad was pulled back to the present by the necessity of saddling and preparing Cornflower for the day's activities. He scooped a handful of oats into a clean handkerchief and deposited the treat for Cornflower next to his own simple lunch package in a saddlebag.

All around him men were preparing to depart. Brad led Cornflower out into the glow of dawn and joined the assembly of men outside the wide smithy doors. The ostler, Eddie, had prepared the horses for Hopkins, Carl, and the two Wingfield men. The four horses were tethered to the hitching rail. The smith stood arms akimbo and brawny shoulders thrown back. The most formidable of men, the smith was regarding the activities of the company of men with a sardonic smile. Thomas Carter seemed to stand like a rock about which swirled the ebb and flow of humanity. Brad followed Carter's gaze and observed the marshal, Carl and the two other unit leaders approaching.

CHAPTER 155 MAIN STREET, SEDONA

"Okay, mount up," the marshal called out. A flurry of activity followed with ample demonstration of the variety of levels of expertise. Jefferson mounted with surprising grace whereas Clayton hopped about a bit and finally accepted a leg-up from the ostler's clasped hands.

Hopkins' directions to the posse were simple. "Stay together. You don't need to ride near your unit leader for now, but later, if I send your leader off somewhere, you are to go with him. Is that clear?"

The strength of the responding cries of acknowledgement betrayed the bottled-up nervous energy. More or less in an orderly fashion they followed the marshal out of town.

* * *

As they were passing The Horn, Jake looked over and saw Lily near the Wells Fargo landing. She was holding a small bundle up and waving for him to come over. He dropped behind and made his way over to join her.

Lily reached up her hand and offered him the wrapped bundle. Thinking she had a muffin or some pastry for him, Jake reached down and took it from her hand. He felt the hard outlines with surprise.

"Take this with you. Just in case," she told him.

Jake stuffed the object into the pocket of his overcoat and reached back to touch her fingertips as she drew back and waved gaily. Her eyes betrayed her and Jake watched her lips form the words, "Be careful."

"I'll be back to have supper with you," he called out and swung the horse's head west to ride after the last of the horsemen.

CHAPTER 156 THE SMITHY

Thomas Carter watched in amusement as the men rode out full of bravado. They were passing in front of The Horn when Miss Lily came out on the landing stage. She raised a hand and beckoned and a horseman separated himself from the others and rode over to her. It was that stranger, Hank or Jake, who seemed to be in tight with the marshal.

Whatever was said was said quickly as Lily stood by his stirrup and reached up a hand to him. She seemed to be passing something to him wrapped in a piece of cloth. Jake tucked whatever it was in his pocket and touched her fingers as she drew back to allow him to ride on.

Thomas wiped his hands on his leather apron and spoke warmly to Eddie Thompson. "There will be some saddlesore would-be cowboys making their way back into town tonight, Eddie. I appreciate the great job you did this morning, and I'll need your assistance again whenever the boys ride back in. Get some rest now and come on back here when they get back if you're up to it. Like I told you, I can help tonight with the livery stable chores."

"I'll be fine, Mr. Carter," Eddie protested.

"Well, we'll see what you feel like later. Go get some rest now," Thomas replied.

Thomas Carter watched Eddie head on toward the dry goods store, above which the Thompsons lived. 'No one would accuse those Thompson boys of being afraid of work,' he thought. Eddie had fed and watered all the horses and mucked out the stalls. He looked around and realized there was no pressing tasks for the moment and few customers left in town.

There was a stage due in the afternoon, but other than arranging a change of horses for Wells Fargo, Thomas didn't expect to have much to do today. This might be a chance to get away for a few hours. He exchanged his apron for a light bush coat and saddled up his favourite mount. He'd pass by the house and pick up his .410 bore coach gun. Thomas didn't like handguns much, but a double-barrel with a slug in one barrel and buck shot in the other is a handy companion.

CHAPTER 157 POSSE, RIDING NORTH

What was hard and small and felt like a gun? In this case Jake thought he knew. Lily had been discrete when she disrobed their first night together, but among other interesting glimpses he had caught sight of the small gun strapped to the inside of her thigh. He suspected that the same, Derringer-style pocket gun was presently resting in his ample pocket.

Usually such guns were single action. They could not be fired, or at least not easily, without first cocking the hammer. Nevertheless, as he traced the outline of the object with his hand thrust deep into his overcoat, he was careful to avoid what might be a trigger mechanism. Some guns could be left half-cocked, and some, like Clayton's Henry rifle, were dangerous even with the hammer down if a primer lay under the hammer.

The small gun in his pocket seemed to be a double-barrel model with two hammers and a fairly large bore. It might be a .44 caliber, though he suspected that it was more likely a .38 or the common Derringer choice, a .41. Without risking blowing off part of his leg, Jake couldn't tell if this particular gun had one or two triggers. Usually there was a separate trigger for each hammer, but a few guns had a selective single trigger.

Satisfied that he knew what it was, Jake turned his mind to wondering why Lily had entrusted the weapon to him. The most likely reason was an attempt to offer him protection. Jake mulled that thought over and found that it led to other more complicated questions.

CHAPTER 158 POSSE, RIDING NORTH

The role of cattle drive boss was one which carried a lot of responsibility. The safety of the cattle and the cowboys was in the drive boss's hands and sometimes the cowboys were more difficult to control than the cattle. Sam had been pleased that Hopkins had named him a unit leader; he felt comfortable in charge of men. If he had any misgivings, they concerned the motley nature of his crew. The youngster, Willard, was quiet and seemingly respectful. Sam knew that Willard had actually worked with some cattle drives and was a good horseman. He didn't know how Willard would react under fire, but everyone was different that way. Sam's grandfather had been in the civil war, which he had always referred to as 'The War Between the States', and had passed on some stories through Sam's father. His granddad had said that some men broke; some turned into heroes; most just hunkered down and got on with combat while hoping to stay alive.

Frank, the town clerk, was as close to being a tenderfoot as one could come while still being a westerner. Sam had heard it said that Frank came originally from Carolina or some other gentrified state. That might account for his prissy ways. Sam didn't know about Frank, but he sure didn't cotton to him.

The real odd ball in the unit was the mortician, Jefferson Brooks. Brooks was just out and out weird. Probably came from messing around with all those dead bodies. Come to think of it, some of those bodies were female. Sam had an image of Jefferson Brooks fooling around with naked female corpses and the idea made him real uneasy. Without wanting to, Sam had an image of Jefferson mounting some pale white corpse and he had to start thinking of something else right away.

CHAPTER 159 POSSE, RIDING NORTH

The members of the posse were keeping together well enough. Now that they were underway, the group had quieted down and they were making good time up the main road. When they came to the spot where Carl had found the hoof prints the night before, Hopkins had everyone hold up while he went forward with Carl to see what remained in the morning light.

There were still some traces at both sides of the road, though the dust had shifted in the light breeze and it was hard to see much. Carl pointed out the direction the tracks led in and Hopkins and Carl tethered their horses and walked a few paces into the dry landscape. Beside some scrub Catclaw Acacia they found a few prints which had been sheltered from the wind and retained sharp outlines. Carl pointed out the indications of new shoes and swore he recognized the gait as Star's.

"Looks like he's headed for Oak Creek, Marshal," Carl declared.

"You could well be right, Carl," Hopkins agreed. "We'll have to keep an eye out to see if he changes direction. In the meantime I'd like you to do something important. I'd like you to send off this telegram and then rejoin us as soon as possible. We'll be following these tracks and our passage will be easy to follow."

Carl had handled his increased responsibility with a maturity which was to his credit. Now Leroy passed him a brief message to be sent by telegraph to the sheriff in Flagstaff. Hopkins knew that they wouldn't be as keen up north to go looking for Lambert, but he hoped that the telegram would at least cause them to be on guard that he might be headed their way. Hopkins and Carl had been involved in a hunt for a 22 year-old army deserter from Colorado Springs named Roy Gardner earlier that year and had met some of the deputies from Flagstaff. They'd never found Gardner, probably they'd never hear tell of him again, Hopkins imagined. Still, it didn't hurt to keep contacts active. Leroy had become friends with Deputy Marshal Joe Wierman, who he considered a good man and a good marshal. He had Carl copy him on the telegram in case he could help out.

As Carl rode off toward Schnebly's combination lodge, post office, and telegraph station with the message for Flagstaff, Hopkins suspected that Carl was being overly hopeful in his certainty that these tracks had been left by his horse, Star, but this was the best lead they had. They returned to the men and Hopkins instructed the group to advance in a wedge with him on point. "If I hold up my hand in a fist, I want you to hold up," he told them. "As you ride up to that bush yonder, keep a bit off to the left. You'll see some tracks in the soil which I have drawn a circle around. Take a look at them. We think those are the tracks of the horse Danny Lambert is riding. Keep an eye out."

As they prepared to move on, Carl added a personal note. "I want that horse back in one piece. If you get a chance to shoot Lambert, make damn sure you don't hit my horse."

* * *

The Artist was impressed. Normally he would have described Carl Munds as mostly a waste of space, but the deputy had picked up Danny's trail sure enough. The Artist knew where Danny was headed. He'd worked with Danny up in Oak Creek canyon before, and knew Danny had a hideaway up Sterling Pass somewhere. He had to be with any group that found Danny. It wouldn't do to have that dimwit shooting off his mouth.

CHAPTER 160 POSSE, RIDING NORTH

Charlie was enjoying himself. This was a great opportunity to show off his horse, his gear, and most of all himself. It was also a good way to build a customer base. These men would have good reason to choose The Horn Saloon as their watering hole.

He thought of Paul Matthews as a regrettable promotional cost. It got rid of the pesky Danny Lambert and attracted cash paying drinkers to the saloon. Hell, Paul only came to town from time to time and didn't drink that much anyway. Wells Fargo would replace Paul and the new driver might be a serious drinker.

Up ahead the marshal signalled for the posse to stop. Charlie quieted his mare and sat up alertly in the saddle. He remembered reading an article in an eastern journal that described someone as having a 'good seat' while sitting in the saddle. He liked the term. He tried to always portray the impression that he was at home in the saddle. He was a decent rider, not like some of these cowboys who practically lived on a horse, but quite decent, and he took some pride in it.

Carl had ridden up to rejoin the posse a few minutes ago. Now he dismounted and was examining the ground. Presently the marshal called for Sam and Larry to come forward. The four men discussed something and then Hopkins came back to speak with Jake and Jesus.

CHAPTER 161 POSSE, RIDING NORTH

'What a pair those two make,' Larry thought as he rode forward to join the marshal, Carl, and Sam. Charlie was all posturing and pretence, anything to make an impression or a buck. Clayton was just the opposite. Clayton preferred not to be noticed, and didn't seem to care about money. Their rifles were as different as the men themselves. Larry itched to try out that rifle of Charlie's. It occurred to Larry that if he flattered the big blowhard enough he might let him.

Sam was down on the ground beside Hopkins. He stood up as Larry came within earshot and expressed his opinion.

"It's a bit hard to be sure in this sandy soil, Marshal. I'd say that Carl's probably right. The edges of the shoes seem pretty sharp. That wouldn't last long, so chances are that this horse was shoed recently and it probably is Carl's horse."

"He seems to have headed north up Soldiers Pass," Carl suggested. "He must be planning to head for the wilderness region of Secret Mountain."

"That doesn't sound like Danny Lambert to me," Hopkins suggested. "He's not really a fan of nature. Besides, he wouldn't last long without supplies. He doesn't even have a rifle."

Sam sort of coughed and said "Well, Soldiers Pass crosses Cibola Pass up north a way. If he went east along Cibola he'd be able to enter Wilson Canyon without traveling on the main road."

"He couldn't travel at night up Soldiers Pass," Larry chipped in. "Don't think he could move very fast at all on that terrain, especially up toward the sinkhole areas."

The marshal considered the situation for a moment. "Maybe his main objective was not to be seen, rather than speed. He probably thinks we'll be looking down south for him."

Sam pointed up Soldiers Pass toward the odd pinnacle of rock visible in the distance. "The turn off for Cibola is north of Thunder Mountain. Soldiers Pass leads right by that peak of rock which looks a bit like a saddle horn."

"Let's take a look up the pass and see what we find," Hopkins suggested.

CHAPTER 162 SOLDIER'S PASS

The posse moved up the pass one or two horses abreast. Brad found himself beside Lars Sorensen. The big lumberman was looking around alertly and commented on the reddish prickly pear and distinctive cactus flowers standing out brightly in the dusty countryside.

"Life is determined," Brad asserted. "The desert plants conserve their strength and then take advantage of an opportune time to multiply. Those flowers were hard red buds on the cactus until we had a bit of rain a few days ago. We encountered a brief spate of rain as we came down the new road in the stagecoach."

"A lot of the local farmers are getting into agriculture down near the creek," Lars ventured. "Lately I've had requests to bring in some drainage tiles to use with irrigation."

"The desert soil has good nutrients in it," Brad agreed. "Just add water and you can grow crops. Farming may become more important than cattle someday."

They had gone only a short way up the pass when the marshal halted the column. He and Sam dismounted and walked off into the scrub brush to the right. They passed through a clump of broom and out of sight amongst some stunted trees.

* * *

In a small open area out of sight from the trail Sam and Leroy discovered evidence of recent activity. The ground had been scraped out into a rough trench a few inches deep where someone had lain recently. A few feet further from the trail behind a low tree the rough ground showed signs that a horse had been concealed for several hours. A small amount of dung had been partially covered over.

They found several hoof prints which showed the same hard edges as those near the turn off point. Clearly the traveler they suspected was Danny Lambert had spent the night at this rough camp site.

"Whoever it was, they didn't light a fire or leave any signs of consuming any food," Sam pointed out. "It was either someone trying to conceal their presence or without any camp gear."

"If it was Danny, he's not too far ahead of us," Hopkins concluded. "We could probably cut him off if we headed directly up river by the main road and cut across to Wilson Canyon."

"Unless he really is headed straight north as Carl suggested," Sam ventured. "He could also stay on Soldiers Pass until he reached Brins Mesa and circle round by Vultee Arch. It's a long way around, but he could descend into the main canyon by Sterling Pass."

"Too many possibilities," Hopkins muttered. "We can't be everywhere."

* * *

Frank was thinking of climbing down for a pee when Sam and Hopkins appeared back through the bushes and approached the posse. Hopkins was looking decisive.

Hopkins spoke quietly to Carl and then addressed the group. "We've found indications that Danny probably camped here last night," Hopkins declared. "We're going to split the posse into two parties and try to cut him off. Unit two and three will go East with Carl and Sam; units one and four, that's my group and Larry's, will continue to follow the track up this pass."

A sense of renewed enthusiasm passed through the posse. Men jockeyed around to arrange themselves near their respective leaders. Hopkins had to call out to get their attention again.

"I remind you that no one is to start shooting unless ordered to do so by your unit commander or unless you come under fire. We're going to try to convince Danny to give up peacefully, but if we meet up with him and he shoots at us or attempts to ride off, we may be forced to shoot him. I want to remind you not to open fire without direction from your unit leader unless you are fired upon. Is that clear?"

There were several responses of "Yes, Marshal", and "Right", but the Artist suspected that some of the men were more of a danger to each other than they were to Danny Lambert.

Hopkins spoke privately to Sam and Carl again and then the two men led their units back to the road east.

CHAPTER 163   CARL'S COHORT

They reached the main road again and turned left. Carl and Sam encouraged the riders to pick up their pace and led the group of seven east toward the narrows below Steamboat Rock.

Frank decided that he should have had a pee when he'd had the chance.

Jefferson was considering the possibility that coming on this manhunt had been a mistake.

Willard was excited by the possibility the posse might actually catch up with Danny Lambert.

Jesus found his thoughts drifting off to the family he had left behind in Tucson and the likelihood that all this was a waste of time which had nothing to do with the rustling.

Jake felt the small gun bouncing lightly against his right leg and wondered about his feeling for Lily. Was he being an idiot? What kind of fool falls for a woman of easy virtue? On the other hand, Jake wasn't exactly a virgin himself. He'd had more one-night stands and casual involvements than he could remember. Besides, Lily seemed by far the most pleasant and sincere person he'd met in years traveling from coast to coast.

* * *

Carl's feelings were mixed. He was proud to be playing a major part in a manhunt; he was miffed that Sam was so prominent. He was furious with Danny for stealing Star. He was concerned that Danny might injure the horse or worse yet get clear away with Star. Then just before the posse split in two, the marshal had done something that made Carl feel like a million dollars.

Leroy Hopkins had spoken to Carl and Sam privately and made it clear that Carl was to be in charge of the combined section. They were to station themselves in hiding at the point where the Cibola Pass met up with the trail into Wilson Canyon near Steamboat. If they saw any track indicating that Danny Lambert had already passed by they were to follow the tracks. If after waiting two hours they had still not seen Lambert, Carl was to take the main Oak Creek route and head north to the mouth of the Sterling Pass.

Hopkins' units would be following any tracks they found and would catch up when they could. If they saw nothing else they would head north toward Devils Bridge and on to Vultee Arch. "Keep your two units together if you can," Marshal Hopkins had counselled Carl. "If you have to split in two you should keep Jake and Jesus with you. We will meet you at Vultee Arch. Even after waiting two hours at the end on Cibola you may get to Vultee before us. You'll be traveling through open country."

"What if one of our groups meets up with Danny?" Carl asked.

"If you hear sustained gunfire come cautiously; if we need help, we'll fire a series of three shots spaced evenly; if you hear four sets of two shots each that will indicate an all-clear. You use the same signals, Okay?"

Now Carl and Sam were leading their combined units upriver. They were making good time on the main road. It was about four miles to the narrows and Cibola Pass was less than a mile north of that on the Wilson Canyon trail. If Lambert did come east along the Cibola they would be there to meet him.

CHAPTER 164 LEROY'S COHORT

Having made the decision to split the posse in two, Leroy put the matter behind him. He had to concentrate on following the trail.

Danny Lambert had only a small head start.

It would be best if Lambert did go east along the Cibola. That would trap him between the two posse groups. To reach the Cibola intersect they would travel only half as far as Carl's group would cover riding upriver, but the going was slow. Soldiers Pass was more suited to moving on foot and only Larry was a seasoned horseman over this sort of terrain.

Hopkins rode forward with Brad tight in behind him. They were both scanning the path and the edges for any sign of hoof prints. Larry was next in line followed by Lars, Charlie and Clayton. If they did catch up with Danny, Hopkins was counting on the superiority of having rifles to give them an advantage. He didn't intend to take undue risks. They would pin Danny down and wait for him to realize he had no choice but to surrender.

Thomas Carter had not watched the posse as they turned at the forks in the road. His thoughts had been on the tasks of the day and getting young Eddie Thompson packed off home. He assumed that Danny had fled toward the south and that the pursuit would go that direction also.

As he rode out of town himself later he didn't see the fresh tracks heading north because he headed due east. His plan was to ride north along Oak Creek and maybe scare up some gamebirds. Grey and white Long Tailed Duck could occasionally be found there. He had set up a sort of mechanized spit mount by the forge where he had roasted chicken in the past. He'd be able to try cooking a duck that way.

His .410 shotgun, loaded with shot and slug, was holstered by his left knee facing backwards. Thomas Carter was unlikely to win a quick draw contest, but he liked to keep the coach gun where he could reach across and draw it in one smooth movement. He wasn't expecting trouble, but Danny Lambert wasn't the only outlaw in the west.

When he got to the edge of the creek he would dismount and reload both barrels with bird shot. It was fine weather for a stroll along the creek, even if he found no ducks. Meanwhile he allowed the horse to proceed at a walk on a long lead and enjoyed being out away from the heat and fumes of the smithy. Two birds struck up a conversation in the nearby bushes. He spotted one of them, a Vireo whose big white eyes gave it a startled appearance. He couldn't see the other bird and knew that the Vireo often mimicked other bird songs, so it might be a totally different bird responding.

The day was still young. He judged that he could relax by the creek for a few hours before heading back to prepare horses for the stagecoach. He didn't expect any trouble.

CHAPTER 165 PROCTOR'S

Something had awakened him. Dr. Pendergast half rose from the bed and looked around as if expecting to see the cause. He had come up to lie down after Frank and Willard left. It felt as if he had just closed his eyes, but the light flooding in through the window suggested that some time had passed. He listened intently but heard no further noise, if noise it had been which had disturbed his slumber.

He had neither bothered to undress nor to get under the covers. Now he felt a bit of chill as he splashed water on his face and neck. Drying his hands he thought about how strongly Brad agreed with Dr. Lister's ideas about washing carefully before operating. The idea had some merit he thought, although there had been great consternation when the theory was first advanced. Many people, even scientists and doctors, had difficulty in believing in things they couldn't see.

By contrast, think of how many believed in angels, fairies, and ghosts without the least visible proof.

Brad had brought a few articles of clothing back with him from the homestead. Now the doctor slipped his arms into a cardigan and moved to the door to go downstairs. His hand was on the doorknob when he heard the outside door closing.

CHAPTER 166 THE HORN

The hotel, indeed the whole town, seemed eerily quiet. The saloon was empty, the shelves cleared of liquor and the beer taps locked. With both Clayton and Charlie off with the posse and many of the regular customers with them, the cook had not even opened the restaurant. There was no stage due in this morning, so the Wells Fargo office was shuttered as well.

Lily had the place to herself.

This was a novelty. She walked out on the stage and cast her eyes east and then west along the deserted street. No noise of hammering arose from the smithy; no activity was discernible from the feed store or lumber yard. The door to Thompson's Dry Goods stood open, but Violet Thompson was engaged in sweeping off the wooden landing for want of something to do.

Lily's attention fastened upon Proctor's boarding house. There was no sign of life there either, but she imagined that Doris and Dr. Pendergast were occupied with the care of Clive. How strange it was to think that Doris was actually his mother. How hard that must have been for Doris to leave her son to be raised by her own mother. But despite all Doris' precautions her estranged husband had turned up to cause trouble, if only by being killed.

'Well,' Lily thought, 'Since I've got some free time I should visit Doris and the doctor. I can pick up a treat of some sort at Thompson's.

She put her plan into action immediately and stepped down into the roadway and headed directly toward the dry goods store.

CHAPTER 167 PROCTOR'S

With Brad, Frank, and Willard off with the posse and the doctor having a little lie down upstairs, Doris was alone with her son again for the first time since he confided in her his suspicion that she had killed Luke Proctor. Clive also told her that Luke had said something which connected Danny Lambert and Charlie Lee. The way Clive had said it made Doris think that Danny and Charlie were in cahoots. Maybe Clive would wake up soon and be able to tell her what he meant.

She touched his brow with her wrist. He had no fever. Surely that was good. The sleeping potion the doctor had given him would put him to rights. His lips were dry; she went to the kitchen to get a cloth and a glass of water to moisten them. As she was returning there was a light knock at the door. Doris set the glass and cloth on the hall bench and opened the door to find Lily standing holding a store-bought pie covered by a checkered cloth.

"Why Miss Lily, come on in," Doris exclaimed. "I wondered who it could be. The town's half empty." Lily stepped into the hall and Doris pushed the door to against the slight wind which had come up.

"More than half empty, I think," replied Lily. "There's no one at the hotel and even Thomas Carter has left the smithy unattended." As if remembering what she was holding, Lily stretched forward her hand and said, "I brought a little health food. They say an apple a day will keep the doctor away; this is a whole pie full of apples, so I hope that will help."

"That was a kind thought," Doris said with a warm smile. "I was just going to put the kettle on. Clive's still asleep," she said turning her head to indicate the parlor.

Lily gave a quick intake of breath. "I hope I haven't come at a bad time He must need his rest after being attacked and all."

"No. no. Don't worry a bit. Dr. Pendergast gave him a sleeping powder and Clive's resting peacefully." As she said this Doris heard a step on the landing and turned to see the doctor coming down the stairs.

"Good morning, ladies," Dr. Pendergast greeted the two women as he descended the stairs.

"Good morning, Doctor," Lily responded brightly. "I've come to visit your patient."

The doctor's attention was drawn to the cloth-covered dish in Doris' hands. "And you seem to have brought nourishment with you." He made a show of searching for the aroma floating on the air and proclaimed, "Apple with nutmeg and brown sugar and still warm would be my diagnosis; you must have been up early baking." As the words left his mouth he willed them back. He was behaving more like Brad than an experienced doctor. He'd been so eager to show off his deductive skill he'd overlooked the obvious. Lily hadn't baked the pie. She lived out of a hotel room. Too late to take it back he could only feel her pain as she responded.

Lily's face glowed slightly in embarrassment. "Sorry to disappoint you Doctor; it's store-bought I'm afraid."

Doris lifted an edge of the red and white checkered cloth to display the artistic basket-weave top crust and the golden brown apple filling. "It looks delicious, Lily. Thank you so much. I'm going to put the kettle on right now. Would you prefer tea or coffee, doctor?"

"I'll have what you and Lily are having, Doris. I'm just going to have a look at my patient and I'll join you presently."

"I'll bring it into the parlor, Dr. Pendergast. Would you help me serve the pie, Lily?"

The two women disappeared into the kitchen and Dr. Pendergast turned his steps and his thoughts to the sleeping Clive on the daybed.

CHAPTER 168 DANNY

The morning sun cast hard shadows across the uneven trail ahead. Danny had decided to stay clear of the main Oak Creek passage to avoid meeting anyone until he had rearmed himself with the rifle and ammunition stored in the old mine. He could also make a bridle-like device out of rope that would make handling this horse easier. Once he had a rifle he could pick off some traveler and acquire a horse and saddle. He had only realized after he rode out of town that the horse he had taken from the Sedona stable was the deputy's. Well, that didn't matter much. He'd trade it for a decent rifle as he headed west. The rifle he had stashed at the mine was a single shot 1873 Trapdoor Springfield. It shot well enough, as long as you didn't need to fire off more than one round, but he needed a repeater.

He had made good time, all things considered. He wanted to reach the mine by early afternoon. With any luck he could pick off a cottontail with the rifle toward dusk. He could build a small fire just inside the entrance to the mine without anyone seeing it. There were plenty of quail and edible birds, but he'd need a shotgun for those. Danny had met an hombre once who claimed he could bring down duck with a handgun. Danny never found out if he could or not; he'd put a slug in the fool's head one night near Broken Arrow.

CHAPTER 169 LEROY'S COHORT

The light wind had made tracking in this sandy topsoil more difficult. Hopkins was examining a mark Brad had spotted just north of the turn off for Cibola. It might be a hoof mark, but even if it was it might be from a different horse. They had arrived at the turn off point a quarter of an hour ago but they had found no indication which track Lambert had taken, or even if he had gone overland in some other direction. Larry had spotted two possible tracks heading east toward Wilson Canyon. On balance Hopkins thought it more likely that Danny had gone east since his ultimate path north would force him to enter the Oak Creek Canyon.

Leroy wondered how much his reasoning was affected by a desire to bring the two sections of the posse together rather than go off into larger separation. He had to make a decision, but he longed for a reason to choose one trail over the other.

"Marshal!" a voice called out from further north on Soldiers Pass.

Hopkins hurried forward to find Lars and Brad bending over a ball of dusty dung lying in a hollow to one side of the trail.

"This looks fresh," Brad declared. His voice was pitched slightly higher in excitement. Brad's mind was racing. What would Sherlock Holmes deduce from this find? Holmes could identify any number of types of tobacco ash. Brad remembered Holmes declaring that he had written a paper on the ashes of 140 different varieties of pipe, cigar, and cigarette tobacco.

The streets of London were filled with throngs of horse-drawn hansom cabs. Holmes used hansom cabs often. And yet Brad could not remember any instance when the great detective deduced anything from the malodorous droppings which must have littered every byway. Perhaps the mixture of feed in a pile of steaming horse balls could have led Sherlock to the stable from which it issued. The size and shape of the feces might provide a clue to the age or type of horse.

While Brad was speculating on the information which could

hypothetically be drawn from manure, the marshal took action.

With one hand Hopkins broke off a twig and prodded the horse droppings. A ball broke open readily and gave off a pungent aroma. "You're right, Brad," the marshal told him. "That hasn't been here more than an hour, I would guess."

Hopkins called Larry to join them at the point where Brad had discovered the scat. He pointed it out to Larry who confirmed that it was recent. "That horse was stable fed, Marshal," Larry added. "There are oats in the droppings. Any working horse on a drive or even just scouting about would have simpler fare."

"I'm surprised at Danny leaving such a clear sign, especially at the junction like this," Hopkins remarked. "Do you think this was left here on purpose to mislead us?"

"Hell no, Marshal," Larry said with a laugh. "Danny Lambert's a nasty fellow, but he's not that bright. I'd say this just means he doesn't expect anyone to be trailing him."

Leroy stood up and dusted off his hands. "You're probably right, Larry. We'll take this fork."

As they walked back toward the horses, Brad was feeling a bit disappointed. The marshal and Larry had drawn useful conclusions from the clue of the horse dung. The marshal had been decisive about a course of action before Brad had even decided how to analyse it. Real life detection was proving more difficult that Arthur Conan Doyle portrayed it in his books. Then Hopkins said something which encouraged Brad. "It's a good thing you spotted that scat. I was leaning toward taking the other path."

BRAND OF DEATH

Part Three: Tracking in the Canyon

CHAPTER 170

Carl moved in advance of the group as their two units relocated east; Sam, perhaps because of his experience driving cattle, tended to hang back where he could keep an eye on things as they developed. Their formation as they moved swiftly east along the main road was anything but military. Nevertheless the contrasting styles of the two unit leaders brought a sort of balance to their progress along the main road.

The towering rock formation known as Steamboat floated into sight. The canyon walls rising above Oak Creek were steep here and the groundcover had altered to reflect the northern Arizona desert conditions. The farther hills were spotted with scrub trees, but the reddish dry soil showed through. There was cover, but a horseman passing across the uplands would have to traverse open patches and might be exposed. Carl found himself scanning the hills as if expecting to spot Danny. With any luck Lambert would still be moving up Cibola Pass toward the turn off to Wilson Canyon. The pass itself was concealed and they too would be out of sight of a horseman traveling parallel to them. They were moving with some haste since their plan to ambush him as he emerged from Cibola depended on arriving at the crossroads before him.

Sam pulled up beside Carl and pointed out the beginnings of the winding path north to the junction with Cibola. "We could leave our horses in the shade and move up to the crossroads on foot. Danny's impulsive, but he's no fool. As he approaches the open area near the junction he'll be keeping his eyes open."

"Will he be able to move at speed though the open area at the crossroads?" Carl asked. "There's no point us waiting on foot if he can gallop right by us."

Sam shook his head in negation of that possibility. "The approach here is pretty steep. He might even be on foot himself. He certainly won't be able to climb that grade quickly. Chances are he'll come on mounted but at a walk."

Carl considered the advice. If Danny got past them it would mean a delay remounting before pursing him, but it would be difficult to hide the horses near the intended interception point. He drew up and gathered the men around him.

When everyone had quieted down their mounts and were listening, Carl explained the plan. "We're going to tether our horses at the mouth of the trail. Give each a handful of water and make sure they're able to reach something to munch on. We will be waiting for up to an hour. We don't want them causing a fuss and alerting Lambert."

A few moments' walk brought them to the small clearing where the trails intersected. Carl pointed out the track they expected Danny to emerge from. He was not used to directing a group and delegating authority, but he realized that the greatest danger was that they would end up shooting toward each other. If Danny came out in the open from the west, they should all have a shot at him without directing a bullet at one of their own. Carl thought that Jake, Sam, and Jesus could be counted on to keep their heads. Frank, Jefferson, and Willard were less predictable.

"What's the plan, Carl?" Willard asked.

Carl made a decision which seemed like a good idea at the time.

"We'll station ourselves in a semicircle to the east of the forks," he began. "I want three groups. Sam, you and Willard find a good point of concealment here at the southwest, Jake, you and Jesus move north on the trail which leads that way toward Wilson Canyon, but keep a sightline on the junction. I'll be directly across from the Cibola exit with Frank and Jefferson. No one is to shoot unless I give the command, 'Fire', and no one is to shoot in a direction which might hit one of the other groups. Understood?"

Carl paused long enough to look at each man and meet his eyes. "Once you are settled in position, pick a point across the open area, a tree or a large rock, which will keep your rifle from pointing toward another posse member. If your aim would take your rifle barrel past that point, don't fire. Even if you have a shot at Danny, don't fire into the red zone."

The men were surprisingly quiet. There were nods all round and Carl added two more instructions. "I will have a view down the trail and will see Danny first if he comes this way. I will wait until he is in the open and warn him to surrender. It is very important that everyone stay out of sight until I issue that challenge. If he tries to run or starts shooting we will take him down. But," Carl paused and added in a serious tone, "If anyone shoots my horse I will not be happy. Aim for Danny's upper body and head."

CHAPTER 171 CARL'S COHORT

Jake and Jesus moved north of the clearing and found themselves a spot that was concealed by some Scrub Live Oak and bordered by a large boulder to their left. Despite Carl's instruction to avoid shooting at each other, Jake would rather put his trust in thick rock.

As they settled into position and checked their rifles, Jesus spoke for the first time since they'd left town. "The deputy has the makings of a good leader. I'm a bit surprised."

"How so?" Jake asked.

"In town he behaved like a popinjay," Jesus explained. "He seemed vain and conceited. I thought he might be too full of himself to lead others. But he has positioned his forces well and given clear instructions without being overbearing. With some military training he could be a good commander."

"He's grown into the position," Jake suggested.

"Yes," Jesus agreed. "Some people thrive with a challenge; others wilt under it."

Jake considered Jesus's words. On the whole he agreed with the assessment of Carl. He was also impressed by the strong insightfulness Jesus displayed. Jake considered himself a good judge of character. It was part of his job to evaluate people. In the last couple of days he had met a fair smattering of people. He was highly impressed by three of them: Marshal Hopkins, Jesus Soza, and Lily. His thoughts shifted slightly as he realized that he didn't know Lily's last name. They shifted more dramatically as he considered his feelings for her.

By connection Jake remembered the object Lily had given him at parting. He lay his rifle down across his leg and drew the small pocket gun out of his pocket. Unwrapped, it revealed itself to be a double barrel gun with REMINGTON ARMS CO. ILION N.Y. stamped atop the rib separating the two barrels. He recognized it as a Model 95 and thought that the engraving of the nickel plating and the white ivory handles made it look remarkably feminine. This type of gun was commonly referred to as a 'Derringer'. With the detailed engraving and ivory grips, the gun would be fairly expensive, probably in the twenty to twenty-five dollar range. He used the built-in extractor and examined the cartridges. The .41 caliber rim fire rounds were shiny. They had been recently loaded. The gun itself was several years old and showed some signs of wear, but Lily clearly took care of it. Even with the three-inch barrel, the total length was less than five inches. It was a deadly weapon which could be concealed in his hand without difficulty.

Jake looked up from his examination of the gun to find Jesus watching him with a smile tracing the edges of his lips. "Be careful, my friend. You may find that lady very dangerous."

CHAPTER 172 LEROY'S COHORT

When the marshal returned with the order to move north along Soldiers Pass, Clayton's first thought was for his own safety. They had set out with thirteen riders, of which at least four were experienced and competent men to have with you in a shoot-out. Now he was stuck in a group of six, of whom only the marshal could be considered reliable. Larry was okay when he had Sam to back him up, but Clayton had never had a high opinion of him by himself. The young Pendergast had to be considered a non-combatant; Charlie Lee was a better dresser than a fighter; and Clayton had absolutely no faith in himself if it came to a gunfight. Lars was an unknown factor, but Clayton had taken a note of his rifle, a 1865 Spencer Carbine 56 Gauge. The rifle was so old it was calibrated in 'gauge' rather than 'caliber'. Lars was carrying a gun that was older than he was. That didn't speak well for his expertise.

On top of everything else, it seemed as if they were the section of the posse which was actually close on the trail of a mad dog killer.

* * *

Lars had watched Brad and Hopkins as they squatted in the trail and examined something Brad had found. He longed to be included in the discovery. He was good at tracking. He'd show them when he got a chance. He'd promised his wife he'd come back safe. He'd do his best to keep that promise. If shooting broke out he'd leave that to the experts, but he wanted to contribute to the effort. He hoped he could do that by assisting in the tracking.

CHAPTER 173 CARL'S COHORT

Jefferson was having a bad spell. They came on him from time to time, but usually he just went off by himself until they passed. Now, as he sat crouched behind a ledge of rock with Carl and Frank, he started to hear the voices.

Frank saw Jefferson's eyes start to roll back. He looked over at Carl, but the deputy had all his attention focussed on the mouth of the path down which Danny Lambert might come. Frank considered saying something, but realized that would do no good. The deputy was no more likely to be able to assist Jefferson than he was himself. If only he could get the doctor's young son to examine Jefferson. But Brad was with the marshal. They were on their own.

CHAPTER 174 DANNY

Danny had been forced to lead Carl's horse through some of the steep sections of the pass because the shale was not stable. Without stirrups or a bridle with a bit to control the horse there was the possibility it would slip and become uncontrollable. This path was the most direct route north, but it was proving troublesome.

Finally he reached the lower slopes which were also more open. He could skirt the highlands near Devil's Bridge and find some cover, but here he wanted to make some time. He was moving ever farther north into an area which was deserted and the last place a posse would be likely to look for him. Besides, if a pursuit had even been begun it would be searching south of Sedona. Still there was no telling who might be wandering in this area. There were latter day prospectors hoping to find a new mother lode. Such a one might wander south into Sedona and mention spotting a lone horseman up this way.

Danny felt vulnerable without a rifle. He was also beginning to experience hunger. He had been hungry as a child and he didn't like the feeling. His hand stole down to his revolver and he stoked the smooth wooden grips. At close quarters his gun would speak for him, but in the open country he needed a weapon which could reach out and fetch a man out of a saddle or bring down a deer or a rabbit. With only three unspent cartridges in his six shooter, he was unwilling to risk a shot at game. He would reach the old mine this afternoon and be able to build a fire to cook something. The quicker he got there the better. He was starting to wish he'd gone straight up Oak Creek. He'd be there by now.

He'd seldom come up this way before though he knew there was a connection with the crease in the hills which led up toward Vultee Arch. He would descend that small valley and enter Sterling Pass from the west. There was a chance he could find some water trickling down that way. The night in the open had done nothing to improve his mood. Danny replayed what he'd done back at The Horn. He'd wasted at least one bullet too many in that smart ass, Paul. One bullet to the head would have finished him off. After he'd done that he could have also killed Sam, Larry, and the big shot Charlie Lee. He could have taken that fancy rifle Charlie was always bragging about and forced the smith to saddle up a horse for him. Someone had taken a shot at Danny as he rode out of town. He should go back and kill whoever that was. He might have to shoot a few people before he found out who that was. That would be fine.

Danny started to imagine killing everyone in town. He pictured himself walking calmly from building to building and picking them off one by one. He drew his colt and admired the cool dull lustre of the cylinder, the precision fitting, the distinctive rear-offset "birds head" grip. Danny had gone to Flagstaff and bought the 1877 with cash he had taken from the dead settlers. It was his first new gun and he knew that Billy the Kid had been carrying a similar gun twenty-five years ago when he killed Pat Garrett. Danny started thinking about his own name. He'd never liked Lambert. That was his father's name. Dangerous Dan or Deadly Dan would suit him better. Maybe if he robbed a bank or something he'd announce his name. 'Aw hell,' he thought, 'better to just shoot them all.'

He was northwest of Brins Mesa when he reached the first open terrain and he encouraged the horse to pick up the pace. First things first. In a few hours he would reach the mine; he wanted to be there well before dark.

CHAPTER 175 CARL'S COHORT

Jefferson was starting to mumble. Carl thought he was speaking for a minute and was about to tell him to hold the chatter. One look at the mortician made it clear that Brooks was having some sort of fit. Carl saw that Frank Green was watching Brooks too.

"Can you shut him up, Frank?" Carl demanded. "What the hell's going on?"

Frank held up his hands palms forward. "I have no idea," he told the deputy. "I've never seen him like this."

"Well, he's got to quiet down. We've got no time for this kind of nonsense."

Frank put a hand on Jefferson's arm and tried to get his attention. Brooks turned his head toward Frank but his eyes were focused on infinity. His lips stopped moving and he just sat there looking remarkably like a sheep staring off into some other reality.

CHAPTER 176 LEROY'S COHORT

The sun had risen far enough to slant down the eastern slope and warm the trail. Lars had dropped back behind Charlie and Clayton and was riding at the back of the group. While the others watched the ground for tracks and in order to find the best footing along the uneven path, Lars was examining the foliage and scanning the horizon whenever he caught a glimpse of it.

The landscape was ambiguous. Oak Creek provided water, brought life to Sedona and the land which bordered the waterway, but a mile or so up slope there was barely enough to support the scrub pine and the desert succulents that clung to the spectacular cliffs and sank roots into rock-dust soil. The trail they were following was twisted, like the Cat Claw, which some locals called the Wait-a-minute-bush. Lars thought both names odd. He suspected that the local name for the plant came from the sharp thorns with which the plant seemed determined to hold you back if you passed too closely.

In the higher elevations which overshadowed them he could pick out some small examples of Hairy Mountain Mahogany. When it had first been shown to him he had wondered why a low, gnarled bush would be called mahogany. He still wondered. The small flowers of both were long gone now. As he traced the edge of a ridge ahead of them a flash of light surprised him. The sun was rising behind them over his right shoulder. The flash of light must be a reflection from some shiny object turning in the light. It could not be from running water. There was no stream at that elevation. It must have been from some metallic object or a piece of glass.

The trail was slightly broader and flat right here. Lars urged his horse forward and moved past Charlie and Clayton to draw up beside Brad.

"I thought I saw a flash of light up ahead," he said to Brad in a hushed tone.

Even though he'd spoken quietly, Hopkins heard him speak and turned to look back. Brad Pendergast waved to the marshal and then pointed to Lars. Hopkins pulled up and allowed Brad and Lars to catch up to him.

"I saw a reflection of light from the ridge up ahead," Lars explained. "It might have been nothing."

Marshal Hopkins looked toward the spot that Lars indicated. It was not far off in a straight line, but the trail ahead seemed to turn to the right and to lead away from it. On the other side of a small valley which lay between them and the ridge, a pathway could be seen snaking through a jumble of rock and up to a saddle which crossed the ridge.

"Someone crossing that divide would be visible from here. If you saw someone they would probably now be on the other side of that rise and moving away from us." He called out softly to Larry who turned back and joined them. The six men sat close together while Hopkins conferred with Larry.

"Where does that notch in the ridge lead, Larry?" he asked. "Lars thinks he saw something up there. Is that still part of Soldiers Pass?"

Larry considered and replied with a nod. "Yep, we're almost at the junction with Jordan Trail and the dry creek which runs down it crosses ahead of us. That rock which sticks up like a saddle horn is called Sphinx Rock. Beyond there is sinkhole country. If Danny is headed that way he must plan to stay well west of the main canyon and head on toward Brins Mesa."

"I wish Carl and the others were with us," Hopkins mused aloud. "I don't want to signal with a gun, 'cause Lambert is probably closer to us than Carl is. He'd hear it and know we're following him. If we sent someone on horseback to get them it would take an hour or more each way and if we keep moving on they'd still be two hours behind us when they got here. We're just going to have to move on and hope they circle up Oak Creek Canyon. Lambert is going to have to go east at some point unless he's heading deep into Secret Mountain. I can't see him doing that. He's not a mountain man and he doesn't have gear to make it through that way."

"It wouldn't make sense, Marshal," Larry agreed. "He left town bareback and without even a bedroll. He'll be heading for a town or at least a homestead to get some food and supplies."

"Well, we'll just follow up this way then. With any luck he'll get himself caught between our two groups. Carl will only wait an hour at most up at the end of Cibola. After that he'll head north and move on toward the Sterling Pass. If we don't run down Danny before then we'll meet up with the rest of our people there."

CHAPTER 177 PROCTOR'S

As the doctor approached the day bed he was encouraged by Clive's relaxed breathing and the fresh complexion which had replaced the pallor of the day before. He leaned forward to take a pulse and was surprised when Clive's eyes flicked open.

Clive focused on the doctor's face and his lips formed an 'O' of confusion. He tried to raise his head and winced in pain. "What? My head hurts."

"Lie quiet, Clive. You've had an accident, but you're mending," Dr. Pendergast cautioned him. He laid a hand on Clive's upper arm and the other on his forehead. There was no fever. The eyes were clear and focused. Yes, he would mend. "Don't move your head too much. I'll give you something to ease the headache." He reached down for his bag and lifted out a brown glass bottle from which he poured a white powder into a short glass of water. He stirred it until it dissolved and spooned a small amount into Clive's mouth.

Clive's lips were dry and he accepted the liquid readily. He swallowed several times before venturing an opinion. "It's bitter, like suphur spring water. What is it?' he asked between the doses which the doctor continued to offer.

"The full name is acetylsalic acid. A German chemist created a stable compound of it to relieve his father's rheumatism. It works well for other aches and pains too."

"What happened to me, Doctor? Did a horse kick me?"

"Do you remember anything?" Dr. Pendergast asked by way of response.

Clive accepted a final spoonful of the solution and closed his eyes. "I know I was in the stable. I can remember the smell and a bright light."

The doctor waited patiently for more but Clive just frowned and lay quietly. Sounds coming from the kitchen indicated the imminent arrival of Doris and Lily. He chanced a quick question while he had Clive to himself. "You mentioned Danny Lambert and Charlie Lee. What made you put those two together?" he asked quietly.

"I've seen them talking together out behind the hotel when I've been exercising horse," Clive replied. "Danny's a killer, and I think Charlie Lee uses him."

Before the doctor could probe for more, the two women came into the parlor. Doris, seeing that her son was conscious, set down a tea set on a tray and hurried over to him. Lily came forward holding a second tray with plates of freshly cut pie. Lily was a beautiful woman. Seeing her standing there, all domestic looking, he felt again a pang of sorrow for the loss of his wife.

CHAPTER 178 EAST OF SEDONA

The air was cool with a hint of winter, but the sun warmed Carter as he leaned back against the overhanging bank. He had thought he might do some hunting; maybe take a duck back to roast by the forge. Now, with the light sparkling on the water he was content to sit quietly and watch the flow of the stream.

Here Oak Creek changed direction and there was an outcropping of rock which caused the current to bend around it to create a backwater pool. Odd bits of flotsam had collected and bobbed in the swirl which held them. Thomas thought a bit about the troubles which had encircled his smithy and stables of late. First there was the marshal asking about Clive and then the attack on Clive as he was mucking out. He'd thought Clive was dead when he first saw him. Well, so had the deputy when it came to that.

Thomas wished he'd been able to do something when Danny Lambert came in all het up and waving his sixgun around. He imagined taking a swing at Danny's head with a hot bar of iron, but a bullet moves pretty fast. Danny would have shot him and probably young Eddie as well.

His mind drifted to the branding iron he'd given to Carl. It might just have been a practice piece Clive was working on, but the reaction of the deputy suggested it was more than just that. He wondered if Clive was mixed up in something. He brushed the question out of his mind and let the water absorb his attention. Thomas didn't like getting involved in other people's lives. He was by nature a loner. You could trust a bar of metal to behave itself; people were unpredictable and trouble as often as not.

CHAPTER 179 PROCTOR'S

"How do you feel, Clive?" Doris asked, her voice full of concern. She took his hand in hers and searched his face.

"I've got a bit of a headache," Clive replied. "Doc Pendergast has given me a magic potion to fix that though. I'll be back on my feet in no time." He paused and then added, "I still don't know what happened to me. What hit me?"

"It seems that you've made an enemy, Clive," the doctor told him. "Someone hit you over the head with a chunk of rock."

"A rock?"

"Well, to be exact it was a piece of petrified wood, but it was just as hard," the doctor explained.

"Say, I've got a piece of that I keep in the stable. Someone gave it to me. Said it was weighing down his saddle bag," Clive told him. "Maybe that's what it was. But who hit me?" As he became more animated, Clive started to sit up and then winced and sank back against the pillow.

"Don't stir yourself too much, Clive. Give the medicine a chance to act," Doris counseled him.

"Your mother's right," the doctor agreed. "Lie quiet for now. We're working at finding out who it was." He beckoned to Lily to bring a piece of pie over to show to Clive. "Lily brought some apple pie. Would you like a taste?" he asked and was pleased to see a positive reaction. He was convinced that an interest in food was one of the most reliable signs that a patient was on the road to recovery. He moved some chairs into a semicircle near the sofa and Doris helped Clive to sample the pastry.

Lily poured tea and Dr. Pendergast sat back and the two women slipped easily into a conversation which ranged from the difficulty in obtaining certain articles through Thompson's Dry Goods store to Lily's sister's declared intention to become a missionary. Then Lily expressed concern for the safety of the members of the posse and Clive asked, "Posse! What posse?"

CHAPTER 180 LEROY'S COHORT

Clayton was continuing to wonder what he'd got himself into. The original posse of thirteen had a comforting mass about it. The splitting of the units left him feeling exposed. The marshal and Larry were good horsemen and knew how to handle a gun. His faith in the rest of the group was less certain.

His employer, Mr. Charlie Lee, looked pretty good sitting tall in the saddle with a fancy looking rifle and side arm, but could he shoot worth a damn? Clayton had his doubts.

Lars was the strong, silent type. He knew his way around a lumberyard. Clayton had watched Lars frame in the new counter in the Wells Fargo office and at work on the extension Thomas Carter had added to the stables. Lars was good with a hammer and saw. Clayton had the greatest respect for his skill as a carpenter. However, he looked out of his element on a horse.

Dr. Pendergast's son was a non-starter. Clayton had overheard Brad Pendergast tell the marshal that he didn't want to fire his rifle. It was good to have a medical person with them, but it raised the possibility that medical treatment might be needed.

If push came to shove, Clayton might have to count on himself. That was really scary; he certainly had no confidence in his own ability.

CHAPTER 181 DANNY

Danny had paused at the top of a rise and looked back along the trail. He had made slow but steady progress so far. He knew that he would reach his destination by early afternoon. He planned to spend the night at the mine and to set out for the Oak Creek pass early the next morning. He'd feel better with a rifle and some more ammunition for his handgun.

There was no real hurry. If the town had mounted any pursuit at all it would be far to the south by now. He would move west avoiding Flagstaff and disappear into the frontier settlements and mining camps. There had been nothing to hold him in Sedona. It was high time he moved on.

He was just turning away to consider the landscape ahead when his eye caught sight of some movement on the trail behind him. He drifted over the brow of the hill and sat motionless scanning the downslope he had recently descended. He watched for a full minute and saw no other indication of human activities.

Finally he turned north and began to pick his way down toward the broken land which lay before him. He felt a pricking of concern about what might have caused the motion he thought he'd seen a minute ago. It was probably nothing important, but he resolved to pick up his pace a little. He moved as quickly as he dared down toward the sinkhole pocked valley.

CHAPTER 182 CARL'S COHORT

Eyes, large luminous eyes regarded him like wells of presence amid the darkness of his soul. They stared into him and drew him down toward them. Now he was falling; they were lifting him. Then, he was lying on his back. Frank was bending over him. Focus shifted; Jeffery realized that he could see Carl behind, above, Frank. Something was pressing against his back.

As his senses return he realized that the hard rock-strewn ground was supporting him. The very Earth held him above Hell, below Heaven. He was still within the vale of tears which terrified him more than promises of paradise could soften.

Frank was speaking. "He's coming around. Jefferson, Jefferson, can you hear me?" Frank called down to him. Jefferson wanted to answer. Strove for words

"Stay with him," Carl instructed Frank. "I'm going to gather the others. Danny's not coming this way. We've got to more on to meet up with the marshal."

Jeffeson sensed more than saw Carl move off. He tried to focus on Frank; tried to answer. Words would not come. He knew he must move his throat, force air up through his mouth and over unresponsive lips; form sounds. He saw the concern on Frank's face. He tried again. Nothing came.

"It's okay," Frank assured him. "Lie quiet. Carl's gone to fetch the others. Lambert's not coming this way it seems."

Jefferson remembered. They were hunting, hunting someone, Danny Lambert. He tried to tell Frank that he remembered, but no words came. It was important that he speak. He had to tell Frank, warn him. He pushed and the words came out in a jumble. "Where ... where are the trees?" he demanded.

Frank looked relieved, but did not understand. "We're up near Steamboat Rock, Jefferson. The trees are small here."

Jefferson wondered why Frank was talking about where they were. Didn't he understand? He tried to tell Frank about Danny. Then when he tried to form words they did not match his thoughts. He'd had a spell like this before, but this seemed different, worse than the others.
* * *

Carl stepped out into the open and called out to the other groups, "Sam, Jake, come on out. Looks as if we've got to move on." As the other men moved out into the open, Carl moved back to stand beside Frank who was partially supporting the mortician.

Jefferson Brooks looked ghastly. Carl thought of the expression 'death warmed over'. It would serve to describe Brooks. He directed his words to Frank. "Can he ride? Do you think you could get him back to town by the main road?"

Frank turned to Jefferson and held him with a hand on each upper arm. "Jefferson, can you ride? We need to get you back to town."

The other four men had gathered around them. Jesus came forward and peered into Jefferson's eyes. He looked at Frank and then held his hand up in front of Jefferson.

"Can you see my fingers, Senor?"

Brooks nodded and then replied, "Yes, yes I can."

"How many fingers do you see?" Jesus asked twisting his hand and displaying three.

"Three," Jefferson replied. "I can see okay. I was just a bit dizzy. Must be the heat."

"Can you ride?" Carl asked. What heat, he wondered? Even with the sun rising above the shrubs and shining down at them it was still cool rather than warm.

"I'll be okay," Brooks responded. "I won't hold you up."

"Frank will take you back to town," Carl told him. "You'd better see Doc Pendergast."

CHAPTER 183 EAST OF SEDONA

The sun was as high as it was going to get, Carter decided. Time he was heading back to town. The posse would be gone most of the day most like, but there was work to be done at the smithy. Reluctantly Thomas raised himself to his feet and stood, arms akimbo, gazing out toward the far bank. Lowering his gaze, he let his eyes slide over the flowing water and found them drawn as before toward the whirlpool of debris circling slowly in the bright sunshine. Shafts of light slanted south to north through the shallow water near the shore.

Lying on the sandy bottom, a few feet out and partially concealed by a coating of algae, was an object which Carter immediately recognised. He stepped back toward the bushes and selected a piece of broken branch. After a few minutes of tentative probing he was able to drag the object to the shore and lift it from the water.

When he had brushed it off and examined it closely, he was certain what he had found. He carried it back up the bank and slipped it into a saddlebag before mounting up and urging his horse into motion toward town. This would be of interest to the marshal. Thomas wondered how it had come to be lying in Oak Creek when everyone thought it was buried in the graveyard.

CHAPTER 184 LEROY'S COHORT

They topped the rise and sat side by side just below the ridge regarding the trail and the badlands which lay before them. There, on the steep downhill slope were the unmistakable traces of a horse recently descending across the dry shale which covered the northern downslope. The tracks were those of a solitary rider who was evidently in too much of a hurry to dismount.

"Looks like someone passed over the track recently. I'd say it was this morning," Lars offered. "The edges are clear; wind last night would have smoothed them out some."

Hopkins accepted the judgement without comment. It seemed likely enough that the passage had been made by Danny, and only a half hour or so earlier. The marshal wondered about the apparent haste. If it was Danny he had taken a route that was much slower than the main road, and now he appeared to be hurrying. What had caused Lambert to pick up his pace? Had he seen them descending into the valley behind him? Had Lars been spotted at the same moment he had seen the flash of light?

"He must have seen us coming after him," Brad suggested, echoing Hopkins' thoughts. Brad turned in his saddle and looked back at the downward slope behind them. "There are open patches where I can see the trail," he added in support of his deduction. "He took a bit of a chance going down that slippery slope riding bareback. You can see some skid marks where he started to slide."

"That shale ahead looks dangerous, Marshal," Clayton chipped in. "I don't fancy riding down that myself."

Hopkins regretted his earlier decision to split the posse. He now needed the experienced horsemen he'd sent east with Carl. Clayton and Charlie were Sunday riders and while Brad and Lars were comfortable in the saddle, they were uncertain combatants. It would be foolish to try to overtake Lambert, but if they laid back and stayed behind him something good might turn up. They had the advantage of rifles. As long as they stayed clear of handgun range they might get a chance to bring him down.

"Shouldn't we wait for Carl and the others to rejoin us before we go after Danny?" Charlie asked.

"Carl's units won't be coming back this way," Hopkins explained. "They will head up Oak Creek Canyon to the mouth of Sterling Pass to meet up with us there."

"Well, what are we supposed to do?" Charlie continued. "If Danny knows we're coming after him he's sure to dry gulch us somewhere in that pothole country up ahead."

Hopkins sensed the reluctance of Clayton and Charlie. He wasn't surprised. Back in town, in the company of others and in the heat of the moment, joining up with a posse had seemed romantic, an adventure. Here, in the full light of day a man could start feeling pretty vulnerable. He knew that these men needed to be given assurance to stay the course. They were nervous now, but if they turned back they would later despise themselves for doing so, and they would secretly resent Hopkins for having witnessed their weakness.

Hopkins settled back in his saddle and looked out over the tortured country which lay before them. He took a deep breath and made a speech to no one in particular, to the emptiness itself. It was as if he were thinking out loud; as if no one had expressed doubts and the thoughts he voiced were already in the minds of all of them.

"There are sink holes and creases in the landscape where a man could hide," he began. "There are spots which a good rifleman could defend against others equally armed. But Danny Lambert is not that kind of man. Danny Lambert is a back shooter and at heart a coward. All he has is a handgun and limited ammunition. We have rifles and all the time in the world. If he tries to stand and fight we can lay back and pick him off from well beyond the range of his revolver."

The marshal turned to Lars. "You're a hunter, Lars. What do you hunt deer with, a rifle or a handgun?"

Lars laughed. "I'd be a fool to try to hunt deer with a handgun, Marshal. I use this rifle."

"What about that fine rifle of yours, Charlie. You reckon that might reach out a mite further than that six gun of Danny's?"

"Damn right it would, Leroy." Charlie responded with a smile of pride. "This .405 caliber Winchester is the same gun President Roosevelt used in Africa to shoot elephants and lions. It will sure take care of Lambert."

"Well, we don't intend to lose the advantage these rifles give us,"

Hopkins said as if stating what they all knew. "We'll track Danny, and if we catch sight of him in the open we'll fetch him down, but we're not going to walk into any ambush."

Sensing the renewed confidence of the party, Hopkins turned to Larry. The man had shown some sense in reading the tracks Lambert had left. It wouldn't hurt to give him a role in decision making. "You know this part of the county, Larry. Where do you suppose Lambert is headed?"

CHAPTER 185 CARL'S COHORT

They managed to get Jefferson Brooks settled on his horse. He was able to mount up with just a bit of help from Sam and Frank to steady him. Once up he claimed to be feeling fine, but Frank thought there was a bit of a slur to his speech.

"Can you two manage alone?" Carl asked. "Willard could ride back with you if you'd like."

Frank stole a look over at Willard and noted that the young man was looking off into the distance as if watching something. It was obvious that Willard didn't want to be detailed off to nursemaid Brooks.

"We'll be fine," Frank declared. "We'll just go at a walk along the main road. If we have any difficulty we'll dismount and wait for you to come back toward town."

Sam had a bedroll tied on behind his saddle. He took it off and fastened it up behind Jefferson. "If you need to, make camp beside the road and light a fire. We won't be out after dark and we'll make sure someone comes back by the road," he told Frank.

Brooks managed a smile as they prepared to ride off.

Frank noticed and felt uneasy. 'Unfortunately, smiling always makes him look predatory,' Frank thought.

They turned out onto the roadway and moved off gently. When Frank next looked back he saw that the remaining five men were gathered near the horses. Carl seemed to be drawing something on the ground.

CHAPTER 186 PROCTOR'S

Doris told Clive about the shooting at The Horn and Lily filled in details about the poker game and Danny's dash for freedom which included a confrontation at the smithy. Doctor Pendergast watched Clive closely as he received the news.

"I've never known Danny to be much of a poker player," Clive mused. "I'll bet Charlie Lee got him involved."

"Why would that be?" the doctor asked.

"Charlie always likes to be manipulating people," Clive explained. "He probably knew Danny would lose and would resort to violence."

"Why would Charlie want to put himself in the line of fire?" Lily asked. "Danny looked as if he was going to shoot everyone when he jumped up and pulled his gun."

"I don't suppose he thought Danny would shoot anyone with witnesses around," Clive continued. "His style is to catch someone off by himself and put a bullet in him from behind."

"Do you think he might have hit you over the head?" Dr. Pendergast asked quietly.

Clive paused and replied seriously, "It's possible. He might have killed my father too, come to that."

There was a sharp intake of air from Doris.

Before she could say anything, the doctor asked quickly, "Did Danny have dealings with your father?"

Clive's eyes slide over to meet his mother's gaze. He sighed and replied, "I don't know about that, but I know he was involved with the rustling, and I saw him talking with Charlie Lee."

CHAPTER 187 LEROY'S COHORT

Larry had been scanning the hills ahead. Now he turned in his saddle and gave a sort of lopsided grin. "Only one place he could be going, Marshal. He must be planning to join up with Oak Creek Canyon up north. That's the only way out. The river can't be crossed easily this far north and if he turns west he'll be climbing up into the wilderness.

Like you said, Danny's no mountain man. He'd die there for sure."

"What's the most likely route he'd take toward the canyon?" Hopkins asked.

Larry took another look at the land which lay ahead and replied, "After passing the devil's kitchen region the land flattens out toward Brins Mesa. There's a dry creek which heads almost due north and may have some pools of standing water at this time of year. The most likely course for a man with a horse is toward the Devil's Bridge and then east down Sterling Canyon. If he thinks he's being followed he might avoid the creek bed, but that would slow him down some."

Hopkins sensed the will to continue seeping back into the men as Larry spoke. Now was the time to give them something to do.

"Well, Carl and the others will be waiting for him if he heads down Sterling. We'll just mosey along behind him and keep our eyes open," he told the group. "Let's all dismount and walk our horses down this grade. There's no hurry; everyone be careful."

As the men dismounted and headed downhill, Hopkins scanned the broken land ahead and wondered if Danny would be foolish enough to try to ambush them. He knew Danny was stupid, but was he that stupid?

CHAPTER 188 PROCTOR'S

The main street lay before him open and deserted. The horse was full of spirits and well aware that they were heading back toward the stable, so Carter had let it have its head a bit on the way back. Now he slowed to a walk as he approached the entrance to the lumber yard. Up ahead he could see a faint wisp of smoke rising from Mrs. Proctor's boarding house.

Dr. Pendergast's buggy was still parked in the driveway. Thomas climbed down and tethered his mount to a rear wheel. As he approached the side door he removed his hat and brushed his thick hair back from his forehead.

His tentative knock was answered by Lily who invited him in with a warm smile. As he wiped his boots she called out, "Clive, Mr. Carter's here to visit. He probably wants you back at work."

Lily smiled broadly as Thomas Carter's ruddy complexion glowed in response to her gentle teasing.

Doris came into the hallway and took Carter's hat. "Come into the parlor, Thomas. Lily has brought an apple pie and I'm just about to brew a fresh pot of tea." Lily ushered Thomas into the parlor while Doris continued into the kitchen.

"Good day, Thomas," the doctor said rising to come forward to take his hand. "Our patient is recovering. He'll soon be back at the smithy."

Carter regarded the young man lying on the sofa and said, "I'm glad to see you mending, Clive. We'll be happy to have you back when you're able."

Doris came back in with a fresh pot of tea and seated Carter in the wing chair beside Clive. Lily brought over a plate of pie and Doris provided Thomas with a cup and saucer. The doctor was amused to observe how out of place the smith, who was perfectly at home with forge and anvil, looked perched on the edge of a chair with a cup in one hand and a plate balanced on his knee.

Talk turned to the posse and the likelihood that they would catch up with Danny. Carter expressed the opinion that Lambert was probably halfway to Mexico and Lily interrupted to say, "Oh, but the posse headed north. I saw them turn up toward the mountains as they left town. They must be heading for Oak Creek Canyon."

Carter replied that he had been back in the smithy by the time the posse reached the forks, but that he had seen Danny turn south when he left town the day before. No one had an answer for the apparent contradiction and the conversation flagged.

More to fill the silence than for any other reason, Carter turned to the doctor and said, "I found something that I think used to belong to you down in Oak Creek today."

"Oh, what would that be?" the doctor asked with interest.

Carter seized on the chance to escape the confines of an overly social occasion by saying, "I should get back to work, the Wells Fargo coach will be pulling in soon. Come out to my horse and I'll show you."

CHAPTER 189 CARL'S COHORT

About the time Carter was opening his saddle bag for Dr. Pendergast, Carl and the remaining four members of his section of the posse were entering the southern portion of Oak Creek Canyon. The floor of the canyon had been well traveled by herds of cattle and horses and the occasional cavalry regiment over the past half century. The way was wide and mostly level. The five horsemen made good time as they rode north toward the mouth of Sterling Pass.

Carl was well pleased to be rid of Frank and Brooks. The town clerk was a bit of a greenhorn for all the fact that he'd spent most of his life in the west. To Carl's way of thinking Frank was a bit of a sissy. The mortician was another matter. Jefferson Brooks was plain creepy. It wasn't just that he spent his time handling dead bodies. Carl was willing to allow that someone had to do that and at least it was honest work. What he found most upsetting about Brooks was his appearance and his odd way of looking at you as if he was measuring you for a coffin with his eyes.

Things were looking up. The four men with him were good riders. Carl was confident of his own horsemanship, but Willard's ability to handle himself in the saddle was impressive. Sam, Jake, and Jesus were all seasoned horsemen. Sam knew the canyon well, and Jake and Jesus looked to be capable riflemen. Willard's shooting ability was an unknown factor, but the Winchester 1873 was a good gun and a reliable one. There was no question that they had Danny Lambert outgunned.

They were moving at speed up the canyon. Even with a bit of a head start and them waiting down near Steamboat Rock for about a half hour, it didn't seem likely that Danny could reach the point where Sterling opened into the canyon before them. If he was coming that way they would have Danny cut off and the marshal would be coming up behind him. Loaded down as he was with Charlie, Clayton, and the young Pendergast, it seemed to Carl that the marshal's units were not as strong as his own. He didn't know if Lars would be much use, but he'd taken a look at the old rifle the lumberman was carrying and guessed that the marshal was a mite short on good shooters. Marshal Hopkins was a fine marksman, but he'd have to count on himself if it came to any serious shooting. Carl was hoping to be in at the capture. He pictured himself directing his units and bringing down Danny. He was also a bit concerned about his horse with Danny riding him. He wouldn't want anyone taking a long shot and hitting Star instead of Lambert.

Sam was out in front for a change because this was familiar territory to him and he was leading the way so they could make more speed. Not all parts of the canyon were safe for all-out galloping, but here in the main cattle trail the land was beaten flat. At last he looked back and pointed off to his left. Carl could see the opening between two steep bluffs which must mark the opening of Sterling Pass. Sam slowed and waited for the other riders to gather beside him.

"That's the point where Danny will most probably be coming out," he told them. "If he's already come out we likely won't catch him, but I'll bet he's still picking his way through the badlands."

Carl had been up the main canyon several times, but Sam was the expert here. He acknowledged it now by asking, "If we make our way up Sterling Pass will he be able to slip by us?"

Sam considered the question. It seemed like he was running his mind over a mental picture he had of the winding pass. After a few seconds of cogitating he nodded to himself and delivered, what was for him a long and detailed account, "There are some places where a single rider who didn't want to be seen could leave the pass and detour around. If he did that while we were moving west along the pass we'd miss him. At one or two spots he could lie concealed in the high shelves of rock and wait for us to pass before rejoining the pass and coming on east." Sam let his eyes drift over the layers of twisted rock that bordered the trail and the ragged patches of Mormon Tea and Shrub Live Oak which clung to the cleft sections of the cliff face where moisture lay longer. Along the western ridge scattered patches of Velvet Mesquite provided a vestige of shade and Arizona Cliffrose eked out a living. Carl could imagine even now that they were observed from some hidden vantage point.

"If we move too far up the main track and he got behind us like that we might miss him completely," Sam concluded.

CHAPTER 190 DANNY

Danny had a feeling. Against all reason, he felt that there was someone, or something following him. He'd looked behind several times and watched for movement without spotting anything, but the feeling persisted.

There was nothing Danny liked better than lying in wait for someone and catching them unawares. He didn't want the same trick played on him and he sure as hell didn't fancy the idea of someone coming up behind him, secret-like.

He'd found some pools of water in the arroyo which ran between two of the large potholes. The horse had drunk its fill and he had slaked his own thirst. There was water at the mine and he felt he was on schedule to reach it before dusk. He was hungry, but he slipped a pebble into his mouth to hold him over. To augment whatever he'd be able to shoot later for an evening meal he gathered a few ripe red prickly pears from the paddle cactus. He was careful to roll them in the gritty sand to remove the spines and then wrapped them in his kerchief. Later he could peel them carefully.

As he topped the edge of the Brins Mesa he moved back from the edge and hobbled the horse. Carefully he crept back and settled to watch the dry arroyo back at the point he'd come along twenty minutes ago. He'd made an effort to leave plain tracks which went off to the west and then rejoined the arroyo two hundred feet or so further along. If there was anyone following they'd be sure to take an interest in that switch of track. Behind him the mesa lay open. If he saw something from here he could hightail it off toward Sterling Pass and arrive well before them. Once again he felt the lack of a rifle. From the edge of the mesa he had a view of the approach. If it were a single person or even two he could pick them off easily with a decent repeater. It would be no great feat to mortally wound a man at this distance, and Danny wouldn't be above killing their horses to stop them pursuing him either.

After counting to one thousand without any sign of pursuit, Danny was about to move on when he saw a movement at the far end of the open patch. As he watched a group of five horsemen moved out into the bare patch.

He could pick out the marshal and he recognised Larry riding along beside him. He easily identified Charlie Lee with his eastern gentleman outfit riding bolt upright in the saddle beside the bartender from the Horn. Charlie didn't count and the others were of little interest. If that was the whole posse he wasn't too concerned. He'd shoot Hopkins first and then Larry. The rest of them didn't amount to much. They'd scatter and run. He was starting to move back from the edge when he recognized the big bearded one at the back. That was the lumberman, Lief or Olig or some fool name like that. Well, what could you expect from a hick town like Sedona. Sedona, a fancy new name for a town that was still nothing but a bunch of red rocks.

They'd come upon the spot where he'd veered off the trail. They seemed a bit confounded by the tracks, even though he'd made them as noticeable as he could. Well, if that confused them they'd have a lot more trouble up on the mesa. The shale up here wouldn't take much of an imprint and he was going to pick up the pace more here too.

He considered trying a shot to pick off the marshal, but they were moving out of the bed of the arroyo now and he wouldn't get a clear shot in the scrub brush which had reared up a bit higher here near a source of water.

Danny slithered back from the edge, removed the hobbles and moved out toward the north. The horse seemed refreshed by the water and the short break. He should make good time to the mine. He wouldn't spend the night there. He'd enter on into the main canyon and head north before the yokels knew where he'd gone.

CHAPTER 191 MAIN ROAD SOUTH

Frank had set a slow pace for Jefferson and stayed close beside him in case another spell came on. Here on the main road Brooks seemed under control. The scant warmth of the day had passed and a light wind had picked up.

Jefferson kept telling Frank that he was feeling fine now and apologised for taking Frank away from the posse. The reality was that Frank was just as happy to be clear of it. He'd showed himself willing to go and that was enough. Let the others deal with the part that involved shooting.

They'd been moving at a gentle walking pace for the best part of an hour and were past the point where the two sections of the posse had split, when they heard a noise coming up behind them. Frank looked back and saw the stagecoach from Flagstaff bearing down on them.

They moved off a bit and Frank raised his hat and waved it in an attempt to get the driver to pull up. Generally the stagecoaches weren't too eager to stop out on the road, what with armed robberies being what they were, but the driver recognised the two men and brought the wagon to a halt a hundred feet or so past them.

The coach had to be carrying some cash or something of special value. There was an armed guard sitting up beside the driver. When Frank drew even with the window of the passenger compartment, he noticed that the gentleman seated inside had taken the precaution of drawing a handgun from his holster.

Frank had seen this driver a couple of times in The Horn and tensions relaxed when he explained that they'd been with Marshal Hopkins' posse when Jefferson had come over sickly.

"I wonder," Frank asked, "If you could give Jefferson a seat in the coach to get into town? I can ride alongside with the two horses."

The driver recognised the mortician as well and readily agreed. Then, as Jefferson was being helped into the seating area by Frank and the traveling gentleman, who had alighted expressly to be of service, the driver reached under his seat and pulled out a small parcel.

"I've got something right here for the marshal, Frank. Is there any chance you could get it to him?" the driver asked.

"What is it? Surely it can wait 'til he gets back tonight? He's up in the canyon by now. The posse split up into two groups and I was with the deputy. I'm not sure that I could even find the marshal now."

Frank argued. He was concerned about Jefferson and didn't fancy heading back into the line of fire either.

"I don't know for sure, but it was brought out to us by a dispatch rider just after we pulled out from Flagstaff station. It's marked personal and it comes directly from the Flagstaff marshal's office. There must be some urgency to it," the driver insisted.

Frank was torn. He really disliked the idea of letting down Marshal Hopkins, but Jefferson needed attention. He tried to remember this driver's name, but nothing came to mind.

"I came back because Jefferson here was taken poorly," Frank explained. "I can't just leave him to go back to town by himself. He needs to see Doctor Pendergast."

"Don't worry, he'll get there safe enough with me, Frank," the driver responded with surprising recall of Frank's name. "I'll be pulling right into town and I'll personally ensure that Mr. Brooks gets medical care."

Frank wavered. He remembered the driver better now. He knew he was considered reliable by most folk and he had even spent an evening chatting with Frank and Jefferson.

"You're most likely to find the town near deserted," Frank cautioned. "Charlie Lee has gone with the rest and taken the bartender. The saloon will be locked up."

The driver paused for a second and Frank flashed on his name; it was Paul, just like "Badger" Paul who had been shot by Danny. 'Funny how the mind works,' he thought. The connection of the saloon and the shooting had caused the name to pop into his head.

"Well, the blacksmith will be there sure enough. We're scheduled to change horses in Sedona, so he has to be there. Thomas Carter's a good man. I'll get Mr. Brooks to the doctor with his assistance."

"You go on back, Frank," Jefferson called out from his position on a seat inside the coach. "I'll be fine. Carter will be sure to help me if I need it."

Frank remembered Thomas Carter with Clive's limp body draped across his massive forearms. The smith was as gentle as he was strong. Jefferson would be in good hands and Frank would look a damn fool refusing to take what was apparently an important dispatch to the marshal.

"Alright, Paul," he said and reached a hand up to take the small package which was wrapped in brown paper and bound with twine.

The driver passed it down to him and Frank saw that it was clearly marked, 'Marshal Leroy Hopkins, Sedona, Arizona – deliver by hand'. It was surprisingly heavy and yet flexible.

The question of how to take care of Jefferson's horse came up. Since they were so close to town the guard riding shotgun agreed to ride it the rest of the way into Sedona. Frank drew back from the stagecoach and waved as it picked up speed and moved off toward town. 'Well, now you've done it,' he thought. 'You'll probably be shot for your troubles.'

CHAPTER 192 PROCTOR'S

Doctor Pendergast was standing next to Carter and looking down at the object the smith had found in the river. It was tarnished and still covered with some sediment from the creek bed, but he recognized it. In his hands he held the silver trophy which he had won when a medical student at some semi-serious fraternity game. It had been engraved, 'Champion' and had not been engraved then or later with his own name to indicate that he had won or for what competition it had been awarded.

Years later, the doctor had dug it out of a chest and donated it to be used for an annual local junior pageant which had been organized for the children of Red Rocks. It had been affixed to a base by Carter and a plate attached upon which the annual winner's name had been engraved over a period of almost thirty years. The most recent name, the last to be engraved, was that of Pearl Schnebly who had been awarded it at the 1905 dog and pony show. That plate with the list of names had come off, apparently been pried off by someone. The action, indeed the possibility of it happening, was beyond mysterious.

The young daughter of Carl and Sedona Schnebly had become enamoured of the shiny trophy which she had received with great fanfare. In her pride, she had kept it close by her bed and her mother had discovered her sleeping cuddled up to it on more than one occasion. When the child had been dragged to her death in a tragic accident later that year, the trophy had been buried with her, or so the doctor had thought. Here it was, resurfacing unaccountably from Oak Creek.

Carter explained how he had come across the trophy and described how a large rock had been jammed inside in an apparent attempt to weigh it down.

"How could it have got there, Doc?" Carter asked. "It was in the little Schnebly girl's arms when they closed the coffin at her funeral last year. I saw it there myself."

Doctor Pendergast had no ready answer. Some of the possibilities which occurred to him were so bizarre they smacked of madness.

CHAPTER 193 CARL'S COHORT

Carl considered his options. Marshal Hopkins and his units were following behind Danny and in effect driving him toward the portion of the posse which sat guarding the mouth of Sterling Pass. They could lie in wait for him here. As far as they knew he still had only a revolver with him. They had him well out-gunned.

But there was the possibility that Lambert would hole up somewhere and engage the marshal and his men in a shoot-out. If that happened the outcome was less certain. Marshall Hopkins had sent the best men with Carl and Sam.

Of the five men with Hopkins, four were townsfolk, and one of those, the doctor's son, could be considered a non-combatant. Brad had voiced his preference not to shoot, and Carl suspected that the combination of his lack of experience and his reticence to shoot anyone would render him of little value except to patch up the wounded.

Lars was an unknown. He was a big man, but big men make large targets. Carl had never seen him shoot that old rifle of his, and it looked about good enough for shooting at rabbits and hoping.

Charlie Lee was all display. Carl doubted there was much to back up his bragging about his fancy sidearm and rifle. The President might own the same gun, but Charlie was no Teddy Roosevelt.

Carl had taken note how little enthusiasm Clayton had for the manhunt. At the first sign of danger the bartender would duck down behind a rock and stay there. Carl had seen him do the same often enough in the saloon when a fight seemed about to break out.

That left only one potential asset for the marshal's combined units: the nominal unit leader Larry James. He was a cattleman and could ride well. Sam Schuerman seemed to set some store in him, but could he shoot?

Carl drew up at the entrance to the pass. He instructed Jake and Jesus to check the southern section of the opening for hoof prints heading out into the main canyon while he, Willard and Sam scoured the northern part of the mouth of the pass. He wanted to ensure that the rabbit wasn't already out of his hole, but he also wanted a chance to talk privately with Sam.

CHAPTER 194 LEROY'S COHORT

Larry was watching Charlie. He didn't trust Lee, never had. Sam thought he was harmless, but Larry had his suspicions that Charlie and Danny were two of a kind. Danny was more obvious about it and more direct, but neither one was to be trusted.

It was as if Danny Lambert were a sidewinder moving across the surface of the desert; he was deadly, but at least he looked deadly and gave a warning with his tail. Charlie looked harmless but Larry had seen the dark side of him on occasion. Charlie was like a flash flood in the desert. You didn't see it coming, but water could suddenly fill a dry arroyo. A narrow canyon could become a death trap for cattle and men alike.

If an armed confrontation with Danny took place, Larry was going to make sure Charlie was not behind him. More than one officer had been shot from behind.

The track they were following had suddenly turned left and climbed out of the arroyo they were traversing. Hopkins had taken the lead and at his instruction, Larry had held back the other men to let the marshal check out the change in direction. The abrupt detour made little sense. The path ahead led in the correct direction. Hopkins told him to keep a sharp eye up the trail ahead. It was just possible that Danny had spotted them and was setting up an ambush.

Not too far forward the terrain rose sharply to a mesa. The footing would be more solid there, but the prints would be harder to follow too. He scanned the edge of the mesa for a silhouette against the sky. The horizon was sharp, close, and empty.

Less than a minute later, Hopkins emerged from the brush. He was a scant 100 feet or so farther along the arroyo. The marshal examined the ground and motioned for the others to come forward but to keep quiet.

CHAPTER 195 CARL'S COHORT

Carl sent Willard on ahead with instructions to go to the north wall of the pass and work his way back checking for signs of someone exiting the pass on the way. As soon as Willard was off and searching, Carl signalled to Sam and drew up beside him.

"I wanted to ask your private opinion of Larry," he told the cattle boss.

Sam nodded appreciatively and responded, "He's a good man, Carl. I've been on many a drive with him and I trust him."

"That's good to hear. I assumed you must," Carl assured him. "What I really wanted to know is how good a shot he is with a rifle."

"Ah, well that's another thing, deputy. And it's funny actually. Larry's as good with a rope or a horse as any cowpoke I've ridden with. He can cut out a steer from a herd with no trouble and he can ride all day and all night too if he has to." He paused and then said with a wry smile, "But I wouldn't let him fire my last cartridge if it was a matter of bringing down some game or starving to death."

Carl winced to hear that. Larry might soon be in the position to take a shot at Danny while Danny was sitting on Star. Carl wanted the horse alive more than he wanted Danny dead.

"That being the case, Sam, I've got a suggestion and I'd like to hear your opinion."

* * *

The Artist wasn't all that happy about how things were going. The way Danny was being penned in he might just get himself taken alive. That wouldn't be good for a number of people.

* * *

Sam's opinion of the deputy had grown during this day. Instead of being all strut and feathers, Carl had shown some good leadership skills. He wasn't afraid to ask for advice and he asked men to do something rather than snapping at them. Now here he was being discrete and consultative. Seemed like a lot of people had underestimated Carl.

Carl outlined his suggestion to Sam. He was thinking of splitting the two units to leave one set of gunmen here to block the exit from Sterling Pass and taking the other up the pass to close on Danny and be prepared to aid the marshal's units by setting up a crossfire.

Sam thought about it and found himself agreeing.

"That sounds like a good idea, Carl. One or two men with rifles could cover the mouth of this here pass. The others might very well be needed by Marshal Hopkins if Danny goes to ground or sets up an ambush. Who you thinking of leaving behind?"

"I thought it best to leave Jake and Jesus. Of all of us they know the lay of the land around here least. Also, they seem to work well as a team," Carl told him.

Willard was working his way up close to them as Carl said this, so Sam just nodded and said, "Sounds like a plan."

* * *

Willard could see that the deputy and Sam had sent him off so they could speak in private. He wondered what they'd had to say, but figured he'd find out soon enough.

CHAPTER 196 PROCTOR'S

Doctor Robert Pendergast did not believe in the supernatural. He was a man of science. If the trophy which everyone believed had been buried with Pearl Schnebly had appeared in Oak Creek there were only two possible explanations. Either it had not been buried with the coffin or, and he hated to think this, someone had dug up the young girl's corpse and tossed the trophy aside.

He didn't want to raise the spectre of a grave robbing before talking to Jefferson Brooks. If anyone would know if the trophy had been buried with the young Schnebly girl or not, it would be Brooks. He was spared from having to respond to Thomas by the fortuitous clamorous arrival of the Wells Fargo stagecoach.

At the sound of hooves coming into town from the western end of the main street, Carter spun on his heel and cried, "Damnation, the stage is in and the horses aren't ready." Rather than mount up, Carter took off running at a good clip while leading the horse by the reins.

The doctor headed back into the house. He stuffed the small trophy into his medical bag which was sitting beside the hall coat tree. 'I'll deal with that later,' he thought.

The two women were still chatting away sixteen to the dozen and Clive was lying quietly enjoying the company and clearly feeling more himself.

Dr. Pendergast went over to check his patient's pulse and to peer into his eyes, but he had just placed his fingers on the lad's wrist and pulled out his pocket watch when there was the sound of a rider pulling up sharply in the drive and a moment later pounding on the door.

Fearing the worst, the doctor strode over to the door and pulled it open.

"Come on down to the stagecoach, Doc, Jefferson Brooks needs your attention," the horseman cried.

From behind him the doctor heard Doris Proctor's cry of surprise and Lily came rushing forward to discover what the emergency was.

"Who's been hurt? Was there shooting?" Lily asked.

"Who's been shot?" echoed Clive.

"Don't tell me Willard's been killed," Doris exclaimed raising her hands to her cheeks and staring wide-eyed at the doctor.

CHAPTER 197 LEROY'S COHORT

When the men of the posse had come up close to Hopkins, he pointed down at the hoof prints clear in the dry earth which formed the middle of the arroyo. "Our rider left the trail, moved through the rough part for a while and then rejoined the path," he said and waited for comment.

"Why would he do that?" Brad asked. "He must have had a reason to leave the path."

"Did he hide something or retrieve something?" Lars suggested.

"He didn't stop or dismount," the marshal told them. "The tracks are even and regular. He just turned into the bushes for a bit and then rejoined the trail." He waited to see if anyone had a suggestion.

"He knows we're on his trail, he was trying to lose us," Brad suggested.

"Not a very successful attempt if that's what he had in mind," Larry commented. He stood in his stirrups and looked on both sides of the arroyo. Low, but steep escarpments closed in on both sides. "No horseman would want to climb those banks without very good need, besides the easiest way out of here is up onto the mesa ahead of us." As he realized what he was saying he looked again up toward the edge of the mesa.

"Exactly," Hopkins confirmed. "He was up on the edge there watching us."

A stir of alarm ran through the others, but Larry just looked at the marshal and said, "Well, now we know for sure that he doesn't have a rifle."

CHAPTER 198 CARL'S COHORT

Carl gathered the men around him. They dismounted so that Sam could make a diagram in the dry earth. It was rudimentary, but it gave an idea of where they were and the path of Sterling Pass. Jake had consulted the map of Oak Creek Canyon back in the marshal's office and Jesus had been up the main canyon twice, but neither had a clear idea of the side passes and general layout surrounding them.

Carl explained his plan to leave the two of them to guard the mouth of the pass and reiterated his caution that if Danny did come riding out they should make every effort to avoid hitting Carl's horse, Star.

Willard seemed pleased to be going with Carl and Sam west along the pass in an attempt to cut off or corner Lambert.

Carl explained that if Jake and Jesus were needed up the pass he would fire three double volleys from his revolver. "If you hear that, move up to join us, but come carefully and keep your eyes open. I'll only use that signal if we've engaged Danny and we want your assistance. If the situation is stable we'll come back down the pass with Danny dead or alive."

"Got it," Jake responded for them both. "We'll hold this position until you signal for us or come back out."

A discussion ensued concerning where Jake and Jesus would station themselves and the signal the posse would give to indicate all clear and that they would be coming back down the pass. At Jake's suggestion both he and Jesus chose positions along the northern side of the opening. That way they could both track a rider's progress and fire without concern that they would be firing at each other.

"That's a good plan," Carl agreed. "My greatest concern is that we don't accidentally shoot one another," Carl explained and then added, "Or Star."

"I wonder who counts more, us or the horse?" Jake asked and everyone laughed including Carl.

CHAPTER 199 THE SMITHY

When Thomas Carter got back to the smithy he found that he had no cause for concern. Eddie Thompson had turned up in time to have the Wells Fargo horses ready for the exchange and had even brought his brother Andy to help out.

Eddie explained that when he'd turned up and found Carter still absent he'd called on his younger brother to assist him.

"I wasn't busy 'cause Mr. Lee's closed up the saloon and gone off with the posse, Mr. Carter," Andy explained. Then he seemed to think this was a good time to apply for future employment and added, "I can help out anytime at all. I know how to handle horses and all."

'These Thompson's are going to own this town and everything around here,' Carter thought.

The driver, Paul, explained that Jefferson had felt dizzy and Frank Green had asked to have him transported back to town by the stagecoach which happened to be passing.

"I promised Frank that I'd ensure Mr. Brooks got to see the doctor," Paul concluded. "Do you know where I could find him?"

"I just came from talking with him," Carter replied. "He's down at Mrs. Proctor's tending to her son."

"Mrs. Proctor has a son?" Paul echoed. "I didn't know she had a son. I've stayed at her place a few times 'cause it's more handy to the stagecoach landing, but I never saw a boy there."

Carter laughed at the confusion, "There have been some revelations lately, Paul. You've seen the boy right enough; he's my apprentice, Clive."

Paul seemed more confused than ever and looked over toward the two Thompson boys hard at work helping with getting the new horses into harness and taking the old team away to rub down, water, and feed.

"Those are my new helpers," Carter explained. "Never mind. You see to your stagecoach and I'll take Brooks down to see Dr. Pendergast."

Carter walked over to the landing stage where a gentleman with a tweed jacket, a bright red vest and a derby hat was standing next to Jefferson who was seated on a pressed back chair and looking paler than ever.

As Carter approached, the gentleman turned and offered his hand. "You must be Mr. Carter, the smith hereabouts. I've heard good things said about your work. I'm David Jones, reporter for the Coconino Sun, formerly the Skylight Kicker, formerly the Flagstaff Sun-Democrat." he declared in a telegraphic manner which brooked no interruption.

"Pleased to meet you," Carter managed and turned his attention to the pale-faced mortician. "How are you feeling, Mr. Brooks?" he inquired. Jefferson Brooks never looked bright and cheery, but at present he seemed completely drained.

"I'm just fine, Carter," Brooks managed. Despite his appearance his eyes seemed clear and he insisted on rising to his feet. "I just got a bit of sun stroke, I imagine. Frank was worried, but I feel fine now."

Carter glanced over at the reporter who was out of Jefferson's line of sight. Reporter Jones looked grim and shook his head in negation.

CHAPTER 200 DANNY

Danny moved quickly across the mesa, past the towering heights of Wilson Mountain on his right and turned east away from the Grassy Knolls and Corrals. Star was feeling refreshed and carried him quickly down into the crease which marked the start of Sterling Pass.

With the knowledge that he was being pursued, Lambert had motivation to reach the old mine as soon as possible. It occurred to him that he might hole up in the mine and count on them not being able to locate him and lose interest. Then he remembered that Larry was with the group. Larry might know about the mine and lead the posse to it.

He couldn't take the chance. If they trapped him there they could wait him out. His best plan was to use the old saddle he had there and equip himself with ammunition and the rifle. There were only six of them behind him. He could move east and if he got a chance he could set up an ambush and pick off Hopkins and Larry.

He had planned to arrive before dusk, but with the spur of the posse behind him, Danny reached the mine by early afternoon and busied himself gathering what he needed and loading it aboard the horse. In a few minutes he was remounted and on his way on down the pass.

CHAPTER 201 PROCTOR'S

Dr. Pendergast calmed everyone down finally and extracted a factual account from the Wells Fargo guard. He told Doris to wait with Clive while he went up to the landing stage where he had learned that

Jefferson Brooks would be waiting.

Lily insisted on going with him. The doctor suspected that she was eager to hear what news had come with Brooks about the posse and Danny Lambert.

They were halfway to The Horn when they met Carter returning with a shaky-looking mortician on his arm. Jefferson contended that he was fine, but all could see that that was far from being the case.

Rather than subject the shaken man to questioning out in the street, the doctor and Lily helped Jefferson to Proctor's while Carter returned to oversee his livery stable.

*   *   *

Doris met them at the door and they settled Brooks in one of the empty bedrooms on the ground floor. Doris had suggested moving a single bed out into the parlor near Clive, but the doctor had suggested that a darkened room would be preferable. He certainly preferred to have some time alone with Brooks. He had some questions for him which needed to be put privately.

*   *   *

Lily was unhappy to be unable to garner any news from Brooks, but Carter had told her that Frank and Jefferson had separated from the posse as a result of Jefferson's spell and that at that time nothing had been seen of Danny.

*   *   *

Clive had been brought up to date about the shooting in the saloon and the posse which had gone in pursuit of Lambert. Now he shared with Lily and his mother his suspicions that Charlie might have been involved in the attack on both Luke and himself.

*   *   *

Lily sat sunk in personal thoughts about Charlie Lee. He had always been fair with her. She had never known him to associate with Danny.

Now, however as she thought about it, she remembered that the card game which had resulted in Paul's death had been suggested by Charlie and Charlie had invited Danny to sit in. She mentioned the fact to Clive and Doris.

*   *   *

Doris expressed the opinion that she had never had any use for Charlie Lee and the news that he'd been collecting rent from Lars on land that had belonged to her late husband was confirmation of his grasping ways.

*   *   *

Dr. Pendergast returned to the parlor. His face was grim and his mouth set.

CHAPTER 202 CARL'S COHORT

Carl, Willard and Sam moved slowly up Sterling Pass. If Danny had intended to descend along this small canyon he might be anywhere ahead. They had to hope that they heard or saw him before he saw them.

The upper portions of the pass, below Vultee Arch, are open and rocky with high cliffs above on each side. It is steep all the way but the lower reaches are heavily forested with tall evergreens and wildflowers covering crests of soil gathered between strangely curved and molded rock formations which seem almost to be flowing glacier-like down the opening between the higher formations of sandstone.

Carl began to doubt his wisdom in entering the pass. Visibility was limited to a few hundred feet or less at times. Danny could already be concealed in these trees and lying in ambush.

He was moving in the lead with Willard and Sam close behind him when he heard Sam whisper, "There, up to the right." The deputy turned to look where Sam had pointed.

*   *   *

Sam's head exploded. His torso jerked back and Sam fell from the saddle. His body rolled slightly downhill and came to a stop against a tree trunk.

*   *   *

Danny lowered his rifle and reloaded. He peered past the broken cliff face which had concealed him from sight. He could see Sam's body where it sprawled in the dappled sunlight. Danny couldn't make out where the other two men were. Sam seemed to be dead. The body lay motionless. In an attempt to draw movement from the others, he fired off two more shots toward the still body with his sidearm.

The horse Sam had ridden had bolted up the steep passage and then slowed to an aimless wandering as quiet returned. The other horsemen had pulled in behind a small thicket concealing the far side of the narrow divide from sight. Lambert moved a bit to his right and could see a chestnut shape reflected in the sunlight. It was the back of one of the horses. There was no one in the saddle. A horse whinnied now again and one of the others responded. The deputy and the other man had disappeared in the underbrush. He'd have to be careful. He had his revolver, but was handicapped by his single shot rifle.

Danny moved soundlessly to his right to obtain a better view down into the lower passage. As he reached the first tree a voice called out to him, "Hey, Danny!"

CHAPTER 203 PROCTOR'S

Lily watched the old doctor. He seemed troubled, but when they had inquired about Jefferson Brooks the doctor had merely said that he would probably recover fine. Dr. Pendergast told them that the mortician had suffered an attack of brain fever from too much exertion and excitement.

"He just needs a bit of quiet in a dark place to settle down," Dr. Pendergast said. He turned to Clive and added, "I gave him some of that powder I gave you. How are you feeling now?"

Clive was much improved in the past hour or so. Lily had noticed his willingness to move his head about and his interest in hearing all about the shooting in the saloon and the pursuit of Danny. She had seen many a cowpoke look in worse shape after a night of hard drinking.

"I'm pretty sure I'll live," Clive responded. "That potion you gave me has taken away the headache. I just wish I could remember more of what happened. Will I remember in time, Doc?"

"You may recover some memory, but probably not everything. It's the body's way of protecting us to have us pass out and to lose short term memory of pain," he told Clive.

"Well, I reckon I've got you and Thomas to thank for helping me, Doctor."

"Carl was the one who found you, Clive. If you're handing out thanks be sure to include him."

"I'll do that for sure, Doctor," Clive said and made an attempt to sit up. As he did so he stopped himself and put a hand to his eyes as he settled back.

Doris moved over to the boy and cautioned him about not trying to hurry things. Lily thought of the old saying, 'a mother is a mother forever'.

While Doris fussed over Clive, Lily observed Dr. Pendergast. He had said that Jefferson Brooks would be fine too, but he seemed pretty worried about something. She suspected that there was something about the mortician's condition that he wasn't sharing with them. Well, she guessed doctors were a little like priests that way. They kept secrets about people and they even sometimes kept secrets from people. She had the doctor to thank for fitting her with a diaphragm to protect her from unwanted pregnancy. Without his help where would she be now? She would in all likelihood be pregnant and on her own. Probably she'd be worse off than Mrs. Proctor had been when Luke Proctor took off. At least Doris Proctor had a way to make a living and could leave Clive with her mother to raise; Lily didn't have anyone, leastwise anyone who could help. Her sister would consider the child as sinful as the life Lily led and shun them both.

*   *   *

While Lily was lost in a brown study, Dr. Pendergast was turning over what Jefferson Brooks had told him. Jefferson would be okay, at least as okay as he had ever been, but the secret that crazy old mortician had imparted to the doctor was one that would haunt Dr. Pendergast for many years.

CHAPTER 204 LEROY'S COHORT

Once they had gotten over the shock of having been so vulnerable, the men with Hopkins realized that Larry was right. If Danny had been armed with a rifle he would have shot at least one of them from the edge of the mesa where it commanded a clear view of the arroyo.

They moved quickly, but carefully up onto Brins Mesa. There was no one in sight, but when they examined the edge of the escarpment where it overlooked the position they had recently occupied on the arroyo, Lars spotted what he and the marshal agreed was evidence that they had been watched from that point by someone, probably Danny.

Lars pointed out how Danny's belt buckle had nicked the sandstone as he crawled forward to the edge and the point where he had scuffed the dusty surface while remounting. The marks looked to Brad like simple weathering of the rock, but both the marshal and Larry agreed with the lumberman's assessment.

"It sure looks like he's headed for Sterling Pass right enough, Marshal," Larry offered. "Up ahead you can see the hard drop-off of Mt. Wilson. The top end of the pass is just past that and off to the right."

Hopkins pulled out his watch and looked up at the angle of the sun, as if to confirm what the timepiece told him.

"I'd say we've got a few more hours of daylight. We'd better close on Lambert or he'll go to ground somewhere. I don't fancy spending the night out here waiting for him."

Charlie and Clayton had stayed in the saddle while the other four scoured the weathered sandstone. Now Brad and the others joined them and the marshal took the lead toward the point Larry had indicated.

CHAPTER 205 NORTH OF SEDONA

When the stagecoach carrying Jefferson had departed, Frank set to considering. There was little chance of him finding, let alone catching up with, Hopkins up Soldiers Pass and beyond. He had no idea which direction they would have gone from where the group led by Carl and Sam had left them. They'd be moving across rough ground unfamiliar to him and he'd probably get lost and eaten by a bear. 'I wonder if they'd name a mountain after me like they did for that fellow named something Wilson who became bear food. Probably not,' he thought.

On the other hand, even if they did, a mountain called 'Green' would just cause people to think of the color, so it wouldn't matter anyway. Besides, he would be dead.

Frank decided that it would do nobody any good him heading up into the wilderness alone and getting lost. At least he knew where Carl and that part of the posse were headed. The deputy had said they'd go to the mouth of Sterling Pass and wait there. It wasn't as if he knew where that was exactly either, but apparently it was on the main canyon route.

On balance, it seemed a better plan to head up behind Carl's section. He could deliver the package to Carl and let the deputy have the glory of getting it to Leroy Hopkins.

Having convinced himself that heading after the group he'd recently left was called for, Frank turned his horse's head back up the main road and set off at a good steady pace. He'd tucked the parcel into his saddlebag and he was feeling a bit lonely out here by himself. The sooner he caught up to the others the better.

CHAPTER 206 CARL'S COHORT

Willard and Carl were peering through the bushes hoping to catch sight of Danny Lambert. Willard looked back down the trail to where Sam 'Shoe' Schuerman lay face down in the dust. He had not moved since the bullet had taken him out of the saddle. If the two other shots had hit him, they had not caused him to move. His arms were flung out above his head and his legs lay twisted as he had fallen. It appeared as if he had made no attempt to break his fall from the horse. Was he dead? He looked dead.

"Do you think he's dead?" Willard demanded of Carl.

"Sam?" Carl asked and looked over toward the limp, puppet-like figure on the ground. "Looks like it. We will be too if Danny gets the chance. Stay focussed. Can you see him?"

Willard scanned the opposite side of the trail. There seemed a million places where Lambert could be. The rifle report, and two shots which sounded somewhat different, had echoed in the enclosed pass and been deflected by trees and sharp angles of sandstone buttresses. He had no idea where the shot had come from or if Danny was still there. Carl had taken charge and pulled Willard to this side of the bushes. The deputy seemed to think that Danny was opposite them in that maze of trees and rocks. Maybe Carl was right; maybe not; Danny could be waiting. or he could have snuck away.

"I can't see anything out there except trees," Willard responded, he spoke quietly so that only Carl, inches away, could hear.

As he started to turn back Carl took hold of his forearm and gave a slight squeeze to attract his attention. Carl placed his left index finger below his eye and then pointed with it off to the left. There was a brief change in the stream of light which fell upon the face of the large stone formation; a shadow had passed over the surface. Willard followed back from that point in the direction from which the slanting sunlight would have come. There was no human form visible, but at that point a growth of large trees blocked the view. The shadows, distorted though they were by the contours of the sandstone, stood out in crisp detail. Willard stared, but could see no further sign of movement.

Carl leaned over and whispered in Willard's right ear. "I'm going to call out to him. Keep your eyes fixed on the shadow about two feet up the rock at the left side of that shadow of the tree trunk." Willard nodded in agreement and fixed his eyes on the spot.

Carl straightened up a bit and raised his head and shoulders slightly. He took a deep breath and bellowed, "Hey, Danny!"

In reaction to the call, almost as if the sound had moved the shadow, Willard detected a widening of the silhouette of the trunk. He tugged at Carl's shirt sleeve and nodded demonstrably. Danny was there, behind that tree.

CHAPTER 207 SEDONA

While waiting for the stagecoach to be ready to continue to its next station, passengers were accustomed to visiting local stores or watering holes to break the tedium of their journey. Thompson's dry goods store was open for business but the saloon was closed up tight. Even the small diner associated with the hotel offered no possibilities today. The cook had wisely decided to make a partial holiday of the day and wandered off in search of wild herbs and berries.

David Jones had an eye for news stories. He had heard of the two killings which had enlivened the usually peaceful Sedona, and he meant to gather some information first hand. Jones had made a bit of a small splash in the big pond of news surrounding the earthquake in San Francisco earlier in the year. He had personally traveled overland and interviewed some of the people caught up in that tragic event. Jones had been involved in writing and reportage for as long as he could remember. His father had been a typesetter and printing assistant and as a youngster David had gone west to make his own way. Time had passed and he was still stuck in the rural fringes, but he was even now on his way to Tulsa to join the staff of The Oklahoman which had been taken over three years ago by Edward K. Gaylord. Jones had met Gaylord and been vastly impressed by the man's energy. He had been offered a position at the paper and was eager to take up the post. Jones had great hopes and he wanted to arrive in Tulsa carrying a fresh story with him.

Since the best spot in any town, the tavern, was closed, Jones headed off to interview the smith and maybe the local stable boy. He sought out the driver first and offered to stand the cost of a hot meal for Paul and the guard at Schnebly's Lodge.

Since Jones was the only passenger traveling to Tulsa today, and had indeed been the only one coming south from the railhead, the driver didn't seem opposed to extending that layover in Sedona for long enough to have a hot meal as the reporter's guest. The two men mounted spare horses and rode off toward the west. They were no sooner mounted and on their way when David Jones engaged Thomas

Carter in conversation.

"I hear tell you've had a spot of trouble in town lately," he began.

Jones was a wordsmith. He could draw details together to write a riveting and informative news story, and he could tell a good tale if it came to that, but he knew well that there was a time for listening. Despite the biblical saying from the time of Moses, you actually can make bricks without straw, just as you can cobble together a newspaper story without facts, but a story with factual information has more staying power. He intended to pick up some details.

"We have had more disturbance than we're used to, that's true," Carter agreed and went on with his examination of the harness and the placement of the horses. He seemed satisfied. The smith nodded his approval to the two young lads and told one of them to help his brother rub down the blown team and to make sure the horses all had hay and water. Then he realized that since the driver had decided to take a layover to have lunch there was no use leaving the team in harness. He called Eddie back and instructed him to get his brother to help unharness the team and put them in the paddock. They'd have a long journey before them once they got started.

Carter turned away from giving Eddie instructions and found the reporter waiting.

"You saw some of the troubles, I heard," Jones prompted.

"Not really," Carter replied and moved over to the forge to check the banked fire.

"Well, I heard you found your apprentice after he was attacked," Jones supplied as a lead-in.

"That was Deputy Munds," Carter corrected. "I was working at the forge here."

"But one of our stringers," here Jones consulted his notebook, "Andy Thompson, sent off a report saying you had carried the injured young man in your arms." He paused and looked at the taciturn smith and demanded, "Isn't that right?"

Thomas Carter looked as if Jones were speaking some foreign tongue. "Stringer . . . Andy Thompson . . . . I carried Clive out to the street right enough, but it's Dr. Pendergast you should be talking to," he corrected. "The doctor's over at Mrs. Proctor's right now looking after both Clive and Jefferson Brooks. He's the one who examined Luke Proctor's body after he was found dead." Thomas Carter picked up a pair of snipes and examined their edge. He looked Jones in the eye and said, "If you wait around the marshal should be back soon enough. He'll be able to tell you the rest."

"There was a shooting in town too," Jones persisted. He consulted his note pad and added, "Some cowboy named Dan Lambert shot a Wells Fargo man. You know anything about that?"

"That happened over in the saloon," Carter said with a glance up toward the general direction of The Horn. Jones knew a dead end when he'd reached one. By the set of the smith's jaw he could see that he'd learn little more here.

Jones considered asking the smith if he could tell him about the whereabouts of Andy Thompson, but he'd noted the name Thompson's Dry Goods over the general store. It seemed like that might be more fertile ground. However, before talking to the stringer and risking a shared byline, he'd like to see what he could learn from Dr. Pendergast. Perhaps the good doctor would be more forthcoming.

CHAPTER 208 CARL'S COHORT

"Here's what we'll do," Carl told Willard. "I'll try to involve him in some sort of communication. At some point he'll either make a dash out of where he's tucked in behind those trees, or he'll try to pick us off." Carl waited for Willard to indicate he understood and then continued, "Either way, we may get a chance to shoot at him."

Willard checked out the tree trunks. There were trees along the steep hills, but none between them and the point where Danny was concealed. The distance separating Carl and Willard from their position crouched behind bushes and Danny's trees was only about 200 feet away. It was not that far for a rifle shot if you had a clear target. Unfortunately there was a problem with Carl's plan.

"I don't have a gun," Willard said simply.

Carl rounded on him in surprise. He took in the empty handed lumber assistant and then sought out Willard's horse grazing contentedly a hundred feet or more uphill. He could see Willard's rifle. It was stuck in the scabbard of his saddle. The other horses were just as far away and only Willard's had a rifle with it. Sam had been riding with the rifle in one hand, as had Carl. He turned toward Sam's body and saw that Sam's rifle had fallen with him and lay in the dust a yard or so uphill of where his corpse had come to rest against the small tree.

There was no point in recriminations now. Carl considered the options and decided that he was probably a better shot than Willard but that it would be good to have them both blasting away at Danny if he showed himself. One of them could try to get to Sam's rifle, but that would likely result in one more of them lying dead. 'Don't blame your tools,' he thought. 'Use what you've got.'

"Okay, here's the plan," he said. He wanted to encourage Willard. A happy shooter is a better shooter he reasoned. "You take my rifle and I'll use my sidearm. If Danny makes a break for it he'll most likely move uphill. There's closer cover that direction and he's probably left his horse, my horse," he corrected, "Tethered up that way."

Willard took the rifle Carl passed to him and nodded vigorously.

"Set your sights on the edge of the tree about three feet up. If he shows himself it will probably be there. But be prepared to shoot near the base of the tree in case he stretches out to fire at us instead."

Willard lay along the dry earth and held the rifle up to sight along it. With his elbows braced and his cheek lying along the stock he presented as small a target as possible. He realized that Danny might be shooting back.

When he saw that Willard was in position, had racked a cartridge into the chamber, and had his sights fixed on the agreed starting point, Carl steadied his revolver with both hands and prepared to call out. He remained kneeling. He would not gain much by lying down with a handgun and he wanted to be ready to react to whatever Danny's response was.

"Come on out Danny, we've got you surrounded," he called out. Even he thought it sounded melodramatic, but what the hell.

The reaction was quick and furious. A rifle bullet ripped through the foliage near where they lay concealed and then it was followed by two more shots from the other side of the trees. 'Damn,' Carl thought. 'It sounds as if there are two of them.'

Willard had fired off two answering shots, but Carl was still searching for a definite target. The smoke from the second two shots hung in the air to the right of the tree, the downhill side. But he suddenly picked up movement uphill. Sure it was Danny, he snapped off two quick shots before the figure plunged into the thicker brush and vanished.

CHAPTER 209 LEROY'S COHORT

Hopkins gathered the men around him to prepare their next step. They had topped a small rise and could see the descent into Sterling Pass lying before them. According to Larry the pass itself was only a couple of miles long, but the lower section was bounded by steep and irregular cliffs and was fairly densely forested in spots. It was a perfect place for an ambush. They would have to go carefully and scan ahead.

As they began to move down the open area, Lars called out. He had found a few scrapings in the loose shingle which coated the rock-strewn hillside. He suggested that Danny may have moved off the main pass and off to their left. Further investigation in that direction led them to some clear indications that someone had recently climbed across the northern gradient and into an area of light brush. There they found an opening which, although narrow at the surface, widened into a primitive excavation. The cave was not completely natural. It had been enlarged by some prospector some time ago in search of the Eldorado of legend.

Lars had demonstrated some good tracking skills without which they might well have missed this old mine. Hopkins and Larry were both good at tracking, but Lars seemed to come to it naturally and had put his skill to good use to help feed his family. The mine itself was camouflaged by some bushes and a large rock which seemed to have been moved at great effort to conceal the opening. A lot of the small-time miners had justifiable fear of claim jumping and worse action which threatened their claim and their life.

When they entered the narrow shaft they could see that the mine had not been operational for a long time, but that it had been used by both animals and at least one human in recent times. Some of the dry soil had been disturbed within the last hour or so exposing moist sections which would dry quickly in the arid Arizona air.

It seemed that Danny had a little hideaway. They found some empty cartridge boxes and signs that Danny had come here and left again in a hurry. The boxes were for two calibers. It seemed likely that Danny Lambert now had himself a rifle as well as his six-gun, and plenty of ammunition.

They spent very little time examining the mine once they were sure it was empty. Leroy was checking his saddle and bridle prior to mounting when the crack of a rifle shattered the silence. The report of the single rifle shot echoed up the pass. The posse members froze in their steps to listen for the sound of further shooting.

"Could be a hunter," Larry ventured, "But it sounded as if it came from down in those trees somewhere."

Leroy trusted Larry's judgement as to the source of the sound. He hadn't been able to place it himself but likely it involved Danny in some way. Most trouble did. He ordered the men to mount up. If Carl's group had made contact with Lambert, they would want some back-up.

They had just started to move back toward the main trail down the pass when the sound of a flurry of shots from that direction broke across them.

"Those were rifles and at least one handgun," Larry judged.

"Move out," Hopkins directed. "I want you to move carefully, but keep up. Move in units. Clayton, and Charlie stay near Larry; Brad and Lars, you're with me. If we come under fire get down, otherwise we'll move together and dismount only if we have to," he directed.

The men all sensed the urgency and responded immediately without comment. The excitement of the moment overrode even Clayton's misgivings.

Almost as if they knew what they were doing, the party of men moved in order down the main pass between towering sandstone cliffs buttressed by steeply tapered hillsides which were increasingly dotted with trees as they moved down toward the forested lower reaches. The marshal's unit led the way. They went on at a brisk walk, almost a canter, which was about all the terrain would allow and every man's eyes swept the passage before him.

*   *   *

The Artist was pleased the shooting had started. When guns go off people die. He planned to make sure that Danny was one of those lying dead when the shooting stopped.

CHAPTER 210 SEDONA

David Jones knocked politely at Mrs. Proctor's side door. If his information was correct he would find one of the victims, one of the casualties, and a major witness to Dan Lambert's violent rampage here. He liked the term, violent rampage. He saw it as a front page headline with his byline below it.

The door swung open and Jones found himself facing a man who looked somewhat familiar. Jones had a good memory for names and faces. He put name to face now and remembered that this was the doctor who had given such insightful information at a coroner's hearing in Flagstaff.

Jones wasn't a hand shaker. He'd learned early in his career that one left oneself open for a fist to the face standing with your best hand forward and your jaw unprotected and jutting out. He smiled winningly and spoke warmly instead. "You're looking good, Doctor. You must be taking as good care of yourself as you do of your patients."

"Hello, David," the doctor responded. "I hear you were kind enough to assist my most recent patient."

"I just happened to be there," Jones replied. "I hear times are turbulent in Sedona. Something to do with a Dan Lambert," he continued invitingly.

Doris Proctor had come up behind Dr. Pendergast and now invited David Jones into the house. The reporter made the acquaintance of

Doris, Lily, and Clive and inquired about the wellbeing of Jefferson Brooks before accepting a cup of tea from Lily's hand and a gingersnap which Doris Proctor brought in on a tray.

"I hear you were attacked by this Dan Lambert?" Jones queried Clive and waited.

"I can't rightly say," Clive responded. "I don't seem to recall what happened."

Jones turned his attention to Dr. Pendergast and sensed that the doctor was not willing to venture an opinion. Rather than press where pressure would not avail, he directed an inquiry toward Lily.

"Did you see this Dan Lambert at all, Miss? From what I heard he shot the driver and rode right down the main street on his way out of town."

"I knew Danny Lambert well enough, Mr. Jones," she replied with a frankness which surprised Jones. "I work out of The Horn. Lambert was a regular drinker there and I was in the saloon when he shot Paul."

Since he had learned that people normally like to speak about themselves and are often prone to exaggerate their role in any 'event', Jones waited for Lily to continue. When she seemed content to leave it at that, he tried to elicit a comment from her or anyone else by leaning back and declaring, "Well, I know Marshal Hopkins by reputation. Likely as not he'll bring Lambert back for trial."

"Then maybe we'll find out if he killed my father too," Clive responded.

"Your father!" Jones exclaimed. "Was Paul your father?"

The flood gates of explanation and information opened with that comment. Although Dr. Pendergast contributed little to the conversation which followed, half an hour later David Jones had what he believed would lead to a series of articles. He consulted his watch and decided that he had enough time to make contact with the stringer for the Coconino Sun. It would be good to put a face to the name, and it occurred to him that it would be good to have a contact in Sedona. Maybe he could interest the fellow in being a supplier of news to The Oklahoman as well, or in place of the Sun.

"Dr. Pendergast," he said as he rose to depart. "I'd like to look up a man who lives here in Sedona, but I don't have a contact address for him. His name's Andy Thompson. Is that the same person who runs the dry goods store?"

The doctor exchanged a mischievous look with Doris Proctor who had come forward to show the reporter out. "That's the right family," he replied, "But Andy Thompson is a young member of it."

Jones expressed surprise. "He can't be that young," he insisted. "The Andy Thompson I'm looking for has been a stringer for the Tulsa newspaper for more than a year now."

Dr. Robert Pendergast let his smile broaden until it looked fit to split his cheeks. "I think you'll find that the Thompson clan is entrepreneurial far beyond their years. Andy Thompson is thirteen years old, going on twenty. You'll find him working now with his brother Eddie, at the livery stable." He paused and then added, "That is, if they haven't made an offer to take it over from Thomas Carter and run it themselves."

CHAPTER 211 CARL'S COHORT

"Did you get him?" Willard cried out. He was excited. The thrill of firing at a human target had overcome any fear he might reasonably have had of being hit himself. The action had taken less than three seconds, and yet he sensed the immensity of the event.

Carl was peering toward the brush into which Danny had vanished. "Can't say," he said out of the corner of his mouth. "Might have."

Willard was pretty sure that he had missed Danny. His first shot to the right of the tree was late; Danny had already changed direction and ducked back. The second shot had been on one of the trees. Willard imagined he had seen it hit and peered at the trunk now to see if he could make out a scar in the bark where it would have entered.

He had enjoyed the excitement. He wished he had been the one to bring down Danny. Well, there was still a chance; he and Carl were the only ones in shooting range and they had Danny on the run.

Then Carl mentioned Sam and spoiled the mood. Willard had nothing against Sam, Fact was Sam seemed a likeable sort. It was too bad he got shot, but it was a far cry better than lying there dead yourself.

"Cover me," Carl told him. "I'm going to check on Sam. If you see anything move up there just fire away at it. None of our group will have made it down here yet."

"They will have heard the shots," Willard pointed out. "That should bring them this way in a hurry."

"The marshal's no fool," Carl countered. "They'll come on alright, but they'll be careful and keep an eye out. We know where Danny is now. We don't want to have him slip away."

Carl took a quick look around and started moving down toward Sam's body. Sam hadn't moved as far as Willard could tell, but he couldn't watch Carl and keep his eyes on the patch of brush where Danny might lie concealed. It occurred to Willard that this might be his moment. He imagined Lambert emerging from the thicket, guns blazing, and he, Willard Wright, the only thing between Deputy Munds and certain death.

CHAPTER 212 EAST END, STERLING PASS

Down at the mouth of the pass, Jake and Jesus heard the shooting and had discussed the number and pattern of shots and agreed that the shooting was too sporadic to be a signal and too light to represent the presence of the rest of the posse.

"Carl's group must have flushed Danny," Jake suggested.

"Yeah, but the shooting's stopped now, so either he's dead or he's run off. He may be headed our way," Jesus agreed.

They settled into position and prepared themselves for the sight of horse and rider emerging into the open at a gallop. If they were lucky they'd take Danny by surprise. If he wasn't expecting an ambush he'd be leaning forward over the horse's neck and trying to make speed as he moved out into the open canyon pursued by the posse, or at least by Carl, Sam and Willard.

They were still waiting several minutes later when Jesus looked south down the main canyon and saw a lone rider approaching at a gallop. He tugged at Jake's dustcoat and they watched the horseman draw nearer.

"That's Frank," Jake exclaimed. "What's he doing back, and in such a hurry?"

There had been no more sound of conflict from up Sterling Pass and if Danny was coming down the pass he was doing it at a walk. 'He might do that if he's killed all three men,' Jake supposed. Since that seemed unlikely and was not a comforting thought, he didn't mention the supposition to Jesus. They just sat quietly as Frank rode northward.

When it looked as if Frank might ride on by without noticing them, Jake stood up and waved his hat to attract attention. Frank saw him right away and slowed his progress before swerving towards them.

Jesus motioned to Frank to come right over to them.

Frank drew up, dismounted and looked around as if surprised to find Jake and Jesus alone.

"Where are the others?" he asked. "I've got a parcel for Marshal Hopkins."

CHAPTER 213 DANNY

Danny was pissed. It was lucky he'd seen those three before they saw him. He might have walked right into it. As it was he'd been able to bushwhack them instead. It was a shame he'd only killed one of them. With a proper rifle he could have had all three.

Now he had a problem.

There was a chance he could pick off the other two and acquire one of their rifles. Trouble was he had to do something quickly. The sound of the shots would have carried a long ways. He knew that it was only a matter of time before the men behind him moved up to surround him. If he waited for that he was a dead man.

The horse he'd stolen in town was tethered fifty feet away up the pass. The saddlebags had extra ammunition and a bit of pemmican. Even if he left the horse he'd want to take the saddlebags. They'd be heavy for what he had in mind, but he'd need them sooner or later.

The two he'd pinned down would think twice before venturing up this way. But since the ones behind him might hurry on toward the shots it would be best if he moved out right away.

Without looking back Danny crept up through the trees. He found Star and unhooked the saddlebags. They didn't feel too bad over his shoulder now, but he knew they'd be a bit of a burden on the hillside.

He considered killing the horse. That would rile up the deputy some and be a payback for the trouble these lawmen and make-believe deputies were causing him. He reached for his handgun and hesitated with his hand on the grip.

It was a bad idea, he realized. They'd hear the shot and have a better idea of where he was. He untied the horse and left it. When it realized it wasn't tethered it would wander off, probably downhill into the bracken. That might help confuse them and put them off his trail. If he could stay out of sight until darkness, he ought to be able to slip away.

Danny snugged his gun into the holster and moved uphill. He steadied the saddlebags with his left hand to keep them from snagging on a tree branch. He was starting to feel the strain, but the sunlight was coming down at a definite angle now. He needed to get clear and stay that way for a few more hours.

He was running out of options, but he had something going for him: desperation. The ridge that joined the heights of Sterling Peak to the Vultee Arch highlands formed the north wall of Sterling Pass. The ridge was steep, there was no way you could get a horse over it short of carrying it, but it wasn't very wide. A man on foot could scale the heights and descend into a pocket which was separated from Oak Creek Canyon all the way north by an extension of the Sterling Ridge. That pocket valley connected to the west with a passage which would allow him to reach Buzzard Springs. It wasn't a route he would normally choose to take, but it sure beat hanging, and he didn't think any posse would be up to following him there.

CHAPTER 214 PROCTOR'S

After the reporter left, Lily declared that she would leave so that Clive could get some rest. Despite his much recovered state, he was clearly in need of some quiet time. Dr. Pendergast went back into the ground floor bedroom to look at his other patient, and Doris started to gather up the dishes. Lily began to help her, but Doris insisted that she could manage easily enough.

"In some ways today seems like a day off," Doris exclaimed. "Usually I have more to do than sit around chatting and drinking tea."

Lily took her leave of Doris and Clive and passed out into the afternoon sunshine. The day had turned out fine. She began to think of the posse. 'Where would they be now?' she wondered. Specifically she wondered about Jake. He seemed a good man. His occupation must take him all about the country she supposed. She was probably foolish thinking that she was anything special to him. In a few days he'd be gone back east and her life would go on. Better not to go having foolish dreams.

As she passed the smithy she looked in the open door. Carter was nowhere to be seen, but that reporter, Jones, was over near the harness rack at the back deep in conversation with Andy Thompson.

Lily mounted the wooden steps leading to the general store. Violet Thompson was rearranging the shelf goods at the back of the store and looked up in anticipation of a customer. The street was quieter than usual today. Most folk seemed to have taken advantage of a chance to turn their attention to personal matters around their homes or, like Carter, had gone off into the nearby countyside to hunt or fish.

"Good day, Miss Lily," Violet greeted her. "It's a fine day today and a quiet one. Can I be of service?"

"I was wondering if your father was about, Vi. I'm thinking of putting in a special catalog order," Lily replied.

"Dad's gone out to Schnebly's with some supplies," Violet replied. "But, I can help you. I'll just get the catalog."

While Violet was going to the back of the store for the catalog, Lily stood by the front door and saw the Wells Fargo driver and guard ride up to the smithy. David Jones walked out to greet them while Thomas and the two young Thompson boys began to harness the team into their stations.

Jones saw Lily watching from the door and tipped his hat. Lily nodded in return. Jones seemed to be considering for a moment and then walked towards her with a determined look in his eye.

He climbed the step and peeked in the door of the store to ensure he and Lily were not going to be overheard.

"I spoke with young Andy Thompson," Jones told her. "He's a bright lad and sure to make something of himself. He's got a bit of a sense of humor too it seems. I asked him if he was going to become a journalist and he told me that from what he'd seen there's not much money to be made by writing, or publishing." Jones paused and smiled in a self-deprecating way. "He may be right at that. My father wanted me to go into the legal profession and join him, but I wanted to become a famous reporter, and here you see me, still trying."

"Maybe being happy is more important than being famous," Lily suggested.

"That's probably true too, Miss Lily. In a sense that's what I wanted to talk to you about before I get on that stagecoach and go on chasing my dream," Jones told her and turned serious.

"Young Thompson told me that there's a Pinkerton Agent in town, name of Jacob Witherspoon."

"I didn't know that was common knowledge," Lily replied.

"Well, it seems young Thompson is uncommonly good at getting information," Jones said and then added, "Point is the boy also told me that you and Witherspoon seemed pretty friendly."

Lily wasn't surprised by that being known. Sedona is about as small as a small town gets, and she and Jake had not hidden their friendship. She waited to hear what avuncular advice David Jones had for her.

Jones seemed uncharacteristically reticent to speak, almost at a loss for words. Then he realised that the stage was getting ready to depart and blurted out, "The thing is, I know Jacob. He's my cousin by marriage. His brother married my aunt's second daughter. So he's my second cousin once removed, or something of that sort. Anyway, I know he's a good man and you seem a nice young lady. Please say hello to him for me, and let him know I'm going to be in Tulsa at The Oklahoman for the foreseeable future."

The driver was climbing up on his perch in preparation to depart and Jones hurried off to climb inside.

As the stagecoach made a wide turn and picked up speed heading out of town, Jones waved from the window. Lily waved back and mused on how long it had been since anyone had described her as a 'nice young lady'.

CHAPTER 215 CARL'S COHORT

Carl was back beside Willard in less than a minute. His report was short and terse. "Sam's dead alright; here's his rifle." He passed Sam's rifle over to Willard and took back his own.

"Nothing's moving out there. Do you think he's gone?" Willard asked.

Carl stared across the open ground between them and where they'd last seen Danny Lambert. The foliage was fairly dense and an almost solid wall ran up the north side of the pass. Well, that side would get the most sun and at the bottom whatever run off there was would collect, he reasoned. Whatever the reason for the thick underbrush, it meant they had no way of knowing if Danny had pulled back up the pass behind the trees or if he was still waiting out there for a chance to pick them off.

While he was scanning the trees he caught a movement out of the corner of his eye. Willard was raising his rifle to his cheek. Carl looked in the direction Willard was aiming and felt his heart almost stop.

There was something moving through the trees. It was something big. Carl threw his arm out and drove the barrel of Willard's rifle upwards just as he fired.

"What the . . . ?" Willard cried out and turned on Carl who had grabbed the rifle barrel with his right hand and was pulling the gun from Willard's grasp.

"That's Star," Carl exploded. "You almost shot my horse."

*   *   *

Hopkins, less than 500 yards west of Carl and Willard pulled up at the sound of the single shot and waited for more. When nothing followed, he said, "I think we need to go on foot from here on. That was very close."

*   *   *

Danny was even closer to Carl and Willard. In fact, the shot came close to hitting him.

He was less than 100 feet up the steep sandstone escarpment, and he was finding it slow going. He wondered for a second if he'd been spotted and someone was drawing down on him.

*   *   *

Down at the mouth of the pass, Jake, Jesus, and Frank were discussing whether it would be possible to get the package to Hopkins. They had just decided that however important it was it would have to wait, when the single rifle shot cut though the air.

CHAPTER 216 GENERAL UNCERTAINTY

Brad was starting to wonder whether he was cut out to be a detective. His sole contribution to this manhunt thus far had been finding a piece of horse shit by the side of the path. Even then it had been Larry and the marshal who had deduced the significance of the scat and decided on a course of action based upon that deduction.

Perhaps he was more cut out to be Sherlock's companion narrator, Dr. Watson. True Watson seemed a bit thick-headed, and he was always coming to faulty conclusions while Holmes gathered the clues and ultimately revealed the solution to the mystery, but it wouldn't be much of a story without Watson, would it?

When the rifle went off Brad was caught daydreaming and snatched back to the reality of the situation. This was no fictitious tale bound in leather to be enjoyed at leisure by the fireside. They were on the trail of a dangerous felon who had killed in cold blood and would kill again if he got the chance.

*   *   *

Lily was wondering if there was the possibility of a normal life after being a working girl. Lillie Langtry, after whom Lily had named herself, had been in effect, a working girl. The difference was that that Lillie had relationships with royalty. Lillie Langtry had gone on to become a famous stage actress and even a Lady of the British aristocracy while Lily, as she had suggested to David Jones, would be content to be happy.

*   *   *

Danny wondered what they were shooting at, since he had decided that they weren't shooting at him. A nasty suspicion crept into his mind and he smiled to think of it. Maybe that stupid deputy had shot his own horse. That would serve him right.

*   *   *

Dr. Pendergast was wondering how he could broach the subject of the silver trophy with Jefferson Brooks without seeming to be accusing him and causing him to become over-excited. But the puzzle nagged at him. He couldn't see Brooks taking the cup out of the child's coffin merely to throw it in the river, but surely the mortician must know something about it.

*   *   *

Jake was becoming uneasy. He wondered if Carl and the other two were even now pinned down and needing assistance. As far as he knew the other section of the posse could be miles away. He and Jesus, and of course Frank too, might be sorely needed. There had been agreement on a series of shots fired to signal them, but what could be going on up there?

*   *   *

The Artist was wondering how he could get himself close enough to Danny to kill him. Even if he did succeed, there was one other problem which might be best solved now also.

CHAPTER 217 PROCTOR'S

Jefferson Brooks seemed to have recovered his normal moribund demeanor. His eyes were melancholy, but clear; his skin had resumed its customary deathly pallor; and his speech was morose, but intelligible. Dr. Pendergast was more interested in the health of his patients than in their general attractiveness, but he was well aware that Jefferson's general appearance suggested Death only slightly warmed over.

He supposed there was no time like the present to ask Brooks about the silver trophy Carter had fished out of the creek. It would be natural to inquire at the first opportunity rather than wait to spring it on him. The doctor also suspected that he would get the most frank response if he asked now.

He had just finished taking the mortician's pulse and still had his fingers across the blood vessels which carried what passed for blood through Jefferson's veins and arteries. The doctor remembered reading about the theories of humours of the blood which preceded the modern understanding of the circulatory system and wondered what an early medical practitioner would have made of Jefferson Brooks. Probably they would have suggested that he had too much bile.

His medical bag was sitting open on the dresser. Dr. Pendergast reached over with a free hand and extracted the trophy as he said casually, "I came across this today. Does it look familiar?"

*   *   *

He emerged twenty minutes later and encountered Mrs. Proctor carrying a glass of water across to Clive.

"Would you like a cup of tea, Doctor?" Doris asked with a bright smile. It seemed that the experience of having almost lost her son had somehow made his presence more precious and allowed her to enjoy the simple act of caring for him.

"Thank you, Mrs. Proctor," the doctor replied. "Between the pie, and cookies, and copious amounts of tea I've consumed today, I won't need to eat for a week," he told her and returned her cheerful smile with one of his own.

"You seem in better spirits now than you were earlier. I know Clive is feeling more his old self. How is poor Mr. Brooks?"

"He's coming along fine now. I'm just going to give Clive a little look over, but I agree with your diagnosis, Mrs. Proctor. He'll be back at work before we know it."

Mrs. Proctor hesitated and then said, "What about your own son, Doctor? You must be worried about him with all that's going on."

"Truth is I am a bit concerned. Danny Lambert is a nasty piece of work. What causes me to be more concerned than I would normally is the good news Brad brought with him when he came west."

"Good news causing concern? What could that be, Doctor?"

"Oh the news itself caused no worries, only joy," he told her with a smile. "It's just that Brad will have more responsibilities. He and Alice are presenting me with a grandchild."

Before Doris could properly react, they were distracted by a call of pain from the sitting room.

CHAPTER 218 LEROY'S COHORT

As soon as they had dismounted, Hopkins made a fateful decision. It seemed best to him that a portion of the posse proceed on foot to investigate the shooting. He suspected that Carl and Sam's units were up ahead and that they had made contact with Lambert. They might appreciate some additional firepower if they had Danny pinned down. Coming down the pass his men might be able to set up a cross fire and force Danny to surrender. He'd prefer to have no one injured, including Lambert. Let the courts make sure he was treated properly. At the same time, he didn't want to chance having Lambert get by them and out into the open again, especially now that they knew he had a rifle. Out in the badlands a man with a rifle could find plenty of points from which to ambush pursuers.

The horses would be left here while a group of the men proceeded on foot. That meant that someone needed to stay back to guard the horses and raise an alarm if Danny got by the advance party. The section of the pass which was passable on horseback was narrow; the group going forward could seal that off. Likewise, two men with rifles stationed here could prevent a horseman escaping. What concerned Leroy was that Lambert might skirt by them on foot and steal one, or all, of their horses. He needed his best guns up front and two armed non-combatants left behind. The choice seemed clear.

"Brad. I know you don't want to shoot anyone, but I need two people to stay here and guard our mounts. Are you willing to use your rifle to keep Lambert away from them and keep him from escaping?"

'This was it,' Brad thought. These men were watching him and would judge both him and his father by his response. The promise he had made to himself on choosing medicine was not as simple as many might think. The Hippocratic Oath is no clear guidance, but rather a traditional promise to behave morally. He had never had doubts that he would kill to protect his family and himself. He believed in acting for the greater good, and this seemed one of those cases.

"I'd prefer not to hurt anyone, Marshal. But I'll use my gun if Lambert attacks us," he replied. All the men had been waiting for his answer. He could sense the release in tension.

Hopkins merely accepted the statement and said, "Okay. Clayton, I'd like you to stay here with Brad. If either of you see Danny Lambert, fire off a shot right away. If you have to, take him down. If we hear you shooting we'll come back to help out." He paused and added, "No one wants to see Carl's horse shot, but Lambert needs to be stopped."

Brad and Clayton nodded in agreement. Hopkins guessed that both would be better left out of the front skirmish line.

The horses were tethered and Hopkins moved forward with his best guns, Larry, Lars, and Charlie. 'Charlie may be no great marksman,' Hopkins thought. 'But that big gun of his will be noticed. Might even shake up Danny.'

CHAPTER 219 DANNY

The loose shingle along the steep northern side of the upper regions was unstable. Danny was forced to move slowly and test each step before shifting his way along it. Any rock dislodged would slide down the rock face and betray his position. He used his rifle butt as a climbing stick, but moving up the slope with the saddlebags was proving awkward. He needed his hands free to move crablike across the uneven surface.

He could hear noises from below and assumed that the trailing party had caught up. He was out of sight for the moment, but he could see down into the pass through large gaps in the foliage and knew that he might be spotted by someone from below. He had to get out of sight. To do that, he needed to climb higher. The sun had moved lower, but there were still a few hours of daylight ahead.

As he crept to his left, across a section of stone worn into jagged teeth by the wind, his right heal crunched off a chunk and he had to hold it in place until he could retrieve the broken piece and set it on a flat surface. He scanned the slope ahead for a stable route upwards and saw that any movement across the broken bits which scattered the possible routes would lead to dislodgements. It would be difficult to climb higher in that direction without causing a rock slide which would give him away. He examined the hill back to the east and decided that it looked more secure. Carefully choosing firm footing, he reversed his direction and moved toward a crease in the rock that appeared promising.

He had only moved a few feet back to the east when he caught sight of movement in a small clearing below. Lambert froze against the rock face and watched as four men emerged into the opening. He could pick out Hopkins in the lead followed by Larry, Charlie, and the lumberman.

They passed on without looking up and Danny moved cautiously forward

CHAPTER 220 EAST END, STERLING PASS

Jake felt impelled to action. Carl had wanted to leave two behind to guard the mouth of the pass; well now there were three. There had been gunfire. He sensed the necessity of reacting. Failing to act is as significant as doing something, he reasoned. He wanted to, felt he needed to, do something.

"Jesus, I think I should go up to find out what's going on," he said and met Jesus' eyes. He saw Jesus begin to smile.

"Of course you do, my friend. You are a man of action," Jesus responded. "Go, find out. We will guard the opening." He pointed up the passage while moving closer to Frank Green. "We will close the mouth of the pass with our good rifles, Frank and I."

Jake could see that Frank was somewhat uneasy with the suggestion. Jake knew that Frank had something which apparently it was important that Hopkins receive. He had ridden up the canyon to deliver it, perhaps he wanted to hand it over in person.

"I can take the message with me and give it to the marshal, Frank. If it is urgent he will get it most quickly this way," he said hoping to alleviate the town clerk's concern about fulfilling his task.

Frank waved his hand dismissively and replied, "It's not that. I'm just wondering if my rifle will be that much use to Jesus here. I sure wouldn't want to be the one to shoot the deputy's horse."

Jesus laughed and replied, "That I understand, hombre. You must continue to live here." He thought for a moment and added, "However, I do not live here. I am sure that we will not injure the horse, but if by chance a bullet does hit it, you can be sure that I will declare that it was mine."

"Does that convince you?" Jake asked. "Chances are Danny won't get this far anyway. But I need to get moving. You can trust me to deliver the envelope."

"I'm just as happy to have you make the delivery," Frank replied and then looked over to Jesus. "I appreciate your words, Jesus, I'll do my best if we have to fire on Danny." Frank opened his saddle bag and produced the small package. "It's not just a letter, seems like a number of documents," he said as he handed it over to Jake. "I've no idea what it is, but apparently it's important."

Jake stuffed the slim, flexible parcel down his back where it was secured by his broad belt. Without a word further he mounted up and rode off.

CHAPTER 221 CARL'S COHORT

Carl regained his composure quickly. The important thing was that Star was here and seemed uninjured. He wanted to go to his horse immediately, but he paused.

Danny was not the kind of gunslinger whose reputation is built on taunting local hotheads into a quick draw shootout which will inevitably lead to the local kid lying face down in the dust and the shootist being celebrated at the bar.

No, Danny was more of a dry gulch bushwhacker who preferred to avoid someone shooting back. It would be just like Lambert to try to lure one of them into the open where he could gun them down.

Carl realized that he still had Willard's rifle in his left hand. He handed it back and said, "Sorry about grabbing your rifle, Willard. I was concerned about Star."

"Understood," Willard replied, but Carl detected a bit of resentment.

'Tough,' he thought. 'The damn fool almost did shoot Star.' Then he attempted to move on by saying, "I'm going to try to get Star without exposing myself. I need you to keep an eye on the bushes just uphill of where Star is now. If Danny shows himself feel free to shoot him."

Carl moved slightly to his right and worked his way across to the other side of the pass downhill of Star. He called out to his horse and gave a sharp whistle by sticking his two little fingers in the sides of his mouth. The horse pricked up its ears and moved toward the sound.

The deputy pulled a handful of oats from a deep pocket of his overcoat and Star took them eagerly. A cursory examination of Star's legs and body showed no signs of abuse and Carl's enmity against Lambert eased somewhat. An old cavalry-style saddle had been cinched onto Star. Clearly Danny had obtained a saddle at the same time he got the rifle he was now shooting. Carl wondered if they were going to find some prospector or hunter lying dead in the rocks south of here.

He moved back to the other side of the pass and tethered Star downhill from the spot where Sam's body lay as a grim reminder. Less blood had run out from the head wound than he would have expected. Lambert's slug had penetrated cleanly but had left no exit point. He examined the entry point and judged that the caliber was a .44-40 or .45; perhaps the cartridge was a Long Colt which was a compromise to be used in both rifle and handgun. It was not very potent in either in his opinion, but a lot of folk liked the versatility it offered if you were loading your own ammunition.

The muzzle velocity of a Long Colt could be fairly low with a light load driving the heavy slug. That could explain the slug remaining in the body. You could sometimes pick up the reflection of the sun from a Long Colt slug in mid-air if the load was light or the powder old. He hadn't seen anything, but he'd been taken by surprise. Danny had only taken one rifle shot. There had been no follow up. Carl wondered why that was. Could it be the rifle was a single shot? If so, Lambert would be vulnerable while reloading.

Carl called out to Willard so the man wouldn't start shooting and then approached the three other horses who had wandered slightly downslope as they grazed. He hitched them up near Star and rejoined Willard.

As he summarized their position it seemed to Carl that Willard retained a stiff-necked attitude. Well, that didn't matter. They still had a madman with a rifle out there which was more important.

He was wondering if he should signal to Jake and Jesus and have them move up, when he became aware of someone moving west toward them from downslope.

CHAPTER 222 PROCTOR'S

Clive, clearly feeling bored with lying about, and in need of using the toilet, had tried to get up by himself. He was lying sprawled awkwardly across the daybed holding his head.

Doris rushed over to him but he assured her that he was fine.

"I'm fine. I felt a bit woozy and came over dizzy-like," Clive explained. "I'm okay now, but my head hurt like blazes when I fell back down."

"You settle back and lie easy now," his mother insisted.

"It's just that I need to visit the john," Clive explained.

The doctor moved up and peered into Clive's eyes before saying, "You have to move slower, that's all. Here I'll give you a hand."

As he moved to assist Clive, Doris retrieved a cane from the hall. "This might help. I got it that time I near broke my ankle when I went rock climbing with Katherine." Doris caught herself up at the inadvertent mention of the doctor's late wife.

The doctor took the cane from her and handed it on to Clive. "I remember well what a good companion you were to Katherine, Doris. Those were good times. Now we put our hopes in our children."

"Nonsense," she replied, accepting his informal comment and

dealing with him with the same familiarity. "You're still an attractive man. Why now that Luke's gone, I may set my hat for you myself."

CHAPTER 223 DANNY

The crease in the sandstone, which had looked so promising from a distance, turned out to be filled with small chunks of weathered rock which moved underfoot and threatened to cascade down the rock face into the lower pass. Danny was stuck. If he climbed any higher on this exposed escarpment he would be sighted from below. Unable to move quickly on the uncertain and increasingly steep slope he would be a sitting duck.

His only option was to descend westward and hope to come down behind the posse members who he'd seen advancing to the east. He had not seen either the bartender or the doctor's son with that group.

A lot of people underestimated Danny because he was unschooled and rough. But he was shrewd in a way which many did not expect. Now he reasoned that the other two must have been left behind with the horses. If he could get within range he could pick them off and steal a horse to get away. It occurred to him that he could shoot up the other horses to reduce the number of men who could pursue him. He'd have to retreat into the western badlands for the night, but it was a plan.

He began to descend, taking every opportunity he could to move to his right as he moved lower. If luck was on his side, he might just have found a way out.

CHAPTER 224 IN STERLING PASS

Jake was moving as quietly as he could, but Carl saw him before he saw the deputy. Up to the left a hat was waved and Carl appeared out of the foliage at the end of the hat-waving arm. He held up his finger to his mouth in the universal hush sign and then motioned for Jake to stay where he was.

Jake dismounted and let Carl come down the path to him and then said in a muted voice, "Frank arrived with something urgent for the marshal. I left him to take my place and brought it up to you."

"Good, but we've got trouble," Carl replied. "We ran into Danny. He shot Sam dead. He's up ahead somewhere. We're not sure how far. "

Jake hadn't known Sam well, but a death was a serious turn of events. Clearly Danny Lambert was a dangerous man. Jake waited to hear what else the deputy had to say. He was the outsider here; let the locals run the show was his usual approach, unless they proved to be incompetent. From what he'd seen of the marshal, Hopkins had his head on straight, and Munds was beginning to impress Jake also.

"I don't like to take the guard off the mouth of this pass completely. Danny could possibly slip by us. He's on foot now, by the way. Star wandered down the pass. He's tethered up yonder with the other three horses. You might as well hitch yours up there too while we decide what to do next."

*   *   *

Danny was crouched down behind one of the last bits of cover before the open section of the pass. He could see the horses about two hundred feet ahead and the bartender sitting on a rock off to the left. He hadn't seen the doctor's son yet, but he had expected to find him here too.

The sun was slanting down the western sky. With it casting its rays toward him he would have to avoid letting it hit him in the face. He'd stand out clearly from this distance.

*   *   *

Once they were into the treed region of the pass, Hopkins had spread the four of them out into a skirmish line. He had instructed each of the men to stay level with him or a few feet back. He didn't want one part of the line to get ahead of the rest. Carl and the others were up there somewhere near and by rights Danny Lambert was trapped between the two forces.

*   *   *

Jake followed Carl and tethered his mount near the others. Carl signalled for him to follow and they moved up the main path. Soon Sam's body came into sight. It was sprawled on its back next to a tree.

Jake noted that the eyes were closed.

"I turned him over to check, but it looks like he was dead before he hit the ground," Carl explained. "I closed the eyes too. Didn't seem right, them staring up and filling with dust."

Jake just nodded and took note of the single bullet hole in the side of the head nearest him.

*   *   *

Brad walked back over the crest of the hill. 'Funny thing,' he thought. 'We all urinate, but we treat it as a very private act. I could have just turned away, but I felt it incumbent to move out of sight.'

Clayton was still sitting where he had left him. Brad wiped his hands uncomfortably on his dusty pants and realized that he had become accustomed to washing so much that it was habitual. It was verging on a fixation on cleanliness.

Clayton saw him approaching and started to get up. Then several things happened at once.

The sharp crack of gunfire broke the silence; Clayton hesitated then fell forward; Brad turned in the direction of the gunshot and tripped. A second shot rang out. It sounded different somehow, but Brad was too busy stretching out his hands to break his fall to think about that.

*   *   *

A head showed above the edge of the hillock. There he was. He'd moved back over the rise for some reason.

He didn't have time to waste. Danny put his plan into action. He braced his handgun as best he could and prepared to shoot the bartender. The man started to rise and Danny let loose before he could get upright. He saw the body fall and holstered his revolver quickly to bring the rifle up to his shoulder. He had to shoot before the other could react and take cover. As he brought the sights to bear, the young doctor seemed to crouch down. Danny lowered the barrel to follow and fired a second time.

Danny cursed his bad luck even as he started to reload. The first shot with his revolver had hit the bartender, but the doctor's brat had fallen forward just an instant before he pulled off the rifle shot. Danny thought he had missed. He had to finish these two off and get a horse before the others came running.

*　　*　　*

Carl and Jake moved up to join Willard who was peering ahead. Jake laid a hand on his shoulder. But, before he had a chance to say anything, sporadic gunfire broke out ahead.

"Marshal must have arrived and spotted Danny," Carl cried out. "We've got to support them from this end of the pass. I'm calling in the others." He pulled out his side arm and fired off three double rounds in the prearranged signal to Jesus to come forward.

*　　*　　*

When they heard Danny's shots down the pass, Hopkins looked behind him in surprise.

Larry called out, "That's up near the horses! Danny must have got passed us. We've got to get back there."

"Hold your positions," Hopkins instructed them. When he was sure they were all waiting he issued instructions,"We're going back to investigate, but keep in line and move together." The group turned back and moved out. Hopkins led then back up the slope at a quicker pace than they had descended.

*　　*　　*

Brad heard Clayton call out, "I'm hit. He's killed me." Clayton was lying face down on the ground and writhing. Brad moved cautiously up across the top of the small rise and knelt down to peer forward.

"Where are you hit?" he called out to Clayton.

*　　*　　*

Danny inserted a new cartridge and slammed the bolt closed as he raised the rifle to sight on the bartender. He was moving. He wasn't dead yet; he soon would be.

*　　*　　*

"With the marshal and the others moving down from the top we can go forward and catch Danny in a cross fire," Carl declared. "Spread out about twenty feet apart and be sure to keep each other in sight. If you spot Danny don't take any chances. If he makes a move to shoot let him have it."

*　　*　　*

"In the leg, I think," Clayton called back.

Brad could see Clayton, but he couldn't see over the rise without raising himself a little. 'I'm out of the line of fire, but Clayton's still in the open,' he realised.

"Roll, Clayton. Roll down this way. He'll shoot you again if you stay up there."

*   *   *

Frank and Jesus heard the group of three double shots stand out clear against the firing from further away.

"That's the signal to join them," he told Frank. "They've come under fire and need help."

*   *   *

Danny aimed for the log-like form of the bartender. He snapped off a shot and saw bits of rock kick up from in front of the target. He reached for his handgun. As he drew down on Clayton, his body gave a final squirm and dropped from sight as if the ground had swallowed it.

*   *   *

Hopkins and his party also now heard the series of shots from the eastern end of the pass. They turned as one to look and Hopkins called out. "That's a signal. Carl must have arrived and be moving up to join us."

Then a rifle crack and the report of a smaller gun came from close ahead and the marshal called out, "Carl will catch up with us. Move forward." He punctuated his command by firing two double rounds from his rifle into the air. He hoped Carl would take that as a message to come on.

*   *   *

Once Clayton was rolling downhill toward safety, Brad ducked down and started to move up to a point where he could peek over the rise. Another bullet hit the ground behind Clayton and spurred him on his way downhill.

Brad risked a quick look over the rise and saw some smoke from gunpowder rising from a copse of bushes. He raised his rifle and fired off three shots toward the spot. He was intentionally aiming low. The marshal and the others were in that direction. A high shot could reach them.

*   *   *

Frank, when questioned afterwards, could not explain the way he responded to the news that Carl and the others needed help. Perhaps it was courage, but he didn't think that was it. He believed that it must have been a reaction to all the emotions which had been stirred up by the excitement of the day.

Whatever it was, he mounted up immediately and rode off without even waiting for Jesus.

*   *   *

Jesus was taken by surprise. He realized that he had spoken with a sense of urgency, but the crazy gringo had rushed off before he'd been able to tell him to proceed with caution.

Now there was nothing for it but to try to overtake him.

*   *   *

The heat of battle had enveloped Carl. He heard the flurry of gunfire from up ahead and he picked out the two-round signal which he correctly assumed came from Hopkins.

"Pick it up, men," he shouted. "Marshal needs us."

*   *   *

Three slugs hit the flat rock in front of Danny and ricocheted past him with the whine of angry hornets. He retreated into the brush and tried to decide what to do. He had to get to cover. He broke off toward the northern side of the pass. There was a chance he could find a route up the hill. There was no need for secrecy now. They knew where he was.

*   *   *

Seconds after the three shot series Brad had let loose, Hopkins saw something moving across from left to right. Then the booming report of Charlie's .405 echoed across the pass.

*   *   *

Carl didn't know it, but the Hopkins' group was a scant fifty feet ahead. He heard the boom of Charlie Lee's Big Medicine and turned to speak to Jake. There was no one beside him. He swung back to his right and realised that he'd lost contact with the other two.

*   *   *

Brad knelt down beside Clayton. The gunfire from further down the pass reassured him. The gunfight was moving off. He turned his attention to caring for Clayton. The staccato firing formed a background against which he worked. The next thing he realized, Hopkins was calling out for him and Brad replied to draw him to the spot where he knelt ministering to the fallen bartender.

CHAPTER 225 IN STERLING PASS

In the aftermath of the shootout, few people could agree on exactly what had happened and where they and others had been, with the possible exception of Brad and Clayton. The young doctor and the bartender from The Horn Saloon believed that they had been within sight of each other throughout the period of armed conflict.

In the dusk of false sunset, after the sun had passed behind the western hills but while the sky was still illuminated by its presence above the serrated horizon, confusion reigned in the obscurity of the wooded section of Sterling Pass. Hopkins tried to maintain order and to preserve the evidence of what had occurred, but even as he was trying to sort things out he realized how difficult the task was.

Vision is always perfect when looking backward; the present and probable future are more difficult to perceive. In retrospect he could see clearly that creating four separate groups within the confines of the pass had been a recipe for disaster. Even within the smaller groupings individuals had disappeared from sight behind trees or because everyone else was taking cover or had their eyes busily searching each shadow for a sign of Danny Lambert.

He had even found himself completely alone at one point.

When Charlie Lee had fired off that cannon he called a rifle, all attention had been riveted on him. But when Danny started shooting back, all hell had broken loose.

Most of the members of the posse had never been under fire. The civil war was a period dimly remembered or, in almost every case, a tale told by a parent or grandparent. They had this day crossed into the fog of conflict and recalled the recent events as through a kaleidoscope of confused images reflecting wishful thoughts and doubts and uncertainty. Their reconstructed recollections were based more on what they thought they had done, or felt they should have done, or wished they had done. Brad knew that their ability to recount what they had actually seen and heard would weaken quickly from its present confused state. They would share stories and before long each would actually believe things had happened as he had unwittingly reconstructed them. Thus stories grow in the telling and legends come to be.

There were a few hard facts which would not alter in the harsh light of the morning sun.

Four men lay dead in the confines of Sterling Pass, this short road to nowhere connecting the western badlands to Oak Creek Canyon. Sam Schuerman, Danny Lambert, Charlie Lee, and Larry James had died during the short period of violent action. It was the purest of luck that Clayton and Brad Pendergast had not been killed as well. In addition to Luke Proctor's murder, and the gunning down of the Wells Fargo driver, Paul Matthews, that was a bad spell of killing. Despite its isolation and somewhat turbulent history, the community of Red Rocks, now Sedona, had been a more-or-less peaceful grouping of settlers who occupied themselves in small-time business, farming, and animal husbandry.

Six violent deaths, and one apparent attempt to kill Clive, within a few days called out for a reckoning. The marshal knew that it would be one tall order to turn the present state of confusion into a reasoned explanation, but he meant to try.

The last members of the posse to be accounted for had been Brad Pendergast and Clayton Edgett. They were together over the small rise at the western end of Sterling Pass. Clayton lay on the ground with a nasty, but non-life-threatening leg wound and some damage to his face from chips of rock which had been splashed up by Danny's errant shot.

Brad described the shootout up on the ridge with Danny to the marshal and Hopkins nodded in comprehension. "Trying to get hold of what really happened may prove as difficult as picking up a slippery licorice whip," he told young Dr. Pendergast. "I'd appreciate you helping Carl and me with the questioning."

CHAPTER 226 IN STERLING PASS

'At last,' Brad thought. 'This is a chance for me to employ my powers of observation and deduction as A. C. Doyle describes his detective hero doing.' Then he had a twinge of conscience and considered Clayton's condition.

"How are you feeling now, Clay?" he asked.

The bartender had been a reluctant participant in the manhunt. Now, however, the spectre of danger having apparently faded away, he seemed more cheerful. He raised himself with a slight grimace and said, "I think I'll live, Doc. My leg's numb more than anything. I think I'd be better if I could stand, or at least sit, though. This sharp rock is digging into my back something awful."

Leroy Hopkins and Brad helped Clayton to his feet and settled him in the rock he'd been sitting on when Danny opened fire. It was on the high point of the pass between Vultee Arch and the main passage which skirted the northern foothills of Lost Wilson Mountain. Clayton seemed quite content to wait there until the posse gathered to begin the trek back to Sedona, but Hopkins promised to send a couple of men up with a makeshift litter to carry him down to the meeting point just inside the forested area.

As Brad and Leroy walked down the slope toward the trees, Hopkins filled the young man in on the major points of what had happened when Danny was flushed in the pass.

"It seems that Carl, Willard, and Sam were the first to come up against him," Hopkins explained. "They were a ways down the pass from us and moving up west when Lambert bushwhacked them. Sam was killed with the first shot and Willard and Carl managed to drive Danny back up the pass. There are some scrapings on the lower sections of the northern cliff that indicate that Danny climbed up a ways. That must be how he got passed us and came up here to attack you and Clayton."

"You said there'd been some difficulty taking Danny down. He's taken then, is he?"

"He's dead and three others," Hopkins replied with a grimace. "I didn't want to say anything in front of Clayton, but I think we've got us a problem. After you held him off here, he came back down the pass with his blood up and his guns blazing. People panicked and things got way out of hand."

"Danny must have put up quite a fight to have killed two more men with the group of you knowing he was coming and had already killed Sam," Brad answered. "That seems odd in itself. Danny was a vicious individual, but I'd never heard tell that he was a great shot."

"That's just it," the marshal explained. "I'm not sure that Lambert killed Larry or Charlie."

"What do you mean? Are they dead or just missing?"

"Oh, they're dead right enough. Charlie Lee's got a couple of slugs in him and Larry's stretched out with a bullet hole in his head," Leroy responded. "It's just odd the way they died. That's why I've gathered all the others together and asked Carl to keep them from talking about what happened until I get to interview them all separately."

'It's just like Sherlock Holmes in real life,' Brad thought. He felt guilty about treating the deaths of so many real people as if they were characters in a detective novel, but sometimes life is as strange as, if not stranger than, fiction. 'I wish my dad was here. Two Pendergasts reasoning together would be better than one. I'll take copious notes and he and I can look them over when I get back to town,' he decided.

"Lead on, Marshal. My handwriting has become harder to read during my studies I'm told, but I can take notes faster now than ever. You do the questioning and I'll try to get down everything."

CHAPTER 227 IN STERLING PASS

Carl had the men gathered in a clearing a few feet inside the edge of the trees. After a full day in the saddle, or clambering over rocks, most of them were content to sit quietly with their backs propped against a tree or large boulder. The exceptions were Carl Munds, who seemed to be taking his task of keeping the posse members from comparing recollections seriously, and Jesus who was standing a few feet off gazing into the shadows.

When he saw the marshal approaching with Brad, Carl came over to them and handed the marshal a package. Brad noticed that it was wrapped in brown paper and tied with twine. It flexed in the deputy's hand and by the way he carried it, appeared to be heavy for its size.

"Frank brought this back from town, Marshal. Jake brought it up to me, but I didn't get a chance to give it to you until now," Carl told Leroy.

"Thanks, Carl. What is it?"

"No idea, Marshal," Carl responded with a shrug to accompany the response, "It came in on the Wells Fargo coach from Flagstaff today. It's marked urgent though."

"You said Frank brought it back from town?" Hopkins said. The question was clear in his tone of voice, and Carl picked up on it.

"Jefferson came over sick just before we entered the canyon. Frank took him back to town and got the parcel then," he replied.

Hopkins examined the package in the dwindling light and replied, "Well, it will wait. We've got a lot on our plate at present. For one thing I'd like you to take Lars and Willard and help Clayton down here with the rest of us. He's got a bullet wound in his leg, so you might be better to rig up a sling to carry him over the rough spots."

Carl seemed pleased to be delegated to oversee the task. He went off to speak with Lars and Willard and a few minutes later Brad noticed Clayton ensconced over near a group of boulders which allowed him to recline in comparative comfort.

Hopkins took Brad to look at the bodies of Danny, Larry, and Charlie Lee. They were all on the north side of the pass and not that far from each other. Danny was partly behind a large rock outcropping, but both Charlie and Larry lay in the open.

Brad examined the position of the bodies and the nature of the wounds. After he had viewed the third of the bodies he shared his observations with the marshal. "As far as I can tell without probing for the bullets, all three men were killed by a large caliber bullet. I know that doesn't narrow the field much, except to rule out Lars, but both Charlie and Larry have been shot more than once. Danny may have wounded them and then finished them off on the ground. It looks as if some of the shots went down through into the earth beneath. I checked Danny's gun, if that's it lying beside him. It's a .45. That could have killed both Larry and Charlie, but I'd like to have my father's opinion. I don't see many gunshot wounds in Boston."

Over the next hour the marshal spoke with all of the men. He even made a point of providing Brad with his own account of what he did, heard, and saw during the period in question.

Carl did the same, so that there was a complete record. Brad took detailed notes of the information provided and promised to make a legible copy of all of his notes the next day. It was getting so dark that Hopkins finally decided to call a halt to the investigation and pick it up in the morning.

"We've got a major problem with the bodies, Marshal," Carl pointed out when Hopkins and Brad were standing to one side with him in confidential conversation. "If we leave them out here overnight some varmints are going to move in and have at them; on the other hand I can't see how we can cart them back to town unless we sling them across the backs of the surplus horses. But that doesn't seem fitting."

"You're right, Carl. These folk are, or were, our neighbors. We'll have to get a wagon out here tomorrow and transport them back to town in a proper manner."

"That means we'll have to mount a guard over them tonight," Carl concluded. "You're going to need some people to camp out here to keep an eye on things."

"There's also the question of Clayton," Brad added. "He seems fine, but he's really in no shape to sit on a horse tonight. Tomorrow, after a rest he might manage it."

Hopkins considered the situation briefly.

"I'd like to keep most of the men here so they can take turns standing guard. I hate to ask you to travel after the full day you've had, Carl, but you're the best person I can think of to carry the news to town and arrange to get a wagon out in Oak Canyon at the mouth of this pass tomorrow."

Carl had been looking worn out, but at the marshal's words he straightened up and replied, "No problem, Marshal. I'll enjoy the chance to ride Star again and get him a good feed tonight in a proper stable."

"I appreciate it, Carl," Leroy replied. "Get Carter to fit you out. Tell him the town will cover his costs. Bring the doctor with you too if he's willing. I'd like him to examine the bodies where they lie."

Carl didn't waste any time. He was ready to ride off down the pass before Hopkins had finished briefing the rest of the posse and instructed the building of small camp fires in strategic spots.

"There's one more body to look at, Brad," Hopkins concluded. "I don't think there's much doubt about how Sam died, but if you're up for it we can go down the pass with Carl and he'll lead us to it."

Brad agreed and he and the marshal walked down the pass alongside the deputy who was exhibiting a certain amount of pleasure in leading Star as the trio walked east.

E. Craig McKay

BRAND OF DEATH

Part Four: Brad Pendergast Investigates

CHAPTER 228 IN STERLING PASS

The examination of Sam Schuerman's body had produced a little new information, Brad realized. He wondered what his father would make of it. Carl had reported that Sam had fallen after a single rifle report from a point in the bushes slightly up the pass from where Sam now lay. The bullet hole was about as big as Brad's index finger. It could be either from a .44-40 or a .45. The bullet had not passed through nor emerged from the other side of the skull cavity with catastrophic effect. Clearly death had been immediate. Carl insisted that the report he'd heard was clearly a rifle rather than a handgun. That would indicate that Danny had acquired a rifle somewhere.

Why had the slug not passed completely through the skull? The high muzzle velocity normally associated wth a rifle-driven projectile would have caused an exit wound. A reduced level of gunpowder might account for the wound, Brad agreed. He admitted that his father was much more familiar with the effects of gunfire than he was, but he was inclined to accept the deputy's theory that a rifle had been used, at least for the first shot.

A second wound had been caused by firing into the dead man. It had passed through the fleshy part of Sam's leg. Carl thought it had been an attempt to draw them into shooting back and giving away their position. This second, post mortem wound differed from the first in apparent size and effect. When hit by this slug the body had been lying on the ground. The entry hole seemed smaller than the first and Brad discovered the deformed hunk of lead in the soft earth near the exit hole. He showed the slug to Hopkins who expressed the opinion that it seemed light for a .45. Brad wrapped the recovered bullet in a wad of paper and slipped it into his pocket for later examination by his father. The fascination Dr. Robert Pendergast had with firearms and ballistics was perhaps understandable given the number of wounds, self-inflicted and otherwise, that a town doctor had to deal with. Indeed, medical practice had advanced greatly over the centuries specifically as a result of surgical experiences during wars. Unfortunately, guns and weapons of all types kept getting more dangerous too.

The inspection complete, they watched as Carl rode off toward town. The marshal and young Pendergast turned their steps toward the camp which was being established up the pass.

"We'll have to transport Sam's body to a spot up near the other three," Hopkins mused. "I don't want to split up the men into two camps. That would force more watches on each man. At the same time, the bodies need to be guarded overnight."

The marshal seemed to be thinking out loud, so Brad walked quietly by his side and let him talk. His own mind was still going over the conflicting testimony the various members of the posse had come up with. It was almost as if no one had experienced the same event.

"Wait a minute," Hopkins cried out slapping the right pocket of his overcoat. "I forgot all about that parcel that Frank brought north. I should have checked that before Carl left for town. Well, there's not much I can do about that now, but I wonder what's in it."

The marshal pulled the package out now and cut the string with his pocket knife. The brown paper was peeled back to reveal a bundle of folded papers. "It's too dark to be sure, but these seem to be maps. There's a note too, but I'll have to wait 'til we get back to the campfire now to read it."

Within a few minutes they caught sight of the campsite and were amused to see the men toasting hunks of ham over the open fire and passing around chunks of cheese. After a full day in the saddle followed by the intense emotion of a gunfight, the fellows were enjoying a chance to relax. 'Humans are very resilient,' Brad thought. 'And it's a good thing too.'

As they entered the circle of light several of the men looked up and nodded respectfully to the marshal. With warm food in their bellies and a sense of camaraderie at having come through something like a battle, they were starting to think pretty well of themselves. Four men had died today, but the truth was that none of them had liked Danny and Charlie was a big-shot hotel owner. None of them had known either Sam or Larry well and, when push comes to shove, they were also glad it was someone other than themselves who had been killed. Even Clayton was feeling full of himself since he was the nearest thing to a local hero because of his wound.

Jake came over as the marshal was squatting down near the fire to warm himself while he examined the papers which had been in the package he had received. There was a note also and he read that over and laughed out loud at what he read. He stood up to share the joke with Brad and Jake.

"That package was from a deputy marshal I know up in Flagstaff. He got our message about Danny Lambert maybe heading north up through these hills and sent me a little present." Hopkins held out the papers to Jake who flipped through them and passed them on to Brad.

"They're maps of some sort," he said. "Look pretty detailed."

"They're high detail ordinance maps of Oak Creek Canyon and the associated territory," Hopkins confirmed. "My contact in Flagstaff thought that they might come in useful for us and sent them down. I guess they would have helped at that, if we'd had them in time."

"It was a good thought nonetheless," Brad commented. "It was intended to be helpful."

"I had some thoughts myself, Marshal," Jake added "Jesus and I were talking over the events of today and we both came up with the same oddity about what happened."

"What exactly was that?" Leroy asked.

Jake didn't exactly look around, but his eyes drifted toward the group of men near them. The men were talking loudly, bragging mostly, about how well they'd conducted themselves under fire. No one seemed to be paying attention to the marshal and the two men standing with him. Nevertheless, Jake moved off a way and drew Brad and the marshal with him.

"I'd just as soon keep it between us for the time being, Marshal. Maybe we could take a little walk out beyond the campfire to talk it over," Jake suggested.

"Let's do something useful at the same time," Hopkins countered. "We need to move Sam's body up here for safe keeping. How about I get the sling they rigged up to shift Clayton and you and Jesus give Brad and me a hand with that?"

Jake agreed and went off to enlist Jesus. Hopkins approached

Clayton, gathered up the jury-rigged stretcher, and threw it over his shoulder. Brad took advantage of a moment with Clayton to inquire about his wound. Clayton replied with new-found bravado that it was nothing.

Hopkins got the men's attention and explained the plan to mount lookout by turns through the night. He intended to be on call during the night, so he designated three teams of the remaining six healthy men to stand a series of two-hour watches during the dark hours, one to tend the fire at the main camp and the other to watch over the dead and keep scavenging animals at bay. Brad and Frank were to take the first watch, Jake and Jesus the second, and Lars and Willard the third.

The scheduling of the watches encouraged men to think of bedding down. While the others began to spread out bedrolls, Hopkins led his squad of body transporters off into the darkness to recover Sam's earthly remains.

CHAPTER 229 PROCTOR'S

His recent examination and consultation with Jefferson Brooks had lifted a load from Doctor Pendergast's mind. Not only had it reassured the doctor that Jefferson was on the way to becoming his normal abnormal self, it also cleared his suspicions of the mortician's possible involvement with the disappearing trophy.

Jefferson was an odd duck at the best of times, but the town doctor had been pleased to find that he had not been guilty of theft of such an unusual type. There was an old country expression, 'Now't so odd as folk' which suggested that nothing in the behavior of man should surprise one. Indeed, Dr. Pendergast had seen some strange things in his time. But at least in this case he had found Jefferson Brooks on the right side of the street. When questioned, Brooks had admitted that he had noticed the disappearance of the trophy from the enfolding circle of the young Schnebly girl's arms as he prearing to screw down the lid. He told the doctor that he had been 'shocked and appalled' and uncertain what to do. The Schnebly family was already suffering from their grief. He had hesitated to draw attention to the missing object for fear of increasing their pain. Finally he had decided that it was best to say nothing and hope that the theft would never be discovered.

Dr. Pendergast had agreed with Brooks that his decision at the time was appropriate and he promised to keep the recent discovery as secret as he could. As he considered the matter later, the doctor decided to seek out the best source of information in town, the Thompson boys, specifically Eddie Thompson, to see if a connection could be made. He set off for the livery stable where he was greeted by Thomas Carter and directed to the stable where Eddie was working away.

A brief conversation with the energetic and well-connected young Thompson provided information which although not directly connecting the theft with any one person, put the investigating doctor on the right track.

Dr. Pendergast had engraved each of the names on the plate affixed to the trophy himself with the aid of a crude pantograph which he had built. The device was first constructed in the 17th century. Called the eidograph and further developed by William Wallace in 1831, it allowed the movement of one pen, in tracing an image, to produce a smaller or a larger copy.

Unlike many physicians, Robert Pendergast had retained a clear writing style. He had written out each name in a large hand and then used a pantograph to inscribe a smaller version of the name of the recipient each year on the silver plaque. He was sure there was a list in his desk at the ranch of the names of the children to whom the trophy had been annually presented.

The fact that the plaque had been removed by someone, probably the thief, made the doctor eager to seek out the original list to peruse the names. He briefly considered riding out to the ranch to look for the list, but evening was coming on. The list would still be there in the morning. He would spend one more night at least at Proctor's boarding house. His patients were both coming along nicely, and he was starting to wonder how the posse was making out.

CHAPTER 230 RIDING SOUTH TO SEDONA

Once he was out of Sterling Pass and into Oak Creek Canyon, Carl picked up speed and made good time. Star seemed to realize they were headed back toward the stable and thoughts of a proper feed may have encouraged him. Carl was in great spirits. Star was safe, Danny was dead, and he'd had his first taste of command. The light of evening lingered long enough for him to reach the new Schnebly road and he was on familiar ground once again.

As he proceeded south toward town and neared Schnebly's Lodge it occurred to him to stop off and send out a telegram to Flagstaff to cancel the alert to be on the lookout for Danny Lambert. He wrote out a brief note at the telegraph counter and had Carl Schnebly himself send it off. Of course, it was big news and Deputy Munds received personal congratulations from Carl and a number of the staff. Unaccustomed as he was to public acclaim, Carl Munds found himself strangely ill at ease. He mumbled something about it being more than just him and was generous in his praising of the way Marshal Hopkins had directed the ambush and how he had just done his part, but as he mounted up and headed off to town it was with a general sense of well-being and contentment at having his efforts recognized.

He'd enjoyed seeing his name and title on the telegram draft. He'd sent it to the deputy marshal who Marshal Hopkins was friends with and who had been copied on the earlier telegram the marshal had sent out when the manhunt had begun.

His mind turned to the preparations for the morning. The first stop would be the livery stable for a number of reasons. He'd have to requisition the use of a proper wagon to take back up the canyon for the bodies, and he was certain Star would be happy to be back among familiar smells and sounds.

Then he'd head over to Proctor's. Dr. Pendergast would still be there, unless he'd had to relocate to care for Jefferson Brooks. Brooks was a loner in a number of ways. He didn't have a housekeeper or even a local woman to come in and do for him. He lived alone with the occasional dead guest in attendance. If Brooks was as bad as he'd looked when Frank took him away, he'd need some major attention.

As it was, Miss Lily was the first person in town that he spoke to. She was seated out in front of the hotel taking the night air when he came down the main street toward the smithy. She called out to him and he drew up out front. He didn't dismount, being in a hurry to speak with Carter, but he doffed his hat and inquired about her health.

Lily laughed and replied, "Been nice to have such a quiet day off. I'm at a loss for things to do. I was just about to rent a horse from Thomas and come looking for all of you." She paused and turned serious. "What's up, Carl? I'm surprised to see you returning alone. I hope there's no trouble."

"There won't be any more trouble from Danny Lambert anyhow," Carl replied. "We won't even have to go to the trouble of a trial; he's dead."

Lily raised her hands to her face in alarm and asked, "Was anyone else hurt?"

Carl immediately realized that he'd started badly. He tried to correct by saying. "Three of the posse were killed in the fire fight, but Jake and the Marshal are fine." Then he remembered that Charlie Lee was one of the dead and added in a serious tone. "There is some bad news. Charlie, Larry and Sam were all shot and Clayton was wounded."

Carl saw a mixture of emotions pass across her face.

"Clayton wounded," she said absently, and it seemed as if her thoughts were elsewhere. "I would have thought that he and Charlie would have kept themselves out of harm's way."

"Lambert ambushed us," Carl said by way of explanation.

"Well, I'm sure glad Marshal Hopkins is okay," Lily exclaimed. "He's a mighty fine marshal."

Carl realized that Lily had been concerned about the welfare of the

Pinkerton man, Jake, but he knew that Lily had an opinion of Marshal Hopkins. He was surprised to hear himself saying "It's an honor to work with Marshal Hopkins," and find that he meant it. Maybe it wouldn't be so bad being number two for a few more years to such a well-respected lawman. He touched the brim of his hat to Lily, then turned Star's head toward the stable and rode on.

CHAPTER 231 IN STERLING PASS

As soon as they were well out of hearing range of the posse, the marshal invited Jake and Jesus to share their opinions about the recent events.

"There are a couple of things which seem odd to me, Marshal. I'm an outsider here and it just may be me finding problems where there are none, but I'll let you judge," Jake began.

They'd brought a small portable lantern with them, but for the moment they could see clearly enough by the light of the moon which although somewhat diminished from full, had risen early and was almost in line with the main passage they were following. Because he couldn't see Jake's face, Brad was going by Jake's tone of voice, but it seemed as if he was hesitant about stepping on the marshal's toes.

"You go right ahead, Jake," Hopkins responded. "I'm always ready to hear another point of view on any subject."

"I'm pleased to hear you say so, Marshal. I think it would be better if I let Jesus go first, though. He had a question concerning Frank Green's behavior."

"I've got a few myself, Jake. But it takes all kinds to make a world, I reckon," Hopkins replied and then added, "Go ahead, Jesus."

The cattleman from Tulsa eased into the subject as if he thought others might not accept his comment in the right way. "It's like this, Marshal. I don't know Frank all that well, but the general impression I got from his behavior earlier today suggested to me that he was sort of timid." He paused and added, "You know what I mean. He was quiet and didn't speak to put himself forward, or act as if he knew better than others."

"He's a bit of a loner and keeps to himself pretty well I'd agree," Hopkins replied diplomatically. "He sort of marches to his own drummer you might say. I've never had any problem with him, either drunk or sober, though, so I've just left him be."

"That's why I was so surprised when he rode hell bent for leather toward the sound of the guns, Marshal," Jesus explained. "It seemed like he had some special reason to be up near the fighting."

Marshal Hopkins was quiet for a few seconds and then responded. "Thanks for telling me that, Jesus. It bears some pondering on."

Brad remained silent, but Jake filled the pause which followed the comment by Jesus by raising another related topic.

"While you were busy with Brad here taking down statements from the men, I've been listening to the chitchat without saying much. Jesus has been doing the same. We've noticed something that strikes us as odd."

"What would that be?"

"I've listened to a lot of men retelling what happened, in lots of towns, Marshal. Folk differ a mite, but on the whole I've always noticed they like to make their participation in any event seem more significant than it was," Jake started off. "I'd be surprised to find it much different here."

"I'd say you're right about that, Jake," Hopkins agreed. "Men tend to blow up their actions, out of all proportions often enough."

"Exactly. Jesus and I noticed that to a certain extent that was true here too, but there was one big exception."

"Who, or what would that be?" the marshal inquired.

"It was more of a what than a who," Jake supplied. "No one made any claim to have been the one to shoot Danny."

Jake let the statement just hang there and Brad felt the urge to suggest a reason for the actions of the men. "Perhaps," he suggested, "they were feeling bad about the deaths of Larry and Charlie and thought that people might think they'd shot carelessly and killed them too by accident."

Jake and Jesus had no response to that, but Marshal Hopkins had a comeback.

"There's a flaw in that argument, Brad," he declared.

"What's that, Marshal?" Jake asked before Brad could.

"Danny was killed by a single rifle shot. Charlie and Larry were shot multiple times with what seem to be handgun wounds. It looked a lot to me like an execution."

CHAPTER 232 THE SMITHY

Carter was surprised to see Carl riding in so late and on Star. The smithy had always been a sort of crossroads of the town, but lately it had been busier than Carter liked. As is often the case with big men, Carter was quiet, even somewhat shy. He liked nothing better than working by himself at his forge and anvil.

Now, however, he greeted Carl and enquired about the progress made seeking Danny.

"I see you've recovered Star anyway. That's good," he exclaimed.

Carl beamed as he pulled up and dismounted. "We got Danny, too," he told the smith. "I'd like to get Star settled for the night in a proper stall again. Give this horse a bit of your special mixture, Thomas. I'll be riding out again tomorrow morning." After a second he turned serious and added, "We're going to need a wagon too. Some other men were shot by Danny while we were taking him."

Carter's broad face darkened as his brow furrowed. "Who was shot, Carl. Were they badly hurt?"

"I'm afraid so. Charlie Lee was killed along with the cowboys, Sam Schuerman and Larry James."

Thomas Carter looked off toward the embers in the forge. He raised his hand to his jaw and paused in thought before saying, "First the Schnebly's tragedy, then San Francisco and now this spate of killing. Seems like a reckoning of some sort. Bad times; bad times indeed."

Carl was taken aback by the depth of Carter's response. He realized that he'd been so caught up in the hunt for Lambert and so relieved by the recovery of Star that the full weight of the events had slipped by him. More to have something to say than for any other reason, he asked Carter if he knew the whereabouts of the doctor.

The smith seemed still lost in thought as he told Carl that Dr. Pendergast had been at the stable earlier but that he'd gone back to Proctor's. Carl thanked Carter, reminded him about Star's feed and the need for a wagon for the morning and headed off through the gathering darkness toward the boarding house.

CHAPTER 233 IN STERLING PASS

Sitting alone, at night, in the wilderness, surrounded by the bodies of victims of violent death, is an activity bound to rouse strong passions in the fanciful mind. Brad did not consider himself fanciful. He thought himself a man of science, for whom speculation was a tool used to deduce, to understand, to solve, the mysteries posed by the forces of nature. Reason could explain the seemingly irrational actions of mankind. He was not credulous; he was not superstitious.

However, as the embers of the small campfire died down, the dim glow they cast was overtaken by shadows which seeped in from the dark avenues of trees and crowded close. He was not completely alone. Not far away, though obscured now by the curtain of night, except for a half-imagined glow of a farther fire banked against the night, others of his party lay sleeping. Night noises filled the darkness, but he felt the lack of another sentient being. No living person kept him company; instead he sat, his back against a tree, and kept a vigil with four shrouded lumps of clay which had been men.

Rough blankets covered each of the still cooling corpses to keep off flies. Neither vacant stare, nor slackened feature challenged him. There were no ghastly images to stir thoughts of the fleeting nature of mortality. And yet, from time to time, night breezes drifted down the pass and stirred small flames among the dimming cinder-darkened coals. Orange and sometimes bluish flickers flared up, as if to mock by contrast the fire of life which burned no longer in these four dead men.

His thoughts dwelt on somber topics and moribund images consumed him. Death conquers all at last. His father, seemingly quite healthy still and with a mind to match, would sicken, and would die, as all who live must do. Beloved Linda, who even now carried his child, their child, would age and illness or calamity would take its toll. All, all would pass away and be no more.

Thoughts came into his mind, unplanned, unwanted. Imagination gave birth to fears that he had been wrong to come west, to have left Linda in Boston. Her mother was with her there, but so ought he to be. They had agreed that he should make the journey to convince his father to join them, to live with them, when Brad had finished his studies and found a place to set up a practice. There had been no thought of Linda making the journey in her condition. Brad had traveled by train to Flagstaff and on to Sedona by rustic stagecoach. It was not a journey to be undertaken by the woman who carried their joint hope for the future. Now, however, here he was up a lonely pass, beside a desert canyon, keeping night watch over men who earlier today had lived with hopes and made plans of their own.

Isolation may dim one's awareness of current events, but it does nothing to stifle the fears which spring from imagination. Brad began to wish that he had sent a message to town with the deputy. He should have penned a simple message for Linda which Carl could have sent off with the official telegram the marshal had consigned to him. His father would be here tomorrow. The town doctor could have brought tidings from Linda from a return telegram. This was the beginning of the twentieth century. The telegraph and even telephone had reached almost every city or sizable town across the country. A network of rapid communication united the nation. Although physical transportation was sometimes tedious, ideas flew from coast to coast.

His thoughts were drawn back to the instant by a sudden noise from beyond the now much diminished globe of light which surrounded the campfire. A grating in the underbrush, perhaps a foot slipping on loose gravel, had been there, on the edge of hearing. The rifle, heavy and foreign to his touch, lay on his lap. Beside him, on the ground lay the notes for the report he'd undertaken at the marshal's urging. His hands now sought the rifle as his eyes peered into shadows peopled by his fancy and his mindspun dangers half-imagined, half-believed, which even as he sat could well be drawing near.

His straining senses heard, or seemed to hear, a labored breathing close at hand. A challenge semi-formed stuck in his throat, and as he sat thus frozen to the spot where chance had posted him, he heard again, and clearer, a gentle swish among the trees as if someone were standing hidden in the dark and watching. Although the fire gave little light, Brad realized that, to one observing from the shadows, he would be revealed. He thought of building up the fire to cast a wider glow, but some instinct held him motionless.

Should he call out? But still he held his tongue, partly in fear of seeming foolish if it were his replacement, either Jake or Jesus, come to take a turn at watching over those who watched no more.

There was another reason he sat mute, he now confessed. He had from childhood carried a strange secret fear of darkness based upon no reason which he knew. No doubt the newest theories of the Austrian, Sigmund Freud, would suggest a childhood trauma of repressed sexual desires. For Brad Prendergast the very thought that he had subconsciously sought sexual relations with his mother was abhorrent. Surely the fear of supposed danger lying beyond the glow of the fire was a more primordial fear of the unknown. Things imagined seem worse than those we know. Each stranger seems a threat; beyond the hill lie dragons.

Brad sat listening and seeking some glimpse of movement. After what seemed an eternity, he became aware of the clear sounds of someone approaching. He half raised the rifle and was about to call out a challenge when the silence was broken by the familiar voice of Marshal Hopkins.

"Hey there, don't shoot me for a coyote."

As if they had never been, Brad's night fears slipped away and mundane reality took shape. The marshal came over and squatted down beside him.

He brought his hand up to his chin and gazed back into the trees from which he had emerged. "I came out to have a word with you, Brad. Something's not right. I don't think Lambert shot either Larry or Charlie Lee."

CHAPTER 234 IN STERLING PASS

For The Artist, sleep did not come. His mind raced with memories of things accomplished and possibilities which lay ahead. The marshal suspected something. He was asking questions and he had that would-be detective, the doctor's son, taking notes. It didn't matter. No one had seen him, at least no one still alive.

Danny was dead. His mouth was shut for good. The cowboys, Sam and Larry, probably had not connected him with Danny, but it was good to have them dead as well. Charlie Lee was too smart to spill the beans and implicate himself, but dead men tell no tales. Wasn't that what the pirates had said? Well, they were right. Charlie would tell no tale, now.

All he had to do was claim he had been nowhere near the place the bodies were found and no one could prove different. His rifle was one of many. The handgun used to kill Larry and Charlie could not be traced to him. It came from far away and long ago. That trail was cold, as cold as death.

His thoughts raced. One loose end remained, Clive. The elimination of Charlie Lee, his tamed killer, and the cowboys had been satisfying and had removed threats. Clive was still a potential danger. Besides, he would enjoy killing Luke Proctor's son.

CHAPTER 235 PROCTOR'S

Dr. Pendergast was up early. Carl had asked him to come north to inspect the carnage. He had hoped that Jefferson Brooks would come too. When Carl had brought the news the night before, Brooks had seemed up for it. The mortician had been enthusiastic after supper and had assured the doctor that he would ride north to aid with an examination of the dead. Brooks was an odd duck, but a good hand with a scalpel and with a keen eye for signs of death. But now there was no sign of him at the breakfast table. Perhaps he was still feeling poorly and was still abed.

Had it not been for his congenital weakness, Jefferson Brooks might have become a doctor himself. Dr. Pendergast was well aware of the nervous disorder which caused Brooks to suffer from spells of brain fever. When he had been young he had been diagnosed as having water on the brain. As long as he avoided stress he was fine. The excitement with the posse the day before had been too much for him, but he seemed stable by bedtime.

For the trip north they would be taking a wagon to transport the bodies, but the doctor wanted to inspect the corpses where they lay. Brad would be a great help and the extra set of knowledgeable eyes which Brooks would lend would play their part as well. Much could be learned by seeing the state in which the dead men lay.

He found Doris Proctor humming cheerfully in the kitchen. Fresh coffee was in a pot and she was mixing up a bowl of pancake batter. Slices of bacon were sizzling and a bowl of eggs sat next to the skillet. Clearly all seemed well in her world. Who could blame her for her good humor? Her son was well and her deadbeat husband was dead. From Doris' point of view, the circumstances of each of the men in her life were appropriate.

"Good morning, Doctor," Doris called out. "I'm preparing flapjacks to stick to your ribs on your journey up the canyon and the bacon's ready to serve. Mr. Brooks is up already. He's had breakfast and has gone to his shop to get some equipment to take with him on your trip. I must say, he seems in better spirits than I've seen him in for a long time."

The doctor bit back the temptation to make a joke about there being a windfall of business for the town mortician. Death was not a suitable topic for jocularity.

Clive was ambulatory, but he was more what might be called 'walking wounded' than in any shape to consider going back to work at the stables. Carter came by to tell Clive that Eddie Thompson and another of his siblings, Carter wasn't sure which one exactly, would take care of the mucking out and feeding of the horses for today again. There was nothing special expected for today since there was no coach scheduled to pass through town. Thomas had agreed to drive the wagon up to the mouth of Sterling Pass to transport the bodies.

Carter was still at Proctor's when Brooks returned with a satchel of devices to aid in forensics. Doris Proctor had invited Thomas to sit down to a proper breakfast. The smith was seated behind a pile of flapjacks lathered with butter and covered with dollops of Doris' homemade preserves.

Doris was encouraging everyone to stock up with energy for the day ahead. When Carl arrived, he too was dragged to the breakfast table and encouraged to have a hearty breakfast, despite his protestations that he'd already eaten.

When the four men were finally able to set off, it was nearly 9 o'clock. There was a sense of a great excursion tempered only slightly by the reminder that there were some bodies of people they knew awaiting them up the canyon. Jefferson and Carter took seats on the wagon. Carl and Dr. Pendergast would be riding their own horses. Star and Grey knew each other well having traveled several times together.

CHAPTER 236 IN STERLING PASS

After a makeshift breakfast, Hopkins organised a search party to gather evidence of the firefight of the day before. He took a position near the middle of the pass and encouraged each member to move slowly in a line down from the upper end toward the point where Carl, Jake, Jesus, Frank and Willard had formed a sort of human wall which marked the furthest east Danny Lambert had traveled. On this sweep down the pass, Jesus was to hold the northern end of the line and Jake the southern extremity while Frank and Lars would be on Leroy's left and Brad and Willard to his right.

"If you spot anything call out," he told them. "If you hear someone call out, hold your position until I investigate and give the order to move on. Keep the person on your right and on your left in sight at all times and don't move faster than the line."

Clayton, who was excused from the line, sat propped against a large rock, but the other seven men were positioned and the policing of the area began. Each item found, mostly expended brass cartridges, was bagged and the location of its discovery noted by Brad Pendergast who Hopkins gave the task of record keeping.

The total area to be scrutinized was less than 700 yards in distance west to east but the exercise took several hours to complete. When the marshal declared the examination over, he sent the posse members back to wait at the main campsite.

"I'll be going out to meet the wagon, in the meanwhile I'm leaving Jake here in charge of preparation of four stretchers for carrying Danny and the posse casualties out to the mouth of the pass. I want everyone to stay clear of the bodies until Dr. Pendergast gets a look at them. Then we'll all be heading back to town. You can get started packing up your own gear."

He drew Brad, Jesus and Jake aside to discuss the findings.

"We found nothing that we wouldn't expect to show up," the marshal concluded. "There was a fair smattering of brass and not much else to show for our search."

"Were you expecting something else, Marshal?" Jake asked.

Leroy Hopkins put his hand to his chin and gazed off toward the men up near the campsite before responding. When he did it was accompanied by a puzzled look and an absent-minded scratch of his neck. When he did speak, the marshal's reply reminded Brad of something from a Sherlock Holmes story about what a dog did, or rather didn't do, in the night.

"It seems to me that we're missing something. But, I'm not sure what that is," Hopkins said. His voice was distant and he sounded perplexed by the situation.

CHAPTER 237 IN OAK CREEK CANYON

Carter and Brooks made an odd couple to be perched side by side on the buckboard seat of the wagon. Thomas Carter was a man of immense physical presence. His completion was ruddy, his eyes clear, his forearms thick and powerful. The reins rested almost tenderly in his hands and he seemed at least twice the size of Jefferson.

Brooks had dressed with uncharacteristic style. Warned by his experience of the previous day, he had donned a fashionable, if utilitarian, dust-coloured overcoat and was sporting a wide-brimmed hat which cast his sallow features into shadow. His pale skin and milky eyes peered forward as from a cave, and blue-veined hands protruded from the khaki sleeves of his coat and rested claw-like on his bony knees.

Neither man was much of a conversationalist. They rode in silence.

Dr. Pendergast was an accomplished horseman. He was accustomed to spending hours on horseback in the varied and ruggedly beautiful valleys and mesas which bordered Oak Creek. He would often have Mrs. Hardy pack a midday snack and spend a pleasant afternoon fishing, sometimes from horseback, and admiring the countryside.

He engaged Carl in conversation as they rode north. Since it was their intention to slow their pace to that of the wagon, and must now choose a route suitable for the wheeled conveyance, they moved easily and drew up occasionally to allow the wagon to keep up.

Carl gave Dr. Pendergast a summary of what had happened, as he had perceived it. He talked of the confusion which had surrounded the final confrontation with Danny.

"It would have been better if we'd caught him in open country," Carl speculated. "But we took him where we could. We didn't think he had a rifle, but come to that he didn't know that we were behind him until near the end. The marshal told me that he thinks Lambert caught sight of the posse just before he reached the pass, but he must have been headed there all along, 'cause that's where he had the rifle and extra ammunition stored."

The doctor asked about the location of each of the members of the party and how Charlie Lee and Larry had apparently come to be the ones to run up against Danny. Carl described the way the shooting progressed and depicted the spot where the bodies of Danny, Charlie, and Larry had been found.

Dr. Pendergast had traversed Sterling Pass in both directions while visiting Vultee Arch and The Devil's Bridge, but had kept to the main path through the pass itself. He thought he knew generally the area Carl was referring to and knew that the sightlines would be broken by trees and outcroppings of rock.

"You said something about Frank that surprised me," he told the deputy. "You described him as charging up to join in the stand-off. Did that surprise you too?"

"Frank's an odd one, Doc. Nothing he does surprises me," Carl replied with a sense of assurance.

"What about Willard and the others? Did their actions seem normal?"

Carl considered the question and replied in a way that showed signs of him maturing into a serious lawman. "The situation was dangerous. People handle danger in different ways based partially on their experience as well as their nature. Your question about Frank Green deserves a better answer than I gave you. I'd say he was scared and trying to act brave. Jake and Jesus were more controlled in their actions. They've both been in tough situations before. They were careful about exposing themselves, but I got the impression that I could count on them. Willard was a little trigger happy at first, but he settled down and followed my instructions."

As they moved into the main passage up Oak Creek Canyon, the doctor wondered what the deputy's assessment of Brad's conduct would be.

He didn't ask Carl, but he would have a word with Hopkins later. He was proud of his son, but he knew that stress and danger can bring out the best and the worst in people. He knew that the marshal would be able to give him an accurate insight into how Brad had dealt with a touch of personal danger.

Carter had been up Oak Creek Canyon before when called upon to assist with repairs to gear and once to a cattle drive which had run into a problem with a chuck wagon, but he was unfamiliar with the pass off to the west where they were headed. Brooks was no more aware of the entrance than he was himself. Carl and the doctor had dropped back behind, so he just kept the team moving along at an easy pace and headed north.

Jefferson had asked a couple of questions about the treatment of metal during forging which had surprised Thomas. Brooks didn't seem like the kind of fella that would take an interest in blacksmithing,

Nonetheless, the mortician expressed a special interest in branding irons. He was curious about the one found in Clive's work chest. The questions were insightful. That got Carter talking about some finer points of tempering and softening of material during the production of objects meant to be used as tools rather than those designed to withstand stress. He was giving Jefferson an example of a set of springs he'd fashioned for a gentlewomen who wanted a solid, but gentle, sway to her carriage, when Carl and Dr. Pendergast rode up.

"Sorry, Thomas," Carl began, "We got talking and I forgot you didn't know where exactly we're headed. You can turn over toward the left here. You can't see it too well from here, but there's an entry into the hills just beyond that sort of cleft in the cliff."

"How far up the pass do we go?" Carter inquired.

"I'll show you where you can leave the wagon. We'll walk up together from there. It's not far and the team would have trouble at some points on the winding trail."

CHAPTER 238 IN STERLING PASS

Hopkins didn't expect Carl to return with the wagon before 10 o'clock, but he wanted to have a private word with Dr. Pendergast and Carl when they arrived. For one thing he wanted to brief them on what had happened after Carl had left for town. He left Jake in charge of the posse and he and Brad rode their horses slowly down toward the mouth of the pass. They'd ride out to meet the wagon. It would have to travel along the main canyon.

On the way, Brad expressed interest in the marshal's expressed feeling that they were missing something. Hopkins was vague about exactly what he thought was missing, but he repeated that it just didn't feel right.

"I'd like to look over the statements you took down when we spoke with the men yesterday. Maybe there'll be something in what they said that will help me put my finger on it."

"I've taken good notes, but I'd like to sit down at a proper desk to transcribe it," Brad told him. "I'll get it to you today if we get back in time."

As they reached the point where the pass widened out, they picked up a bit of speed and moved east into the canyon. Almost immediately Hopkins spotted the dust from the wagon and the two riders set off to intersect it.

CHAPTER 239 IN OAK CREEK CANYON

As Brad and Leroy approached the wagon, Carl peeled off and galloped out to meet them. Leroy saluted his deputy and made a comment about a night in town having done wonders for both Carl and Star.

"We both had a bit of a feed-up, Marshal," Carl replied with a broad smile. "I may relocate to Doris Proctor's boarding house on a permanent basis."

"It would be a big improvement over your present housing, that's for sure," Hopkins agreed. Carl had been living in a room over the courthouse for a year. It was cheap, but dreary and the marshal doubted that he was eating well.

"Who's that riding shotgun next to Carter?" Hopkins asked, squinting off toward the wagon. "Don't tell me you brought one of the Thompson boys." The figure seated on the narrow plank seat looked so diminutive next to the blacksmith that it took a moment for Brad and Leroy to realize that it was Jefferson Brooks beside Carter.

Rather than head back directly, Hopkins convened a briefing in the paradoxically private setting mid-canyon. He found that, during their meeting in town, Carl had given the doctor the major details from the day before. The marshal recounted results of the morning's search of the pass. Then Dr. Pendergast looked over Brad's rough notes, decrying as he did the disintegration of Brad's penmanship. Soon he was satisfied that he had a grasp of the situation and expressed interest in examining the bodies for physical evidence. As they mounted up and prepared to move off together, Hopkins took a moment to tell the doctor of his concern that there might be a killer amongst those back in the pass.

"I'm inclined to agree with you, Leroy," Dr. Pendergast allowed. "I'll be able to judge better after I see the victims."

CHAPTER 240 THE HORN

The news of Charlie's death was not exactly a blow to Lily. However, it did pose the question of what she would do next. Her position at The Horn was more that of a free agent than an employee. She rented a room and worked the saloon on her own terms. Charlie had been happy to have her there because she brightened up the place and brought in business. A lot of the cowpokes liked to be able to buy a pretty lady a drink. A happy cowpoke was a source of money for a saloon; Charlie had processed an eye for opportunity and a taste for money.

For Lily, Charlie had provided a safe working environment and paid her a stipend based on how many drinks were sent her way. Extra money she earned from special services was her own. Lee had never asked for or expected a kickback. He was content with his own business and let her manage hers.

Now there would be changes. New management might have other ideas. Lily knew that some of the bars and saloons operated more as a bordello or bawdy house. She wanted nothing to do with that.

Besides, she had prepared against something like this. Lily had put away a good portion of the money she'd earned. Her only expenses had been her room and board and the occasional addition to her wardrobe. She took a hard look at her account book and decided that she had enough to start her own business. The question was what sort of commerce could she undertake?

She had neither aptitude nor interest in farming. From what she'd seen of agriculture, it involved back-breaking work with uncertain results at the best of times. Based upon what she'd seen and heard about animal husbandry, the large cattle drives were becoming a thing of the past and a woman would receive no welcome in any aspect of the business.

She had come west to escape the drudgery which going into service or working in a sweatshop offered. She would rather run a boarding house as Doris Proctor did than go back to the tiny sittingroom and endless toil that she had left behind.

She had read about professional women who were making a place for themselves alongside professional men. But those women had sprung from money. They had received education in law or one of the respectable occupations which were opening to women. She had no such qualifications and no way to attain them.

If she was going to earn a living wage it would have to be based upon those skills and that knowledge which she possessed. Her capital was not large, but what she had must be used to advantage.

CHAPTER 241 IN STERLING PASS

Brad assisted his father and Jefferson Brooks in the physical examination of the bodies of the four dead men. The putrefaction of their remains was in an early stage and since there was a light breeze drifting down the valley which constituted the pass, the task was not as bad as it might otherwise have been.

Dr. Pendergast made his own survey of the wounds and took note of the entry points and likely caliber of each of the bullet holes. After he had satisfied himself he listened to Brad summarize his own findings and diagnoses. The older Pendergast made no comment about Brad's hypothesis of the gun used for each wound and the likely manner in which it was delivered other than the occasional nodding of his head and grunts of agreement.

Jefferson Brooks had brought with him some tools useful in measuring the diameter of lead slugs which had not been too badly distorted by impact and the internal dimensions of entry holes in material which had retained its general shape. He also had a miniature set of scales which allowed him to weigh the bullets to compare them to the known weight for the guns posse members had carried and used.

The doctor spent a portion of his time talking to members of the posse about general impressions they had gained as well as listening to their tales of their personal contribution. Brad noticed that many of the group now remembered acts of bravado and courage which they had failed to mention the day before. He concluded that the tale had grown in the telling and would continue to grow until it bore no resemblance to what had actually occurred.

At a certain point Dr. Pendergast announced himself satisfied and turned the mortal remains over to Jefferson Brooks to prepare for transport. Hopkins set up work details and had the men so assigned work under the mortician's direction.

CHAPTER 242 RIDING SOUTH

The two Pendergasts rode south together and during that short passage down Oak Canyon discovered that the forced separation occasioned by the son's studies in the east and the father's continued practice of medicine in the Red Rocks region of Arizona had brought them both to a realization of just how strong their emotional bond was.

Their physical similarities were not at first glance apparent. Brad had much of his mother's grace and delicacy about him. Robert's sturdy frame was more representative of the mixed Welsh and Norman ancestry which the family recalled through their oral history. Like most immigrants, the Pendergasts had lost track of their exact lineage. Robert's own father had often joked that the letter 'R', which was missing in their spelling of their surname, from the more common 'Prendergast' version, had been sold by an ancestor to buy passage to the Americas.

It was a concordance of intellect and shared life experiences more than simple geneology which formed the foundation of their shared ethical and ideological natures. Brad had been drawn to the same medical calling early in his boyhood, and the two male members of the family had spent so many hours in shared experiences in the wild and strikingly beautiful countryside in which they lived, that it was not surprising that they now seemed more like brothers than father and son.

Problem solving had long been an activity which fascinated them both. Now they found themselves facing a real life mystery which had an urgency about it which was not unlike their common struggle to diagnose and cure the illness of their patients.

During the ride south, they turned their efforts to that mystery.

CHAPTER 243 BRAD'S ACCOUNT

The description of the shootout as transcribed by Brad Pendergast

Note: I have rendered the accounts to provide a comprehensible report rather than attempting to quote each person verbatim. Occasionally I have added comments in parenthesis for clarity. – B. Pendergast

Lars Sorensen: We headed down the pass. I was with Marshal Hopkins over to the right, that would be the south side of the pass, and I could see Charlie and Larry moving down across from us. We were coming into an area with very steep cliffs on the north, where Larry and Charlie were, and sort of uneven hills on the south where I was with the marshal. The pass was starting to widen at that point and we started to get further apart.

We were hoping to catch Danny in the pass between us and the mouth where we thought the other sections of the posse would have set up an ambush for Danny.

Then we heard gunfire break out behind us, up near where we'd left the horses and the marshal right away said we should turn back because Danny must have got behind us somehow. Then there was a series of shots from further down the pass that was apparently a signal from Deputy Munds, because Marshal Hopkins told us to move back up to protect the horses.

We were heading that way in a hurry and I lost sight of Larry and Charlie in the thickets. We were still in the trees when I heard Charlie's big gun go off and then there were revolver slugs coming through the underbrush at us. I think that must have been Danny shooting because all the posse were carrying rifles at the ready. Mind you, in among the trees a rifle wasn't much better than a handgun.

I couldn't see very far ahead and I was staying low what with bullets flying every which way. I tried to get a sense of where Danny was firing from, but sounds came from all directions. It almost sounded as if he was both in front, up the pass, and behind me. I know that it was probably just the echoing up close to the steep cliffs, and like I said, Danny was the only one likely to be shooting with a handgun.

Even though I must have been pretty close to Danny, I never caught a glimpse of him. I don't shoot until I know what I'm shooting at. Fact is I never fired off my rifle at all.

I heard Charlie Lee's big gun go off at least twice more and then there was a whole lot of rifle firing. Toward the end there were six or so shots over toward where we found Charlie and Larry dead. I suppose that was Danny going berserk just before he was shot himself.

The shooting became ragged after that and it wasn't clear if there was anyone shooting back or not. Marshal Hopkins had to call out three times before everyone stopped firing, though at the end Danny must already have been dead.

Marshal Leroy Hopkins: I directed Brad and Clayton to stay back and guard the horses while four of us advanced east down the pass. I told Larry James to keep to his left and hold close to the northern edge of the pass. We expected Lambert to be headed east in order to get out into Oak Canyon. It seemed unlikely that Lambert would turn back west, but possible that he might hole up along one side of the pass. Our intention was to keep Lambert in front of us and drive him toward the mouth of the pass where I expected Deputy Munds to be lying in wait.

When the shots from up near the horses came, it became clear that Danny had either slipped by us, or had never entered Sterling Pass. He may have hidden somewhere in the rocks and let us go by him. I wasn't aware that he was on foot, and I am solely responsible for the decision which led to the confusion in the pass which ensued.

A series of three double-shots sounded from down the pass and I concluded that Deputy Munds had indeed shut off that end of the pass. It was of paramount importance to prevent Lambert from getting to the horses, so I directed Lars, Charlie, and Larry to turn back and get up to assist Brad and Clayton.

When we headed back west through the top of the pass we heard three quick shots fired from a rifle. I thought at the time that it might have been Danny shooting at Brad and Clayton, but based on the fact that the rifle he had was a bolt action single-shot, and from what I was later told by both Brad Pendergast and Clayton Edgett, those shots came from Brad's rifle and resulted in Lambert breaking off his attack and coming back down the pass toward our line of four.

I was then on the left, near the south side of the pass and I saw someone move quickly through the woods above us from north to south. Visibility was limited by the underbrush, the shadows cast by the setting sun, and the gun smoke which drifted down the pass. I could hear shots along the northern side of the pass which at that point is a steep wall of rock. I attempted to re-establish contact with Lars, but could not see him anywhere.

I moved east and north in an attempt to keep Lambert from going back toward the ridge where Brad and Clayton were with the horses. There was a great deal of firing going on. I had a view down the open section of the main passage through the pass and at one point I spotted Deputy Munds and the Pinkerton agent, Jake Witherspoon, coming west to support our position.

When the shooting eased off and became sporadic, I called out for everyone to hold their fire. Finally there was no more shooting and I was able to move to the northern wall where I discovered the bodies of Charlie Lee, Larry James, and Danny Lambert. Danny appeared to have been killed by a single shot, but Charlie and Larry had been shot several times.

While I was inspecting the bodies, I was joined by Jake, Jesus and Carl. We did a head count and found all the other deputies to be present with the exception of Brad and Clayton. I left Deputy Munds to settle the men in a clearing and to break out some food.

I found Brad up on the ridge tending to Clayton who had a leg wound.

Note: since Lars Sorensen and Marshal Hopkins were the only two surviving members of our posse at the top of the pass, with the exception of Clayton and myself who were on the ridge just east of the pass proper, I have edited the reports of the remaining members of the posse to record aspects of the gunflight which they observed from behind Lars and the marshal. – B. Pendergast

Willard Wright: Carl sent me across to the north side of the pass to watch for Danny trying to sneak down that way. The rock wall is sheer on that side, so Danny would have to go between me and the deputy to get by.

I fired off my gun once into the air to signal to Carl that I was in position. Other than that I fired no shots because it was hard to see and I knew Hopkins' group was up ahead of us. I didn't want to be shooting in the direction of our own men. I held my position until I heard the marshal call for us to cease firing. Then I came up the north side of the pass through the trees and found a number of the men gathered around the bodies.

Frank Green: When Jesus told me that the signal meant the posse needed assistance, I came forward as quickly as I could. I wanted to show that I was willing to help out. Then when I saw Sam's body lying in the dirt, I thought maybe I'd better take it easy.

I moved up through the trees, but I didn't see anyone at all except Carl. He motioned for me to go to the other side. There were shouts and the sound of gunfire all over up ahead, so I stopped when I was as far forward as I thought I could go. I could see Carl and the other two fellas over on my left, but I'm not sure if they saw me once I was in place. I was trying to stay low.

Carl Munds: I established a position with Jake guarding the south side of the pass. That's the only open trail where a horseman could approach at speed. Willard was over on the other side. I had him fire off a single shot when he was in position and instructed him to hold that side of the pass.

A little later we heard a rider approaching from the east. I assumed it was Jesus and Frank since I had fired three double-rounds earlier to signal to them to come forward. The rider stopped down where the others were hitched. When he came forward on foot I saw it was Frank by himself. I gave him a hand signal to go over and join Willard at the northern wall. I saw him go over and then both he and Willard were out of my line of vision. I knew they were there to block Lambert, so I made sure that Jake and I could do the same on our side.

A couple of minutes later Jesus rode up at a slower pace. I sent Jake back to meet him and instruct him where to tether his horse. Jake brought him forward and the three of us started to move up ready to intercept Danny if he broke through the marshal's line.

Jacob (Jake) Witherspoon: I came forward to Carl after Frank came back with the express package. Carl said there was no way to get up to the line with the marshal, and that we'd be better to set up to intercept Danny Lambert if he got hold of a horse and tried to ride through.

A little later I saw Frank arrive and after that Jesus rode up. Jesus came forward on his horse and Carl sent me back to 'Tell that idiot to get down off the horse before he gets shot.' Those were his words you understand.

After that we just waited and listened to the shooting up ahead until the marshal gave the all-clear.

Jesus Fernandez Soza: When we heard the signal to move up, I told Frank what it meant. When he heard that, he didn't wait for me. He was all het up and took off like a man racing to his funeral. I followed on behind and met up with Jake and the deputy.

We spent the rest of the time there on the lower part of the trail.

Clayton Edgett: The young doctor went up for a pee, and I was watching the horses. Just when I saw him returning I started to get up to take my turn when something bit into my leg. It didn't hurt right away but I heard a noise and I sort of fell down. Then I heard another shot and something hit me in the face. Apparently it was stone chips. Anyway, Brad started yelling at me to roll out of sight and I did. I heard shooting nearby and saw that it was Brad shooting. That kind of surprised me, him being a doctor and all. Then he came over and bandaged me up and stayed with me. We heard shooting, but never saw Lambert again. I'm right sorry about Charlie and the others, but we were totally out of it.

Bradley Pendergast: After I saw Clayton shot, I ducked down and tried to see where the shot came from. Then when there was a second shot I figured it must be Lambert and I called for Clayton to roll out of the line of fire. I fired three shots off toward Lambert's position, but I know they were all into the dirt. I heard the slugs whining as they ricocheted away. Still it must have scared him off, because the next we heard the shooting was all down in the trees.

Nothing else significant happened where we were. Clayton and I stayed put just west of the ridge and sometime after the shooting was done Marshal Hopkins came up to check on us.

Note: At the request of my father, I have also prepared a list which indicates the guns which were present at the shootout in the pass and who was in possession of each gun. – B. Pendergast

CHAPTER 244 REUNIONS BACK IN SEDONA

The death of Danny was greeted by most townsfolk as an end to the 'troubles' which had disturbed their relatively peaceful existence. Clive was mending, Luke was more or less forgotten, Sam and Larry had been only occasional visitors to Sedona, as had the stagecoach driver, Paul.

On the whole, the town was ready to move on.

It was at The Horn that the sea change was most apparent. Clayton had been transformed into a somebody by virtue of being shot by Danny Lambert, and he blossomed in the limelight into somewhat of a celebrity. His rise in prominence at the saloon was facilitated in a large measure by the absence of Charlie Lee.

The other big change at The Horn was the departure of Lily.

Doris and Lily had formed a bond of their own during the period of turmoil. Caring for Clive and aknowledging her true relationship to him had given Doris a sense of well-being which she had hardly realized was missing in her day-to-day life. The death of Luke Proctor, and the financial bonus it provided, closed one chapter of her life and encouraged her to turn the page and open another.

Lily had herself taken stock and made a decision which had been long developing. She moved out of The Horn and took a room at Proctor's boarding house where Doris was pleased to provide food and lodging in return for Lily helping out with the business.

Both women knew the arrangement was likely to be of a short-term nature while Lily decided what she would do next.

The Thompsons got on with the business of business, perhaps looking forward to the opportunities created by the absence of Charlie Lee.

Jefferson Brooks seemed to have fully recovered and was actively engaged in the service of the recently deceased.

Frank continued to be Frank; Lars returned to family and lumberyard activities; Willard spent more time at The Horn, perhaps basking in the same sense of importance which Clayton had derived from the activities with the posse, and Carter continued to pound out iron into useful things.

However, beneath the apparently calm waters, a current was stirring. Hopkins, Carl, Jake, Jesus, and the Pendergasts were still at work.

CHAPTER 245 A CONSULTATION AT THE RANCH

Jesus Soza, Pinkerton agent Jake Witherspoon, Marshal Leroy Hopkins, Deputy Carl Munds and the two Pendergasts presented a pretty picture gathered in front of a cheery fireplace. They were seated comfortably sipping tea and munching homemade shortbread cookies. It had the air of a cosy tea party.

It was, in fact, a very private meeting arranged by Dr. Pendergast at his ranch. The men had gathered in the doctor's parlor at the select request of the doctor. Upon arrival at the ranch, they had been warmly welcomed by Mrs. Hardy and provided with tea and cookies before she left them to their meeting. The doctor informed them that they were to receive two reports prepared jointly by himself and his son. First to be presented would be the results of the medical examination of the bodies. That report would be followed by a summary of testimony gathered by Brad Pendergast.

"I'd like to present the facts we have first so that we can discuss the ongoing mystery with a common fact base," the doctor explained.

"What mystery?" Carl asked. "Danny killed Paul, Sam, Larry, and Charlie Lee; we killed Danny; end of story."

"There is also the question of the murder of Luke Proctor and the attack on Clive Harrison," Brad interjected.

"Okay, Danny did that too. He's dead. Sounds like a happy ending to me," Carl insisted, waving a piece of shortbread in the air as if in support.

"We also don't know exactly who killed Danny," Jake pointed out.

"As far as that goes, who cares?" Carl went on. "As far as I can see, the only reason to find out who actually shot him would be to pin a medal on that man. You seem to forget that Danny was shooting at us. Besides, he'd already stolen Star. Horse thievery alone merits hanging."

Carl was in high spirits. The succesful elimination of Danny Lambert paired with the safe recovery of Star had, momentarily at least, brought back his old habit of jumping to conclusions and making rash judgements which had often characterized his apprenticeship as a law officer,' Dr. Pendergast thought.

Over the next hour, it took the combined efforts of Jake, Jesus, and Marshal Hopkins to calm Carl and convert him back into the more thoughtful deputy he had recently grown into.

At length, all the persons present at the meeting were convinced that there were questions raised by both the medical examination and the physical evidence which required more investigation.

It was agreed by consensus to proceed to a combined inquest into the recent deaths and to give Dr. Pendergast a free hand to conduct an inquiry into the entire affair.

A date for the inquest was set and it was agreed that, by limiting the persons present to a select group, the two lawmen with the aid of Jake and Jesus would be able to handle whatever developed.

CHAPTER 246 BROOKS' MORTUARY

The moribund atmosphere provided by Jefferson Brooks' offices, served to remind Frank of the extent to which life and death had been brought into close proximity over the past week.

In general, he had to admit that events had turned out well enough. He was pleased and surprised at the speedy return to normality which both his friend Jefferson and the townsfolk in general had demonstrated. His own status in the community had been improved by his actions in joining the posse. Best of all, Danny Lambert was dead.

When Dr. Pendergast had contacted him and arranged to meet with Jefferson and himself at the mortuary, Frank had been concerned, perhaps even a bit apprehensive. However, the doctor assured him that he was simply preparing for an inquest, as required in such matters, and was in the process of going through the formalities in a timely fashion.

Frank noted that Brooks quickly fell in with the doctor's proposal for a single inquest as being most efficient.

The appropriateness of his own presence at the inquest, both in his role as town clerk and as a recent witness to events and participant in the posse's search for Lambert, was obvious.

Following the meeting, Frank walked back toward the courthouse with a sense of confidence that all was well.

CHAPTER 247 THE RANCH

Brad Pendergast was looking forward to the inquest with great interest. The meeting in one room of all the main persons involved in recent events would provide him with an opportunity to employ his powers of observation and deduction. He and his father had discussed the physical evidence and the events of the past few days several times. Brad had expressed his opinion that the behavior of Frank Green was not that of a normal man. Riding back to join the posse on the excuse of delivering a piece of mail struck Brad as irrational and completely out of character for the town clerk.

On the one hand, Frank had claimed to be worried about Danny Lambert attacking him; on the other, at the drop of a hat, he became bellicose and raced into battle. He had shown himself victim of fairy-tale fantasies and dramatic mood swings to a degree bordering upon what the new Austrian alienist, Sigmund Freud, would call "hysteria". The new theories of Freud were all-encompassing. Many doctors now believed that almost all medical conditions could be traced to problems rooted in the subconscious.

Brad had confided in his father that he believed Frank might be suffering from an imbalance in what Freud called the ego, id, and super ego. Dr. Pendergast expressed interest in hearing more about what Brad thought of Dr. Freud's theories. However, he had also asked Brad if it could be just that Frank was trying to gain some respect from the other men who were part of the posse. Brad had tried to explain how repressed sexual desire for his mother might be manifesting itself in Frank's attempts to imitate the manly behavior of other men. Brad's father had listened to Brad's diagnosis with attention, Brad thought. Perhaps the old doctor was not too stuck in his ways to enter the twentieth century after all.

While remaining reticent about expressing his own opinion about Frank's behavior, and the actions of other members of the posse, Dr. Pendergast encouraged Brad to observe all the people present at the inquest for signs of irrational behavior.

Brad was pleased that his father found the summary of testimony by the posse of interest. In fact the doctor asked for a copy for himself which he said he intended to edit and use at the formal inquest which would consider the deaths of Luke Proctor and Paul Matthews as well as Sam, Larry, Charlie, and Danny. He was further surprised when his father asked him to prepare a list of rifles and handguns which had been present in Sterling Pass during the shootout with Danny. Brad was convinced that the mystery of all the deaths could most likely be found in abnormal psychology. He knew that his father was of the old school of physicians who looked for physical causes for everything. No doubt that explained his fixation on facts about guns and physical locations of people.

He promised himself that he would observe the reactions of the people at the inquest closely and try to diagnose their inner motivations.

BRAND OF DEATH

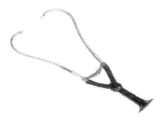

Part Five: Diagnosis by Dr. Pendergast

A note handed to Brad by his father just before the inquest.

These are questions we need to answers in order to solve this mystery.

Luke's killer, Weapon, Opportunity - time and place, Motive ?

The attack on Clive, W. O. M. ?

The branding iron ---- Who made it?

The object Carter found in the creek! Who took it from the casket? Who put it in the creek?

Who shot Sam, W. O. M. ?

Who shot Charlie? W. O. M. ?

Who shot Danny? W. O. M. ?

The rustling of cattle. Who was involved?

CHAPTER 248 INQUEST AT THE RANCH

Uncertainty and mystery were strangers to most of those gathered. They were men and women of action, accustomed to dealing with issues quickly and directly. The idea of a formal inquiry was foreign to them. Nonetheless, Dr. Pendergast commanded respect in the community. They had come when summoned.

The central room of the Pendergast homestead had seemed vast to the young Brad, as big as all outdoors, his mother used to describe it. Now it seemed almost crowded. The seating arrangement of those present had been subtly contrived by Dr. Pendergast and he had enrolled Brad and Mrs. Hardy to ensure that each was in his or her place. The doctor was seated in his favorite chair near the fireplace and Marshal Hopkins sat to his right opposite him across the hearth. A burlap sack was lying on the floor tucked between the doctor's chair and the lip of the fireplace. A small table with a chessboard and a box of pieces sat between the two men. That table and chessboard had been the focus of Brad and his father over many years. Today it would serve a more moribund function.

Miss Lily and Doris were on a love seat to the doctor's left. In order to accommodate everyone, the sofa had been drawn over to the right of the marshal and additional pressed-backed chairs brought in from the kitchen. Deputy Munds, Jake and Brad were seated on the sofa near the marshal and Clayton reclined at the far end. The other men, Jefferson, Frank, Jesus, Willard, Carter, and Clive were strung out in a semicircle on pressed-back chairs facing the fireplace. Jefferson was between Clayton and Frank.

<pre>
          Lily   Doris Clive
                    Carter
  Dr. Pendergast   Willard
                         Jesus
      Leroy   Frank
                       Jefferson
        Carl Jake Brad Clay
</pre>

"I've looked over Brad's transcript from the statements of the posse members, and found it instructive," Dr. Pendergast began.

He drew a folded sheet of paper from his breast pocket and read it in a clear voice.

"Salient facts from transcript of Brad Pendergast:

Lars Sorensen:

I was with Marshal Hopkins over on the south side of the pass.

I could see Charlie and Larry across from us. I lost sight of Larry and Charlie. There were six or so shots over toward where we found Charlie and Larry dead.

Marshal Leroy Hopkins:

I was near the south side of the pass.

Looked for Lars, but could not see him anywhere.

Spotted Deputy Munds and Jake Witherspoon coming west up the pass (on south side).

Discovered the bodies of Charlie Lee, Larry James, and Danny Lambert (North side).

Found Brad up on the ridge tending to Clayton who had a leg wound.

Willard Wright:

Carl sent me across to the north side of the pass.

Held my position until I heard the marshal call for us to cease firing.

Frank Green:

Came forward as quickly as I could.(south side).

Saw Sam's body.

Carl motioned for me to go to the other (north) side.

Could see Carl, Jake and Jesus over on my left.

Carl Munds:

With Jake guarding the south side of the pass.

Willard was over on the other side.

A couple of minutes later Jesus rode up.

Jacob (Jake) Witherspoon:
Came forward (along pass) to Carl.
We (Jake, Carl and Jesus) set up (south side) to intercept Danny Lambert.

Jesus Fernandez Soza:
I met up with Jake and the deputy (south side).
We spent the rest of the time there on the lower part of the trail.

Clayton Edgett:
He (Brad) came over and stayed with me.
We heard shooting, but never saw Lambert again.

Bradley Pendergast:
Clayton and I stayed put just west of the ridge. After the shooting was done Marshal Hopkins came up to check on us.

The people present had listened attentively as the doctor read the summary of the report. Here was a tale of an adventure of which they, and people they knew, were a part.

When the doctor finished reading the account he drew his eyes across the faces of all those present and nodded with satisfaction.

"Now," he told them, "I would like to make use of a simple chessboard to create a physical representation of what we have heard described. "Based upon the statements by the men and the few observations of them by other members of the posse, we can see as indicated by the position of these pawns on the chessboard where each person told us he was. In some cases we have collaborating statements from others to confirm the locations," the doctor explained.

Setting the edited transcript aside, the doctor took one-by-one twelve white pawns from the box and arranged them on the board as shown below.

Dr. Pendergast's representation of positions of posse members

-------------------------*Northern edge of the pass*------------------------

               Larry   **Willard**

               Charlie

                                   Frank

   Brad

West   **Clayton**   *East*

               Lars   **Carl**   **Sam**

                        Jesus

               Leroy   **Jake**

-------------------------*Southern edge of the pass* ------------------------

After he had placed all the pawns on the board, the doctor added, "Although the pass is irregular, the section containing the pass may be considered more or less rectangular with north at the top and running West to East toward Oak Creek Canyon. Danny's movements are presumed to have been along the northern edge and the hillside running up north of the pass. I've placed Larry and Charlie up near the northern edge where their bodies were found, and I've shown a space between Willard and Frank and another between Marshal Hopkins and Lars because they lost sight of each other. I've also shown an open area between Lars and Charlie and Larry and between Frank and Carl for the same reason," he explained.

"Danny's body was found near the position of Charlie and Larry, but we have reason to believe that he moved around and staged attacks upon Carl and Willard down east and Brad and Clayton up west as well as going north of the area designated by the edge of the chessboard to climb the hillside and bypass Marshal Hopkins' group at least once." As he spoke the doctor indicated with his finger the probable movement of Danny Lambert along and above the top edge of the chessboard.

The six men seated on wooden chairs had leaned forward to see better what the doctor was doing and gradually they all drew their chairs nearer and tighter. The circle of faces was intent on his statements and actions.

"We know that there was a certain amount of confusion during the shooting," the doctor acknowledged. "In fact, almost everyone was out of sight of the rest of the party at one time or another. Even the marshal here was on his own for a while." He waited for any objection to the statement and then said, "So, I'm going to use black pawns to replace the men who were in the company of someone else, or at a known location, throughout the action."

He took the box of extra chessmen in his hand and began at the side of the board nearest him, the side which designated west.

"Brad, you were with Clayton throughout the period of shooting. Is that right?"

"Yes, I bandaged his wound and stayed beside him until the marshal came to get us," Brad affirmed.

"So you can vouch for Clayton's location," the doctor clarified, "Who can vouch for yours?"

Clayton raised a hand and said, "Well, I can, Dr. Pendergast. I was with him, just like he was with me."

"But are you sure he was there all the time?" the doctor continued. "Brad told me that at one point you sort of dozed off."

"I may have," Clayton confessed. "I was worn out and it was pretty warm lying in the sun like that."

"That being the case, I think we'll have to leave Brad's marker as a white pawn," Dr. Pendergast stated and looked over at Brad for confirmation.

"Logically that makes sense," Brad agreed. "But, you can replace Clayton's marker with a black pawn. There's no way he could have moved much on that leg."

"That's your medical opinion, is it?" his father asked with a measure of humor and pride.

Brad confirmed his certainty and Dr. Pendergast replaced Clayton's white pawn with a black one.

"Moving on then," the doctor continued. "As I've already noted, Marshal Hopkins was out of sight for some time, and just as he was out of sight, so was Lars. Their pawns will remain white."

"What about Charlie and Larry?" Lars asked.

"We have no knowledge of their movements and they also were out of sight of all of us until their bodies were found. Their pawns remain white as well," Dr. Pendergast explain. "Willard and Frank were also concealed from sight by foliage from time to time, I believe." Again he looked around to see if anyone had a contrary opinion. Then he continued, "Carl was out of sight of Willard at the same time that Willard was out of sight of Carl, so Carl's pawn also must remain a white one."

"Wait a minute," Jake interrupted. "I was with Carl."

"You were with Deputy Munds after you had come up the pass by yourself, Jake," the doctor corrected. "Likewise Jesus was with you and Carl after he had come up the pass by himself. The same rules must apply to all. The only other person who deserves to be designated by a black pawn is Sam Schuerman. Sam had the best of all possible alibis; he was dead."

The doctor set the box of extra pieces down on the table again and surveyed the board. There were only two black pawns indicating certainty of position. All of the others were still white.

"That hasn't proved much," Carl commented. "We know next to nothing."

"On the contrary, we now know what we don't know. That is how we will arrive at the truth," Dr. Pendergast said with a secretive smile which suggested that he for one already did know the truth.

CHAPTER 249 INQUEST AT THE RANCH

Mrs. Hardy wheeled in a teatable replete with sandwiches, bran muffins, and icebox cookies. The attention of all shifted suddenly to the pleasurable sharing of food and drink. In the pouring out of cups of tea and coffee and the piling of comestibles on plates, all thoughts of death and enigma retreated into the background.

Each of the participants in the inquiry into the events surrounding the death of Danny Lambert and three other men, filled his or her plate and mingled as if at a strawberry social. Jake was overheard to tell Carl that this was the most enjoyable inquest he had ever attended.

Finally each person returned to their original seat, like obedient students in a schoolroom. The doctor sat nursing a cup of tea and taking the occasional nibble at a cookie cut in the shape of a prancing pony. Mrs. Hardy was congratulated on her baking, cups were refilled, and with a general sense of well-being, the doctor resumed the process at hand.

"I have been provided with a few items by Marshal Hopkins. They may or may not all have relevance to the inquiry, but I'd like to hear what each of you may be able to add about them," he announced and reached down into the burlap sack which had hardly been noticed by most in the room.

Drawing forth a piece of petrified wood, Dr. Pendergast explained that it was thought to have been the object used to strike down Clive Harrison. He explained that although there was no clear connection between that occurrence and the death of Danny Lambert, he'd like to know if any of them had seen it before. He passed the rock-like object across the table to the marshal who passed it on to Carl and it began to travel from hand to hand around the room.

"Clive has told me that it was left in the stable by some customer some time ago and Carter has confirmed seeing it there, though he has no recollection of who it was who had originally pulled it out of a saddlebag and set it on a ledge beside one of the stalls," he told the assembly as the fossil made its progress around the circle.

Most of the people present had seen the piece of petrified wood before and passed it on without comment. Clayton spent some time hefting it in one hand and holding it up to the light, but he had nothing to add. Willard remarked that he had seen the mineralized fossil in the stable. Doris admired it and passed it on to Lily who remarked, "I think one of the prospectors had a collection of small pieces of rock which looked similar. He was telling everyone who would listen that it was a clue on where to find sources of underground water. Someone asked him why that would be interesting and he shut up as if that part was a secret or something."

"Half the prospectors are half crazy and the rest are plain loco," Carl said with a laugh at his own witticism. He seemed to realize that his comment was out of place and quieted down.

When the specimen made its way back to Dr. Pendergast, he set it down on the hearth.

"I asked Brad to prepare a list of the firearms in the possession of the men in the posse," the doctor told the listeners. "All the men who were part of that posse are here today. I'd like you to look over the list and check to see if the description of your personal gun or guns is correct, but I'd also like you to look at the complete list and see if anything seems odd to you. I've made copies so that there is one for everyone. Please take your time and read over the list carefully."

So saying, he nodded to Brad who rose and walked around the room giving a copy of the list to each person.

Prepared by Brad Pendergast. Edited by Dr. Robert Pendergast

	Hand Gun	Rifle
Leroy:	Remington 1875, S.A. .45 L.C.	Winchester 1873 .44-40
Carl:	Colt Army S.A. .44-40	Winchester 1873 .44-40
Jake:	Colt model 1905 .45 ACP	Winchester Model 1895 .30-30
	Derringer .41 caliber	
Jesus	Colt Army S.A. .45 L. C.	Winchester Model 1894 .30-30
Brad:		Winchester 1873 .44-40
Sam:	Colt S.A. Army .44-40	Winchester Model 1892 .44-40
Larry:	Colt Army S.A. .44-40	Winchester Model 1892 .44-40
Willard:		Winchester 1873 .44-40
Lars:		Spencer Carbine 1865
		Gauge 56 Spencer
Charlie:	Remington 1890, S.A. .44-40	Winchester 1904 .405 caliber

Clayton:	Henry 1st model 1862 .44 rim fire
Frank:	Winchester 1873 .44-40
Jefferson:	Winchester 1873 .44-40
Danny: Colt Army S.A. .45*	Model 1873 Trapdoor Springfield .45-70-405 Cavalry carbine

* Special Note, Robert Pendergast, M.D.:

(1) The revolver, a Colt .45, was found lying next to Danny. In 1875, the cartridge for the Colt Army .45 was shortened so that it would also function in the newly adopted S & W Schofield revolver. It was designated "Revolver Cartridge" and loaded with 28 grains of black powder and a bullet of 230 grains. The Bénet primed cartridges were manufactured until 1882 then replaced by reloadable cartridges with brass cases and external primers similar to those found in this gun.

The rifle, a Trapdoor Springfield, is a single-shot breech-loading rifle which would be suited to close contact but slow because it requires reloading after each shot. Rounds could only be fired about 10 seconds apart. The copper shell casings, found in Danny's pockets and on the ground near the locations from which he apparently fired at Sam and later Clayton and Brad, are much older than the brass shells which were adopted after the battle of Little Big Horn because the copper shells tend to jamb.

(3) There is no indication that anyone in the posse had a shotgun with them, but it is worth noting that Carter and some other men in town have .410 gauge shot guns. The .410 shotgun is capable of firing a slug of the same size as a .41 caliber.

The list of guns excited some interest in the men present. This was something they could get their teeth into, their attitude seemed to be saying. For several minutes there was complete silence as each studied the detailed description of munitions. Finally they seemed to have satisfied themselves and sat back to hear what would come next.

When he had everyone's attention again, the doctor asked, "Is there anyone who has a correction or addition to the list for the handgun or rifle he had with him that day?"

There were some mumbled replies of general agreement, but no one offered any suggestion that there was anything wrong in that respect.

"How about the firearms listed for the others in the posse?" Dr. Pendergast prompted.

Lars spoke up, "I know S.A. means single action, as opposed to the new double action where you just have to pull the trigger to cock the hammer and shoot," he began. "But what's this designation ACP beside your .45 Colt, Jake. Is this something new?"

Jake looked at the doctor for permission to answer and when the doctor nodded he replied, "It sure is, Lars. Colt's produced what they call an 'automatic'. ACP stands for Automatic Colt Pistol. It's not a revolver but a self-loading handgun in which the recoil is used to automatically load the next round and cock the hammer ready for firing again. It's fast, reliable, and accurate."

Although it had been Lars who first asked about Jake's pistol, a lot of the other men now expressed interest and for a minute it seemed that the inquest would turn into a general discussion of guns.

Jake held up a hand to silence the questions being thrown his way. "I'll be pleased to demonstrate the Colt .45 ACP for you gentlemen, but since the good doctor requested that we not bring any firearms with us to this inquest, we'll have to arrange that for another time."

Once order was restored, Dr. Pendergast asked if there were any other comments about the list. "What about Danny's gun?" he prompted. "Marshal Hopkins told me he thought there was something funny there."

Clayton was the first to speak up. "I'd say the marshal was right about that, Doctor. I was in the room when Danny gunned down Paul, the Wells Fargo driver. Danny fired off three quick shots, and I didn't see him stop to cock the hammer once. He just drew and fired."

"That's right, Marshal," Lily chimed in. "That gun Danny wore was special. He told me once that it was the same gun Billy the Kid used."

Frank Green lifted a hand and when the doctor told him to go ahead did so with a bit of nervousness obvious in his voice, but with a great deal of certainty in what he said. "I took a good look at the sidearm Danny usually sported," he said looking around the room. "It was a Colt model 1877 "Thunderer" double action, with a loading gate mounted on the frame. It looked a lot like the "Peacemaker", except for its special rear-offset "birds head" grip."

There was a stunned silence when he finished and every eye in the room was on him. Marshal Hopkins was the first to speak. "I didn't know you were a gun expert, Frank!" he exclaimed.

"I take an interest in anything that threatens to kill me, Marshal. Danny and his guns were the greatest threat in town to my safety."

The doctor smiled in appreciation. "Did you happen to notice any other details about Danny's gun, Frank?"

Frank reddened a mite and looked directly at the doctor as he added, "I did some research. That's how I could tell exactly which model it was. The model 1877 was offered in three calibers which were nicknamed "Lightning", "Thunderer", and "Rainmaker". The 1877 "Thunderer" in .41 caliber was the preferred weapon of Billy the Kid and it's what he was wearing when he was killed by Pat Garrett in 1881."

Dr. Pendergast reached down once more and drew a bundle of cloth from the bag beside him. He unwrapped it carefully and produced a revolver. He held it up and announced, "This is the gun that was found with Danny's body. Is this his usual handgun, Frank?"

Frank leaned forward and looked doubtful. "It doesn't look like it," he ventured.

The doctor turned to Leroy. "Marshal, can you confirm that this is the revolver found beside Danny Lambert's body?"

The marshal took the handgun and made it 'safe' by checking each of the six chambers. The single action .45 was notorious for being inherently dangerous when loaded since the hammer rested up against the primer of any cartridge in line with the barrel. He examined the gun carefully and replied that it was the same gun that had been found lying near Danny's hand. The doctor instructed him to pass the gun to Frank so that he could look at it closely as well. Frank took the gun in hand and after a brief examination reiterated that it did not seem to him to be the same gun that Danny usually carried.

Clayton asked to look at the gun and he in turn vowed that it did seem to be different from the gun he had seen Danny with. Clayton admitted that he didn't know much about guns, but that he didn't think Danny's gun had the 'dimples' in the side of the cylinder that this revolver did.

At his point Frank spoke up again and explained that the notches in the cylinder were for advancing and locking the cylinder in place for firing a subsequent round. He agreed that he was sure that Danny's regular sidearm lacked those notches, consistent with a Colt model 1877 "Thunderer" double action.

A number of the other men then crowded around to make their own inspection of the gun. After a few minutes, Hopkins recovered the revolver and set it on the small table in front of the fireplace. He spoke quietly to Dr. Pendergast who nodded in agreement and then in a clear theatrical voice, which seemed to fill the room, the marshal repeated for all to hear, "We've got us a problem."

CHAPTER 250 INQUEST AT THE RANCH

"As the Marshal so succinctly puts it," Dr. Pendergast told those gathered, "We've got a problem." He paused to allow that statement to sink in before proceeding. "It would seem that Danny had a different gun with him in the canyon than he usually wore. There could be a number of reasons for that; I'd like to see if we can solve that question. But, first I'd like to review another aspect of the encounter in Sterling Pass. I'm going to read off the names of the members of the posse and try to determine which of you fired off one or more of your guns during the shooting." He turned aside and asked Hopkins to make a note beside each name of the number of shots fired by each.

Brad was amused to see the marshal draw his small notebook and stub of his pencil from a pocket and prepare to take notes.

The group settled down and the doctor took up a sheet of paper with the list of guns and owners. In a clear voice he began to call on each to respond in turn.

The marshal stated that he had fired two shots from his rifle as a reply signal to Carl, but that he had not fired his .45 Long Colt at all. Carl had fired both guns, the rifle in an attempt to hit Danny and the handgun as a signal device. Jake stated that he had not had occasion to fire at all. Jesus also said that he had not fired at all. He estimated that he'd heard twelve shots in total, but all before he heard Charlie's big gun fire for the first time. Brad reported that he had fired three times into the ground in front of Danny with his rifle to drive Lambert back.

When the doctor came to Sam's name there was an awkward silence until the doctor called upon Carl to account for Sam. Carl testified that neither of Sam's guns had been fired and that when examined later they had been found to be fully loaded.

The same procedure was applied for Larry with Hopkins testifying that both of Larry's guns had been discovered fully loaded and that the barrels were clean indicating that neither had been discharged.

Willard stated that he had fired only one shot. "That was to signal to Carl that I was in position. That was the only shot I fired. I turned in all my ammunition minus that one cartridge when we all got back to town."

Lars said that he had not fired his rifle, and had no pistol.

"The next person on the list is Charlie Lee," the doctor told the assembly. "I understand that a number of people heard Charlie's big gun fired twice. What about that, Marshal?"

Hopkins affirmed that the Remington .44-40 of Charlie Lee was still in his holster when his body was discovered and that it was fully loaded and had a clean barrel. The .405 rifle had been fired twice but the bolt action cycled only before and after the first shot. "The empty shell was still in the chamber when I found the rifle lying on the ground beside Charlie's body," he stated.

Clayton and Frank both swore that they had not fired their rifles and Jefferson said he wasn't sure what had happened to his rifle. "It just slipped my mind what with examining all those bodies," he told the doctor.

At this point Thomas Carter told Dr. Pendergast that he had given the rifle to Deputy Munds when he arrived with Star that evening. Carl agreed and stated that he had unloaded and stored the rifle away and that it had been clean and fully loaded when he prepared it for storage.

Dr. Pendergast thanked everyone for their information and turned an inquiring glance toward the marshal. Leroy Hopkins passed his small notepad over to Dr. Pendergast who examined the page displayed and nodded solemnly and made a note on his own documents.

"There are one or two other items I'd like to pass among you. I'd like to hear from anyone who has any familiarity with or knowledge about either of them." So saying, the doctor drew up the edge of the sack beside his chair and extracted the hammer which had been used to bludgeon Luke Proctor and the strange branding iron which had been found in Clive's work chest in the stable. He passed the branding iron to the marshal to circulate and handed the hammer to Lily who was seated closest to him on the loveseat.

CHAPTER 251 INQUEST AT THE RANCH

Brad had been watching Frank intently. Now he thought he saw a slight widening of Frank's eyes as the hammer was placed in Lily's hands.

"This is the weapon that was used to kill Luke Proctor," Dr. Pendergast said by way of explanation. "There are some marks on the bottom which might help one of you identify it, if you've seen it before."

The marshal, Carl, Jake, and Brad glanced briefly at the branding iron and passed it quickly from one to the other since they had already seen it. Brad rose to pass it to Jefferson and walked on to bend forward to whisper into his father's right ear.

"Frank perked up when he saw that hammer." Brad was facing the fireplace and was sure that no one but his father could hear him.

The doctor nodded in acknowledgement but his eyes were fixed on something, or someone behind Brad's right shoulder. Brad couldn't be sure, but it seemed as if he too was concentrating his attention on the town clerk.

"It seems odd that he would know so much about guns, especially Danny's gun," he continued.

"Still waters run deep," the doctor replied. "Be careful now. Watch and wait."

Brad returned to his position on the couch. Jefferson and Frank had the branding iron between them and Jefferson was speaking rapidly to Frank in a low tone. He seemed to be becoming agitated and Frank was trying to hush him.

Doris was holding the hammer out to Clive, but Clive had half risen from his seat on the chair furthest from the sofa, and had his eyes on Frank and Jefferson. The other three men were also turned toward Frank and the excited mortician.

Suddenly Jefferson pushed Frank's hand away and he spoke in a clear voice, "No, I will not be quiet. I'm sure it was the same design."

CHAPTER 252 INQUEST AT THE RANCH

Hopkins was watching Clive. When the young man started to stand upright the marshal checked on the readiness of Thomas Carter and Jesus Soza. Both men were well positioned to intervene if needed. He looked to his right and confirmed that Carl and Jake were ready also.

Jefferson raised his voice again. This time he was looking toward the marshal. "I've seen this pattern before, Marshal. Charlie Lee had a piece of cowhide with this brand on it. I saw Danny Lambert give it to him out back of The Horn."

Frank was holding the branding iron in his right hand and Clive made a sudden move toward him. Thomas Carter took hold of Clive's arm and said something to him. Clive looked at Carter in astonishment and stood still as Jefferson took the brand from Frank and held it forward toward the fireplace where Hopkins and Dr. Pendergast sat as if audience to a performance.

"How did you come to get a good look at the brand on the cow hide?" the marshal asked.

"Pure curiosity, Marshal," Brooks responded. "I saw Danny give Charlie a rolled up piece of something and I was curious. Charlie looked it over after Danny handed it to him and then gave it back to Danny. After Charlie went back inside I saw Danny toss it into the trash barrel at the corner of the building as he went around toward the front of the saloon."

"And you pulled it out and had a look," Dr. Pendergast finished.

"That's exactly what I did," Brooks agreed. "I wondered why Danny would be showing a cattle brand to Charlie Lee, but then Danny did a lot of crazy things. I pulled it out and looked at it and then tossed it back in the barrel. But this is the design; it was pretty complicated for a brand, and I'm sure this is it."

"The branding iron was found in Clive's work chest at the stable," Marshal Hopkins announced, looking at Clive. "He may be able to tell us more about it."

"Can I take a look at that iron, Marshal?" Clive asked. "I may know something about that."

Marshal Hopkins signalled to Carl who took the branding iron from Jefferson Brooks and carried it over to Clive where he stood beside Carter.

Clive examined it and said, "I made this, Marshal, here's a mark I make on my work." Clive indicated a small "CH" stamped into the handle. "Sam Schuerman commissioned it and I fashioned it for him. I haven't seen it since I gave it to him months ago. How did it get into my work chest?"

CHAPTER 253 INQUEST AT THE RANCH

There was no immediate answer to Clive's question. Then the eyes which had been on Clive swung back to Dr. Pendergast when the doctor announced, "The same person who put that iron amongst your tools killed Luke, Larry, and Charlie."

"You mean that Danny Lambert killed them all?" Brad exclaimed. "But you forgot Paul and Sam. Danny killed them too."

"Danny killed Paul Matthews and Sam Schuerman sure enough," the doctor agreed. "And it is likely that he has killed others as well. But, he did not kill Luke Proctor, Larry James, or Charlie Lee." Brad looked at Frank; Frank was watching the doctor who had put his hand into his vest pocket and drawn out a cloth bag.

"Frank," the doctor demanded, "Since you seem to know so much about firearms, I'd like you to look at these four lead bullets and tell us what you can about them." As he said this Dr. Pendergast loosened the drawstring and poured four distorted slugs onto the chessboard amongst the pawns.

Frank came forward and examined the pieces of lead. He picked each of them up and then set them down in two groups. There were two slugs in each group.

"They seem to be of two different types," he said. "I'm not sure what each of them is, but there are certainly at least two different sizes."

"Indeed there are," the doctor agreed. "I have measured their diameter as best I could considering their present deformed state, and I have weighed them. It is my opinion that two of them come from a .45 and two from a .41 caliber." He paused and added, "The smaller slugs were taken from the corpses of Paul Matthews and Sam Schuerman. The larger ones were among those which killed Larry James and Charlie Lee. Both Larry and Charlie were shot with a .45, almost certainly this gun lying beside me now. But Danny did not have that gun with him. It was brought to the pass and left beside him by someone who was part of the posse. That person is in this room right now."

Exclamations of surprise issued from a number of lips, but, amid the confusion which ensued, the voice of Dr. Pendergast cut like a sword of justice cleaving through a fog of uncertainty. "That person's name is written here."

The doctor had risen to his feet and was holding aloft a shiny rectangle of metal.

Brad had his attention on the object his father had in his hand. He heard an outcry behind him and as he swung back he saw Jesus and Carter grappling with someone and the marshal cried out, "Hold him. He's the one."

CHAPTER 254 POST MORTEM

N.B. The following occurred some time later after an arrest had been made and the accused locked up in the jail awaiting trial.

Marshal Hopkins, Carl, Jake, Jesus, and Brad were gathered by the fireplace at the Pendergast ranch. Dr. Pendergast wanted them all together as he explained his solution.

"Okay," Brad admitted, "I confess that I was taken completely by surprise. In fact, I'm still unclear as to how you knew who had killed Larry and Charlie."

Dr. Pendergast smiled and replied, "As is the case with most puzzles, the solution seems obvious once you are shown how it can be solved. But I think you will find this enigma even more self-evident than most."

"But, I had all the clues you had, plus I was an eye witness to some of the events, and I still don't see how you did it."

"Let us return to the chess board," the doctor said invitingly and they all gathered around him as he sat in his favorite chair.

As he spoke he laid a finger on each pawn and discussed the person represented by each. As he dismissed a pawn as a subject of discussion, he laid it on its side.

"Carl, Jesus, and Jake I eliminated as suspects with opportunity.

I did not do so because they were ostensibly part of the official law force; officers of the law can be, have been, guilty of offenses before now. I eliminated them based on the fact that they were together at the time that Larry, Charlie, and probably Danny were killed. They, with the exception of Carl, were also together when Clive was attacked, and I was convinced that the attacker of Clive is also the person who shot Larry and Charlie, but leave that aside for the moment. We will concentrate on the killing of Larry and Charlie, about which we all agree the same killer was responsible." He paused and continued when greeted by nods all round. "Although Danny was probably also killed by this person, it is possible that any one stray of the other rifle rounds hit Danny. In any case, Danny's death is not the significant factor.

"Brad and Clayton were in fact well out of the action. I exaggerated, with Brad and Clayton's complicity, the possibility of Clayton dropping off to sleep. That wound hurt like hell. Clayton only got to sleep that night after three stiff shots of whisky which he is unused to drinking.

"Brad and Clayton were together during the shooting spree down in the pass. In addition Clayton was painfully, if not seriously, wounded. I personally examined the nature of his wound and am certain that he could not have made the trek down into the area where Danny was found near the other bodies without opening up his wound again. In addition, both Brad's and Clayton's boots were clean. One of Clayton's boots was removed. I was shown it the next day by Marshal Hopkins. By contrast, I noticed right away that the boots of all the bodies and most of the posse were caked with dry clay, or smears of clay, from the section on the north edge of the pass.

"The final proof that neither Brad nor Clayton was the person we were seeking is that both were in public sight when Clive was attacked. Clayton was in the saloon and Brad was in the marshal's office with Leroy Hopkins, Jesus, and Jake.

"Since Marshal Hopkins was in the office at that time, I eliminated him as a prime suspect even though his revolver caliber would have otherwise included him."

At this point Dr. Pendergast began removing the pawns he had touched while delivering his lecture. He looked around and said in a satisfied tone, "You will note that the field of suspects has become somewhat more limited."

Only three pawns remained on the board. They were those pawns that represented Lars, Willard, and Frank.

Top of chessboard representing northern edge of Sterling Pass

Willard

Frank

West   *East*

Lars

Bottom of chessboard representing southern edge of Sterling Pass

"We can see that in the murder of Charlie and Larry only these three persons had opportunity," Dr. Pendergast concluded with a smile.

"Surely you didn't suspect the marshal," Brad objected.

"It's not a question of what I believed likely. At this point I was merely attempting to eliminate possibilities. Anyone I couldn't rule out had to remain on the list of possibilities."

Brad was about to protest again, but Leroy Hopkins held up a hand and said, "That's fair enough. I'd like to hear how you did decide who was the killer."

"Very well, let's move on to the matter of availability of a suitable weapon," the doctor suggested.

CHAPTER 255 POST MORTEM

"Brad, at my request, produced a list of the weapons each person is believed to have had in his possession. Each individual agreed as to the list being an accurate account of what he had," Dr. Pendergast began. "The problem is that there is both a missing gun and an extra gun when it comes to Danny Lambert."

"How is that?" Jake interrupted. "We know what guns Danny had."

"Do we?" the doctor asked mischievously. "What were they?"

"We found a .45 Army model Colt and a Winchester rifle."

"Right," the doctor agreed. "He was found lying next to a single shot Winchester 1873 in .44-40 caliber, the same caliber fired by most of the posse. I have no question about the rifle. It is in keeping with his firing of single rounds followed by a number of handgun shots. We also found empty shell casing which could have come from that rifle at locations from which he was reported shooting. He fired once and took down Sam. Then later he fired from a handgun toward Sam's body and another toward Carl and Willard from a rifle before following up with several more rounds from a handgun, correct?" Dr. Pendergast aimed the final question at Carl who nodded agreement.

"What bothered me was that no empty shell casings were found from the .45 Colt."

"He was busy shooting and moving," Brad suggested. "He wouldn't take time to reload until he got clear."

"That makes sense, but he had to reload sometime, and we found no spent shells to match the copper spent cartridges found in the gun beside Danny."

"Maybe he didn't reload," Carl suggested.

"But, he must have. He fired six shots into Charlie and Larry and we know he also fired at least another six either at Carl and Willard or at Hopkins' group when they cut off his retreat east," the doctor explained. "What's more, we found no other rounds to fit that .45 revolver in Danny's pockets or saddlebags."

"Maybe he discarded the spent shells and only had six left when he opened up on Charlie and Larry," Carl suggested.

"I considered that," the marshal interjected. "Jake, Jesus, and I went over the areas Danny shot from and the likely path connecting them. There was rifle brass from a .44-40 at each location, but no .45 shells in copper or brass."

"That's correct, Carl, the marshal tipped me off to that anomaly," Dr. Pendergast added. "Tell us what you did find, Leroy."

Before replying, the marshal shoved a hand into his pocket. He pulled out a small cloth sack from which he poured out a handful of brass. "We found a number of shiny .41 empties, just where you would expect Lambert to have reloaded."

There was a stunned silence into which Dr. Pendergast voiced the obvious question, "And where is the gun which fired those rounds? And, in case you don't think that finding the .41 caliber brass proves that Danny had his .41 with him, I compared the slug that Lambert wantonly fired into Sam's body as it lay in the dust. It was deformed, but I'm certain it was .41 caliber."

CHAPTER 256 POST MORTEM

"So, there was a missing gun and a new gun," Dr. Pendergast declared.

Brad and the others were examining the .41 caliber brass as if somehow it held the answer.

The elder Pendergast leaned back in his chair and said, "Even if we accepted that Danny could have retrieved the .45 revolver from the old mine when he got the saddlebags and the rifle, we'd still have to wonder why he would discard a double action handgun which he liked and had just used for an old .45 single action for which he had very few rounds. And if he didn't discard his double action revolver before he was shot, what happened to it and why was it exchanged?"

He waited a moment and then answered his own question. "Someone removed Danny's handgun and replaced it with the old army Colt. Whoever did that had killed Charlie and Larry with that gun before leaving it beside Danny so we'd think Danny had shot Charlie and Larry as well as Sam." Dr. Pendergast picked up a chessman and turned it absently in his fingers as he added, "What's more, I believed that that person had also committed the murder of Luke Proctor and the attack on Clive."

"What could be the connection?" Jake asked.

"At first I thought, as Brad suggested, that the killer of Luke Proctor had something against the Proctor family. Then I reasoned that while Luke had been simply killed, Clive had been tied to the rustling as well. That suggested a more detailed plan."

"How do you deduce that, Dad?" Brad exclaimed.

"The whole point in drawing attention to the branding iron which was left among Clive's things was to make it seem that one of the rustlers had killed Clive. Charlie Lee accidentally complicated that plan by involving the rustlers in a game of poker together and making it impossible for any of them to be the one who attacked Clive. Oh, and you have an alibi for that time also, Marshal, if I needed another reason to clear you. You were with Jake, Brad, Jesus, and me. We can vouch for each other," he said and smiled.

Jesus had been listening quietly. Now his eyes widened as he heard the doctor mention the rustlers.

Jake, however, was first to put the question into words. "Do you mean that you have solved the mystery of who was making off with some of the Soza cattle as well, Doctor?"

"I think so," Dr. Pendergast replied. "I think that a court order to reveal the controlling interest in the front company that registered that new complicated brand and has been selling Jesus' family's cattle as their own will turn up Charlie Lee's name."

"And this Sam and Larry, they were involved too?" Jesus asked.

"Danny Lambert was also part of the gang. I think that Paul Matthews may have suspected something and Charlie wanted him out of the way."

"So, he had Lambert kill him," Brad concluded.

"Well, I don't think Charlie directly ordered that shooting. I suspect that he just got Danny into a poker game with big mouth 'Badger' Paul and let nature take its course. He probably didn't expect Danny to kill Paul so openly. Normally if Danny became annoyed with someone he would have waited and ambushed him somewhere. Charlie underestimated how annoying Paul could be. Danny couldn't wait to kill him."

"But Larry, Sam, and Charlie all joined the posse," Brad objected.

"There was too much at stake. They wouldn't care if Danny got away, but if he was going to be taken, he might talk. He had to die."

"So who killed Charlie and Larry if not Danny?" Jake asked.

"I think that that was yet another member of the gang who saw this as a way to get clear," the doctor replied. "Besides he had another score to settle with this town. That's how I came to realize who was the killer of Luke, Charlie, Larry, and probably Danny."

"Hold on, Dad," Brad burst out. "If I've been following this closely, you've just eliminated Marshal Hopkins from the list of possible killers, but Lars, Willard and Frank are still possibilities. Am I correct?"

"Absolutely," Dr. Pendergast agreed. "Who would be your choice of those three?"

"I've always suspected Frank Green," Brad declared, "And just now you ruled out the marshal on the basis that he had witnesses for his location at the time Clive was attacked. If that is sufficient we can rule out Lars and Willard as well. They were together at the lumberyard when someone hit Clive with that piece of petrified wood. Frank is the only one with opportunity."

"On most days that would be the case, but Lars had given Willard the afternoon off. Neither Willard nor Lars has an alibi for that time either. Besides, I was about to talk about motive."

CHAPTER 257 POST MORTEM

Before he laid out the motive he believed was the driving force of the killer, Dr. Pendergast had the good grace to admit how he came to have the inside track.

"I must confess, Brad. I had a piece of information which turned up while you were with the posse. That missing piece of the puzzle helped me fit it all together."

Dr. Pendergast leaned over and lifted the edge of the burlap sack which had concealed so many of the exhibits used during the inquest. It seemed there was one more item. Before he brought out his hand, the doctor paused and said, "For reasons which will become clear, I'd like you all to agree not to mention what I'm about to show you." He made eye contact with each of them and receiving tacit agreement proceeded.

All eyes were on the old doctor as he brought out a tarnished trophy mounted on a wooden base.

Hopkins was the first to recognize it. "That's the Spring Fair children's prize that was buried with Pearl Schnebly. Don't tell me you dug up her body."

"Nothing quite that ghastly, Marshal," the doctor assured him. "It was found by Thomas Carter in Oak Creek. I have kept this discovery quiet because I don't wish to cause any further pain to the Schneblys. Mrs. Schnebly was driven almost to distraction by the tragic death of her daughter, there is no need for her to learn that this object was removed from the casket before it was buried."

"But who would do such a thing?" Brad asked. "That is a cruel and pointless thing to do."

"As far as that, it wasn't taken with intent to hurt anyone. I believe that it was taken by our killer. He valued it highly, but it was his private secret. You will notice that the plaque with the names of winners has been removed. I believe that the man who took this trophy removed the plaque and still has it. He must have realized that to keep the whole trophy was too dangerous in his situation," Dr. Pendergast explained.

"Why would that list of children be important to the man who killed so many?" Marshal Hopkins asked.

"I think I know," Brad responded. "The victims must be related to the winners."

"No, that's not the connection, though you're close. I showed you the list of names which were engraved on the plaque. Do you recall any in particular?"

Brad stared at the vacant spot on the base his father held as he tried to remember. "I know there were a number of the Thompson clan among the winners, but no other name stands out," he replied.

Dr. Pendergast set the little trophy down on the chess board and said in a solemn tone, "That plaque was important to a former winner. It was taken and kept because his sister's name is on it."

Carl couldn't restrain himself. "You're saying that all these men were killed over a prize given to children. I swear, I don't understand what's going on. It seems like everyone's mouthing crazy talk. The mortician was next to raving when we were up near Steamboat Rock, and just the other day Thomas Carter as much as told me that Sedona was cursed. He claimed we were facing a 'reckoning'."

"A 'reckoning' is not a bad way to describe what's driving our killer, Deputy. Revenge is a powerful motive. Our killer had been hurt by this town. He wanted to even the score.

"Thomas Carter found the old trophy in the creek. A rock had been jammed into it to weigh it down and the trophy itself discarded once the plaque had been pried off. I thought that was significant, so I sought out my master list of the names of the winners." Dr. Pendergast drew a folded sheet of paper from the inside pocket of his smoking jacket. He held it in his right hand like a sceptre and punctuated the air as he delivered his diagnosis.

"Even when I looked over the list, the answer did not leap out at me. There were 27 names engraved on that trophy. Many of them were members of the Thompson family. Those Thompsons are go-getters, I'd be surprised if every one of them doesn't amount to something."

His voice held them. They listened as one while he spoke of darkness.

"The trophy wasn't stolen by someone who has and is succeeding; it was taken by an individual who felt he had been passed over, treated badly, even persecuted. Somewhere among these names is a connection to an individual who the town has forgotten, but who has not forgotten the town. Someone who resents, perhaps even hates, each one of us."

CHAPTER 258 POST MORTEM

"I thought you claimed the killer's name was on the trophy," Brad corrected. "Not his sister's."

"It is," his father insisted. "His last name is the same as his mother and his sister, both of whom are now dead. He shared the same first initial as his sister."

Brad picked up the silver plaque and ran his finger down the list until it reached W. Wright.

"But if Willard's sister won the trophy, why did that make him want to kill people?" Hopkins asked.

"Willard's mother was Wanda Wright. She left town with Luke Proctor because she was carrying his child," the doctor explained. "Willard was that child. Proctor later deserted them when they were in a shack out in the bad lands west of Tucson. Willard's sister died that winter and his mother became consumptive. Willard was raised as an orphan. He vowed revenge on Luke Proctor and everyone connected to him."

"Wait a minute. That means that Willard killed his own father, and he's Clive's half-brother," Brad pointed out. "Was he trying to kill Clive too?"

"I suspect that he had a struggle with that," the doctor mused. "His blow was tentative and Clive survived. Then the hunt for Danny came up and Willard saw a chance to strike back at a number of people at the same time."

"But how did you get hold of this plaque?" Brad asked. "You said it had been pried off the trophy by Willard."

"So it was. This is a replica," Dr. Pendergast explained. "Since I had a list of the names and had engraved the plaque in the first place, it was easy enough to make a duplicate. I counted on Willard believing that I had somehow found the original where he had hidden it and all was revealed. He did and panicked. In fact, I believe that we will find the plaque hidden among Willard's belongings in his room. He has had no opportunity to dispose of the gun or to hide the plaque in some other location since leaving the canyon."

"Are you planning to tell Doris Proctor and Clive about all this?" Hopkins asked. "Seems to me that that would be a difficult piece of knowledge to live with."

"That's why I restricted this meeting to the six of us," Dr. Pendergast explained. "I'm hoping we can keep the relationship of Willard to Clive and the fact that the trophy was stolen rather than buried with the Schnebly girl quiet."

Hopkins and Carl were quick to voice their agreement and Jake and Jesus promised that they would never speak a word about those aspects of the investigation. Dr. Pendergast locked eyes with his son and received a quick nod of concurrence.

Epilogue

Willard Wright was well represented by a lawyer from Flagstaff who did his best to have him sentenced to concurrent life sentences, but Willard was his own worst enemy. During the trial he made several threats against the people of the towns of Sedona and Flagstaff and the judge and jury deliberating his guilt.

Whether because they feared that he meant what he said or whether they just thought he was not capable of being reformed, the jury found him guilty on a straw vote without leaving the courtroom. The judge delivered a penalty of death by hanging two days later and Willard went to the gallows unrepentant. He even informed the clergyman who walked to the gallows with him and the masked executioner that if he survived the big drop he would hunt them down and kill them too.

The twin secrets the six men shared was carried to the grave with each of them. Hopkins retired several years later to form a security consultant partnership with a friend in Flagstaff. Carl became Marshal. Jake and Lily went east together, married, and opened a bar and grill in Philadelphia. Brad returned to school and completed his studies. He, Linda, their daughter, Doris, and Dr. Pendergast moved to a town in the midwest where the Doctors Pendergast opened a father and son medical practice. Clive became a co-founder of the Carter and Proctor Livery and Custom Metalwork business and prospered. The rest of the town proceeded in their own way, as folk are prone to do.

Appendices

The appended material may be of interest.

The material includes details about firearms described, or relevant to the preceeding story and a brief historical note about Sedona. It has been gathered from various sources which include infomation in common knowledge or in the public domain.

A list of guns used at one point or other during the novel

Posse: Hopkins: Brad, and Lars; Carl: Jesus and Jake; Sam: Willard, Jefferson, and Frank; Larry: Clayton and Charlie

Handguns and rifles known to be used by posse members:

Hopkins:	Remington 1875, single action .45 Long Colt and Winchester 1873 .44-40
Brad:	Winchester 1873 .44-40
Lars:	Model 1865 Spencer Carbine Gauge 56 Spencer
Carl:	Colt Single Action Army .44-40 Long Colt and Winchester 1873 .44-40
Jesus:	Colt Single Action Army .45 Long Colt aka Peacemaker and Winchester Model 1894 .30-30
Jake:	Colt model 1905 .45 ACP and Winchester Model 1895 .30-30 (also had Lily's Derringer) Remington Model 95 .41
Sam:	Colt Single Action Army revolver .44-40 and Winchester Model 1892 .44-40
Willard:	Winchester 1873 .44-40
Jefferson:	Winchester 1873 .44-40
Frank:	Winchester 1873 .44-40
Larry:	Colt Single Action Army revolver .44-40 Colt and Winchester Model 1892 .44-40
Clayton:	Henry 1st model 1862 .44 rim fire
Charlie:	Remington model 1890, nickel plated, single action .44-40 with custom black walnut grips with inlaid mother-of-pearl Winchester 1904 .405 caliber

(Armed characters not part of posse)

Thomas Carter   .410 shotguns
          N.B.   A 410 shotgun is capable of firing a .41 slug
Lily: Remington Model 95 .41
                      a double-barrel pocket pistol
                      (commonly called a Derringer)
Danny: Colt model 1877 "Thunderer" .41 caliber
                      (double action made in 1900)

Colt Single Action Army revolver. In 1873 the service cartridges were copper cased .45 center fire Benét inside primed "Colt's Revolver Cartridges" loaded with 30 grains of black powder and an inside lubricated bullet of 250 grains. They were manufactured at Frankford Arsenal Philadelphia, PA, through 1874. In 1875, the cartridge was shortened to also function in the newly adopted S & W Schofield revolver. It was designated "Revolver Cartridge" and loaded with 28 grains of black powder and a bullet of 230 grain. The Bénet primed cartridges were manufactured until 1882 and then replaced by reloadable cartridges with brass cases and external primers.

Danny's 1877 D.A. pistol. It had a three-position hammer, just like the 1873 SAA, with safety, half-cock, and full cock notches. It likewise had a cylinder pin mounted through the center of the frame, a loading gate mounted on the frame, and a rod ejector mounted on the barrel. To the untrained eye it might look a lot like the famous peacemaker, except for its signal rear-offset "birds head" grip which gives it a very distinctive look (almost certainly in imitation of the Webley Bulldog's grips). The frame is somewhat smaller than the SAA, and the section of the frame in front of the trigger is pinched, as were the Webley Bulldog's. There are no locking notches on the outside of the cylinder. Instead, the locking notches are on the rear face. The Model 1877 was offered in three calibers, which lent them three unofficial names: the "Lightning", the "Thunderer", and the "Rainmaker". The 1877 "Thunderer"" in .41 caliber was the preferred weapon of Billy 'The Kid' and was the weapon he was carrying when he was killed by Pat Garret in 1881.

Some History of Sedona

The naming of Sedona

Theodore Carlton 'Carl' Schnebly met and married Sedona Arabella Miller in Gorin Missouri in 1897, on Sedona's 20th birthday. Sedona's father was against their union, despite Carl's prominent family, college education, and successful hardware business partnership with his brothers.

In 1901, Carl's brother Ellsworth was teaching school in Oak Creek Canyon. He wrote to his brother and asked him to join him in red rock country. When the family departed Missouri, Sedona's father wrote his daughter out of his will, not wanting her to move away and to "Indian country". Carl arrived in Camp Garden as it was called, and bought the Owenby's 80-acre patented homestead along the creek. Sedona and their two small children arrived a few days later on the train to Jerome Junction. At first, the family lived in an old bunkhouse on their property. Carl was energetic and built the family a 2-storie home along the banks of Oak Creek, near where the road crossed the creek. The family grew produce and settled into their new life.

Carl took his fruit and produce to Flagstaff up the Munds trail. It was a 2-day trip up and a 2-day trip back. Carl and his brother worked on improving the primitive road, which other residents worked on sporadically, hoping to reduce travel time to Flagstaff. After delivering produce, Carl often brought back visitors and the Schnebly home became known as a good place to stay and have meals. When things were especially busy, they set up tents and rented them to guests. Carl also had a supply of bacon, flour and tobacco that he sold.

Schnebly often picked up mail for locals on his trips to Flagstaff. So, in 1902 he applied to the Postmaster General to establish a post office there. After submitting "Oak Creek Crossing" and "Schnebly Station" as names and getting a rejection, Ellsworth suggested that he submit Sedona's name. This was accepted and Sedona got its first post office - and its name - in June 1902.

The tragic death of Pearl Schnebly

The Schnebly's third child was born in 1903. Sedona was busy with laundry, cooking and cleaning for her family and their many guests. She also led non-denominational church services in the family home. The family seemed touched with good fortune.

In 1905, Sedona was herding milk cows with her son Ellsworth, daughter Pearl and baby Genevieve. The story is that little Pearl looped her pony's reins around her neck as she stooped to examine something on the ground when a cow suddenly took off for the house. She was dragged to death when her pony dashed after the cow. After that, Sedona became melancholic and the doctor advised that Carl take her away from the sadness.

They moved back to Missouri and later homesteaded in Colorado. Three more children were born. When their cattle died in a blizzard and of anthrax, and Carl became ill with influenza, Carl and Sedona moved back to the community that bore Sedona's name. They both worked. Sedona administrated the Sunday School and helped establish the Wayside Chapel. Carl was often called the town's 'honorary' mayor. They lived the rest of their days there and are buried in the Cook Cedar Glade Cemetery in town.

Now available in large print on Amazon worldwide

A tale of parallel worlds

by the author of the Hit Trilogy and Brand of Death

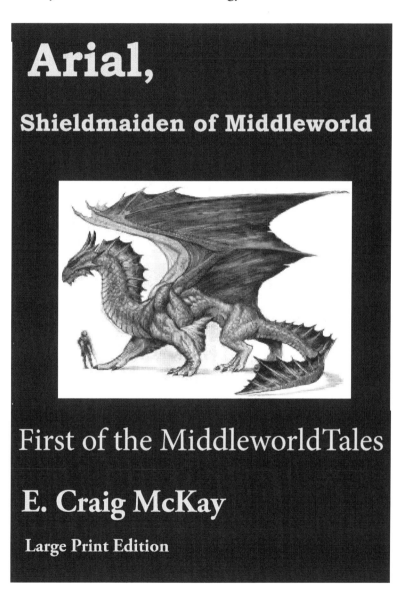

Arial,

Shieldmaiden of Middleworld

First of the MiddleworldTales

E. Craig McKay

Large Print Edition

published by *Greenleaf-Underhill*

E. Craig McKay

Brand of Death

Made in the USA
Charleston, SC
26 September 2014